INVERCLYDE LIBRARIES

D0234480

First published worldwide in 2013 by
Andrews UK Limited
The Hat Factory
Bute Street
Luton, LU1 2EY

www.andrewsuk.com

Praise for Neil Rowland's writing

A substantial, profound and funny novelist - **James Wood**
(Literary critic for The Guardian, then The New Yorker and New Republic)

Fresh and cliché free - **Jill Dawson**
(acclaimed novelist and a tutor at UEA Writing Course)

A very accomplished writer - **Karolina Sutton**
(Curtis Brown)

A confident and original writer - **Jo Unwin**
(Conville & Walsh)

This was a real page turner - riveting - **Paul Harrison**
(University of Bedfordshire)

...the plot was original, very interesting and not like much else I have ever read. I didn't know what was going to happen or how it would end - **Michael ki-Fun**
(writer)

The concept and story is a fascinating one - **Donald Winchester**

To friends and family

Acknowledgements

Thanks to Paul Harrison for being a first reader, offering encouraging criticism and advice. Also to Michael Ki-Fun for reading the script in a constructive way. Abdul Ahad and others for nagging me to keep writing. Richard Taylor for his literary passion over the years.

James Wood, Jill Dawson, Louis de Bernieres and all those people who have encouraged or supported my writing, in smooth times or rough.

Thanks to Paul Andrews for getting the monkey off my shoulder.

Special thanks to Will Hilton (www.willhilton.com) for photographic images

THE CITY DEALER

1

Clive couldn't remember to save his own life.
He knew that he should.

Clive Pitt was a 32 year old merchant banker at the famous British company of Winchurch Brothers, at the heart of the City of London. He'd been head of M & A (mergers & acquisitions); involved with asset purchasing, corporate reorganisation and even defence. His talent had been cherry-picked at an early stage and, following his internship, he made a rapid rise. Clive's origins were from the north of England, but he'd adapted to his London career with aplomb and found that it offered all that life can afford.

Clive had the sensation of high flying above the square mile. He peered down at the towers below, at the Gherkin on Saint Mary Axe, the Cheesegrater in Leadenhall, The Shard in Southwark, the rising scale of financial organ pipes. Until he hung so far above that dogleg of the Thames, that all the shapes below were hazy through broken cloud. Still the perspective across London was more superb than from the highest niches of any of those constructions. Objects on the ground, including buses and taxis, jetties and bridges, were on a tiny model scale.

It was definitely one of his "my life is flashing before my eyes" moments. There was a feeling of euphoria as if he was just experiencing the common dream of being able to fly. But he was able to feel a noisy rush of air about his face; powerful currents around his limbs. Previously, he had jumped out of an aircraft to raise funds for charity. He had overcome terror to bungee jump on a trip to New Zealand with his family. He had looked out across the Grand Canyon without any thought to abseil. Similarly Clive had stared through the glass curtain of Niagara Falls without any inclination to squeeze into a wooden barrel.

This experience was too real, too superbly scary, suspended in gaping space above the City, as if from the thumb and forefinger of an invisible giant, with only the super jumbos going into Heathrow above his shoulder. These flying machines so close that they exaggerated the void and a terrifying drop underneath.

There was not time to look back along the Thames to fully enjoy the view, even if he was inclined. There wouldn't be such a soft landing, or a parachute, he considered. What if his wax wings became gluey and sent him hurtling, crashing back down to earth, with a discrete splash?

Except that he didn't plummet. Instead he felt himself swooping, gliding and swinging downwards, drifting and circling. There was a swooping motion, in the way he had been lifted, but then he began to descend more gently, to drift and to circle like a leaf. Soft and beautiful, as long as he could shut off the noises and smells; the clamour and frenzy of the City. He didn't sense much speed or weight, until he touched the ground again, as softly as a baby in a crib.

Above their heads pedestrians hadn't taken much notice of him. Probably they were focused on their typical daily routines. Clive had been indistinguishable; just as you might ignore the swoops of a seagull. There was disbelief when he landed on his toes, as deftly as a trapeze artist or flying ballet dancer. The nearest person to him, when he touched down, seemed totally astounded, as if witness to a miracle. A particular suited business woman, full of awe, asked how he had achieved this remarkable stunt, but Clive himself didn't fully understand.

For a while he staggered, shadows clawing inside his mind. He felt he was at risk of passing out, right in front of people, and then how could he recover? His insides were churning violently, while he stood in a strange posture, stock-still in an open armed gesture towards the sky. At first passers-by wanted to check his welfare, interrogate him or to simply express wonder, admiration. However, this knot of humanity quickly moved on, back into their busy lives. Soon there was nobody thereabouts who'd witnessed his re-entry to the City.

It took him a long time to orient himself after this bizarre experience. He had an impulse to lie down on the pavement and to go to sleep: but this would be as fatal as a soldier trying to rest in freezing weather. What had he been doing beforehand? After long consideration he realised that he was hungry and must be out on his lunch break. This was the time to reintegrate with his working routine, and to recover his bearings. Clive realised he wasn't wearing his suit jacket and neither did he possess his work cases. Logically this indicated that he had broken away from his job for a while, and that his possessions must be around his office. Clive puzzled why he shouldn't be able to remember that precisely, without delay.

The narrow and dusty streets of EC1 were even hotter than he recalled. People had shed layers of clothing to try to cool off. Arms and shoulders were exposed, as ties were loosened and blouses unbuttoned, on what was a sweltering afternoon. Clive had done likewise, and yet his shirt was soaked through. Whatever people were doing in the east of London, they sought temporary respite and refuge from the heat, craving shade or any draught or even a vent of cooler air.

Accordingly Clive turned off Cornhill and pressed into his regular café, feeling perspiration instantly freeze and shrink on the skin of his face within the shop's shadows. He placed his arms on the counter and allowed himself to re-familiarise. He asked for his typical double espresso and Panini, with a filling of smoked salmon, fresh as if pulled out of the River Ure that day.

Yes it was great to return to his regular office pattern, those familiar haunts and paths of his job, after that amazing scare. He was reassured to be back among fellow City workers, as bodies squeezed into the café for a caffeine fix and calorie count. However, one of the guys working at the place gave him a filthy look. This negative and suspicious glance spoilt Pitt's feeling of getting back into the old groove. This guy was recognisable to him, and may have been Italian, Greek or even Romanian. In a great city like London you didn't stress about ethnicity. Clive knew that he often shared some matey banter across the counter with this guy. He could recall a shared joke about the daily grind, the private lives of footballers. But not this time - this time the man was edgy in his behaviour, suspicious, and made Clive feel like a heel scraping. What exactly was his problem? What was going on there exactly?

Whatever the cause, Clive returned outside, into the pattern of side streets. He intended to eat lunch at his favourite square, finding welcome shade under tree canopy there. Why didn't he check his watch and be sure there was enough time? He was pleased to get out of the crowds and traffic. Afterwards he could join friends for a drink at their favoured bar, *The Banker and Flower Girl*, clock permitting.

The recent experience of flying and plunging was still affecting him. How would he explain that sensation to others? They would argue he was guilty of over-working, over reaching himself in the bid to excel. While all the guys at Winchurch Brothers were expected to work hard, few were as driven as Clive; as they would tell him. This had led to resentment and criticism among some colleagues, he suspected, as he had been rapidly promoted in the organisation.

Yet even in these criss-crossing old back streets, within the original medieval maze, containing shops, bars, restaurants, storerooms and varied businesses, City people went about their complex tasks, running in and out of doorways, which no doubt led to offices similar to those he'd left behind. Clive got an inkling of unease about his job, as if there was a negative factor about his entire career. He was oddly nervous about the prospect of going back to the office that afternoon. It was unusual to have enough time to be out to lunch. He had to remember where he'd broken off.

He didn't have any trouble finding his way around; the City was mapped into his mind. Perspiration streamed down his forehead, from a thick blonde fringe, stinging burnt blue eyes. Recent expensive hair styling was coming unravelled, but he was already too distracted to bother. He threw back another take-away espresso on the move, in one gulp, then crushed and tossed away the paper cup. His heart was still doing uppercuts into his rib cage as he paced along the next street. He wiped the sweat from his eyes and further loosened the collar of a bespoke, monogrammed shirt.

The idea was to reach the square and sit down, drink something icy, try to cool down. He anticipated the refuge of manicured bowling greens and flowerbeds, surrounded by that Lord Mayor's luncheon of architecture. There he might reflect for a while, watching sports men and women, breaking their trades to spin their wooden globes, in that oasis amidst the hubbub.

2

Before he could make any more progress he was obstructed on the pavement. He was deliberately blocked off by an enormous uniformed guy, a coated and booted giant, square shouldered as a concrete block in North Korea, with a shiny peaked cap pulled over black shades.

Clive gradually took in the situation. He realised that this corporate giant stood in a catching position close to a limousine - an immense black limousine. This suggested that he was a professional driver, or even a chauffeur. The limo was comprised of no less than three compartments, with a long antenna at the rear, like a whip. Yet this was not the showy type of limo that people hired for significant birthdays or other glitzy celebrations. This model belonged to a significant personage and it was not ridiculous or improbable in shape or function. The car had an unusual, even other-worldly sleek design, curiously of no recognisable manufacturer: anyway Clive didn't recognise the make and he had a decent knowledge of cars.

"What's going on here then?" Clive asked. He approached the brute and found that his route was cut off.

"There's nothing to be suspicious of," the giant replied.

"What's your problem?" Pitt objected.

"I don't have a problem, do you?" the driver said politely.

Clive resolved not to be intimidated. There were many pricey marques around town. Clive had an expensive motor himself, as you'd expect in his job.

"I said get out of my way!" he persisted.

Despite Clive's determination, the chauffeur did not step aside. The guy was blocking him tenaciously, surprisingly agile. He danced on his toes and did a little cage-fighting shimmy to stop Clive from out-manoeuvring him. Clive had played rugby himself when younger, and he knew many dirty tricks and sharp moves. But this guy was equal to everything and large enough to throw a motorway over. Clive was up against a uniformed terminator.

"Come on, mate. What are you trying to pull?" Clive demanded.

"No need to get upset sir," the driver insisted.

"Why don't you go and take a piss or somm'ut?" Clive suggested.

"No need for that sir, I'm on an empty bladder right now."

"What's your beef with me?"

"Don't get upset," he argued, offering shovel hands.

"I'm on my lunch. I need to get back. How am I going to explain this?"

"*My* boss is waiting patiently to talk to you."

"What does he want with me?" Clive retorted, standing square to the guy.

"Just behave like a gentleman, Mr Pitt."

"How do you know my name?" he wondered.

"Although this is a polite form of no choice," the chauffeur considered.

"Nothing in the world's going to make me get in that car," Clive assured him.

Reading Clive's growing panic, the driver changed tack. "Consider this a form of business, sir."

"Nobody gets into a strange car with people they don't know."

"You've never seen a car like this before, have you? This is a limousine among limousines; like the one that occasionally figures in your fantasies."

"How do you know about my fantasies?" Clive asked, seeing himself doubled in the guy's ovular shades.

The chauffeur squeezed a door open - at the central section. It eased open like an oiled luxury safe deposit box. "Jump inside sir. You don't want to be rude to a brilliant, talented young man. My boss just wants to have a little conversation with you."

"What does he want to speak about?"

"This and that, sir."

Clive searched for any available help in the vicinity, but strangely there were no options. "Just like the movies, huh," Clive commented. "A big Mafiosi boss? Some new guy in town from the CIS regions, with his personal gas line on the table?" he wondered.

"You don't want to prejudge him. He just wants a little chat and then you're free."

"How do I know what you're up to? I don't negotiate in the back of limos. He's wasting his breath."

"No need to be hostile, Mr Pitt."

"I need to know who your employer is."

"No cause for agitation. We'll drop you back to the same place, to the exact paving stone in fact. Now come along, Mr Pitt," he said firmly. The driver put a huge leather glove on Clive's bare sweaty arm, nodding suggestively at the plush interior. "Hop inside and let my governor have his fill. Let's keep him satisfied."

The car's long black door reached across the pavement, blocking his way like another strong arm. Finally Clive was forced to follow instructions. Then the door was snapped behind him with barely a sound. He was immediately sealed into a silent compartment, with intimate smells of luxury, like a pretty girl aroused. Again he was battling with his heartbeat, trying to regain composure and not to plunge into a vortex.

Clive sank into a creamy leather seat, attempting to control his breathing and a strange light headedness. He was reassured by being able to observe outside shapes through reinforced tinted windows. But nobody could possibly see him inside the car from outside. There was toughed reinforced glass in front and behind. He couldn't see the driver once he had returned, presumably, to his seat. Neither did he see whoever was sitting in the compartment behind, within the third and final compartment of the stretched limousine. He could only sense "them", without identifying them.

Soon there was a purring sensation, as the engine started up, followed by smooth and soft movement. They were apparently setting off on a tour of the square mile.

A suave and correct voice, like the big brother of all CEOs: "Good afternoon Mr Pitt, greetings."

Clive's nerves turned to steel; as if this time he was going to fall hard from the sky and finish up like the butcher's scraps.

"You getting a bit hot under the collar, my dear young man?" the velvety voice continued. "Did I interrupt your daily routine?"

"So why don't you get to the point?" Clive asked.

"You have a reputation for being blunt, don't you, Clive. Isn't that right?"

"Why don't you show your face, for starters?" Pitt suggested.

"My face doesn't belong to you, Mr Pitt."

"I don't do business like this. What do you want?"

"Scrupulous as ever, huh? Would you care for a drink?"

"Let's get the thoughts off your chest first...whoever you are."

There was rich sardonic laughter. "Take a whisky from the cabinet in front of you. Reach down. Don't you appreciate what my Scots are doing up there with their mud and rain water? Who are we to complain, when they are performing miracles for me?"

"All right, just a drop, as you are offering," Clive agreed, thinking that whiskey would maybe help.

"Take advantage of the world's goods. Your precious metals aren't going to last forever."

"I'll take you up on that," Clive said.

"Consume them, while you can still extract them. Make sure the Chinese haven't stuffed them all into their overcoats. There's an ice bucket in the left cabinet, if you look."

He tried to snap the steel trap of his elbow joint.

"Yes, rather hot today isn't it. Warming up nicely anyway."

"You have air-conditioning," Clive reminded him.

"You don't feel comfortable at Winchurch Brothers; do you Clive...not any more. The old chap with his rather touching, if hilarious attachment to his slutty daughter... while we are talking of hot and sticky situations," he chuckled darkly.

"As far as I can remember, which isn't very much," Clive said. The inability to recall made him perspire even more.

"No, something has fucked with your head. You need to understand your place, Clive," replied the gentleman. His voice was changed electronically, Clive understood - disguised - before it came to him.

"So who am I talking to?" he stated.

"Excellent whiskey though Clive, isn't it. It's from my own distillery in the Highlands. Such potency from absolute purity."

"I can taste the quality of course," Clive agreed.

"Only the best for you City boys and girls, am I right. I can see that you are a young man with nice vices," remarked the gentleman.

"Is that the right?" Clive replied, bristling. "On what basis would this be?"

"Pour yourself another one. There's time, I can assure you, before we are done here."

Whiskey tackled the stress of recent experiences, although it only exacerbated his thirst, which was flaming up. Despite this luxury and the sumptuousness of his seat, Clive was feeling understandably on edge. Dark glass surfaces hemmed him in on all sides.

"Now you can explain what this is all about?" Clive suggested.

"You have to be wondering," he agreed.

"Does this refer to my work?"

"You focus too much on your job, Mr Pitt. You fucking *obsess*."

"Sometimes I can agree with you," said Clive.

"You have to squeeze the tit of life. Get as much as you can!"

"Maybe I need a change," Clive admitted, taking another sip from the glass. "Offer my services elsewhere."

"Excellent, that's the spirit!"

The drink was doing a bit of talking, but Pitt liked what it was saying. He'd wanted to discuss the shortcomings of his employment for a long time. Unfortunately at this point he couldn't recall what they were. "I'm up to here with everything at Winchurch Brothers at the moment," he added, for effect.

"Right, Clive! Variety is the spice of life. Don't let the bastards get you down. Particularly that pompous little prick at the top table, huh?"

"So you have a job proposal here? Some useful information for me?" he wondered.

"This is much more interesting," said the gentleman, with warm confidence.

"Maybe you are a scout?" Clive said.

"I definitely have a strong interest in you," he returned.

"If you have a proposal, then I need to know your name... and who you work for?" Clive pressed.

"I don't work for anybody. I only work for my fucking self. I could be the devil as far as you know. I am the devil to you... or your nemesis...your destroyer at least. Kill before you are killed. Well, that's among the many other names, not to mention nicknames," he said, "and other unflattering names."

Ice did a dance into Clive's lap. His whiskey didn't look so good soaked into a trouser leg. "If you're trying to scare me mate, then you've done a good job."

"You're not going to piss your pants are you, Clive? That would be a shame to spoil them."

"All right, mate... now you've had your fun, let me out of here,"

"Keep calm in a stressful situation Mr Pitt. Don't you enjoy chatting to the devil... the devil in the details? I understand that my publicity has been atrocious."

"What kind of unhinged maniac are you?" Clive demanded.

There was dark laughter from behind. "A devious devil, that's me, Clive. From when I was a brilliant little chap, barely an evil idea had crossed my almost innocent mind."

"You're the biggest head-case I've come across," Clive insisted.

"You're still a relative innocent yourself, aren't you?"

"Yes, you're doing a brilliant job at scaring people. That must have something to do with impressive props and a bass voice. Looks as if you've got a little synthesiser rigged up there...if I'm not mistaken."

"Evil geniuses should be entitled to a little style," he retorted.

"Is that right? So you hired the limo to give me a shock?" Pitt wondered.

"Why should I *hire* anything, apart from people?"

"OK, mate, let's hear your proposal and then let me out."

"Agreed Clive. As my driver promised, we shall return you where we picked you up...to the exact paving stone," he promised.

"If you don't mind, as I've duties and responsibilities."

"Then you'll find that the fun and games start for you. That is one of the little charms of my powers. You still have some work to do for me. You still have to appreciate my dark arts. It must come as a bit of a shock. It always does," the gentleman told him. "I was always the boss. I was always pulling the strings, you see."

"OK, as you like, you fire away! Then we can get this over with!"

"Fix yourself another drink. You spilt the last one," he observed.

"But I don't want another drink," Clive replied.

"Suit yourself, Mr Pitt. Didn't you see the benefits of alcoholism on your working classes? How could the polite people run their own estates and affairs, without booze, Pitt? What are the people offered these days? It is more complicated," mused the synthetic voice.

Even while these tones came from behind him, Pitt couldn't turn around to investigate. He continued to look rigidly ahead, and the tinted thick glass was impenetrable. Even if this was some kind of nutcase here, it was not the type of nutcase he wanted to encounter.

"Presumably you're super-rich or mafia... you're having fun with me. Not working for a living is your way of keeping occupied."

"Don't fool yourself, Clive, because the super-rich have plenty to do in these times. We're at the top of the pyramid, a smart little band, even after the pyramid has crumbled under our feet."

"I would rather be the guy I am, than some fruitcake in a stretch limo, going about the streets of London in a hearse, describing himself as the devil," Clive replied.

There was electronic laughter in bass tones. "Why didn't you join our party? You were lucky enough to be introduced. Were you too fucking dim to see that? Shouldn't you know that, if you are so brilliant? No wonder you are taking your crumbs of comfort, in the face of oblivion."

"Do I know you? *Should* I know you?"

"Should you?"

"It's true that I feel lost at the moment," Clive agreed.

"But you *are* lost, Clive, my big beautiful young man. Your time has already been appointed," he said.

"You can seriously be fired for talking crap."

"Now you are really having a laugh, aren't you?"

"So you play your game. Let's finish it soon."

"Your notion of the game is fascinating to me. An arrogant techie like you probably knows how it works! How very amusing and pretentious these ideas can be. The universe really operates on an even sillier principle, similar to a game of tiddly winks."

"Tiddly winks?" Clive retorted.

"Yes, that's right, tiddly winks," he chuckled. "A charming little British game, a legacy from your old empire, I think... which shows moral seriousness, in this fallen universe! The Royal family play this game while they are sitting on their thrones, I can assure you."

"This is definitely a wind up," Clive argued.

"How does that sound to you? The truth is usually ridiculous, Pitt."

"Look, I have to return to my desk. Just drop me, will you? So I can get out of this mean-machine of yours." He peered out of smoky windows trying to delineate milling crowds, normality, beyond.

"You're sure that's a clever idea? To go rushing back to your little desk job?" he said, giving an extra dark roll to his vowels.

"You said that you have a question for me?" Clive reminded him.

"Don't worry, I never forget a face. Do you?"

"Just questions," Clive retorted.

"Well, not so much a question as a proposition. Actually more like a dilemma than a proposition."

"This is doing my head in," Clive said.

"I love abstractions. Either you will agree to go forward a year in your life, or alternatively you will have to go back a year."

"That's amusing," Clive said ironically.

"I'm pleased to provoke your rebellious interest at last, Pitt."

"Just imagine how things might be... if I have another try. I could get up my courage and ask the family to relocate to the Far East with me. Just for starters. I might have put in for promotion, rather than sticking where I am," he ruminated.

"Never a good idea to stick about. You wanna go back a year in time?"

"You claim to have such powers? You must be completely out of your mind," Clive concluded.

"Don't you understand the power of information? You will have to make the choice."

"It's a creative proposal, but I'm not interested."

"You have to, Pitt, and you made a choice. Unconsciously, if you like it or not, you have already chosen."

"I refuse," Clive insisted, seeing only his own reflection exactly reversed.

"You must be exposed to this process," the voice stated.

"I'm not doing any time-travelling," Clive told him.

"Why should you be so hostile to that idea? Haven't you heard about that precocious child Albert Einstein?" he replied.

"Let me outside."

"Your life is different. Are you not interested to step outside and find out?"

"I'm not going to be shaken up like this."

"You went through a black hole, Clive. Didn't you feel yourself fall? Now you have to see where your ridiculous efforts have taken you."

The limousine drifted to the kerb and eased to a stop. Clive was invited to alight and he didn't refuse. Indeed he was returned to the exact paving stone, except that the chauffeur didn't come to instruct him this time.

3

The afternoon was still very hot, if not hotter than ever. Clive told himself that the macabre encounter was an elaborate prank. No doubt he'd soon discover who was behind it. Was this dark joke the brainchild of a colleague or of a hidden enemy? Maybe the perpetrator was waiting to come forward.

He stared down the street as the 'devil's limousine' glided away, coiling back into the boiling flow towards St Paul's.

Initially Clive was able to read off the car's plates; even to commit them to memory. Yet suddenly, disconcertingly, all the characters jumbled up and he couldn't recall them. Here he was, with a degree in economics and mathematics, not able to memorise a plate. He dealt in algorithms every hour of every working day. He stood watching for a while, disconcerted, shielding his eyes from the glare, long after the vehicle had vanished.

Clive felt a tremble of unease pass through his entire body. He was shaken after that banter in the limo. Whoever was that sinister guy?

A high level figure who wanted to scare him? A guy who liked to deploy symbols of power, enormous influence and wealth, merely to play games? At some level he might be able to laugh about this experience. It could offer an amusing and scary anecdote for his wife and their friends. What would his father have thought about this craziness, if he was alive? A father who had warned Clive, when he was recruited by Winchurch, about 'playing with the devil' in London. His job was very different to what his Dad had known. It was far removed from offering secure loans towards a new kitchen or a three piece suite. Family and friends would laugh at this story and, if they were being at all honest, understand why he was so shaken.

Phew! It was so damned hot outside. *As hot as hell*, he jested darkly to himself. He was trying to brush off that unsettling encounter. Yet his knees buckled as he walked along, there was a sliver of ice in his heart. He was then finding the crowds as he turned back in to Aldgate, knowing that he should return urgently to his desk. There was an intimidating quality to the City, as the streets stretched long and hard ahead of him - as if he'd been miniaturised. His eyes were burning in the sunlight that glistened off every shiny and hard surface and caught in the trapped traffic smog. He had been taken away from himself and suddenly he didn't properly belong in the world.

The whole sky went white and poured blindingly into his vision. So his progress was erratic, almost alarming to passers-by, as he reeled about in the red heat and wobbled along smoking pavements. The light rolled into his mind in a tidal wave that knocked him off his feet. It took minutes for this wave of molten heat to crash over and for shapes to reassemble.

Fortunately he knew these streets like a worn treasure map. Indeed they have proven lucrative over the previous decade. Despite the whiskey inside him, there was a strange taste of fear, like scorched bone. The usual afternoon business would have to wait a bit, he decided, until he regained his own balance. He was so much out of sorts that he had to leave his urgent affairs for a while. The screens on his desk, his double triptych of sacred binaries, would remain unattended, like saints without an audience.

While he was in this dire state he had to take further time out. He needed the cooling balm of sociable company, a fix of familiar and friendly faces. He had to get off the hot street and escape his hot memories. He knew that some colleagues frequented *The Banker and Flower Girl*.

He negotiated a blindingly dark yet pleasantly cool stairway. Sagging limestone steps lead down into a cellar wine bar. Sporadic laughter and conversation bubbled up from the shadowy room below, until he joined the dingy but convivial melee. His vision needed time to adjust to darkness.

The Banker possessed a density of vintner's atmospheres, and was a frequent refuge to the staff of *Winchurch & Brothers*. A mellow artificial light and fat candles cast a waxy lustre over crumbling ornament.

But where were his colleagues today? He didn't recognise anyone, even within his colleagues' favourite alcove. The bar was busy for the time of day. Customers gathered around rectangular tables and along an oaken bar, hot and weary from a morning's toil and rumours of job cuts.

Nevertheless he fought his way to the counter and waited to get served. There was no Ann Elizabeth here or Douglas, nor Pixie or Albert, not today, but he could take comfort from the absolutely normal scene, as he observed people socialising. Otherwise he couldn't remember the names of his closest friends. He could take his time over a bottle of ale and try to figure out his rare situation.

However, when he'd finished a beer, and put a hand into his pocket to draw out his wallet, Clive was startled by the result. When he searched there was no cash inside or any of his own cards. Incredibly he found a *company* credit card, tucked away in one of the flaps. It was no prank or mistake; it was authentic plastic embossed with *Winchurch Brothers* and account numbers and details. A thrill of anxiety tingled his nerves and reached the ends of his fingers, as he turned it over and over. Could he really be in possession of his boss' plastic? On principle Clive had not used a company account for private transactions.

Clive changed his next order to a glass of wine, a Sicilian Shiraz, and opted to pay with Winchurch's credit card. Not having any means to pay himself, he would declare everything on his return to work. But he knew he was potentially making a big mistake, because the transaction would be easily traceable. Yet it was not part of his character to walk out of that bar without paying.

Then amazingly, when he was obliged to pay, he tapped a pin code and the card was approved. He must have known the number - or his fingers did. On occasions we remember as unconsciously as we can forget. After a tense delay the pin was verified, no problem at all, and his receipt was torn away. He was shocked and elated at the simplicity, like a short selling asset stripper.

The barman seemed to recognise him, but didn't give a dirty look, not like the guy in the café. The new situation was puzzling and most untoward. What was even weirder was the discovery that, in another compartment of his wallet, he was in possession of condoms as well. There were a clutch of *ribbed and dotted* specimens pushed under a flap. What was he doing carrying rubbers on a work day? He was a happily married man, who'd started a young family already. Maybe some guys behaved like that, but he wasn't one of them. Could he trust himself or anything? At least he was wearing one of his own suits - or the trousers of that suit. That was as far as his self-confidence stretched.

Shaken, puzzling, he took his glass of wine away and sat down. He tried to reassure himself about the situation, while in that friendly crowd. Laughter and conversations in the room buzzed in his head; as if his blood pressure was shooting high. He was nervous, even though he was a regular and all the patrons here were City people. All the time he'd been sitting on his boss' credit card: maybe it was a stolen one. How, and when, did that get into his possession? The new wallet seemed to belong to him, as it was to his taste and contained personal details, such as a now out-of-date rail pass. It was the credit card that was definitely hot. Although it had been very cool when paying for his drink.

Clive wasn't able to enjoy himself. He grew oppressed by his unusual disorientation. Therefore he finished off a final glass, ducked through the low exit and ascended back to the street. Again he was whacked by searing heat, not only the noise and ferocity, as he confronted those alienating thoroughfares of east London. This was not a typical impression for Clive, as by then he was excited by the City and the challenges it posed. Today the

City was made from glinting concrete, glaring glass and metallic paving stone; that denied him any comfort or progress.

When he turned into the required street he noticed two female employees from Winchurch Brothers strolling towards him. Probably they were returning from an outside appointment. Clive picked up his step, thinking that he might return to the office with them, to hide his lateness from managerial displeasure. Perhaps these ladies could offer a few clues about his new situation; and he could ask why nobody was in *The Banker and Flower Girl*. He noticed that particularly beautiful lady again, with whom he'd previously worked. What was her name now?

Clive was shocked when, after they saw him, the women reacted with horrified surprise; even putting hands up to their mouths. They wanted to run away it seemed, just at the sight of him. But somehow they were frozen for a while, too scared to even move. Clive watched their expressions in amazement, shocked and afraid himself. He felt a new perspiration over his brow and a rising chill in his blood.

"What's the matter ladies?" he announced.

"Oh my god, Clive?" gasped the other.

"Come on, give me a break. Stop piking me, will you?" he pleaded.

"What are you doing here?" Pixie Wright said. Yes, that was it.

"Don't you know?" he replied.

"Are you in your right mind?" she returned.

Pixie was an incredibly elegant blonde: he was confident that he'd spoken to her a few times. She'd a cool rippling figure and an even more excellent head for figures; under that semi-beehive hair arrangement, like an old time girl vocalist - Diana Ross or Martha Reeves say - or perhaps, outwardly, a Hitchcock heroine.

"Why shouldn't I be?" he declared, offended.

"It isn't safe for you around here," she gasped.

"What's the matter with everyone today?" he asked.

"What can you be thinking of?" she said, breathless, panicked.

They confronted each other on the pavement, with heavy crowds dividing around them, in a state of astonishment.

"What are you trying to tell me?" he pleaded. Pixie Wright assumed a degree of familiarity and even concern. But like unfamiliar code, he was unable to interpret meanings. He stared dumbfounded into her eyes, lost in her mystified expression, complex with untranslatable feelings.

"I'll literally scream until the cops arrive," declared Olivia Pearson.

"That's just your style, isn't it," Pitt commented.

"Try me, Clive. Go on!"

Yet for some reason he was more interested in Pixie - she held a secret.

"Clive!"

"I'm the guy who should call for a policeman," Clive insisted.

"Don't you threaten us, you disgusting creep!" Olivia yelled.

"That's charming, isn't it," he complained.

"How did you get out of that place? I mean, did they release you, or did you escape..?" Pixie asked.

"I've got no idea... what you're talking about," he admitted.

"You have to get away before it's too late!"

"Too late for what? I was hoping to slip back with you," Clive explained.

"Slip back where?" she puzzled.

"I forgot all about the time. I'm chronically late."

"Did you lose your senses?" Pixie replied.

"You can't get shot of me that easily," Clive retorted.

"They were trying to eliminate you. Why expose yourself to that risk?" Pixie insisted.

"Eliminate? Me?"

Her hypnotic eyes rounded. Her white blonde hair seemed to evoke both extreme youth and old age. "They are trying to take you out. It's insane to return to the office now!"

"Why do they want to kill me?" he urged her.

21

"Perhaps the idea...I'm not certain though...is to make it simpler for them."

There was information to pass on, but it was lost to him.

"Leave her alone! Go away!" shouted the other woman. Rage and fear pushed her to edge of control. Then Pixie pulled her away by the arm, as if for her own safety, until both women scurried away.

"They all seem to be losing their minds today," Clive said to himself quietly, as he observed the pair as they threw themselves into the revolving doors of the Winchurch Building.

4

Had he said or done something out of place in the office? Could that offer any explanation?

Plainly it had been a hard morning at work; in fact the previous weeks had been difficult, as far as he remembered. The details were hazy, he merely had a general if compelling impression. There had been a complex and difficult merger happening; a leveraged and unsolicited bid. The pressure of that deal had got to him lately, he knew; it tingled on his nerves like the feel of nicotine or coke for an addict. It had been an exhausting twenty-four-hour piece of business, on which he was asked to lead. Handsome profits for the company if he succeeded, if he handled things correctly, but big pressure and risks too. Wasn't this a fact you had to live with? Nothing could justify the reaction of Olivia and Pixie, outside the very doors of the firm. He wasn't directly their manager, but he was certainly one of their bosses. He had certainly been Olivia's mentor for a year; this was how she repaid him.

Pitt was shaken, disturbed, by the hostility of their reaction. But their horrified response seemed completely in earnest. So what had people been saying about him; what was he supposed to have done? The City was always crackling with rumour and gossip, breaking reputations as it crunched numbers and chewed statistics. Was it all part of the prank that started in a black limousine, with that guy joshing about being the devil?

"But she implied that they're trying to kill me," he recalled, allowing her warning words to resound. "Can she be serious?"

Well they'd almost succeeded, hadn't they, on the evidence so far.

Maybe this was an elaborate office joke after all. During his first years at the company, his boss, Sir Septimus Winchurch himself, had highly approved of his impressive, rapid progress. Sep had been impressed with Clive from the beginning in fact; with his sharp mind, his eager attitude, exemplified in a strapping physique and fresh good looks. Sep made a point of starting him off in a more responsible role and at a higher salary, with bigger bonuses, than the other graduate intake, once his internship period had concluded.

The shrewd old chap, a doyen of the City (among the last of the old school) regarded Clive as a brave musketeer on the markets; just the talent to take his company into the new global era, and to accommodate a new political world order. Even so he had a few doubts, as Clive was "a northern outsider", whose background didn't exactly stack up, compared to previous company policy and conventional recruitment practice.

With the passing of over a decade, Clive thought, at some point thereafter, Winchurch had taken exception to him. No longer seen as the brilliant golden boy from an admirable grammar school outside a northern town. The boss had grown regularly irked by his progeny's strict ethics and scruples (that came from a tight, respectable family background) which were not in tune with an unregulated financial era. The old chap was not tolerant of occasional miscalculations, or misjudgements, that even directors were guilty of. Such errors had been inevitable, a calculated side effect arguably, considering the fast and unpredictable nature of this 'casino' side to the business.

As far as Winchurch was concerned Clive didn't belong to the trustworthy list of schools and universities. Sometimes it could be down to the precise college. Pitt's mathematical intellect, his eager charisma, his rugged physique even, had been appealing attributes. Clive gave them the sense that he could not only survive in the financial bear pit, but savage the dogs and wolves. He could hold his own in that sphere of gargantuan egos. But the old chap always questioned Pitt's nerve, doubted his sympathies, at the sharp end of a crucial negotiation. This was even as Sep needed his experience and expertise to close out a complex deal. Did Pitt truly understand that *Winchurch Brothers* was more important than anything to him, Septimus, than even his own flesh and blood?

Clive lingered on the pavement outside HQ. He stared up at the sheer glass surfaces of the building, brooding over the morning's events. His colleagues would be laughing at him, if they intended to test him through an office hoax. If so then it was the most elaborate prank they had ever pulled off. He was puzzled why they selected him for a joke, considering his status in the organisation. His talents and achievements in the company had been respected by colleagues and staff, not only by his boss, the board and significant shareholders. This had not only been true during the tony times, but after the debt bubble burst, as the big bang went into reverse, and practically sucked the FTSE back to a dot.

Pitt wasn't going to be intimidated by some maverick who wanted to severely embarrass him or even to wreck his career. It was a Friday anyway, almost the weekend, according to his calculation, so he was entitled to go home early. This action would undermine the unknown practical joker; it would deny him a triumphant scene. Clive did not recognise the time of day, or even the changes of seasons; but on this occasion he would absent himself. Maybe he would let his wife know of these plans and book a late flight to Rome or Paris. She would be delighted, as they rarely had the chance to arrange spontaneous holidays. Unfortunately he couldn't find a phone in his pockets to make a call or to communicate with. Did he lose all those techie devices somehow, or had he left them on his desk?

Still he would get in touch with her somehow. If there was an office scam, then it would turn cold as sliced meat by Monday morning. Most likely somebody would call him later to explain the ruse and to apologise. They would grovel and be shamefaced, because this had been miscalculated from the start. It was a dangerous game to try to make fun of an associate and a key-holder.

But these explanations didn't quite convince. Despite such bravado, he feared that something had flipped. It came as a shock to believe that any colleague wanted to humiliate him. He took a deep breath and slipped back into the Winchurch building.

There was no option but to retrieve his jacket, briefcase and other personal belongings. Most likely he had left everything in his locker, as he didn't like any clutter around his working space. It was a bit sneaky to return back into work like this, but Pixie's warning words had affected him. She said that someone was out to eliminate him. The threat was vague, yet at a subliminal level, Pitt had believed her.

He wasn't noticed. In place of the regular doorman, Harry (a man devoted to racing pigeons and the Arsenal) there was a craggy substitute security man, Harry's vacation stand-in, unlikely to identify Pitt. This was a bit of luck, as the reserve desk guard wasn't interested in Clive's jerky movement across the lobby, but was instead fascinated by a multiple array of security screens, as if he was enjoying the most expensive media package.

Clive decided to take the service stairs. He didn't wish to hang around waiting for an elevator either. There were multiple flights and he still risked bumping into a junior colleague. It was a crazy proposition, but he sensed that his role, his status within the organisation, had gone awry. He wasn't going to ignore the warning offered by Miss Wright, even if it didn't typically respond to verbal rumours or tip offs.

Super rapid elevators ran up the core of the building, while the stairway was empty. In fact he didn't know who did use the stairway. Clive could hear the machinery's ecstatic whining as he trudged up the hollow well. He only encountered one person during the entire ascent. But he didn't recognise that individual and the nervous looking guy didn't recognise him either. They hardly acknowledged each other. To discover a character he had not met in the building before, on the back stairs, was also a strange phenomenon.

Clive reached his usual level of the building, puffing as if reaching the finish line of a peaks walking challenge. Hesitantly, for once, he pushed through port-holed doors, rather like serving doors in a restaurant (he always thought) and nervously entered the next corporate space. Somehow his normal work place had transformed into a danger zone, full of hidden questions like landmines.

A mental warning sign stopped him from going further. The male locker room that he patronised was at the end of the next corridor. He fixed his glance and set off directly, keeping soft feet, as calmly as his heart and lungs allowed. There was no reason to veer off into a trading area. He had every right to behave out of character, to set off early for a long weekend, however unfamiliar. That's exactly what he intended to do, to wrong step them. This hadn't been such a great day at the office so far. He wasn't going to extend his hours like an ambitious intern. He didn't need to insinuate himself like a graduate Trojan.

Clive felt the presence of his colleagues, the whole eyes-focused-front shirt sleeve culture. Obviously his desk would be unoccupied in his absence; temporarily abandoned; who could take his place now? Was it even possible to replace him, given his portfolio, his expertise, his involvement? Those people would be wondering what had taken him, as this was not his normal pattern. Despite such risky behaviour, there was no need to be afraid, despite Pixie's warning.

Perhaps he should just show up and try to explain. This wasn't like misbehaving on a boys' night out. He picked up the normal bustle of financial traffic. The office continued as usual, just beyond thin walls and divisions, amidst a spectral hum of information technology. Even his boss was only a few divisions and walls away. His heart skipped a beat, hurtled like financial tickers over Bloomberg screens. He strayed across a glass division - a screen of etched crystal that had been presented by a Swedish client - that surely revealed his outline, a smoky ghost, if people gazed up for a moment.

What made him tread carefully when he could afford to swagger? Did he really have a reason to be nervous around here; considering he was Winchurch's head boy and protégé, or had been?

Pitt strode stealthy as a cat burglar, before he darted into the locker room. He took a breather, adjusting to a humid enclosed space, like a heart chamber. He faced regimented lines of lockers, grey and mute as the morning cleaning shift. Yet there was an equal risk of being discovered, if it was dangerous to be found. Clive searched in his trouser pockets and was relieved to find a set of keys. The ring contained the appropriate swab to open his locker.

Except that there were many other keys and passes, which he couldn't remember adding or accumulating. What was going on with his head? On the other hand he did tend to collect keys and gather junk. It was one of the gripes of his missus. At least he was able to pick out the swipe which could open his locker.

After opening the box he stared confusedly at various contents. There was a loud check jacket on a hanger, two flowery kipper ties and a yellow nylon shirt. Not only did these not belong to him, but he wouldn't be seen dead in such a get up. Clive had good taste in clothes and was scrupulous in presentation. If there was a new occupant of the locker, who'd exchanged possessions, then he had not disposed of, or reprogrammed, the previous swipe. That was careless security as Clive well understood, in an age of corporate espionage.

However, at this point he had company; there were steps and voices at the entrance; two guys had entered the room, to join him. Fortunately Clive was hidden from view like a street robber between the tall avenues of steel. The pair chatted, slacking, enjoying themselves, while Pitt froze to attention in the adjacent aisle. He recognised the voices of colleagues, and obviously they'd recognise him.

"I need another change of shirt. The air conditioning is buggered. If it gets any hotter I'll be wearing my French swim briefs."

"On for tennis, Sunday evening? Don't forget the sun cream!"

"Definitely, chum, always a pleasure to smash your balls over the grass."

"No chance, Jonny, 'cause my back spin's deadly as a knife. You'll get your balls served back in cubes, matey."

Clive identified the first speaker as Martin Abrams, and his companion was Jonathan Spence. He didn't want them to discover him playing truant, if that's what he was doing. Could this pair be responsible for the practical joke?

"We shouldn't piss about here. We'll be noticed if we're gone too long. There's the Singapore deal, and then I have to refer quotations back to Shanghai," said Abrams. "Just let me splash my face…"

"I've got a fresh shirt," Spence informed him. "For once it's not the old geezer who's making me sweat. You know we're fortunate the establishment didn't collapse. We are meant to be grateful. This is the afterlife, remember?"

"Who could have predicted Pitt turning up? Right in the street, outside the very building. He was supposed to be under lock and key, according to rumour."

"Not satisfied with nearly wrecking all our jobs and careers."

"Wants to come and have another try!"

"Incredible, if it really was that crazy dick and not a case of mistaken identity."

"We've no reason to doubt Pixie, our Miss 'Head and shoulders'!" Abrams had a cocky way of talking from the back of his throat, as if he could spit at the world to prove his superiority. "She's not one of the ditzy chicks!"

"Pixie Wright wasn't the chick who identified him… although she didn't or wouldn't contradict Olivia's account either," his sidekick recalled.

"Why should we disbelieve her? It shows that Pitt is still in play. They said he was dressed for work, like the day he was expelled. Do you think he's working for a different company? He must have found another position."

"Anything's possible. He wants to fuck us from behind this time. That would confirm the rumours…and his footprint on trades…his thinking is unmistakeable."

"You're paranoid as fucking Hitler. The old geezer has the information and contacts to take him out," Spence bragged; as if he had the boss' ear.

"Anyhow, the old Sep will be furious to learn about this," Abrams considered.

"How long has it been since Clive disappeared?"

"Shows he hasn't left the country, or anything more drastic," Abrams joked. "Nothing would surprise me in regard to Pitt."

"Why wasn't he eliminated already?" said Spence. "Y'know, that's the rumour."

"A guy like that is usually disappeared...*eventually*," Abrams agreed. "Nobody lick's Sep's bollocks, only Sep. He was a particularly self-opinionated, arrogant provincial dick, I think we all agree. Didn't get a proper upbringing."

"Oh, totally...totally pompous and self righteous dick...in the known financial universe. As an associate he was leading a charmed life...because he was a key-holding prick face...he had them over a barrel on the deal.,, He had the inside track and a seat in the main room...before he fucked it up."

"Smug dick stuck in the air. Why let some oik loose on high worth stiffs? Trouble was for Sir Sep, that Clive knew stuff here. They let him too deep. Where did he store all that info? In technical terms he was going places we couldn't fucking dream about. That's the problem, he was the code sorcerer...and he kept us away from the black magic. Maybe he's being protected."

"Would anyone wish to touch that northern dick now?"

"You reckon he's diced meat?"

"Yes, I do mate. They'll rip off his balls and stuff them in his mouth."

"It annoys me to think he's doing toy time for a rival. What do you think? The idea of Clive still playing and dashing around the globe...makes me want to fucking puke."

"I reckon he put the frighteners on our ditzy chick 'secretaries' to give us a warning. That's the type of pomposity you expect from an arrogant northern pleb... here on a scholarship from his fucking little grammar school."

At this point their voices dropped off; as if they had caught a sound and were listening out for something.

"Hey, Abrams, do you smell alcohol...whiskey? Isn't it?"

There was a humming pause. "D'you know, I think I can...I'd swear by your big spunky balls that I can smell whiskey."

"Who's the fucking dipso at Winchurch's, then?"

"That you around there, Mike? Mikey D? You big dicked fuck...what are you pulling?" Abrams guffawed. "You trying to scare the shit out of us? We're talking about Pitt again, you shitfaced bastard."

"Now he's trying to grope our females in the street!"

Laughing violently and derisively the young men left. But Clive was amazed by the conversation overheard.

Hard to explain this by saying Abrams and Spence were taking a vicious stunt further. They left him with the impression that his situation had radically altered. The idea of moving or shifting in time was not far fetched. There had been a kind of earthquake under his professional life. He'd achieved a different outcome. Clearly he had not gone back a year. Instead he had jumped forward in time, or perhaps lost a whole year, as warned by that sinister fruit in the limo.

Yes, he may have suffered this involuntary gap year. Or at least that potent idea had been suggested to him. There was as yet only flimsy evidence to establish this (only hearsay) but he'd suffered an ominous, threatening alteration. Had he really met that dark gentleman, that evil force in the universe, that we choose to call, among other tags, "the devil"? Or more likely it was a powerful individual who had a stake in wrecking his reputation? In destroying his position at *Winchurch & Bros* and trying to blow him away?

Pitt began to rummage the interior of the locker (his old locker), none of which pertained to him. Yet he found a selection of items to confirm that twelve months (a significant period of time) must have elapsed. In the pockets of that comedian's jacket there was a dry cleaning ticket, bus tickets, a stub for an Aerosmith reunion gig, a receipt for flowers and a badminton club league table. In the bottom of the compartment he found a commuter style fish 'n' chip newspaper. Sure enough it displayed the same date, only exactly a year ahead.

Clive scanned the pages obsessively, from a blind impulse and rising panic, not out of curiosity. Many of the columns were taken up with ecological stories - droughts, mass exodus and movement. All the usual cheery Armageddon snippets that we try to stash under our Afghanistan rug. The topic of these news reports had not changed, yet he got a sense of intensification after an interim, like a tropical sun going behind a cloud to emerge with greater intensity.

He skimmed through pages of scandal and gossip in growing panic. Did he fear there was an article about himself? Was he going to read about himself? Get a distorted summary of the strange disaster that had befallen him? There was a new Home Secretary in place, after the previous occupant spent more time with family. There was a change of manager at the football club he supported.

Luckily he couldn't spot anything about himself. He supposed that it was very unlikely to get the information in that basic analogue manner. Was it really true that he'd stepped out of the world and then been pushed back again? He felt like a passenger of a ship who'd missed his sailing and tried to race on to the next port.

His likely predicament began to oppress. He'd taken a short journey into the future, with an effective loss of memory, to find circumstances thoroughly changed. He had gone through a black hole, an information wormhole, suffered a temporary annihilation. This was an explanation for his peculiar encounters and sensations of that day.

For he then did not simply vanish into thin air, he was (apparently) very much present, making decisions, locked in a pattern of behaviour. During that lost year he was without the ability to judge his actions, or to retain memories. Certainly that didn't imply that the year had not happened.

Hopefully nothing too serious or damaging had passed during those absent twelve months. But he wouldn't like to bet on that prospect, in either a private or professional capacity.

5

The east London streets looked unchanged; only with an added heat shimmer dancing over surfaces. The City had evolved over centuries, absorbed social and political change, been destroyed by wars and bombs, by leaps and increments. Yet all the usual sights and scenes were made strange to Pitt, dislocated in his mind, due to an interruption of twelve months, this blind spot seared into his brain.

There was a newly finished building across the road, born to the world, that he remembered under construction; a hive of industry, surrounded by cranes and platforms, and filled with hard-hatted construction workers.

Should he return to his desk and try to explain his predicament? Could they not believe his experience of disorientation, even amnesia? Such characteristic boldness might have ended his confusion. But a sense of danger and of unanswered questions restrained him. Going back to work would be like bursting into a meeting without a brief on any of the participants. The ironic and hostile attitude of Martin and Jonny implied that a blind reunion wouldn't be smart.

Clive remained unnerved by his limousine meeting with that big shot. He wanted to return to his family and seek out human company. After the death of his father, just a couple of years back, his wife and son had become more important. Both his parents had now passed away. He couldn't be so naïve as to surrender to his enemies. For all he knew these might include his boss and, he thought, trying to interpret past actions, disgruntled former clients.

Pixie Wright had referred to death threats. Should he take that idea seriously? That his life was imminently at risk? Why did he instantly trust her judgement, when she'd warned him? Returning to the Winchurch building, mentally in the dark, he'd risked advancing the end game; whatever the game might be.

So he'd been mistaken to think that his job, his career, was a place of sanctuary for him; not to talk about having a job for life; exciting and well rewarded. On the contrary, it might be the very source of that danger. He was excluded from the company, despite his previous position: all the signs indicated this negative switch around. Pitt was a radiation leak to the firm, as the financial world order had entirely changed in his absence.

During the hours that followed Pitt wandered the City streets, torturing his memory, through blank light and empty shadows. For the first time since he had relocated to London as an eager graduate, he felt alienated in the glinting money canyons of the City. He was locked out from his career, suddenly an exile or even an outlaw in this town, without any mental purchase on why or how: reduced to tramping the arteries from Lime Street to Liverpool Street, as if he was on a temporary contract or even hired by the hour. But these aimless exertions gave no extra insight. This fretful wandering merely baffled him. He was encouraged to indulge destructive emotions. In this suffocating dusty heat he merely worked himself into a molten sweat.

He surely had a wild, dishevelled, bloodshot look to match his internal turmoil. But he tried to keep as calm as possible, keeping his fight or flight responses in check. He thought this could even be a question of survival. He was determined to protect himself, by staying sane, to face any new challenge or threat that came along. These were the type of character traits and skill sets that *Winchurch Bros* had sought; and which training and development policies had promoted for senior staff.

Clive reached a resolution - a decision. The next step was to see his wife. There might be some value in talking to his wife. They had been together for five years now. They had a four year old boy. They were extremely happy together. They were a happy little family. God he had to see his boy again. How could he begin to explain this to Noreen? How would she react? She might know more about this affair, as her head was still in the right place. Clive was still very much in love with Noreen; she would stick by him - she was a cracking right-on girl.

Presumably she'd be able to describe the missing experiences and consequences to him. No doubt, as far as Noreen was concerned, he'd been an active agent over the past year, living and breathing; very much present and responsible for his behaviour. The reaction of family and friends would depend on exactly what had happened to him. What had he been doing in all that time? He'd lost his job, fallen out with former colleagues and alienated his employer - what more?

This was big enough. Could there be more? On the other hand, if his dismissal from *Winchurch Brothers* was just about a personality clash, or an ethical difference of opinion, then there was no shame attached. He'd lost that prestigious position and, during the period of his employment, he'd surely made millions for Winchurch (and hefty bonuses for himself).

Pixie, and other former colleagues, implied that he might have another job, as a whole year had gone by. For all he knew, at that very moment, he was employed by a different, rival organisation. He could have been poached by a competitor, tapped up by a bigger player. Then he'd have an office to go to and an even better career. Perhaps that was why the boss, Sep Winchurch, was angry with him. If there was anything in that positive spin, then Pitt didn't need to worry. His gorgeous wife wouldn't be upset, worried or even frustrated by his behaviour. The security of his family would be assured, along with the global financial system. Then everything would come up smelling like an oligarch's girlfriend.

Whatever the truth, he had to return home at some stage. Pitt couldn't torture himself by hammering out the paving stones, exhausting his ideas about the square mile. Hopefully the missus would have some explanation for this nightmare; a thread out of this dreadful day he was barely aware of leaving or entering. She'd be able to refocus and re-place him.

At least he knew the way home, even while his memory was wrecked. That would have spoiled this devil guy's sense of fun. Clive hadn't lost his senses or instincts. Perhaps that was illogical, yet anyway he had some route back. He knew all his faculties were intact; his earlier memories, life's overwhelming store of information. Everything was at his fingertips bar the year in question, which had somehow been encrypted for security reasons. He had lost the password to his life, but who wanted to engineer this, to control his life, his ideas, and his movements?

Clive found himself going down the Bank tube station. He was into the typical daily throng and there was nothing untoward in that aspect. Normally, before, he had a yearly pass to cover his daily commute. Noreen and he gave up their City apartment after the birth of their son. Unfortunately he had to pay for a ticket that evening, because the travel pass was of course out of date.

On this hot evening it wasn't a false note to go without a suit jacket. Still, he knew that it was lost, along with many other possessions, and that was humiliating and infuriating. It wasn't so much the wasted fittings at his favourite tailor shop behind the Royal Academy of Arts. Not surprisingly it was the feeling of being divided or incomplete. Without the jacket and a briefcase he was stripped of status and felt like a pariah. Was the loss of personal items any accident? Where had he mislaid these possessions? What was going on with his head, that he didn't have a clue where?

It was obvious that other commuters thought that he was out of sorts. Something really awful had happened to him; or he had seen it or witnessed it. He'd habitually worn his self-confidence and prestigious job lightly. He was able to glide through his commute, protected by his assured status, absorbed and buoyed by his powerful work. The sense of being professionally finished now shattered his public confidence. His volatile demeanour betrayed this fact. He began to shuffle with the moving crowd on the concourse, to hide within the stampeding current.

Clive took a descending elevator, keeping tightly to the right side, an alien surrounded by aliens. Bemusedly he studied alternating electronic advertisements. There was a big new American show in town, straight from Broadway, that Noreen would have enjoyed. Most of these advertised events and products were familiar to him, despite a superficial change of imagery and message. He drew attention to himself with his paranoid look, which was a disconcerting sight for people passing on the ascending escalator. Nothing could be taken for granted or looked at in the same way. The whole world of signs, machines, noise and people, was threatening, as if he was about to be chewed and discarded.

On the subterranean platform commuters stood about in typical restless postures. He was highly aware of people's tension within that heated crush: checking of watches, pacing, mutterings and peering into tunnel abysses. Until the tube train, building compressed tension, burst and clattered into the station, with a metallic shriek like a dinosaur. This train was a new model he hadn't seen before, with different colours and design. Sliding doors hissed back. There was hasty exiting and entering. Pitt squeezed among the influx. He tottered into a space before the vehicle lurched back into that abyss. This was a place where people generally didn't wander but trusted in the dark.

Clive found himself participating in the familiar game of eyeball footsie. Sometimes he brought his reader or tablet with him, but that was either left in a desk drawer (at his previous or present employer's) along with other possessions; mislaid with his jacket and cases. He felt that he was completely cut off or, conversely, buried up to his neck. God only knew where his briefcase was at this moment, or his essential communication gadgets.

He stared deeply into space, disconsolate; unconnected. He struggled to compose his strong, if bony features; his breathing, the perspiration. He realised that nobody wanted to look in his direction. They were even less enthusiastic than on a normal day. If he was not invisible then he may as well be.

The train left those sooty tunnels behind and emerged into the open air, and the harsh light. They rattled between stations, with fizzes of electricity, as if the wheels ran on the gums of a dragon.

They were carried deeper into outlying countryside, dusty and scorched, all the way towards the end of the line, where Pitt lived.

During this stage of the journey school kids hopped aboard, unruly and loud, after another testing day in roasting classrooms. Their demonic laughter and jostling energy took over the carriage, like a giant skateboard, until they got off again and restored semi-rural silence. Strangely he preferred the noise of these anarchic kids to the City's indecipherable clamour.

He felt he was suffocating, locked into his own mind; he could kill himself. But he wouldn't listen to negative voices. Clive had never considered killing himself. He refused to give in to such weakness, despite intense pressure. It was the intention of his enemies to make him despair. They wanted him to believe there was no point to (his) life. He felt their influence, whoever they were, even if he was entirely confused, as he felt the effects of institutions behind the individual.

The train clattered into his regular station; with its familiar Victorian canopies and pots of geraniums. On the narrow platform an elderly lady blocked his path with a trolley, frustrating his attempts to pass. Despite such aggravation he maintained his patience and nerve, to get through to the ticket office. Without considering his actions he set off into an adjoining car park, along with other commuters. A march out to the motor was normal at the end of a working day.

Cars glittered and shimmered in the car park like oil drums in the Sahara.

But when he arrived at his customary spot his brand new sports coupe was not waiting. Other drivers were taking off, emptying the area, while Pitt began to stride about desperately, tired eyes roving, wondering if his motor was stolen. He thoroughly searched other areas, but his vehicle was definitely not there. What should he do, call the police?

If he had another job, unbeknownst to himself, then he'd still expect to have a car. He would be commuting to the City; he would be parked up underground and should expect to collect his car; return home to his family and a relaxing evening.

Pitt assumed that he must own the same car. He still had the gadget to countermand security and open it. If there was a conspiracy going on, then this was the latest most infuriating twist. Definitely there were some individuals at work who would find this situation amusing.

Abandoning a near empty car park Clive decided to catch a bus. He was accustomed to taking cabs around central London. The last time he'd taken a bus was in New Zealand on holiday actually, when they'd got lost one evening in the mountains. Noreen was undertaking her *Lord of the Rings* pilgrimage. A local bus wasn't an appealing swap for an air-conditioned dream machine. Allegedly A/C contributed to global warming. That was cruelly ironic wasn't it, because you needed A/C while trapped in an over-heating planet. Fortunately the bus didn't take too long to arrive, which was fortunate in this quiet area. The fare was paid and he found himself a window seat. Somehow he felt hidden, as if people should not be able to see him. Yet his anxious presence was recorded in their evasive looks.

The high-street was thronged and the bus filled up. It was that part of the day when everyone was trying to get home for dinner. Passengers were forced to stand in the aisle, suffering in solid heat behind glass. It was a meandering route, through hamlets and villages, nearly an hour before the stretchy vehicle reached the old town. By the time Clive stepped off, seeking out his district, the bus was completely empty; they lived at the edge of town.

6

Pitt felt alone in the dead quiet. He set off along a country-style remote lane, punctuated by large properties. These places were concealed behind high trees and hedges, with scorched gardens beyond, some with water-sprays, like trying to soothe the cracked skins of parched elephants.

Clive was now beginning to feel some effects of heat exhaustion, with sunburn on his face and neck (he didn't have a hat) as well as dire thirst. Why did he forget to buy a drink in town; apart from beer and wine? The fierce evening sun felt like a metal rod through the top of his crown to his knees. His mind and thoughts had a quality like molten glass, swirling away and shifting shapes.

Drawing nearer to home he grew apprehensive, considering what he could expect. What was the condition of his marriage under these strains? Was she used to him returning home late these days? Had they been going through strains and conflicts in their relationship? Clive thought that was most likely. There had to be some change at home, from the huge shift in his professional life. Like the two sides of the brain itself personal life had a double aspect.

Clive finally reached his gravelled and high hedged lane, an estate agent's whimsy, which led towards his house. They had put so much work and money into fully restoring this eighteenth century terraced property. They'd exchanged an apartment on the Thames near Greenwich for this impressive old place.

On the outside the red brick was attractively crumbled, with bay windows and climbing roses over a deep porch, presently in prolific flower. The interior was surprisingly spacious, yet adapted to contemporary living, with a large garden at the rear. They hadn't found time to fully develop the long back garden as yet. They'd wanted a garden for their lad, but Clive had been too absorbed by the office; they were both too busy bringing the boy up.

Pitt noticed that his car was not stationed on his drive either. If you'd left or lost your car somewhere then the fact tended to bother you. This loss or theft was a big enough grief to him. With a reeling mind he began up his own garden path. He had a front door key ready in his hand. But when he inserted the key and tried, it wouldn't work. The locks were changed! Somehow he expected this, but it still came as a shock. Had Noreen changed the locks? Was that to protect them? He looked about the place, cold with confusion in the baking afternoon, feeling like a dead man.

There was no reaction to pressing his door bell. He knocked on the sturdy cottage-style front door (purchased from a demolition sale) and waited there anxiously, or expectantly. There wasn't a reaction to these blows, and he tried again, harder. Noreen was most likely far up the garden, looking after Josh, playing some instructive game with him. She would be sitting out there, not exactly sunbathing, but enjoying a shady place beneath wisteria. In the morning she was busy with her charity work, going through the accounts, after putting in some hours at the computer for her own business.

Pitt thumped their authentically eroded wooden door again, and gazed up towards upper latticed windows, where climbing roses twisted and tangled. She'd definitely changed the curtains since yesterday, and placed some erotic art on the sill too.

Clive wandered around to the side of the row, and began to call out Noreen's name, towards the gardens. He understood that this was an optimistic chant, even on a regular day. Then after another crescendo of "Noreen!!" he eventually drew a response from one of their neighbours. An elderly widow next door, Gemma Buckingham, who risked a narrow chink, one eye, to investigate the commotion he was making at his unscheduled return.

"What are you trying to do?"

"Yes Gemma. How are you?" The eye merely blinked with no response. "Where's Noreen this evening? Isn't she home yet?"

"What's that to you?" she challenged. She was a plaid skirt held in with a pin type of girl.

"I can't get into my own house. What's going on Gemma? When did she change the locks?!"

"There's another couple in there now. A lovely couple," she explained. "Dr Shipman."

"How can that be? Another Shipman?"

"Dr Shipman's at his surgery and she's gone to the gym," Mrs Buckingham informed him.

"You mean that Noreen isn't living here anymore? You're telling me that we don't own this property?"

"Absolutely not. You're out of luck I'm afraid."

"Is that the case?"

"If you are asking."

They'd always had a testy relationship with Gemma Buckingham; who thought that having babies was a liberty and complained about cries in the night or moving about on floorboards. Basically it was their moral fault to want a family, as if human beings should be purchased in a hamper from *Fortnum*'s. She was making a principled stand towards quiet extinction; she was the eldest of six spinsters.

"We moved?" he asked. "Where are we supposed to have gone?"

"Noreen went to America."

"I can hardly believe this."

"Without you, you dreadful man," she intoned.

"It's terrible! With Joshua?" He addressed a narrow strip of person; which was all she considered respectable.

"Of course she went with the child. She couldn't abandon him. She wouldn't leave him to live off benefits. She isn't that kind of person." As if Mrs Buckingham cared what kind of person his wife had been.

"What got into her? To go off like that?" he urged.

"She got thoroughly sick of all your carryings on, Clive. And who can really blame her? Thanks to you she couldn't even stay in the country, or wait for a divorce. Now please leave before I call the Police."

"Gemma, don't go yet please, don't go!"

"Look at the condition you are in now, Clive. You have no moral boundaries. What have you been doing? God help us."

"You see there are a few details that I am sketchy about. I promise not to keep you long. I understand that you are reluctant to speak to me."

"You're responsible for your own actions, aren't you?" she said.

He thought about the idea. "You didn't say exactly why my wife left me," he reminded her.

"Starting to have some regrets are you? You should have considered your marriage at the time, while you were going off the leash. The bird has flown," she announced ironically. "What a Christmas that must have been, all on her own."

"Which Christmas are you referring to?"

"Joshua wondering where his Daddy was. Why did you abandon responsibility? The poor woman couldn't tolerate the situation any longer."

"Sounds like a merry little time," Clive said. "But what's she doing in America? The US you mean? Whereabouts is she in the US?" he considered. His world was revolving.

"All I know is that she has another chap."

"She's run away with another bloke?" he exclaimed, reeling.

"A good looking chap. I believe he bred pedigree dogs."

"A dog breeder?"

"Yes, at first they went to Dumfries, and then he decided to move the business to America."

"How did he get a Visa? I don't believe this."

"If you want my advice you won't try to find her in America. She deserves another chance to be happy. Leave her in peace over there. She was never happy with you."

"Well that's a complete lie," Clive replied.

"Who could predict that you'd show up here again?" she considered.

"How did our little Josh respond to all this?"

"Don't you blame yourself?" she told him.

"That's what I'm trying to discover," he replied.

"There's nothing to find out," the woman complained.

"Noreen was always big on America. She talked about going there, as soon as the right job came along," he recalled to himself, trying to make sense of these unknown events. "But sometimes it was Boston, sometimes New York, then in another mood San Francisco or even Seattle."

"Why didn't you consider the consequences at the time?"

"At what time? I can't make much sense of what you're telling me. It's too bizarre. Maybe this is all a lot of gossip," he concluded. "Where did you get your information?" he challenged.

"This conversation has come to an end, Mr Pitt. Your big City bonus won't buy back your wife, will it? It didn't guarantee your family or your happiness, did it? Now you'll have to reassess your rotten values. I would advise you to leave my neighbours' property before I finally call the police. Get yourself off, while you still can."

Mrs Buckingham retired behind her thick door. There was a risk she'd retrieve her antique mobile and contact her local constabulary. That's exactly where she kept her telephone; in a small cupboard in the kitchen. He wondered about waiting for the new occupants of his house to return; this nice young medical couple Dr Shipman and his loyal wife. But he knew it was advisable to leave the area quickly. Sometimes you didn't want the truth, or you feared to understand the nasty details of what you had.

7

What were his plans now? Not back to London, because he couldn't face a reverse journey. He couldn't depend on the idea that old friends remained friends, if he could be sure. You couldn't just turn up at their homes or offices asking questions. He experienced the anguish of losing all his friends at a stroke. In fact he wasn't even sure who his friends were any more. He felt himself melting down under this new disconcerting feeling; this sense of groping about helplessly in his memories.

But there was one guy he knew, who lived in the next village. Calling back at the house had returned the memory. Douglas Breadham was a very open minded corporate lawyer, a complacent, self-centred type of man and a *bon vivant*. Douglas was trained not to ask personal questions or even questions of character; anyway not in an emotional or judgemental way.

Sometimes it was difficult to know Douglas' opinions or how he thought. This trait was surprising as Doug enjoyed his liquor and certainly dabbled in drugs. None of that prompted a loose tongue or any personal confidences. He overrode any negative effects through a sporty lifestyle and promiscuous sex, usually with high class hookers from Africa or Eastern Europe.

Douglas could offer a refuge and maybe an explanation for this ordeal; this nightmare of shifted time and squandered ambition. Doug might shed light on that strange guy who'd snatched him from the street, if he dared to introduce the topic.

Pitt began to retrace his steps away from 'home', along meandering, leafy streets. These no longer belonged to him, even though every turn was mapped inside his head, as were his memories and experiences of living as a young couple, with their beautiful son and an excitingly upward future. Were all their dreams and hopes completely undone? Their aspirations ruined, and Pitt potentially leaving the district for good? Could he even refer to Noreen and himself as a "couple" anymore?

Think about them as a family? Shockingly his wife had left him and decamped. She and the boy were relocated in the States somewhere. He was truly stunned and devastated by this turn of events. He trudged, almost blind with grief, the breath torn out of him; feeling stunned, oblivious to himself.

He might be seen by other neighbours. If there had been irregularities, or a dispute, then the police and the authorities would want to interview him. The lane was private and very quiet, particularly around evening time, during the post-commute period. They'd recognise him from the local pub, because Noreen and he would go in there some evenings. As a couple they made an effort to socialise and get to know people. During the spring and summer they would sit out in the garden, so that Josh could play on the swings and frame.

There had been some scandal at work and home, judging by the reaction of their neighbour. Noreen had been a popular woman in town, as she ran her charity, she organised fetes and raised money locally, using her business expertise. Noreen must have carried through the house sale rapidly. Even though a year had passed, she must have been determined to complete. Pitt maintained control; he had trained himself from an early age to avoid self-pity. He would get to the bottom of these sinister mysteries. That's how he had survived and flourished at his job, with the same attitude of mind, placing his vulnerability at one remove.

Then as he was walking he was passed by a guy, about the same age as himself, with two young children, a boy and a girl. Clive acknowledged them faintly in this state of mind. As he later recalled, he even raised a hand in a partial wave, with a friendly glance. The normality of this encounter brought no comfort. If anything the sight made him sad because it reminded him again of his son and former wife; of everything he'd lost. This was a husband and a father, and Clive no longer belonged to that club, or sector of society.

Presumably this chap had picked his two kids up from school and was walking them back home. He was leading his kids by the hand and had passed by in a few seconds. Clive didn't recognise this family and it seemed as if they didn't recognise him either. He wouldn't have thought anything more about the fleeting encounter. Yet then Clive felt a heavy blow across the back of his shoulders. He gasped before the sudden impact. This ripped across his bones and muscles, pitching him on to the ground, electric cables running down his arms, as he tasted thick hot dust. What a nightmare, the guy had knocked him to the floor.

Clive simply could not stay on his feet, in the face of this blow. It took him a few moments to record the shock, and to sense the injury, of this attack. To begin with he didn't connect such violence with the guy who had passed; and who appeared so normal. It might have been a lightning strike, for all Clive knew.

Then he rolled over, tried to keep conscious, and he was looking up at this same man. The expression wasn't friendly; he was leaning over menacingly, glaring with a mad eye, holding up a stick, more like a stave, ready to crash back down on Clive's skull. The guy's two children were stood to the side, watching impassively, just waiting for their Dad to finish the job. What had triggered this hellish experience?

There was a quick instinct that led Clive to swivel, just as this stave club, like a pick axe handle, swung down at him again. Rather than demolishing Clive's skull as the guy intended, heavy wood thudded against ground to the side; with such force that the guy jarred his arms. The man winced, began to puff, to struggle, even while busting a gut to take him out; straining every sinew to kill him. Clive was near exhaustion point, but a fight for survival renewed his strength. Suddenly the right hormones were flowing; he was responding vividly to every twist and turn.

Clive found enough agility and energy to avoid attempted blows to his head. These were beginning to reduce in force and accuracy as the guy tired. The enormous orange orb of the sun found a hole in the trees ahead. As evening drew on, as the struggle continued, its sharp rays pierced through branches, which burst violently into the attacker's eyes. His head jerked up in an effort to see around these blinding needles, battling to keep his weapon aloft and to take fresh aim. He reeled about somewhat, trying to reorient himself and keep his victim in place.

This was a brief opportunity for Clive to gain the initiative. He threw himself and made a low tackle to the guy's knees, bringing down his opponent in a grunting heap, into the dust. He'd always been a good tackler for his team, despite often playing on the wing, and he held this opponent fast.

The small children took this opportunity to come forward. In defence of their Dad, or whoever the man could be, they began to kick Clive with determined concentration. Clive felt their small shoes punching between his ribs. The guy was down with him in the dust, trying to scramble to his knees, keeping a hold on the pickaxe handle - if that's what it was - and hitting out, striking again. Clive reached to his side, clawing desperately, and his hand found a lump of rock - or actually a lump of decorative mineral - which was placed there to mark the entrance to somebody's driveway. Clive took a happy grip on this found object, which he brought thumping down on the guy, as hard as possible. Clive didn't realise that he had struck the guy in the face until he saw a crushed nose and Technicolor, spaghetti-western streams of blood.

Moments after this the children ran off. He saw their vanishing backs, as they scrambled away, panicking on their bony little legs.

8

Pitt found his way back to the main road. He was afraid of having killed that guy, he couldn't explain the horrible attack, but was happy to escape with his own life. The bloody, ruined image stayed with him, even on this terrible and strange day. He was in trauma. Had this been a consequence of mistaken identity? Had he looked at that guy in the wrong way? Managed to antagonise a psychopath with a friendly wave? Or was he part of the conspiracy to 'exterminate' him, as Pixie Wright, that brilliant girl from the office, had openly warned him?

Clive scrutinised a yellowing bus timetable and sat to wait. In terms of public transport this was not exactly Piccadilly Circus. But it was too far to Douglas Breadham's place to consider walking - at least not without a proper pair of boots and maybe hiking gear. So he attempted to regain his balance and take stock. In some ways it was best to keep moving, to prevent negative ideas forming, to stop shock from setting in.

He was forced to sit waiting in the bus shelter for over two hours. Only an occasional car ripped past, including a crowd of teenagers who offered him the finger for daring to raise his thumb.

The late sun pulsed down as if worshipping itself, with no feeling of nurture. At least he was slightly sheltered from the evening heat. But the sunshine had saved him earlier, when that psycho had been blinded, and so he gave thanks to the sun, with pagan intensity. What chance was there of passing that lost year with no greater crime? He had merely been defending himself against violence: That was the sort of misdeed that could be forgiven and forgotten. Douglas would keep an open mind about these bleak adventures.

His thirst raged and he was soaked with sweat, which chilled him in spite of the temperature. He gazed across a roll of coconut matting textured fields beyond. The tree canopy was singed and wilting, afflicted by general die back, even at the height of summer. He felt as if all the sap of life had gone. He enjoyed fishing, but probably the rivers were down and invaded by poisonous spumes. What was the chance of following any of those outdoor sports now, which Noreen had originally interested him in, when the natural world was apparently under severe stress?

At last he caught sight of an approaching bus - a chugging charabanc - as nobody around here used public transport. Clive raised his arm as a signal to the driver, then felt bolts of pain and ripped nerves, branching along his arms and shoulders.

His supply of small change was running down. Fortunately he had enough and hadn't spilled everything in the dust, while playing gladiators with that mysterious thug. The bus was near empty at this stage, getting to the end of its route, yet serving every little settlement. He sat quietly, controlling a trembling hand, trying not to be disturbed. He waited until the bus finally lurched to a standstill, at the nearest stop to his friend's place, the "green" of Ashsilt village, outside the local pub and shop. It should have been a rapid walk the rest of the way; perhaps about five minutes by car. In the circumstances the walk across a country mile would take him longer. There was no alternative.

Pitt continued along tracks, over stiles, down lanes, taking short cuts where possible. The sun was forging to impressive metallic hues. He came into sight of the high iron gates to Breadham's country mansion. The juicy rewards of Temple Bar hadn't been completely drained away, he considered, viewing this mouth watering estate. Clive assumed that his friend should be at home by this hour. Doug's huge car collection was parked over a wide tarmac driveway. Soon he would need to return his valuable vehicles to their garage (something more like a hangar) for security. Pitt also kept his eyes open for larger German dog breeds, which were another hobby of Douglas'. A group of would-be intruders had given those canines a scent of human blood, a few years back. It had already been a rocky day for him, without adding extra sport. But he couldn't remember when he'd last visited this place, or exactly why he was drawn.

Douglas' place was a converted seventeenth century mansion, donated by one of his trusted advisors. The house rambled over extensive grounds, fallen handsomely into its joints and foundations. Doug had bought the house at auction, after the last financial crash, when the original dot coms were popping and bursting like champagne bubbles.

The house had been built as a hunting lodge, designed for those sophisticated aristocrats with a taste for animal blood. After the revolutionary wars it had been extended again, made into a family residence, by a banking family.

Clive was hoping to finally access his messages, jump back on the information train, so to renew contact with the outside world. Doug might be able to illuminate him about all recent events. Pitt was hopeful that the barrister wouldn't be influenced by negative stories about him. Douglas would require a proper brief, unrelated to outright character assassination.

Fortunately those high front gates were open at this stage of the evening. There were security systems in place. There was no option but to cautiously approach, despite the risks. Clive got as far as the front door and put his thumb into the chime. He could hear dogs yapping and snarling somewhere at the rear of the estate. There was a whole kennel complex, a paradise for highly bred psychotic mutts. A long wait was enforced without reply to his summons. However after a long pause, a near aristocratic delay, he picked up an opening procedure, with the sound of bolts, catches and chains being released.

Clive found himself scrutinised. This time he faced a grudging pair of male eyes. The entire world was gazing at him from around the edge of a door, it seemed. He knew these eyes to belong to Doug's butler, or manservant (or whatever his exact job title). This guy's responsibilities for house and garden went much further than the original job description, handed to him by the agency, several years before. Pitt always found the concept of a man servant hard to accept, even though it had been adopted abroad, and was not outdated in some City circles. But whatever the morality of keeping servants in the twenty first century, this guy's silk Italian suits did a lot of talking.

"Hi, Reg."

"Mr Pitt?" Distaste was brilliantly stifled.

"I realise it looks strange... to turn up like this. Sorry to impose myself on you, without an invite. I was caught out in town and don't have anywhere else to go," he explained, helplessly. "Look at the state of me, mate."

Even Reg was shocked by his appearance. "Have you been in some kind of scrape, Mr Pitt?"

"Definitely. It's all been a terrible accident. But I can't explain everything that's happened to me. I need some help from your employer."

"Do you. Has it really? You don't seem a hundred per cent."

"Mr Breadham will be able to advise me, I shouldn't wonder."

"You do look in a state," he considered. "You don't look your complete self, Mr Pitt," Reg decided. He continued to retain that chink, through which to scrutinise an untimely and unsavoury caller.

"Tell Douglas that I'm here, will you? If he has heard anything about me, then I would like to get the inside track. Do you understand? Maybe he can tell me what's been going on in my life."

The butler's guard was dropping and a little more of him was showing. Nevertheless he imparted the following information with relief:

"You didn't choose a convenient time. Mr Breadham is not at home," he stated.

Reg was about to push the door back, but Clive physically insisted that he didn't, with the use of his foot; a distressingly scuffed Church's shoe.

"What's the reason for a frosty welcome?" he said. "Why your sudden formality? Been keeping your ears open lately, Reg?"

"Mr Breadham is in town this evening, sir. He's on lady business."

There was contact between their fingers on the door edge.

"Is that the case? Is he, now? When do you expect him back home?"

"Why, in the morning, as usual," Reg said, very professionally disguising clenched teeth and straining muscles. "When might you expect him?"

"Then I can stay over for the night... this night. If it isn't too much trouble," Clive suggested.

"Not without Mr Breadham's prior permission, you can't," Reg insisted.

"You're going to turn me away? What's wrong with you? Don't you recognise me? I was a regular visitor and mate of Mr Breadham's," Clive reminded him.

But judging by Reg's reaction, the relationship had changed. No longer could he present a careless air of good humoured confidence. He could only guess at a wild and filthy appearance, showing the trapped anxiety of an insect in treacly amber.

"It wouldn't be proper, would it... to invite you for the night," Reg explained.

"The house must be empty," Clive replied.

"We haven't prepared a guest room."

"How so? Doug's away in Chelsea, isn't he, entertaining one of his nerveless girlfriends? Sorry to be so frank about this, but..."

"I'm not employed to make any judgements about my employer, Mr Pitt, and it's not obvious that they would be negative anyway," Reg said.

"Why don't you try to contact Mr Breadham?" Clive said. "Tell him about my predicament tonight. On my behalf. That's a fair suggestion, mate."

Reg found this idea amusing. "Mr Breadham can't be disturbed in the evening after a long day in court."

"Straight up? At least he's got a roof over his head. I've discovered that I don't have my own home and that my family has gone to the USA. I don't mean Disney Land either!"

"I can see you are in a distressed condition, Mr Pitt. We are most sympathetic, but unable to help," Reg told him.

"You are prepared to turn me away Reg? I don't have anywhere to go this evening."

"I'm sorry sir, but we're not a hotel."

"What do you mean?"

"I am only following my employer's instructions, in regards to unsolicited enquiries."

"Doug's going to have your guts for this," Clive warned, "and be warned, you can trade in your little Ferrari right now."

"Come back in the morning, sir. Maybe Mr Breadham will see you then," he suggested, "whatever you have to say for yourself."

"It would seem you're pretty stubborn about this, Reg. All right, don't press your panic button, leave it alone... I'm going away now. Just promise me that you'll not call the police, or raise the alarm in any way. Give me a chance, will you?"

"All right Mr Pitt, if you leave the property, I shan't press the hot line or let the dogs on to you," he agreed.

"You're surpassing yourself aren't you Reg, in the old charm school," Clive commented.

"Good evening Mr Pitt."

At which he secured a substantial oak door (which contained fragments of musket shot), and went through security procedure in reverse. Clive had noticed that smile of contempt or pity playing around Reg's conceited lips.

Clive stood about the front facade, calculating his options, considering a next move. He thought about staying on the property, to explore the grounds and other ways of entering. But Clive knew this would draw attention to himself, as Reg would carry out his threats, with his finger on that hot line to the local police station. Breadham had contacts with the rural fuzz, to safeguard expensive paintings and other expensive objects that might be exchanged for a Caribbean island. Therefore Clive had no option but to return down the drive, back out into the fields beyond, with the thought of trying his luck in the morning.

He tried not to think about that mansion with its numerous vacant guest rooms. But he gave a kick of frustration to the gate post on his way out. He really considered breaking in. Normally the trained hounds would be friendly to him - after being introduced and knowing his scent - but not if he attempted to shin uninvited up Doug's Restoration beams. There was a sun house at the rear, a type of folly, but this also had a security system.

The sky grew black and heavy, and in a few minutes a violent rain storm began. Within moments he was drenched through, hair plastered down his face, although the rain was warm. There was no bus back to town at this time, and it would be pointless to try to go back to London. Ironically he knew there was still a company credit card in this wallet; no reason to think it wouldn't be accepted by a hotel. The problem was that he didn't know of a hotel in this area. He was warned about credit details allowing his enemies (or whoever they were) to locate him. So far they only knew that he'd taken a drink at *The Banker and Flower Girl*. He couldn't take any more risks until he was briefed. He preferred to stay in the vicinity of Ashsilt village, waiting for his friend's return next morning.

By nature Clive was up to a challenge. It might have been exciting to sleep rough in other circumstances. The last time he'd slept under the stars had been in New Zealand - a year ago, or was it two? That was with the advantages of having the right equipment, keeping in contact with the outside world, with proper food and clothing. Here he was virtually in rags and beginning to freeze in pelting rain, as the temperature fell with the sun. Violent rainfall swirled about the distant Chiltern Hills. This was not comfortable. With job gone, home gone, family emigrated, he allowed himself a moderate measure of bitterness.

On a regular Friday evening Noreen and he would have a round of golf or go for a run. If they could get a babysitter they would go and catch a movie. This was all out of the window now and Clive was stricken. He trekked over the burnt out fields, which yet had sudden pools of flood water in the middle; the English terrain resembling some different country, or even planet. A throbbing purple sun re-emerged out of black funnel clouds: it sliced the atmosphere open like a hot saw as it slowly sank. Suddenly life was unnerving and difficult to recognise or to manage. You could hardly feel comfortable with the air you breathed, or tried to breathe. Clive was shocked to stumble over dead animals and birds, littering the caked earth.

Before nightfall (the twilight was long and allowed time to explore) he managed to find a place to sleep - inside a barn, on a rickety loft. He tried to sleep in meagre straw, beneath a patchy roof. As a result he endured the small hours shivering, with the stars glittering icily and a chill mist gathering. Equally he didn't know who could be about, searching around, trying to kill him, as the girl from the office had warned.

9

At dawn Clive struggled to his feet, rubbing his face, blinking in astonishment as the lineaments of his predicament returned. His head was splitting, muscles tight, body aching and tender. He stumbled back down a hay loft ladder and, returning over the rutted desolate fields, posted himself at the gates of Breadham's mansion. Soon he noticed Reg spying on him from an upstairs window, sticking his nose around a drape. Fortunately there hadn't been police sirens during the night. Clive was allowed to wait for his friend's return unmolested, hungry, exhausted, and trembling; in a woeful physical condition: like a whipped dog indeed.

Douglas was unlikely to return at the crack of dawn. Breadham would have spent the night at his Chelsea apartment, overlooking exclusive water, not far from the old Stamford Bridge (where he had an executive box), as well as a stake in the hotel. Didn't Clive have a shaky memory of accompanying him to a match once?

No doubt the lawyer would be enjoying breakfast with the fortunate lady concerned (depending on your point of view). However it was now the weekend and so he would return to Gatemead, to tend to local business and pleasure. No, Doug didn't like socialising with his easy conquests; he wouldn't hang around in town too long on a Saturday.

The dawn chorus fizzled as morning heat gathered. Giant storm puddles had evaporated, leaving a misty veil around tree tops and hills, which gradually burnt away. Suffocating humidity was beginning to build. It was after eleven that Pitt, slumped on the floor without shade, finally heard an approaching car. He noticed a following cloud of dust forming and dispersing. It sounded like one of Breadham's cars, as there was a kind of sophisticated snarl; a whine of slick revs. This was the kind of car that was constructed by guys in white suits in a dust free environment.

Shortly afterwards a high performance yellow Morgan came snarling around the corner, emitting subsonic sound frequencies like the roar of a lion. Pitt had a glimpse of his friend's very contented expression behind the windscreen, fully enjoying himself, shifting gears with the sensation of control, equal to any Persian king on a chariot. Then there was an unmistakable expression of amazement, or disgust, when Doug caught sight of Clive, or of some ragged man: as he noticed a large bedraggled figure, stood about at the gates, in a miserable and impoverished condition.

Doug didn't recognise Pitt at first. He was just shocked by this probable vagrant, some interloper peering between the bars. Yet Breadham kept both himself and the machine under tight control; pulled up smoothly, before exiting warily to investigate. He was used to dealing with violent criminals or gangsters, or simply devious crooks, but ordinarily guards or police stood by to prevent contact. There was genuine concern as well as shock as he fully recognised his associate, Clive Pitt, beyond the pale and wasted. Breadham calculated quickly as he came around the beautiful car, caressing its wing, how to deal with this potential threat.

"My god is that really you, Clive Pitt?" he observed, peeling off Ray Ban aviator shades.

Obviously he had not been communicating with Reg.

"Doug, I've been stuck out here all night," Clive gabbled.

"Where did you come from?" Doug wondered, taking him in.

"You're the only guy I can depend on," Clive told him.

"Do you think so?" Doug replied, nonplussed.

Pitt shrugged helplessly.

"Look at the state of you? Where's Reg got to, anyway? He should have hopped down here to open the gates. What am I bloody paying him for?" He stared irritably along the driveway as if he too was excluded.

"I need your help mate. I find myself in a dreadful spot."

"What's keeping him, do you know?"

"Literally, mate, I don't know where I am."

Breadham looked him over apprehensively. "You've been missing for months, and now you show up here. Where have you been in all that time?"

"That's the whole point," Clive told him. "I was relying on you to explain, to fill in some of the gaps in my memory."

An ironic smile touched his friend's lips. "You shouldn't have disappeared off the map. Then you wouldn't need me to do the talking," Doug retorted. "Are you really trying to claim memory loss?"

"I've lost track of everything that's happened to me, over the last year."

"Judges in my experience are not sympathetic to pleas of amnesia. That's one step short of extra-terrestrials in their book."

"What about contact with the devil?" Clive wondered. "At least I encountered a maniac who claims that title."

Breadham gave a jump, laughed and took in Pitt's bedraggled appearance again. "Let's continue this discussion indoors. What are you talking about? You didn't bring any cops or heavies on your heels did you?"

"I had to sleep in the open last night, or as good as. The cops may be searching for me, I don't know. But I was attacked last night, when I returned home."

"Don't you realise that there's nothing for you at home any longer?" Doug said.

"I discovered that for myself," Clive confirmed.

"Who do you think attacked you?" he wondered.

"I suspect they don't want the police to be involved somehow. This was a private individual who attacked me," Clive explained. "It was totally weird...some ordinary guy and his two kids."

"Sound quite unusual," Doug considered. "A description?"

"Just somebody apparently on the way home, collecting his kids from school. But I get a sense that individuals and organisations are looking for me. That may sound paranoid to you, but they are certainly out there."

"So why did you sleep rough, when you could have been staying in the house?"

"Thanks for the consideration, but Reg wouldn't allow me inside last night."

"Oh god, so Reg wouldn't let you in? He made you spend a night under the stars? Maybe he heard some talk... and you don't look so appealing... so he was afraid to allow you in," Doug reasoned.

While he manually opened the gates, Clive was less charitable in his assessment.

"Hop into the motor and we'll drive to the house, shall we? You're a bit filthy, but allow me to make amends...for my man servant's inhospitable attitude...with a charitable offer."

Clive ducked down and felt paradoxical relief in the air-conditioning. They glided towards that mansion, cushioned from the seething oiled efficiency of the Morgan's engine.

Reg showed his face again, upright as he strolled to welcome them, wearing a different silk suit.

"So sorry, Mr Breadham, I completely forgot to unlock the gates for you."

Wasn't he a touched spoiled? He took his severe ticking off in good grace, while getting a coded approval in Breadham's tone. The idea of a comfortable mansion being completely vacant, while Pitt slept in a drafty barn, very much appealed to Breadham's sense of humour.

"What's wrong with your damn memory anyway, Reg."

"Where's the best place for us to talk?" Pitt asked, as they came into the oak lined hallway. "The billiards room? The smoking room?"

"There's plenty of time to talk things through. You look terrible Clive, so go upstairs and run yourself a hot bath immediately. Then we can discover what's on your mind."

"You want me to soak in the bath?" Clive replied.

"Yes, why ever not? I would offer you a change of clothes, but we're not the same size. Never mind, I'm sure we can arrange your couture later. Borrow one of my bath robes and Reg will give your things a quick laundry."

"We don't know, do we, who might come knocking on the door for me," Clive said. "You keep firearms and your dogs, but is that any defence?"

"You really are in a paranoid condition, Clive. You can't think properly looking like that," Douglas advised. "No man can think straight while un-bathed and needing to polish his shoes."

"I don't think our discussion can wait, Doug."

"Come along, Clive." Breadham's narrow features quivered, either in response to body odours or as a nervous reaction. "This has to wait because I refuse to talk until you are clean. You've not the only one who has to adjust. You suddenly appear at my house, looking for explanations, when for months you have been evasive. It's like you vanished and only your name existed, as a kind of ugly rumour," Doug told him.

"Really? What's the truth of this ugly rumour? Have I been like a ghost for this past year? Do I have to read about myself, or learn about myself from others?" Clive despaired.

"Sorry to put this so bluntly, but I absolutely refuse to open my mouth, except to recuperate with a drink," Doug insisted.

"Make sure you unlock your gun cabinet," Clive added.

"You should really keep a check on yourself," Doug said.

A change of clothes and a scrub down didn't sound a bad idea, following that long night alone: shaking and tumbling out of his mind. Only someone mentally robust was able to keep body and soul together, and try to calculate an escape strategy. After all investment banking could be a highly physical business. The company recruited with the consideration of stamina, concentration and quick thinking, not academic qualifications and high IQ alone.

But there were further shocks to his system when he tried to get on line in Doug's study. He realised that all his electronic accounts, either professional or social, had been frozen or deleted. He couldn't network or make any useful contacts; he was unable to search any information about himself, despite his technical expertise and strategy. He had been eradicated from virtual presence. Frustrated in that area, he tried to retrieve archived media stories relating to the affair.

There must have been a cover up, a block or a blackout, as he didn't turn up any interesting or relevant news. An electronic wall had been constructed around the ZNT deal, following its conclusion. Perhaps his other devices were still in his suit jacket somewhere; lost or abandoned. Or they were left in a departure lounge or hanging on the back of a chair in a mysterious office: picked up and stored as lost property that went unclaimed. Without his vital electronic devices - stripped of memory, contacts and agendas - he was out of the network, a disconnected 'squawk box'; a manual worker standing at a street junction in Silicon Valley. Intellectually he'd been 'kettled'.

Clive stepped back from those blind XD display units, trying to squeeze angst from his mind and rigidity from his limbs. He decided to get that hot bath, do some thinking, as he was a mess; while Doug fixed himself another drink. Or perhaps a cold shower would be more effective. Hot water was dependable and reassuring, in the absence of knowledge or strategy. He could hear water gushing, from the bathroom already. In passing along the landing he offered Reg a silently expressive look. The servant didn't even flinch and danced away with jaunty steps.

Pitt enjoyed the steamy luxury of his friend's bathroom, comparing favourably to a drafty, splintered barn. There were baskets of ready soft towels and an impressive selection of quality gentlemen's products. In a deep tub he closed his eyes, breathed deeply, and almost drifted away. He was only brought back to consciousness by a sense of panic, a rapid arrhythmic heartbeat. Sloshing water over the brim, he burst back up through the suds, slipping around until he found his feet, as if afraid of drowning. Gasping, gulping, he fought to regain composure and clarity, watching his featureless image in a full length fogged mirror.

10

Clive found his way back down the twisting oak staircase, gripping a thick banister. He had an idea about how to get around the house; which must come from previous visits, he assumed. He ambled back into the sitting room, garbed in a floral silk Japanese robe and pointed slippers that Reg had left out. Reg did not linger around to help their guest into these clothes; as a luxury servant he made himself invisible.

Breadham was awaiting him in the back lounge, dressed smart casual, seeming to be agitated. The financial lawyer clutched a dimpled tumbler of single malt and surveyed the distant horizon of his knotted and floriferous grounds. This particular room was filled with hunting mementoes and trophies, portraits of dead Jacobeans and Restoration fops, accumulated by previous owners of the estate. Doug gave a jump when the banker entered the room, as if this reunion with Pitt was a nightmare rather than an unexpected pleasure.

"Ah, here you are at last!" he declared, with false surprise. "Did you enjoy your soak in the bath? Come here and sit yourself down," he offered.

"You're still cool about having me here?" Clive asked, padding over.

"To imagine that I am sheltering a fugitive," Doug commented. "I suppose that implicates me already. I could be struck off, regardless of our past relationship." He forced an ironical guffaw.

"Wait a moment, Doug, before we talk about my situation... Look, I found something else very strange. When I was having a shave, when I cleared the mirror, I noticed a scar....on my face. Under my left eye there, do you see?" he suggested, leaning forward. "It's like somebody thumped me one, don't you think? The guy was wearing a big ring on his forefinger, whoever he was."

"Oh yes. That must have been nasty. But how can you be so specific?" Doug said.

"'Cause it's bloody obvious, mate, that's why. It must have been a while ago, because it's closed up...although not smoothly. I didn't get stitches in that."

"That scar may have been caused by an accident," the lawyer argued. "By any daily mishap."

"Do you know anything about that?"

"I don't have a close knowledge of your physiognomy," Breadham remarked.

Clive looked at him doubtfully. "So you don't know if anybody thumped me at any stage? Someone with a big fist and a ring on their finger?"

"Why should I?" Breadham replied, tipping back the heavy crystal tumbler again, as if whisky could disguise a bad taste.

"You're a top City lawyer, aren't you? You may have some inside information...if something happened to me."

"Inside? Regrettably I'm unable to account for your scrapes," he replied.

"Well, it's definitely strange," Clive insisted. "I didn't get this by having a bad dream!"

"There's no need to obsess, because it doesn't show very much," Doug told him.

"Is that the point? Do you think this is about vanity? For a start you might explain something about my situation. Then I can leave, because you're not comfortable," Clive offered.

"Who says I am not comfortable, old chap? Why don't you fix yourself a drink too?" Doug suggested, pacing up and down, in front of the wide window.

"Not at the moment. It wouldn't help."

"Something to smoke perhaps? Pharmaceutical? Top quality."

"No thanks, mate, not interested. I've never been interested in taking drugs."

"Suit yourself," he said, with a hint of disapproval. "Of course you must be ravenous. I'll ask Reg to magic breakfast for you. He's an absolute whizz in the kitchen."

"Later, thanks. Right now we have to talk."

"In Reg you see domestic service rationalised to the finest margins," Doug argued. "The climbing roses are more trouble than he is, frankly."

"What happened to my wife?" Clive bluntly challenged.

"Your wife? Her? What do you imagine happened to her?" Doug risked.

"I don't know," Clive said, levelling his bloodshot gaze. "D'you have any idea why she went away?"

"You don't know?" said the lawyer, astonished.

"The last year, I am not aware of its passing," Clive confessed.

"You stick with your amnesia claim," Douglas realised. "But if you lost your memory how did you manage to return here?"

"There are different levels of memory, I guess," Pitt replied.

"I can't explain your thoughts and actions," Doug told him. "I can't fill your shoes."

"Just help me to put my shoes *back on*," Clive suggested. "Allow me to re-assume my identity... find out who's been knocking me about."

"What *do* you know? What *can* you remember?" Doug prompted.

"I remember going out to lunch... about a year ago. Then I am falling...I am afraid of smashing to pieces at the bottom. Suddenly my body is caught...my tumble is halted and I'm suspended there, in space. Then I am looking down on my life... literally flying above the City... and the whole world, for that matter."

"A type of hallucination then," Doug said. A hint of distaste spoilt his smile.

"For a bit I have an eagle eye view. Next thing I know, I'm down there like a sewer rat. I'm back in circulation, thinking about my regular life and job. When I return to the office I discover that my life is destroyed. Job gone, home and family gone. I've been fired by the firm, at some stage. God knows what the reason was."

"You claim to have no knowledge of the background?"

"Just a bit of malicious talk overheard in the locker room."

"Are you saying you actually went back to the Winchurch building yesterday?" Doug replied, staring at him.

"Why not? I've been employed there for ten years. I still worked there, as far as I knew."

"How did you manage to avoid security and... and escape?" Breadham asked.

Clive blinked hard, raking his almost dry hair. "Did you expect them to keep me prisoner then, mate? As I already explained, I intended to return to my desk as normal... then I overheard locker room gossip. I did bump into two colleagues on the street outside. I couldn't get much sense out of them. To be honest, they reacted as if I was some monster dredged up from the bottom of the lagoon."

"Were these male or female colleagues?" Doug wanted to know.

"Female, if that's relevant," Pitt complained. "What's notable about that fact? Trading algorithms don't discriminate for gender."

"Didn't they try to raise the alarm? Did you recognise these girls? Who were they?" the lawyer persisted.

"Definitely I recognised them...Pixie and Olivia. The trouble is that they recognised me as well," Clive said.

"They were afraid of you?"

"What's been going on with my job lately? Do you think my recent experiences are connected to work? My recollection is hazy...scrambled," he considered. "It seems as if I have been taken out of the system. They extracted me like a processor."

"We're not in the same profession," Breadham pointed out.

"Fair point, but we work in the same geographical location," Pitt replied.

"So does the shoe shine," he cut back.

"When I returned 'home' yesterday I discovered that my wife had left me."

"A very peculiar business, admittedly," Breadham observed.

"I found out, from a neighbour, that Noreen ran off with another bloke," Clive confided. "That's impossible to get my head around. I didn't see that one coming. She left me and took Josh with her. They've emigrated to America!" he declared.

"Seattle, Washington State," Doug confirmed.

Clive was amazed. "You already know about this?"

Breadham nodded steadily. "You had no prior warning?"

"How did she manage to sell up? More than half was in my name! How was she able to tidy up her affairs so quickly? Then obtain a visa, get permission to remain in the States?" Clive puzzled.

"These are all excellent questions," Doug agreed. "Your wife had a remarkably fast schedule. Didn't she need your agreement at many stages, and your signature? Did she have contacts to cut corners? It would be fascinating to know how she pulled that off," he argued.

"Then help me to discover the truth. Help me recover my mind."

"Perhaps her lover assisted her...pulled strings with the right people. He was a businessman of a kind. It's conceivable that he had legal contacts."

"On what grounds did she leave me?" Pitt wondered.

"Noreen called by here to talk about her plans. I was surprised to see her. I didn't believe she would confide in me... that we were ever close enough."

"She obviously trusted you with sensitive information, mate," Pitt said.

"Noreen explained that she and... her new gentleman friend... were leaving for Scotland. They had bought an estate around Dumfries. The guy thought conditions would be better for business. Then I got a message from a contact to say they were relocating to Seattle. He'd got family in America already and a cousin offered him a job... didn't your wife already have a sister in the States somewhere?" he wondered.

"Why did Noreen leave me? What got into her head? Did she give any reasons?"

There was a rueful expression on the lawyer's face. He didn't relish the topic.

"Was it because I got fired?" Pitt asked.

"Losing your job is the least of your problems," Doug mused, rubbing his chin.

"How did you work that out?"

"I can see that you don't remember a scrap of this," Doug said.

"Not a bit. I could die from ignorance."

"Noreen left you before Christmas, after she discovered you were having an affair."

"Me? Having an affair?" He slumped down into the distressed hunter's seat.

"You'd already left Noreen, effectively, to live with another woman."

"Who was I seeing?" Clive pressed. He felt the silky texture of the robe floating over his goose-bumps of astonishment.

"It was one of the girls in your office," Doug explained. "Noreen told me she was completely disillusioned. She was terribly distraught, when she came here, to give me the news. Her response was to relocate to the States. Make a new life for herself over there. Not to look back over her shoulder. I'm sorry to have to tell you this. You have my condolences," he added, watching Pitt's anguished expressions.

Both men dropped into a short, shocked silence - one retrospective, one recent.

"Noreen didn't waste much time, did she," Clive observed.

"No," Doug regretfully agreed. "She was very decisive and didn't hesitate. She had known the other chap for quite a while. She knew what she had to do apparently."

"Noreen and I were sweethearts. We had a child together. Josh is such a great boy... the little bugger looks the spit of me, you know. Am I ever going to see him again?" he despaired. "This is just dreadful."

Doug couldn't find an answer. He expelled a helpless breath.

"How could Noreen do that? This is totally shocking. If she had an affair I might be able to forgive her. Where does this leave me?"

"I can try to find the relevant legal documents," Doug offered. "That's far from my own specialism, but I can ask a family solicitor on your behalf."

"That I had a relationship with a woman at work... that's equally astonishing to me."

"I can see that."

"Do you have any idea who it was?"

"Unfortunately you didn't talk about your office affairs with me. I never met this other girl friend of yours. You didn't have much to do with me. I'd ceased to exist for you," Doug said.

"What am I going to do? What would you advise?" Clive pressed.

"Your only approach is to think on the women at work, considering who the most likely candidate is...for you to have had an affair with."

"Are you serious? I'm trying to think. Is there a girl at the company, with whom I was particularly close?" Clive considered, rolling his eyes to the ceiling.

"Try to cast your mind back, because she may be able to help you."

"Unless this is just an innuendo," Clive considered. He thought hard, like someone twitching their fingers into the corners of a dark recess. "So I didn't tell you the name of this woman?"

"You began returning home late from the office. Later than normal, that is. Then, Noreen told me, you began staying away all night, and she suspected you. You slipped up and you didn't show any remorse. You'd lost your moral compass, so to speak."

"This is hard to recognise. What can I say?"

"You refused to talk to me about your affair. While you visited you sat morosely in that armchair. That's right, where you are now. You didn't tell me the name of your girlfriend. You never listened to a word I said. Then you drove off again."

"Does that sound like the Clive Pitt you know?"

"You fouled up your career in a big way. You grew too bold, too conceited, and too arrogant. However you want to describe that syndrome. You were a shambles."

"That's what it looks like," Clive admitted. "Obviously I wasn't very happy. Now let me think, who was I having an affair with?"

"You truly don't remember which girl?" Breadham marvelled.

"Not Miss Porter with the horsey grin and unaligned eyes. Not Janice, not Dorothy. Listen to this appalling sexist bilge," he remarked. "I'll be calling them the 'ditzy chicks' or 'secretaries' before too long, like a few of those other troglodytes on Winchurch Brothers' trading floor," Pitt complained.

"What are you talking about?" Doug wondered.

"When I first joined the company, as an intern, I would join in with that banter. Then I began to think for myself. I began to protest against that macho culture. The only woman I really liked, you know, in that way... would be Pixie Wright," Pitt considered, "she's not only beautiful, but she's a brilliant woman, dealing with risk."

"There you are Clive; you have a candidate," Doug said.

"I felt weirdly connected to her yesterday," he recalled. "She was shocked to see me, and afraid at first... but when she calmed down a bit she wanted to warn me. She told me it was dangerous to be there... she claimed that the company was trying to eliminate me." Clive considered. "How do I get my head around *that*?"

"Is that what she said? It was probably an exaggeration," Doug argued.

"Yet there was something between us," Clive recalled, stretching out his long muscular legs.

"So was your girlfriend?" replied the lawyer. "This was the girl."

"Pixie certainly takes a good likeness, I can't deny," Clive said, thinking with a smile.

"You're starting to brag about her already," Doug noted.

"That was only in the office. I took my worries to her sometimes, as far as I remember. She was concerned, she listened to me. She understood what I was talking about," Clive recalled.

"Can you remember what you were concerned about?" Breadham asked.

"Not the precise details...but they are coming back to me. Pixie understood my logic."

"In what ways did she understand your logic?" Doug pressed.

"The ways of doing business were not healthy. That's really vague. But did our relationship go further? I guess it's possible... it has to be possible... but the idea of cheating on my wife, throwing away our family life, still sounds ridiculous. After all I was happy with Noreen. But according to you I completely lost it... I had a relationship with a girl, and the wife couldn't tolerate that...so she packed her bags and flew off to the States," he agonised.

"Of course it's easy to have your head turned by a pretty girl. Pixie Wright is the likely candidate. You need to find out for sure."

"Maybe I can patch things up with Noreen," Clive agreed.

"You are guilty of other transgressions," Doug said.

"How's that? '*Transgressions*'?"

"For heaven's sake," Doug declared. "I'm a man of the world, aren't I... and I'm not upset because you had an affair. What you have to face up to is far more serious, let me tell you," Doug argued. The lawyer's sharp eyes shifted across a cool legalistic mask.

"Well for me it is quite serious to betray my wife, after six years of marriage, I can tell you, mate," Clive insisted.

Doug's glance floundered, as if a chink of ice had attacked his back teeth.

To disguise this rare confusion, he strode back towards his drinks cabinet. He began to fuss with a collection of bottles as colourfully cosmopolitan as his clients and cars.

Clive followed the man's movements uneasily, as if he was mysteriously detached. He could only allow himself to wait, to sink back further into buttoned sections of the cracked old chair.

Doug returned, pensive, reluctant, washing alcohol around perfect teeth, avoiding immediate eye contact. He swished his straight, greying blonde fringe, as if to bedazzle a judge. He took another substantial glug of liquor before twinkly eyes found their way back to Clive's questioning glance.

"What I am trying to say," Doug said, in a strange voice, constricted and lower than usual, "is... that... you are known to have committed a rape."

Instantly a dam of blood fell away from Clive's mind. It was a sensation like turning to liquid and draining away into the ground. He was slipping away from consciousness again, while taking a back exit from the human race. "Rape? Me, a rapist? You have to be pulling off a sick joke." But the lawyer didn't look as if he was swapping jokes, sick or otherwise. "That's impossible, Doug. Isn't it? How can anyone believe I am capable of such an act?" The tension in his voice broke. The eerie disturbing sound didn't seem to belong to him.

"I don't like to think of you that way either," Doug said

"Who could the victim have been? Did Pixie accuse me of this?"

"No, it wasn't Pixie, or whatever girl you were sleeping with. You are quite wrong in that assumption. The girl you in fact attacked was Emily Winchurch. Yes, that's right, your boss' daughter. 'Fraid so... that's how you brought your house down," he explained, wincing.

"Noreen knew about the accusation?" Clive asked, entirely shaken.

"You couldn't accuse her of making an error, could you?" Doug retorted. Although criminal law was not an area of expertise.

"Where did this rape take place? When did it happen?" Clive returned. His features were contorted as if he was forced to chew poison.

"At the beginning of summer, it must have been. I suppose it was back in May."

"Are you part of this prank?" Clive asked, shuffling his mind under the turbulence.

"Do you imagine that I am joking about such an allegation?" Doug returned. He was presenting his poker-face-to-the client look.

"The daughter couldn't mean anything to me," Clive argued, horrified.

"Did she have to 'mean' something to you?" Doug pondered.

"What do I know or care about that girl? I probably only met her a couple of times in my life! She looked a bit of a rebel to me that was all. Winchurch had problems with her, didn't he? He was embarrassed by her antics and didn't know what to do with her."

"That wouldn't justify a sexual attack. Just because she was a tart and rebelled against her background," Breadham argued.

"Definitely, definitely not," Pitt agreed, afraid of being incriminated. "That's why I am telling you this, because I don't know her. What she is like. I don't believe that I've ever talked to her before. The idea that I attacked her is just plain bonkers. I'm really not that type of guy anyhow. Do you think of me like that?" He put a forefinger to his temple.

Doug was pacing out a different pattern. "Who knows what we are capable of, shall we say?"

"What are you trying to suggest, Doug? But why did they want to discredit me? What exactly was I working on at the time?"

"She is said to have resisted her attacker. Maybe she gave you a bash on the head, which would account for memory loss," Doug suggested.

"To hell with a bash on the head mate, I don't know the girl, even if she did accuse me of this... this awful deed!" he added in disgust.

"You took her into some woods, not far from the Winchurch house, near to a village in Buckinghamshire, from what I understand."

"You don't honestly think I was responsible, do you?"

"The girl was in a mess, severely traumatised. Her father had to send her off to recover at a specialised psychiatric clinic. As far as I know she's still being treated there and... she's under further observation... having treatment," Doug explained.

"Unthinkable. Never. They've got the wrong guy." Clive shook his head, eyes downcast, wringing his hands; sensing that his identity was in equal danger to the traduced girl's.

"It looked a very convincing crime at the time," the lawyer remarked.

"If they've got proof, I will have to accept blame. But at the present moment I totally doubt the story," Clive argued.

Gradually he got the outline of the accusation against him.

"Is it really as unthinkable as you claim, Pitt? Excuse me for being frank," Douglas insisted. "We can both agree, I would say, that you have a sharp eye for the ladies...or you certainly had that reputation, judging by the company gossip."

"Before I fell in love...with a particular girl...and tied the knot," Clive reminded him. "Are you a mate of mine or are you not?"

"That is the way it has struck me, in the past, if I can be so bold."

"Are you crazy? I'm shocked to hear that Doug."

"Don't be offended Clive, but I know that you have lustful looks for beautiful women," Doug said.

"Even if that's true, what about it?"

"Do you imagine that other chaps don't notice your propensity?"

Pitt made a dismissive noise and chuckled sardonically. "Come on Doug, I am no more likely to rape a girl than you are. How would you feel if such an accusation was thrown at you?"

"Sorry to disappoint your self-image, Pitt, but that's the way your attitude has struck me," Breadham said.

"That's a caricature that can be levelled against any man," Clive answered. "Even against you."

"That's how you are going to defend yourself, is it?" Breadham wondered.

The lawyer was relieved that he never dealt with men labelled as common criminals, particularly sexual criminals, in his section of the law.

"Of course we desire women, if we're straight, but we don't take them by force. Things can get a bit out of control for City boys, after hours, as I have observed. I always backed off those dodgy situations. I know the limits," Clive insisted. "I totally reject any accusation," he added, trying not to despair.

"Emily Winchurch was raped among trees near her home, and she accuses you of that act. What's more you were present on the evening of the crime. You were on intimate terms with her before this attack took place."

"How did you work all that out, mate? How d'you remember, when I've forgotten?" Clive asked. He was numb with shock. "Do you have inside information or something?"

"There were numerous witnesses... at Winchurch's house in the country. Politicians, businessmen and diplomats, were present."

"I was present at Septimus Winchurch's country estate?"

"At Close Copse House in Buckinghamshire. A handy part of the country to hold some real estate. It was a rare honour for Winchurch Brothers staff to be invited to Septimus' home... to help him to celebrate."

"What was he celebrating, God help us?" Clive wanted to know. "We were at the point of bankruptcy at one stage."

"His role in the successful conclusion of another City merger, with a Swiss based hedge fund. Well, if you can't remember your role... it's all done and dusted now... I don't imagine that's significant any more. After this big merger the company made a profit, compared to huge losses since the last crash."

"Yes, there was a big merger... that must have been a significant bit of business. Only a year of my life is in the dark!" Clive retorted.

"You hadn't better torture your mind," Breadham suggested, knocking back the rest of his glass.

"I didn't like the look of the deal. Isn't that it? There were aspects of the transaction that looked dodgy to me... actual details are extremely hazy. What was the background of that? What was the data? I was investigating the initial share price, making a presentation at a public meeting to the employees."

"Well, you turned up at Winchurch's garden party...and got hitched up with his daughter," Doug added, as if preferring the topic.

"I know that the boss has an estate in Buckinghamshire. So he invited me there to attend a garden party? I've no conscious memory of that either. How can I tell if any of this is true? Seems as if my brain is scrambled."

"Your memory loss plea sounds convincing," Doug admitted. "Not sure if anybody else will believe you. There's a lot of evidence against you... but we have encountered unlikely turnabouts of the truth before. Sometimes the most incriminating evidence is finally shown to be deceptive or illusory."

"Thanks Doug, I knew you would not condemn me so easily," he told the lawyer firmly. Yet he had the sense of clinging to a free sleeve in a storm.

"Well, I always try to keep an open mind. However, you are looking very out of sorts. Why don't you get some fresh air, before the temperature rises? All this must have come as a shock. You have the look of a trauma victim."

"You know that I have strong ethics. I think my worst behaviour was a bit of rough sex, with a girl I met in a club in Shanghai. That was before I tied the knot. Well, she took me back to her apartment afterwards...it was in a shady district of the city. Her grandmother was in the next room. Can you believe that? I wasn't proud of myself. But it was entirely consensual, for the record."

"As far as you can remember," Doug commented.

"Yes, right Doug, I can remember. I have recollection of that experience. There's a table-dancing club, a full on place...some dive off the Farringdon Road. Some of the guys would go. I joined them...once or twice... but that was just a night out with the lads...a birthday celebration. We got there in the small hours and I didn't know what we were doing, to be honest with you."

"Come on, stop beating your brains, Pitt. You need to get out and stretch your legs."

"Apparently the boss wants to stretch my neck now," Pitt argued.

"Apparently you've had a bit of a scare," the lawyer conceded.

Pitt reluctantly took a turn around the lawyer's territory. He still wore that silk kimono, and a pair of matching slippers, like a hoity-toity invalid. Clive fluttered in the hot breeze like an irradiated butterfly. They explored together along sharply cut crazy paving over sprinkled lawns. Humidity rose, the horizon shimmered, but they were safely distanced from the dead heat of recent afternoons. The garden's fresh colour was a relief to the eye. Doug employed a father and son gardening team, and he kept his sprinklers running over grass and flower beds. All was maintained and sustained to the utmost, in contrast to the withered condition of the surrounding countryside. Indeed this was a shocking contrast, like golf courses in West Africa.

"Compared to that dirty blot against my reputation," Clive said, "who bothers if I had an affair with a girl in the office?"

"Still, it would help to know the identity of that girl," Breadham argued.

"She wouldn't be thrilled to see my face again, whoever she is," Clive remarked. "That was how Pixie reacted to me Friday afternoon!"

They stood at the apex of a little wooden bridge over an artificial stream. Exotic carp raised their sensuous lips to the surface and made circling ripples.

"If it's Pixie then she can explain more. She can tell you the type of man you are. You can free yourself from this predicament."

"I'll turn barmy if this can't be sorted out... forced to the margins of society like a criminal. I'm inclined to follow your advice... speak to Pixie... in the hope she's the right person."

"Perfect strategy, because you need an alibi," Doug suggested.

"But she isn't going to welcome me back with open arms. She was totally horrified to see my face again."

"You have to speak to her. See what she knows. Try not to drag her in after you. As a former colleague, I am inclined to support you, but the law doesn't follow. Especially in this case, when all your intuitions appear to be founded on practically nothing."

"They might be trying to discredit me, to destroy my life. But the Winchurch family didn't seem to bring the law into this," Clive reminded him. "Where were the coppers in all that time?" he asked. "Doesn't that strike you as bloody peculiar?"

"I don't know, Pitt. That's not my concern," Doug replied. "Maybe this wasn't a crowd control issue," he suggested. "At times of crisis a powerful individual has to sort out his differences like a gentleman."

"Which century are you living in?" Pitt retorted.

11

Clive stuck around Doug Breadham's place over that weekend, hoping for a profitable hunch. Then early that Monday Doug dropped him back at the tube station. Pitt had decided to make a return trip into the City, pending further investigation. They set off early, tensely, while the air was cool, as Doug had a busy schedule to fulfil, with hearings and meetings in the square mile.

In town on Saturday he'd purchased new clothes for Clive, though he was careful to throw away receipts and even packaging, as if this linked him to the disgraced banker. Yet on Sunday he'd gone out speed surfing with friends and lunched with them as planned. Of course he didn't invite Clive along. Pitt tried to talk about old times in the evening; falteringly, beating out the dark regions of medium-term-memory - that lost year - as if scaring grouse from undergrowth.

The idea of returning to the City disturbed him; his life was upside down. He was without a position, virtually unemployed, as he understood. Thanks to Breadham he was wearing another well fitting suit (made from the wool of a dozen Australian lambs), newly soled and repaired Church's shoes. He was snug again in a pair of black silk Thomas Nash boxers. Also Doug had placed a new wallet, containing spending money, into the fresh cut trouser pockets. Clive appeared like normal, as if returning to a secure job, but his whole life was decentred. Now he was obliged to step back into that danger zone to discover what had really happened to him. Regardless of risk, he had to debunk his legend as a dishonest banker, a deviant personality, even as a sexual criminal.

"Don't try to contact me," Doug insisted. "Best not to. Even top lawyers don't enjoy a charmed existence," he argued, as he released his Ferrari.

"Aren't you going to offer me your contacts," Clive pressed.

"Far too dangerous, Pitt. Give me some wiggle room, will you?"

"What are you afraid of, Doug? Do you regard me as toxic?"

The lawyer fixed his gaze. "Precisely in which situation would you intend to contact me?" he challenged.

"I don't know exactly, yet," Pitt admitted. He noticed as they drove into the small town; which was the nearest settlement with a train link to the capital.

"It's too risky! They know that we are already associates. They will be curious what we have discussed. They will be watching out for something like that."

"You admit something's going on," Pitt noted.

"Whatever tight spot, you don't want to have company."

"You don't want to be seen with me?" Pitt concluded.

"Can you blame me?" the lawyer replied. A ripple of discomfort went through his sharp profile. "How can it help?"

"I look like a million dollars anyway," Clive remarked.

"Don't think anything of it," Doug told him.

"No, I won't," he replied. "You're throwing me back to those wolves, even if I have a clean shirt."

His tetchy attitude had the effect of disconcerting Doug. Breadham was one of the most polished dissemblers in the entire profession. That was the closest Pitt dared to a description of his limousine encounter with that hidden power broker with a disguised voice; who had sent him spinning on the roulette wheel of time.

Pitt was dropped outside the tube train entrance, seeming to blend in with the bustling early-hour commuter scene. As soon as he snapped back the long car door, like a fearsome red jaw, Breadham ripped away, even with a squeal of rubber. If by different means, they were both heading for the same area of east London.

Inside the building Pitt tested his company credit card and found, as expected, that it had been stopped. He dipped into Doug's cash gift to pay for the journey instead, trying to separate a wad of fresh notes, much to the incredulity and alarm of the desk assistant; as if he was attempting the buy the network.

He shuffled about on the platform, waiting with the others, as if finding protection in a crowd. Compared to the Beijing subway, he considered, the London underground resembled a rusty old bicycle with a hard seat. There was a recognisable feeling of being crushed and isolated in the mass; but concealment added to his security. This claustrophobic recipe now included an unfamiliar ingredient of unpredictability and danger.

Pitt could sense peril about him; yes he could smell danger like bad stock; even if the exact quality was not yet established. On the surface of things the daily commute to work looked harmless, but normality was a sinister illusion. His nerves told him that his new 'reality' was menacing; peripheral warnings nudged his subconscious. Even the surface of his skin warned him to remain at a high alert. In the metropolis he knew that murders could happen in public in daylight; and he couldn't be sure that anybody would intervene to help.

Could there be somebody tailing him on this journey? Did that explain his instinctive unease and sense of being not quite alone? Or was the danger more concealed than this? Why was Breadham so eager to get rid of him and to stay out of touch? What kind of old friend was he, anyway? Sending him out like this, naked to the markets to be butchered, in a new suit and silk tie.

Clive alighted at Bank and followed the tunnels to the surface; he held his place in the frothing tide, as humanity met finance. For all this Pitt visually blended and was not suspicious to others. He cut a strong, rugged, lithe figure; he was a tall striking fellow, strong shouldered and confident with his shock of stiff blonde hair. He retained the outline of his last expensive haircut, in a Sweeny Todd joint around the arcade. That's if you didn't meet the troubled gaze of his cracked, swivelling blue eyes. His beautiful new suit and clothes drew admiring or grudging attention, even in the City's anonymous morning hustle. To other people he had a trim and energetic image, like a guy who knew the reason for all this stress and effort; who'd had a happy weekend with a loving family. Now he was returning to his high status desk. You only had to look at this guy to understand he must be a powerful player. But what was lurking under that pricey barnet, as an old East Ender might ask?

His heart thumped and his mouth was dry, acid splashing about his stomach, as he emerged from a subway. 'Scrapers and hyper-baubles loomed into the sizzling bluish haze above him, as if they'd ruptured the sun. How should he orient himself about the square mile? Pitt didn't know if he had a job, or his own office - somewhere. He was lost, but he was not a reflection in a mirror. It was hard to know how fast to walk. He was a sapper in a minefield, a jobless and homeless stiff; a mere individual in that mass of commercial purpose. He'd never been intimidated by the City before; in fact, after acclimatising himself, it had danced joyfully in his blood. He had the feeling of being anonymous now but, much worse, notorious. He was sought by the invisible hand of the market.

Pitt had to identity the woman he'd been going out with - allegedly. He had to find that mysterious girl, so that she could tell him more about the missing year. She would have to brief him about those lost episodes at work and play, because he'd completely lost the plot. The oppressive sense of guilt and shame was not a useful clue.

To start up, where did that scar under his left eye come from? The mysterious jagged wound, roughly healed, was a symbol of his predicament. That was entirely sinister, like the sick tension in his stomach, the fuzziness in his head, tuning out into blackness from time to time; an overall feeling of being completely out of sorts, like the onset of chronic fatigue.

It might be hasty to fix Pixie Wright as his possible lover. He didn't retain any memories of having had an affair with her. If you slept with someone, he obsessed; you'd surely remember something about them, about the whole experience, right? Did he recall her signatures; such as her underwear preference, the feel of her skin, her erotic temperature, her sexual mannerisms and techniques? He was being pushed into fantasy land here, visiting a lad's porn site of the imagination, just trying to think about it. Intuitions could be amazingly insightful, but they could also be disastrous and lead to further trouble; he should know that in his line.

He had vague memories of talking to her in the office; being friendly; of confiding in her. They had shared concerns about the company; about the way of conducting business for their clients; gradually the substance of these objections was coming back to him and settling into detail.

That's essentially what they were up to, even after the big crash, the 'casino economy'. There was always some rusty nail working against his conscience. He'd been concerned about phoney deals and fabricated products, in what he'd called 'virtual finance'. These annoying, stubborn scruples of his no doubt came from his Dad, from his background, he supposed; although he was implicated all the same.

A hard-working, conscientious father, who'd seen him through university; who had not insisted that he follow into the building society. From his Dad he got the idea that finance was a force for good that changed lives and careers. He came down to London full of ideals, not just greed and ambition. City finance should be dynamic, able to get the people and the country's economy moving, roaring, again. The financial system provided vital resources for enterprising people to launch their ambitions or to build their enterprise; helping them to employ other people and to create prosperity for others too. Pitt's drive and ability had been recognised by Winchurch, hadn't it? He was offered an internship, then a full time job on excellent terms. What profession could be more exciting and worthwhile? What other business could be so dynamic, rewarding and creative? Pitt and his young colleagues were considered the brightest and best the country can produce. Talent and hard work deserved high rewards. High IQs married to quick wits merited generous annual bonuses. They provided vital expertise; an essential service and resource. Finance is the fuel of the economy.

Being attracted to Pixie was not so ridiculous - only the idea of trying his luck. She was sexy and fascinating: her voice alone was a complex perfume. She was tagged "the head and shoulders" girl in the office, for her ability to read the peaks and troughs of various commodity prices. But Pitt shouldn't have been free to flirt; and "the head and shoulders" girl was already dating another guy. Furthermore she was a favourite of their boss, not only for her abilities as a banker, but also due to her looks and charisma. Pixie Wright could do no wrong in the eyes of Sir Septimus, even during the most turbulent market conditions.

No doubt these hunches, or neural prompts, had some basis, but it wouldn't be easy to face her. Last time, when he'd shown up in the street, she had been as amazed as she was terrified. Despite being impatient for the truth, Clive knew it would be fatal to break into the office again. He physically craved to confront his former colleagues, demand to know their intentions and what was going on. The job was trained into his nerves, by practice, education and routine. Pitt was a junkie for the stimulus of market risk. At this point he was playing with more than the markets. This time he wasn't gambling just with other people's capital.

Clive called into a coffee bar at a precinct across the road. He broke into another of Doug's fifty pound notes to afford a cappuccino and a Danish pastry: the staff here were used to large denominations. It would have been different in Halifax, when he returned to visit relatives. He took his purchases over to a thick rounded glass window (as if bullet proofed). He perched himself on a high stool there, where he obtained a long view of comings and goings. Either he resembled a shark in a tank or the sharks were outside. Or was he a slaughtered calf in formaldehyde? Was this the golden calf that had been exhibited in a glass tank for the amusement of diners?

The shopping precinct outside, reaching up the cobbled lane, had certainly undergone a facelift - since he was last present. He got many unfamiliar messages from the environment, subtle changes, as if returning from a posting abroad.

Pitt watched the denizens going about their business. Did he belong among them any longer, and if so then exactly how, and where did he fit? Even though he looked the part, did he have any position in the financial world? The whole recognisable street scene looked counterfeit - as counterfeit as many financial products during the boom years - as if his amnesia was more real; as if the lost year had solider outlines. Pitt was the man out of sync and trapped in a double-exposed mind, like a primitive 3D print out.

With the morning dragging on, as he grew fatigued and bored, he spotted another top of the range BMW. This model resembled a killer whale and it halted at the kerb outside the Winchurch building. A brown uniformed chauffeur emerged from the driver's side and moved around the car, where he let out his passenger with a flourish.

In a second Pitt recognised his old boss; the very man whose daughter he was alleged to have attacked. There he was back in the flesh, the same as ever, even while the whole situation and relationship had changed. Sir Septimus Winchurch was a short man, barely five feet tall; yet spry, dynamic, rounded on his nimble little legs. He dashed around the limo, sprang to the pavement, towards the rotating door at the building entranceway. A perpetual smirk of knowing good fortune gave his face a friendly expression, as he flipped back a proud, rococo wave of tightly-crimped sterling-silver hair.

Pitt found it most surreal to observe the financier again in these extreme circumstances. It was most surreal to believe that Winchurch detested him; even though he'd been so taken with Clive as an intern. Pitt had been a favourite for many years, advancing into a high position of trust; an embodiment of the knighted banker's shrewd pick of character.

But if Clive was responsible for the terrible crime against his daughter, why didn't Winchurch prosecute him? Why did the financier dither and waste time about the issue? Sep was a known advocate of traditional criminal justice, including a return to the death penalty. Pitt should have been rotting away in prison, or even swinging at the end of a rope. Certainly he'd be in that position if there had been a referendum and change of the law as Sep advocated. Perhaps it was the ignominy and scandal, knowing his own daughter was the victim, which prevented Sep from turning to traditional justice. But then what else did he have in mind for Clive - the perpetrator of this outrageous crime? Clive didn't have the answers, but why he was still at liberty, allowed to roam and prowl the City's lanes and alleys?

Breadham argued that the financier avoided doing his dirty laundry in public. Indeed such a family scandal might prove ruinous to business, putting off new clients and alienating existing ones. The markets didn't operate through sentiment. If there was a scandal attached to the firm, sullying their reputation, then investors would avoid Winchurch Brothers like a street hawker with forged lottery tickets.

Pitt also knew that he was being pursued by other people or interests. There's been that guy near to his old home, walking two kids from school, seeming harmless and ordinary at first, who'd attacked him with a stave. Maybe this would-be assassin was part of an organisation hired by Winchurch. Then he was tormented by an after image of the guy's smashed face, streaming blood into the dust. The attack was singed over his mind's eye. If only he could remember the lost year so vividly, he complained.

Pitt observed as Sep disappeared between spinning glass doors into his company HQ. Perhaps the CEO really had hired people to get rid of him, to satisfy an instinct of revenge and, most pressingly, to safeguard business.

The hours of the working day agonisingly elapsed. Pitt continued to wait, to stake out the building, waiting for movement. He hoped that employees would not be told to stay to work extended hours. That would depend on business. He even felt hungry and considered a dash to an Indian place in Smithfield Street. He had a favourite restaurant around there. But he knew that it could be a mistake to leave. Why spend so much time watching, only to risk missing something?

By this hour the shape of pedestrians formed long shadows. At last people began to emerge from Winchurch HQ; a trickle becoming a tide, as staff headed for home. The majority kept regular hours, although some had a day for night session. Clive picked out a senior analyst by the name of Jane Grant, who often socialised with Pixie Wright. These were the women so disdainfully referred to as "secretaries" by some male employees at the firm.

Pitt realised that there was a risk of being noticed. He was visibly perched behind the glass of the coffee shop. What a shock that would prove for them, but probably bigger for him. Cohen, Spence, Abrams, Bradshaw would be leaving the building soon, as reflections began to shift.

Pitt continued to wait patiently. He had plenty of time for the moment.

12

Jane Grant gestured and smiled to friends, and then set off along the street by herself. Clive thought she might offer information about Pixie. Therefore he dashed out of the café with the idea of following her. Pixie and she had been close in the office; they went regularly to a gym together, and to a specific sushi restaurant at lunch; or it was brought up to them. They had socialised at Inferno in Clapham and were known to frequent Movida, when Jane obtained a suitable inside squeeze.

Pitt trailed on the opposite side of the street, the shadowy side. There was no sign of Miss Wright at this point. His strategy was not to approach Pixie in the street again, because she already knew he was around: she would be nervous and wouldn't appreciate a second look.

Pitt took advantage of the gathering rush hour crowd; keeping his distance, staying concealed from the young woman. Equally he tried to maintain a view of her, as if finding a spy hole in the moving wall of bodies, buses, taxis and other vehicles.

Even though it was a preoccupied hour, he was getting suspicious looks. The working population was heading underground, on the way back home; in anticipation of families, children, spouses, partners or simply their own company.

Miss Grant vanished into the Underground system. So that Pitt forced his way across the road, going after her, through choking traffic, with a predictably encouraging response from irritated drivers. He was lucky not to be chewed under wheels and axles, but reached the other side and lunged into the station.

There was a contrast in light which forced him to wait and allow his eyes to adjust. His vision was more sensitive than usual, he felt, with that left eye slower to focus and adapt. This small defect must be related to the cicatrize underneath. Somebody had punched him - punched his lights out - wearing a chunky ring, or rings. The wound had healed up, so the blow must have been struck months before; not by that psycho in the lane. From the recent, closer to home, he had sore ribs, an abstract set of bruises and tightness across his shoulders. What sort of vicious, malevolent game was he embroiled in here? It was all because he was trying to prise the candy from their fingers?

When this visual fog began to clear he scanned the vicinity - which was the immediate area of the Underground station. Fortunately he picked out Jane's trim, flame haired form in the crowd. She moved ahead to join a queue at the turnstile, ready to swipe her pass. Like many other people, she was already mopping her face with a handkerchief. There was a risk she would be swallowed up, while he was snagged at the surface, drawing a blank.

But then, as chance would have it, Clive saw Pixie just metres away from him. She had come into the station, and was positioned, dangerously, uncomfortably close. She would surely recognise him, as he was in a frozen posture in front of her nose. Pitt felt himself bristle like a hedgehog. He didn't dare to move even a muscle, as if forced into a game of statues.

By some miracle Pixie didn't notice him, although her eyes passed over him. She was positive and brave in her job. Her cool was legendary. She had exerted a calming influence on him, particularly when he offered criticism of the company. Pitt somehow felt he knew this woman well. So had they been a genuine item? They were probably a harmonious duo, if that was the case, he thought.

At some point he had to speak to her, if he wanted to get the truth. He remembered that she had worked with him, at certain stages. She had been sympathetic to his attitude. But she wouldn't like to lose her job, would she? Had she been willing to put her neck on the block? Or should he know better?

What if he was wrong to make conclusions about Pixie? If she hadn't been his confidante and lover, as Doug Breadham and he had speculated? If that theory was right, then why was Pixie still trusted or even employed by Winchurch? Wouldn't she be sent flying out of the revolving door, even if she had always been the boss' blue-eyed girl? Although the actual colour of her eyes was green, he recalled. How did he remember that? Her eyes were as green as a healthy English lane in its former summer prime. This was as amazing recollection - perhaps it was wrong - gleaned from their former association?

Either she would have resigned or been fired, if she was implicated with him; or if she was having an affair with Pitt. Or had they really been engaged in collaboration against Winchurch Brothers? Sir Septimus would have discovered such goings on, equipped with a blind-sight, even though he had a soft spot for Pixie, by all accounts.

Only luck saved Pitt from being recognised by Pixie in the station. Somehow she had an inkling that something was amiss, but she couldn't isolate a particular reason. But she required a little extra time just to compose herself, and remember what she was supposed to be doing. After all she'd already had a recent encounter with Pitt, and like a marked note he was back in circulation. She understood he was back in the game; that it wouldn't take him long to resolve his focus.

Perplexity rippled her brow. He was glad to find her, because he'd been afraid she was away from work. She might have taken some leave, gone on holiday overseas: perhaps she'd taken up Winchurch's offer to enjoy his heart-shaped island in the Arabian Gulf. That was the type of value added perk she could draw on, if Sep wanted her out of the way.

On the contrary Pixie wasn't vacationing; she must have had a busy day at work, very much up to her head and shoulders. It was a big assumption to think that she could trust Pitt again, or that he could trust her, assuming there was any truth in the story as presented so far.

Clive remembered their first introduction. This had occurred during his induction as an intern, when he was shown around and introduced to people. There had been instant mutual warmth between them, as her smile communicated to her other features, justified when they got to know each other. She was two years older than him.

Clive tracked her on a downward escalator. She kept to the right and didn't run down the left. She had a distinctive hair style, which helped him. There was the regular grind and groan, as trains arrived and departed along tunnels below, like enslaved beasts. Two lines of passing humanity, rising and falling, avoided making eye contact. It looked and sounded like hell, but was merely daily routine. Clive no longer held down a regular job, as far as he gathered, and so he didn't have normal life to humanise these dreadful places. As ever during a heat wave, the Underground was badly ventilated, offering only a hot, dry, suffocating air. Some girls wore dresses as revealing as negligees. Men might have worn tee-shirts and shorts if they were allowed. Instead they wearily hooked jackets over the shoulder and rolled shirt sleeves over biceps, as if modelling expensive wristwatches.

Pixie reached the bottom and filtered out to the platform. She clutched a Vuitton handbag and gazed nervously about the cavern. Was it merely the heat and atmosphere that had disconcerted her? Clive kept his distance, while scanning the environment, maintaining an idea of her whereabouts. She would assume the worst about his motives. When the next tube train arrived, he lost her in the press to embark. For several stops he had to jump in and out, searching different carriages. He didn't know her whereabouts, or if she was even on board.

Perhaps she had already given him the slip. Maybe she had changed or disembarked, as part of her connections. He almost gave up and felt resigned, as if giving himself up to the darkness. Could he find a hotel for the night and play the same game of catch tomorrow?

He stood about the carriage, trying to think about his next move, hanging disconsolately to the handrail like a condemned prisoner. Where did this leave him? What should he expect from the evening? His palm was sweaty in the leather strap, as he held on for dear life, staring into space, not sure how this was going to turn out.

13

When the train pulled up at a west London station, however, Clive saw Pixie. He spotted her as she went gliding outside, past the train window. He was startled back into movement, before the doors slid against him. In fact he was forced to prize the doors apart. He pushed through the crowd, jostling, looking over the stream of heads in front. Pixie's elegant heels picked off the Way Out steps. Giving chase to a lady was an uncomfortable role to be cast into. But Pixie was back in his reach, along with the hope she offered, to obtain a full explanation of the lost year - even an escape route.

At the surface she hesitated, as if struggling. She stood about a flower stall, looking around, just as if she was being alerted by an extra sense this evening. Or maybe she was simply recouping energy, considering the best route home, after that steamy tube ride. A tide of humanity and traffic continued to flow around. Pitt came to the top of the stairs and watched her, only fifteen metres away. What was she going to do next? Would she decide to go home, as might reasonably be expected? Or had she already made other plans for the evening? Was she going out to socialise with friends, or even with her boyfriend?

Much to his relief she finally decided and set off purposefully. These spontaneous reflexes could have been fateful for her. What if she was being followed by someone less favourable to her? By the same people who were following him? She touched and considered some bouquets but didn't buy any.

Had she sensed his presence? However, she hadn't looked around to find out who might be there; or had been afraid to try. Briefly she seemed to consider taking a bus home. The out of town guys always jumped into their cars, but as a Londoner she preferred public transport. Clive slipped out of view, as far as he was able, even trying to shrink to the shape of a little old man. Fortunately she also dismissed the idea of flagging down a taxi, as with catching a bus. Pixie decided she would like to walk home.

The evening was fine, indeed too fine. Ozone shimmered over surfaces like spirituous fumes. Pixie was 'wearing' a delicate white chiffon dress suit, with a subtle blue piping. The garment was as light as tissue paper, showing the frail strapping of her under garments; although she still seemed over dressed for this rare summer. Men too had no qualms about showing their naked bodies, chests and midriffs, like Colombian salsa singers at the beach.

Pixie floated and clipped along the street on long thin heels. She hooked her jacket on a little finger and held it over her shoulder. Clive might have removed his jacket too, but he was too focused on his deeds. He pursued her with scrupulous care, noting the grace of her bared neck and arms.

She was less sun tanned than you'd imagine from this hot summer. Of course she was trapped in that office all day, which explained her paleness. She definitely hadn't been invited to Sep's special island that summer. This explained why she chose to walk home, to find some fresh air if it became available. Somehow her physical beauty was exciting and familiar to him - which was really hard to explain. It wasn't ignorant lust, but a secret knowledge. Her presence gripped his senses and compelled his mind. There was a lovely unique quality to her. Could she describe a missing narrative for him?

Soon Pixie turned off into quieter streets, taking her deepening shadow and Pitt with her. Her pace dropped and she was enjoying her time. The evening was finally beginning to cool and allow human activity; restaurants and bars were becoming busy. If Pixie decided to call in somewhere, it might be easier to approach her and to chat. Instead she kept walking. She reached a set of park gates and decided to cut through. If this was intended as a distraction or just a short cut, Clive couldn't tell. He followed in her wake, hastening his step.

Clive drew so close behind, he was practically breathing on the back of her neck. Her distinctive white blonde hair had more or less survived and was set into a perfect shape, like a pearl; indeed like a female vocalist from that classic pop period.

Every now and again they came across another person, or group of people, either passing or taking adjacent paths. Fortunately they didn't give him away, or notice anything particularly suspicious. Pitt was very close to her, but there was nothing menacing about his body language. Sometimes people at a further distance seemed to notice Clive's tracking figure. From there it may look as if something was threatening about that large young guy trudging behind her. Pixie didn't notice. She was caught up in her own thoughts.

Traffic noise tended to mask any sounds. Generally the park was empty. Yet he waited for a more sheltered spot.

Pixie scanned the broad sun browned area of the park. At some point she had a sense of the untoward. Perhaps she finally got a sense, a flicker, of someone behind. She kept her cool and attempted to continue as normal. Then, recognising Pitt's features in a few seconds, her gaze registered shock and terror. She hadn't actually been terrified when he showed up outside the office. Rather she had been startled. But this was different, as he conjured himself in a menacing light. For Pixie it was like stepping out of the forest and confronting a pouncing bear.

In the first instance he tried to talk; or he opened his mouth. In the next moment she took a deep breath; she prepared to either scream or call for help. She didn't react calmly to his presence. What could he do? She was about to shout out for rescue, or as a warning. Clive watched her begin this terrified pantomime. It would surely lead to his apprehension. He was forced to reach out and do something to stop her. Even if this was spontaneous, he knew, with the serious allegation against him, that such an aggressive action was dubious - or even incriminating. But he dreaded who would answer her call. His large knobbly hand clamped over her mouth, as her fingers reached up and tried to peel him away.

Nevertheless she attempted to cry out. He felt vibrations against his fingers, like breath going through a reed. She was then grunting and squealing through his hand. He could feel the enamel of her teeth rubbing on his skin, as they attempted to bite but failed to cohere.

She began to jab her stiletto Court shoes into his shins. Sharp pain branched through him. In further struggle they were thrown into a shrubbery of poisonous and spiky plants, which monopolised this section of cracked earth. Nobody wanted to intervene or take any notice of their struggle. Clive was horrified at the turn of events, as he only wanted to communicate with her. But she was perhaps entitled to fear the worst.

She still had a grip on that pricey handbag, and made attempts to strike him around the ears with it. The shape of her hair was disarranged, threads flying in all directions. Her delicate clothes were also a complete mess, fabric torn and smeared. Somehow one of her shoes was dangling from the lower branch of a dead ash tree, like a festive candle holder. Clive needed all his strength and bulk to subdue her, even as these actions made him sick. He was sorry if he'd hurt her in any way, if only her pride. But he was battling to decipher the code that had put him into amnesiac darkness.

"Are you all right Pixie? No intention of harming you," Clive gasped.

She was gasping. They were both sat exhausted on the dry earth.

"Desperate measures," he argued. "Really bloody sorry!"

She drew up her knees and tossed back her head. Her deep eyes, a lovely green, Clive thought; as green as the Atlantic off America, rolled backwards, as her lungs still found the atmosphere too thin.

"You can rest easy with me. You can trust me a hundred percent. If you're not prepared to open up with me... you get me? ...then I am lost. Nobody else can put back the broken pieces inside my head," he argued.

Pixie was regaining calm, as she didn't shout for assistance.

They sat on their bottoms, side by side, rubbing cuts and scratches. For ages they were out of breath amidst flattened botanical specimens.

"You opted out as a human being," she stated.

"How did you make that out?" he complained.

Her face was smudged and hair flew away in every direction, crazy as candy floss pulled out of the drum with a stick.

"Why get me further involved?"

"How can you say that?" Clive objected.

"What were you thinking of?"

"I'm not going to hurt you," he objected.

"You already did. Is this how you treated that girl?" she speculated.

"Don't believe those slanders," he replied.

She fixed him in her sights. "How long have you been following me?"

"Since the office," he admitted, beginning to mop his face with Doug's silk hanky.

"I knew something was wrong!"

"You did?"

"You creep. *You absolute creep.* Can't you leave me alone?" She wiped her face, her neck and hands too. She tried to push her toes into the remaining shoe.

"Here, let me get that other one down for you," he offered, jumping up.

"Aren't you satisfied with the damage you caused? To everyone who ever cared about you?" she told him.

"That's a matter of total grief to me," Clive remarked.

She dipped down to replace her shoe - which was only mildly scuffed. "What are you doing back here? You were supposed to be locked up in a secure ward, or out of the country."

"Sorry to disappoint you Pixie," he said, ruefully.

"I'm not disappointed exactly. More like completely disillusioned."

"Oh, really," he thought. "I'm sorry."

"You should be sorry. Look what you did to me. Chasing me around and, you know, wrestling me to the ground."

Clive was somewhat alarmed by her reaction. He remembered Pixie (as far as he did) as a calm and reflective lady. Pitt kept reminding himself. This cool quality encouraged him to confide in her. Such anger was completely against her nature, despite his extreme provocation. She had a way of lowering her eyes and then raising them again, boldness fighting with shyness, that had captivated him.

"Where have you been hiding out, anyway?" she asked, brushing down her pale, now smeared, skirt.

"I've not been hiding out," he insisted. "To be honest, I don't really know."

"Why didn't you keep in touch? Don't pretend you don't understand how to do that."

"I have to ask you some vital questions, right now," Clive admitted.

"This seems totally irrational, or surreal," she commented.

"Equally for me," he replied, as if empathising with her.

"Are you tired of being a fugitive? Run out of places to hide? Is that it? You've come back to face the music?" she accused.

"Yes, maybe that's it. I wanted to face the music. I am like, totally knackered right now, to be straight with you... but I've not been running as long as you imagine."

Did he have a passionate affair with this woman? Pixie Wright? Been ready to cheat on Noreen and, ultimately, abandon his family, his beautiful young son Josh? To risk everything, betray solemn vows to himself as well as the vicar?

Pixie was a beautiful picture; she was appealing in looks and intellect, and (presumably at one time) very sympathetic to his views. He already heard a note of complicity in her voice, fluting and refined, beneath those initial cries of outrage. So was this so far-fetched? Or was it merely a response to her vulnerability and his notoriety?

"Look," Clive said, "we shouldn't hang about here, visible to the eye. There could be somebody following me, just as I trailed you. Let's find somewhere else to sit, shall we, and talk this through. At least as far as we can," he remarked.

This time he offered a hand to help her. "Certainly, let's go then, I didn't choose to sit here," she objected. "Normally I choose a seat. You definitely have form with the ladies, don't you think?"

"I didn't intend to be rough. I didn't want to give myself away."

Their rumpled look drew bemused expressions from a scattering of fellow park-goers. A kindergarten group gazed bug eyed at them while licking ice-cream cones. Luckily for Clive there had been no "have a go" heroes in the park. Pixie had composed herself by now, and was back to her usual self.

14

Clive felt numb and subdued as they strolled; as if the whole traumatic day was catching up with him. She was a woman who enjoyed her composure, but she hadn't been thrown to the ground before. Not as far as he knew. They both looked a mess and fought to regain self-possession.

"Why have you come back?" Pixie asked. "Or should I ask how you have achieved this?"

Clive lurched backwards in his mind. "I haven't got a clue about all that. I've had some strange experiences. I'm still shaken," Clive mused.

"Don't play games with me Clive," she warned. "Not with me."

"This is serious. I experience periods where reality gets confused. There's a continuous buzzing in my ears. I kind of hallucinate and get blind spots. It's like suffering the after effects of being beaten up."

She obviously believed he was exaggerating, to cover his behaviour. "Can you say where you've been? When did you decide to abandon your responsibilities?" she complained.

"I can't say." He tried to burrow into the tunnel of clouded memory, hoping for reminders. The park was expansive, but he was in a hedged maze.

"When was the last time you saw me, Pixie?" he wondered. "You know, before this evening that is."

"You seriously need an answer to that question?"

His hammered bloodshot eyes conveyed total bafflement.

"It was only a couple of weeks ago," Pixie told him.

"Really?" he absorbed the news with amazement.

"After you had raped that poor girl!" she explained.

"You insist that I am a rapist as well," he said miserably.

"That's just a small word, is it? But it was more than a little word for her. How can you not understand the consequences?

Why did you turn out to be such a heartless kind of monster?" she objected.

"I can only draw a blank," Clive suggested, uneasily. He strode stiffly by her side, moderating his step to stay alongside her. He realised that his jacket was ripped at the elbow.

"You want to erase the experience?" Pixie challenged.

"No, I am only trying to bring it back," he insisted. "Sometimes you try to bring back a nightmare, in a bid to understand yourself. That's what I'm trying to pull off here."

"You forget who you are? That's what you are claiming?" she replied.

"How can I know myself?" Clive said.

"What that girl went through! And you entirely betrayed my trust," she reminded him.

"Why should I need your trust?" he wondered. "In what way?"

"I saw you as a man of honour... how was I taken in by a man again? ...when you stood up to them. How could you abandon your campaign? Why throw your case away? By indulging such base instincts?" she accused, clutching the bag tighter.

Pitt was crestfallen. "I'm completely out of your network."

She pulled her arm to slacken his grip. "Let me free, will you, Clive."

"All right, Pixie, I'm sorry for that...if I was holding you too tight," he said.

"Why did you behave in such a nasty... such a beastly way, when you'd already collected a damning report against them? You literally, you know, compiled an entire dossier of evidence against them."

"At what stage?" he said. "Then in what regard?"

"You could have exposed the take-over," she told him. "You raised questions of governance... if you had behaved in a professional manner."

"You are referring to a significant acquisition?" he replied, some outlines clarifying in his mind.

"Certainly, it was the ZNT takeover. It was a landmark deal. Sep gave you the lead on the negotiations for that acquisition. Our team was heading up the agreement. You had the job of advising on buying a controlling interest of the pharmaceuticals group," she confirmed. "What's the matter with you?"

"Which particular company are we talking about?"

"British Imperial Pharmaceuticals," she informed him.

"That's right, a significant global player," he considered.

"You told me to work with you, while I was on your team... as the deal was going through."

"You're implying that this was a leveraged buy out? Somehow I objected?" Pitt urged.

"Yes, but they concluded the transaction... in your absence. This is a Geneva based hedge fund. ZNT purchased the BIP shares at below market rate... during the divestiture... that was a nice piece of business for that particular fund... and the upshot was... that Winchurch rescued his company, literally drew his chestnuts out of the fire...which covered his losses since two thousand and eight," she explained.

"No doubt big commissions and bonuses for those staff still involved," Pitt speculated.

"Certainly," she agreed. "Including you...or should I say us?"

"So we had to blow the whistle on the deal, did we?"

"Correction. You blew the whistle, Clive," she informed him. "Why do you think that I'm still here?"

"So if I decided to expose their transactions, they'd regard me as the death-ray."

"Is that how you like to see yourself?" she replied. "But Mr Death Ray, what happened to the evidence? Where did you put your dossier? You jeopardised our effort to expose corruption by attacking Sep's daughter. You sacrificed our investigation by taking revenge on the Winchurch family. That was, you know, the stupidest and vilest act you could have dreamt up."

Pitt stared at her in horror.

They kept to the pathway and strolled around the park perimeter. To the casual observer they presented a careful and thoughtful pairing.

"Whistle blowing is a dangerous game," Clive said. "That's like stepping off a high building to join the lunch queue. Presumably the people in Geneva were near to closing that deal?"

"The hedge fund managers were very confident of success. They were in close contact with Septimus," she recalled.

"The people in Geneva would not be impressed by my actions."

"*The people in Geneva*, as you describe them," Pixie said, "have mafia figures as partners, money launderers, trying to go respectable by purchasing BIP... buying into numerous world famous brands in the pharmaceutical business."

"All right then. This explains why I was gathering evidence against them. Why I was determined to stop the deal going to completion. We were surely crazy to take them on!" Clive exclaimed, going crab-like to her side to avoid a low branch. They skirted a cluster of oaks and beeches, around the perimeter of a seared cricket pitch.

"Septimus was involved to keep us, that is *his* firm, afloat. I guess that employees should be grateful to him. It's an old name, from back in the time of the promissory dinosaurs," she said.

"Those were desperate days following the credit crunch," he recalled.

"They urged us to be more daring, more risky in these times, if we wanted to keep our bonuses, our life style, and our global position."

"Like some ageing footballer ...flattering to deceive?" he remarked.

"More like a London version of Lehmann Brothers, to be precise... and Sep didn't want to share their fate. Neither did his staff want to collect their few belongings into a cardboard box and leave...with camera flashes as a curtain call."

"My heart bleeds for them all, Pixie," he said. "We hit the triple dip and we threw away a lot of chips...or should I say 'chits'?"

"Admittedly the markets were running out of control," she agreed.

"It was more money than the old lady could print," he objected.

"Winchurch Brothers may not have survived as long as that," she told him.

"Then we reached the point of no return, as bad debts chased bad debt," he protested.

"You have some memory at least?" she wondered, looking at him in a challenging way.

"Why should I suddenly turn into a liar?" he asked.

"ZNT have the capital reserves to gain a hold. Septimus is prepared to broker these deals," Pixie recalled.

"The old chap was going to save his company... and our jobs. Only in the process British people would lose theirs...the same with all copyrights, patents and installations in this country ...stripped and removed abroad. They could launder their ill-gotten profits from criminality," Pitt argued, animatedly "... transferring profits to sympathetic tax regimes, running off shore, in personal and corporate terms... with liberal employment law... more so than here in the UK."

"You are able to sketch the deal," she remarked.

"Unfortunately I have lost the script," he added, rubbing his burning eyes.

"You took your opportunity with that young girl," Pixie recalled.

"This again? That's a total misrepresentation," he argued. "That's their version...my enemies' version."

"Then how Clive?" she challenged.

"Look," he said, "I have a complete memory blank about that girl.... about what I am alleged to have done to Emmy Winchurch," he insisted.

"That would suit you, wouldn't it?" Pixie said.

"They make these accusations, all right, but this crime took place in a dark period...in my mind. That's why I had to get hold of you again," Clive explained.

She turned to him with hostile incredulity. "Don't give me the old lie that men aren't responsible. Are you one of those cave men with a degree? That struts and preens around the floor of Winchurch's? Calling us 'secretaries' and such rubbish? Next you will be telling me that she deserved it. She had it coming to her, right?"

"But, you see, Miss Wright, I really don't remember anything about that," he insisted.

"Not only aren't you responsible, Mr Pitt, but you don't remember," Pixie said.

"Exactly right, 'cause I have no memory of what I've done," Clive reiterated.

"Let me go. Let go of me! I had no idea who I was getting involved with!"

"But I tell you I have lost my memory for the year gone by."

"You destroyed all the work we were doing...researching, collecting data...evidence. You left me exposed. Fortunately they decided to leave me alone. I'm sorry Clive, but a loss of memory is too convenient."

But a measure of perplexity was added to her response. They began to take another lap around the park, as they edged about the truth.

"Why did I come back like this?" Clive said.

It was strange to describe his experience as "coming back". But it was easier to accept his claim of amnesia than a tall story about a guy in a limousine, who described himself as the devil.

"You couldn't stay hidden forever. It suits you to return at this point."

"Sure, it suits me to discover that I've been booted out of my job, lost my home and that my wife and son have emigrated to the Pacific North West," he smarted.

Pixie allowed him to deal with his evident grief for a few minutes.

"Why did Noreen decide to leave me for this guy? A guy I remember as no more than a friend of hers from the village. Don't you know anything about that?"

"You told me it was sensitive. You didn't want to discuss it."

Yet delicacy kept him from asking Pixie if she was his former girlfriend. Had they really been an item? He always thought it was strictly professional.

"Don't give me a hard time, Pixie. You have to understand this... that I found myself flying above the City skyline... as if hallucinating."

"I suppose you came down again, in both senses of the phrase."

"After that I was bundled into the back of a car. I meet this freaky guy, a right nutcase, and then I was pitched a year into the future. Definitely these negative events didn't happen like you said."

"How did you lose your memory? Did an apple fall on your head?"

"Don't try to make fun of me Pixie. Why should I invent such a story? Why did I wander back to the Winchurch building? Under the very nose of Sir Septimus Winchurch... that diminutive legend of the City!"

"Clive, short of faking suicide or hiding overseas, I was convinced you'd be back in touch with me, eventually," she argued.

"Were you?" he replied, surprised. "Maybe I'm determined to unscramble this mystery," he argued.

"You think you can finish this off?" she said. "From where you left off?"

Clive absorbed this information carefully, staring at her. They must surely have been living together, he registered.

"But if I am guilty of that crime.... if I was looking for your help... why did I take such risks?"

"I stopped trying to explain your motives," Pixie retorted.

"Do you imagine I am so crazy as to gad about the trading floor at Winchurch's? Is it the usual style of a hunted man?"

"I was too worried about my own safety," Pixie told him. "We were brave to challenge our employer, so you are capable of risky moves."

"When I attempted to speak to you... last Friday... I was just looking for moral support. You see, I decided to go out to lunch for some reason... then it got extended and I lost all track of time. Hasn't that ever happened to you? Now I am told about a sex crime," Clive said, grasping his temples, shielding his eyes from a horizontal sun. "They've got me in this moral noose."

"Forget about amnesia, Mr Nice Guy, we are approaching insanity."

"Is that what you really think?" Loss of sanity would have to be his plea.

"Don't believe the criminals who employed us," he argued. "Follow your own judgement."

"But Clive, I watched you walking away with that girl."

His head jolted back. "That isn't possible," he declared, frozen to the spot.

"It isn't? I literally saw you," Pixie said. She was colouring, and the muscles of her neck were under strain.

Clive was shaken at the horror. Yet he couldn't begin to doubt his own veracity, in the middle of a crisis. He couldn't let himself fall apart, with this bombardment of negative data.

"You honestly think I'm the type of guy who rapes someone?"

"How can we talk about a type of man?" she proposed. "Many of you guys get out of hand...you don't know when to stop."

"Is that right? I wonder why you bothered with me!" he commented.

"Oh, a very good question," she agreed, taking some of his sting.

"Then would you have a stab at answering it?"

"It didn't occur to me that you could be violent. It's true that you didn't treat me that way. Even though we had our disagreements, as you may remember... mostly tension under pressure. Not until this evening," Pixie reminded him. "Sadly I didn't have a clear idea about you."

"You need to trust your instincts. Obviously you find these allegations hard to believe. You don't think it's in my nature. What more do you need?"

"I don't have a privileged view into your impulses."

"Let me assure you, I don't have these impulses."

"Are you sure about that?"

"I didn't attack Emmy Winchurch. I don't know who did, but it certainly wasn't me," he insisted, staring at the ground. "Why would I risk everything?"

"You honestly believe someone else did this?" Pixie demanded.

"Obviously, I do."

"Can you name this other guy?"

"Not yet," he admitted.

"Are you going to prove that?" Pixie asked.

"Why ruin our investigation? You said so," he recalled. "Why disgrace myself and get myself fired...from what was the job of my dreams?"

"Clive, you got fired for opposing the deal...for threatening to send evidence to the authorities. They terminated your contract before that crime."

"They did?" Clive said. "Just for doing my job well?"

"As you put it before, you were the death ray in the room, capable of wrecking massive investments and they had to remove that danger," Pixie recalled.

15

They walked around a knot garden, so as to talk further. There were bowling squares and an evening baseball match was going on. Clive felt it was safer like this. They were making progress. He had to account for an entire year of his life.

When he touched on the subject of an affair, she didn't contradict him. Pixie hadn't expected to see him; while to him she was a mysterious figure. Their closeness was like a rumour, a mere fancy or innuendo. He was at the mercy of her memory, perhaps even of her imagination. The past was a fabrication, he realised, in the retelling; even as she was careful with the details of her account.

She wouldn't have considered he was capable of rape. How could you say that any man is so predictable? Did Clive know what he was capable of in a given situation? This was uncomfortable for her to think about, but it had to be done. How did his synapses react in extreme circumstances? He had been under severe pressure both at home and at work. He had set himself against the deal and his boss. All his beliefs and assumptions had been shaken. He had been pushed into dark crevasses of his psyche.

She didn't hate or even fear him (due to their former intimacy) but she was very hurt by his betrayal, after their collaboration on dangerous work. What exactly did they find together? They gathered detailed evidence of fraud, corrupt governance, illegal share activity, huge unexplained revenues. The latter funds were paid to Winchurch personally; including commissions, kickbacks. These were large enough to draw the company out of receivership. These were transactions paid secretly by a leading member of the ZNT hedge fund. This a guy called Viktor, who had deep pockets and, it was widely rumoured, a hidden former communist party slush fund. A ZNT delegation regularly flew into London to meet with Sep,

Clive, Pixie and the rest of their team, to discuss the deal and to develop a new portfolio of UK assets.

"We lost the old geezer millions, but that's what they employed us for," Abrams used to joke, during the crash. "I'm already doing a trade on big boxes from the supermarket."

Via the ZNT brokerage Winchurch gained extra revenues, even drawing on future natural resources at the Arctic, if anyone cared to inspect the small print. Winchurch negotiated a cut of that float, as an investment for the future; as a gift to his grandchildren, some rainy day. Although he was required to place ZNT people on his board in return.

Septimus got wise when Clive turned rogue. Pitt had expressed doubts, objections, to his face, but there was no immediate hint of whistle blowing, treachery and betrayal. Pitt had managed to hack into encrypted files known as "deep space". This turned violent, because Clive sought personal revenge, by attacking his family, his precious daughter. This brutal action had wrecked his case against Septimus and associates. No wonder that Pixie had been disillusioned with Clive.

Pitt heard her account; listened to the drama of his professional life. He was amazed at the conspiracy, as he was aghast at breaking a lover's pledge. Maybe he'd been out in the wild for too long, he couldn't say. The way she lowered her gaze, brushed the tops of her arms; broken inflections in her voice, nuances in her gaze. This was suggestive and oddly recognisable, as if recorded in his nervous system.

"You fall in love with a man thinking he is one person," she declared, "only to find out that he is another."

"I am the same man," he insisted. "Honest, I'm being up front with you. But I remember as little about us, as I do about Emily Winchurch!"

"Whoever you are, I was entirely deceived by you," Pixie insisted.

"You are so different to my wife," he declared. "Why would I carry on with another girl?"

"Do you expect me to answer that?" she told him.

But he knew that men don't have an affair with a woman who resembles their wife. It is, typically, because the particular girl is different to the wife that the man is tempted. He believes she's a lost opportunity freshly presented. Noreen had a similar experience with that guy in the village, didn't she? He was supposedly a good friend who turned into something more. He didn't much resemble Clive, but she decided to make off to Seattle with him. In his current predicament these irrational impulses of life began to prey on his mind.

"How could we have liked each other, slept in the same bed for months, been intimate, you know, while now you can't remember anything?" she puzzled.

"I wish I had the answer," he told her.

On one level Clive's claim of memory loss was not unfamiliar. Wasn't it a common strategy of men when they dump you, she considered: when (in the pathetic secrecy and obscurity of their own heads) they decide to drop the relationship and move on? Even at her age she'd known a few guys who had forgotten all about her, starting with her first great love in Switzerland. These amnesiac males wouldn't be able to relate their experiences either. Men claimed to suffer this deep process of mental and emotional laundry. They forget everything so that relationships vanish into a black hole.

"My idea about losing a year is an illusion. In truth I didn't vanish," Clive stressed. "Even if my head was elsewhere, I was there in body, if you get me."

"I'll certainly need some time to adjust," she replied.

A baseball tumbled over the straw field to his feet; which he scooped up and tossed back, to a grateful waiting crowd.

"It feels almost mad to come back again," he remarked, mopping his face.

"Where do you think you were?" she asked.

"I can't rightly say," he admitted.

"There are rumours about where you went...what they did to you."

"Then there was my encounter with that crazy devil character... yes I met him at the end of that dark period. When do they claim I attacked Emily Winchurch?"

"At the end of May, it must have been... if I can remember exactly," she puzzled.

"It's like they tried to take over my thoughts and actions. They tried but didn't quite succeed. What were they trying to achieve?" Clive despaired.

After the park they hid inside a vandalised bus shelter, to allow a heavy shower to pass. A group of youths hustled at the next corner, self-consciously threatening, furtively offering packages to passers-by. They shot confrontational gazes towards the couple. Yet in the present situation these fears dwindled to nothing. The two financiers were aware of a greater menace. Their energy was focused elsewhere. They were looking back into a past closeness. Oddly the youths understood this distraction (almost otherworldly) and chose to ignore them instead; as if the couple and they were lost in different zones.

Through precise information, that only Pitt might have recalled (except that he failed to) Pixie began to be convinced by his story of amnesia. She was unnerved at her credulity; she almost kicked herself; but could not avoid making such a conclusion. There was a period of vagueness in his mind, during which catastrophic events had occurred. Either he was cunningly or foolishly candid, but she didn't recognise such character traits in him.

He knew nothing about sensitive events and times - until she explained. Had a *metaphorical* apple fallen on his head?

Pitt realised that she was beginning to believe his account. If only he could explain his memory loss, rather than pretending it was an act of God (as she put it). He described again, in more detail, his encounter with a satanic figure in the back of a stretch limo. There was a risk of scaring her with the story, but it sounded no less bizarre than his other impressions.

Not that she believed he'd faced the devil. She was a rationalist and a talented mathematician and economic analyst. She understood that they were playing mind games with him. Certainly his memory had been interfered with and they had disorientated him. On that score he couldn't have invented the whole story. There was a fantastic element to his version, but she didn't think he was a fantasist.

They kept these personal, contradictory views, as buses came along and they waited for passengers to disembark. They sat on the plastic bench, leaning forward in anxious postures.

"There were no witnesses to this attack on Emily," he said. "It is just my word against hers isn't it ...and the rest of them."

This argument didn't impress her. "You think she's invented this?"

"Was I even aware of what I was doing?"

"That doesn't prove your innocence," she argued.

"To be honest, I have no more awareness of innocence than I do of guilt," he told her.

"Maybe they brainwashed you," Pixie suggested.

"If I was brain washed then my mind would be empty and my thinking patterns disturbed."

"Aren't your thoughts disturbed?" she argued.

"I seem able to reason effectively. Don't I? My recall of life before this year is hazy... yet my mind hasn't been wiped. My long term memories are clear and absolutely normal. Well, at least as clear and normal as most people's. Until I stepped into that limousine and talked to that guy," he mused.

"It's disturbing and frightening," Pixie admitted. "They picked you up and wiped your mind, under the power of suggestion."

"Who knows, maybe you hit it on the head. It would be simpler to believe that I had encountered the Devil."

"Don't be absurd, darling. There is no devil figure. Not that I can believe in."

"Maybe I really was acting in a destructive and evil way, Pix, even though we thought we were doing some good," Clive

113

said, confusedly. "Maybe we were completely out of our depth. Where did it get us?"

"Don't let them get to you. It entirely suits them, to transform you from a principled guy into a criminal. I watched you going with Emily that evening. But something could have happened. Someone may have been there too, and intervened. You may not have been alone in there with her."

"You may be right, Pix. I appreciate your input... I was confident you would have faith in my true nature," Clive told her.

Again those young guys, trying to sell drugs to passers-by, hanging about on the corner, chose to evade Pitt's glances.

"How would you respond if I didn't?" she asked. "Let's go home, as I'm getting chilly out here." She clutched the tissue fabric of her jacket.

"Fair enough," he said, relieved.

"Let's go home then, shall we?"

"Does that imply that we were an item?" he asked.

"It was another concluded deal. I don't mind telling you," she replied.

16

Pixie's apartment was in a1930s art deco styled blocked, that overlooked the park. The city was rich with architectural treats, yet these were also bricks and mortar ghosts, observing the great city's changes; like petrified ancestors forced to exist among us in the "here and now".

Pitt was surprised that she trusted him enough to invite him back. This was not a light invitation, given the allegations against him and his besmirched reputation.

When they arrived he noticed that her apartment had undergone recent renovation and redecoration. The interior ran along minimalist lines, in a colour scheme varying between gauze white and battleship grey. There were many vases of flowers in French art nouveau vases; camellias, lilies and pots of orchids; yet while the place was chic, it also gave a blank echoing feeling that amplified Pitt's sense of isolation and unease. There were none of the friendly homely touches he expected.

"Don't you like the re-design? You can relax because my boyfriend is away, working in Paris."

"You ditched me three months ago. Then you meet another guy?"

She offered her bubbly pure laugh. "You're the only man in my life, are you?"

"I've lost my wife, my child, our home. Did you understand that?" Pitt wondered, seeking her eyes.

"Are you sure I'm exactly the girl you should be telling?" Pixie suggested, plucking off her shoes and going about the smooth floor in stocking feet.

"You didn't waste time forgetting all about me," he remarked.

Pixie gazed at him curiously, to test his seriousness. "Bertie and I have known each other for several years now. Why do I have to justify seeing another man, to you?" she wondered, tossing her lamentably soiled jacket.

"Did you introduce me to him, y'know, when we were..?"

"Yes you were introduced to him...a couple of times. Bertie and I became friends during a skiing holiday. A romance developed soon after that on business in Frankfurt. After all the recent upset, you know, we kind of fell into each other's arms."

"Right, but I don't remember this bloke either!" Pitt objected.

"Why should you?" she told him.

"What does he do for a living then?"

"Bertie's collaborating with the electronic composers Air... they're working on a government commissioned project... he's over in France now at their studio. He's trying to persuade Bjork to sing over the space opera sections."

"You live with this bloke?" Clive asked. "When he's not gone off somewhere?"

"We have a busy schedule, between us," she admitted.

"Definitely sounds like that," Clive observed.

"Is that too much of a scandal for you?" she retorted.

She slinked on her soft feet over a hard polished, chequerboard floor, as she covered her considerable living space.

"But I don't want a threesome," he objected.

"Are you crazy? No danger of any threesomes. He isn't returning to London over the winter. Creatively he's in a different universe. Although he literally calls me every morning and evening, to see how I am...to say that he loves me."

"Then take your calls, just as normal," he told her.

There was no use showing lack of trust by trying to restrict her. She had the power to betray him at any moment, he knew that; assuming that he hadn't betrayed her - consciously or not - by simply getting back in touch.

"Make yourself at home," she invited. "Why don't you..? Sit down and relax, okay? You look all done in, to be honest," she said, looking him up and down again.

She noticed that his eyes were sore and troubled. He kept wiping his face anxiously, and there was a coat of perspiration over his features, like shellac, sticking strands of hair.

Pitt followed her instructions and selected an Art Nouveau armchair.

She moved about the apartment room to room, tidying and rearranging. After this she disappeared into her high-tech kitchen for a while. She brought out a pot of coffee and a plate of chocolate brioche.

"Presumably I've been here before," Clive suggested. "I've spent time in your apartment."

"No, Clive," she replied. She placed all the objects on her smoked glass table, and settled on a white leather sofa unit. "I moved into here with Bertie, actually. Hard to believe I am the same girl really. No, we - you and I - lived in a small flat in Hampstead. Don't you remember? Literally above that little antiques shop... don't you even remember where we lived? We always felt vulnerable there. It caused a lot of tension between us."

"Certainly sounds unlikely, because I hate antiques as much as the minimalist style," he confessed, grumpily.

"You prefer a rustic farmer's cottage, I suppose. The time we had together in Hampstead has vanished from your thoughts? How weird all this is, Clive... whatever has happened to you!" She rubbed the top of her arm, as if freezing in the A/C.

He grimly tore brioche between his teeth. "Not a thing, Pixie. I keep telling you. Not even you," Clive admitted again.

She took a few moments to pour.

"That's a really charming thing to say... even if it's true. You guys know what to say to a girl," she told him. She elegantly poured him fresh steaming coffee, from a long pot with a curlicue design. She brushed a few crumbs from her lap into the palm of her hand and poured them back on to the plate.

"Did we really have a flat in Hampstead? About a lot of old furniture?" he asked. "Next you'll be saying I restored an old Morris Minor and rode about town in a tweedy suit."

"Oh yes, Clive, you definitely lived the role," she replied, mischievously.

"What did you do to me, eh?" He rubbed a flake of skin from his sunburnt nose.

"You haven't changed so much," Pixie said. "Anyhow, you needed somewhere to hide away from Septimus and his associates. They were very keen to talk to you, after you threatened to scupper their landmark agreement."

"How come they didn't follow *you* home?" Clive asked.

"I still shared a place in Camden... we made sure that I moved about... and I would take a cab to you in the evening. Jane and the other girls would cover for me. Even though they had no idea what they were hiding. That was a strange and dangerous period. We always took precautions."

"You're still taking a risk, aren't you?" he concluded, savouring the short strong coffee.

"They didn't suspect me. They blamed you, even if they did suspect. Septimus regarded me as another of your gullible victims."

"Well Pix, I've definitely lost communication now," Clive bemoaned. "I'm totally cut off from all sources and contacts."

"You can have a try with my devices later, if you'd like."

"Thanks Pix, I appreciate that. I'll try to set up a VPN."

"You can get around security," she encouraged.

"I don't remember that flat in Hampstead." He began to rub his features in bemusement again. "How can you tolerate this new place? I like the flowers and contemporary art, but it's like a doctor's surgery here."

"Trust you to think of flowers!" she exclaimed. "As for the art, it cost me a small fortune and...and no matter what you think...this isn't your home."

"Why should I particularly mention flowers?" he wondered.

"When we were together," she explained, "you were buying me flowers all the time. Literally all the time," she emphasised. She turned away to conceal the rise of colour to her face.

"Was I really? Me? Flowers?" he repeated in amazement.

"Why not, Clive?" She returned her attention with widened eyes.

"I'm not in the habit of buying women flowers, am I? Wasn't I the 'love em and leave em' type?" he rebutted.

"Certainly the leave them type," she agreed, mysteriously.

"Fair point," he stated.

"Maybe you don't understand yourself as well as you think."

Pixie leant back into a relaxed posture and watched him down her pert nose. "You should believe me, as I was gracious enough to accept your little story."

"Exactly what kind of bloke was I then... back then... when we knew each other... from your point of view, like?"

She glittered nervously. "To tell the truth you were more in love with me," she explained. "Yes, Clive, you were quite intense... passionate actually... but sweet too. You definitely enjoyed giving love tokens...yes, buying me flowers. You seemed happy and relaxed with me... when we could be. Although we had a terrible lot on our minds," she recalled.

"That's a safe enough proposition."

"But I can be quite tough too, and I can take pressure. We brought work home with us. Yes, we were afraid they'd follow me...that I'd lead them back to you. We loved each other and we took risks. You were very loyal, strong, until you let us down and ran away."

"Don't you believe me, when I say you have nothing to fear?" Clive emphasised. "I wouldn't hurt you or anyone. Not deliberately."

"What if I can't believe your version?"

"Now I'm history. Do you believe that?"

Clive noticed a photograph of her dark handsome Frenchman, in a heavy silver frame on a Noguchi coffee table. Pixie had an entire archive of soundtracks and videos of them together.

"That's a photograph of Bertrand," she said, following him.

"So you bought this guy at a spot auction," he complained.

"Hardly, as you were out of circulation... and on the run from a rape charge."

"You can't let me forget."

119

How could he be envious? Was he really crazy? He didn't consciously know this woman. This episode was related back to him. He couldn't recall being intimate with her, or even drinking coffee with her. Why should he care about her new lover at this stage? In the long term she wasn't even his type.

"Now you're going to have to do some talking?"

"How? I've been doing my best," she told him.

"I need your help to fill in some mental blanks," Clive argued.

"How many do you have?" she said.

"Please, you know, talk as much as you like. Tell me everything you know. Will you? I'll just pour myself a bit more coffee...sit back for a while and listen. I won't even interrupt, I promise."

"All right then, Clive, if you'd like."

17

So Pixie continued her narrative. She began to describe his recent past as accurately as she could, while trying to relax; to remove stiffness from her legs and her neck. She related how Pitt had been made an associate; how she was assigned to work on his team, in regard to the deal.

"You approved that I had been thrown out of finishing school," she reminded him. "I swore you to secrecy that I never obtained my diploma," she quipped. This was a reference to an unfortunate experience in a restaurant that had her expelled.

They struggled to keep their colleagues in the dark about their assignations; nor to arouse suspicions about their professional collaboration. They tried to meet in unlikely places to maintain secrecy, such as the church at Greenwich Hospital, in a disused corner of Smithfield market, the planetarium at the Observatory, the Serpentine Gallery, the Freud museum; as well as numerous quiet pubs and restaurants in the district around their flat.

"It literally added an edge of excitement," she recalled - she shuddered involuntarily. "Sounds like that, doesn't it?"

Clive had brought along incriminating evidence against their company and ZNT executives, for her to verify. This evidence included many stolen documents, hacked emails and other recorded messages, all copied and categorised. They were operating within a sense of peril, as if security guys could burst in with Uzis or Kalashnikovs at any moment, to curtail their activities.

Yet Septimus had invested too much in her; on a personal and professional basis, to connect her to Pitt; or couldn't bring himself to do so. To doubt either of them in fact was to doubt his own judgement, in appointing and rapidly promoting them, almost as a pair. While his company's survival was at stake after the crash of 2008, then fighting for survival in the financial shake down, he was focussed on trying to restructure. He was working twenty four seven to rescue his world famous family business; to achieve that vital ZNT deal, and the lucrative partnerships it offered in future, even if concessions were required.

Septimus couldn't imagine that Pitt, so deeply trusted and respected, so crucial to negotiations, would turn into a traitor. He had taken Pitt under his wing, as a virtual college boy (he liked to think), from offering him an internship, recognising his talent and making him an associate. Sep went on his instincts, his trusted hunches, even though Pitt was a raw provincial recruit. The financier had confidence in more than Pitt's ability to conclude the deal. The young banker had Sep to thank for his position, for everything he had achieved. Therefore the financier had no suspicion concerning his employee's underhand activities, just as it was an illusion to say that the City could be successful *and* clean, after the crash and global readjustment of power and currency reserves.

"You became besotted with me, as we worked together," Pixie explained.

No doubt intense danger had encouraged their attachment. He even followed her home after work, to feel close, when it was too dangerous to be seen publicly together.

"The situation resembled this evening... except you didn't throw me into the shrubbery in those days," she recalled.

"For the record, I believe that you threw me. Did our office affair destroy my marriage?" he asked.

"You enjoyed spending time with me. Also it was essential to develop our case against Winchurch. You needed my help to compile a water-tight dossier... which could be presented to the FCA or SFS... or whoever we decided. I was the only person on the team you could trust. But I'm not sure of the exact sequence of events."

"If you're not, then how can I know? Did my wife leave me because she found out about us? Or she was unable to manage the stress involved?" he wondered.

"Your wife was also having an affair. She decided to leave for the States, taking your son with her... you explained as much to me. You were reluctant to talk to me about her... or about your marriage in detail. You preferred to keep quiet about your family as a whole. I assumed that was normal practice," she argued.

"Well, sounds as if we were a proper couple, even sharing our work responsibilities," he suggested.

"I didn't want to pry, but there was more going on under the surface," she suggested. "That was my feeling."

Even though Clive kept silent about his marriage, as if it was too painful to mention, he would grow depressed about the break up.

"You were equally obsessed with exposing Septimus and in love with me," she claimed, arranging ivory chiffon over her thighs.

"It looks as if I didn't refuse your charms for long," he admitted, squeezing his jaw.

He may or may not have been the innocent party in the break-up of his marriage. This wasn't the first time, by all accounts, that he'd pursued Miss Wright. The idea of lacking control or judgement was disgusting to him. Had he recited those vows at a country church for nothing, as deceitful as a mynah bird, as he sought to impress that flock of friends and family, bearing pointless witness? He considered himself still in love with Noreen. He still possessed all the essential feelings, a deep bond of trust. So that abandoning the lad and his wonderful lady felt entirely brutal and worthless.

"How could I be so callous?" he brooded, shaking his head.

"You were determined we would break the deal together," she recalled.

He regarded Pixie as a smart, sexy girl, whose sophisticated, somewhat elite background appealed to him; himself coming from a more regular provincial background. He remembered the impact she had made on him, on first introduction at an internees luncheon. As an already married man, with his first child on the way, he was ashamed of his wide eyed excitement about her. Could he be so impressed with a bit of high polished glamour?

A predatory attitude was a part of the often testosterone-fuelled atmosphere at Winchurch's. He didn't know directly, but there was probably a similar macho culture at other City firms.

But he didn't blame that culture entirely, as he could always choose. Pixie herself was stirred by his rough northern machismo, as she saw it (compared to the sons of government ministers and financiers perhaps) just as she was impressed by his bright mind and professional confidence (contrasting with his gauche social persona - on joining). Her life experience made her identity with his upright northern values and his type of principled rebellious stance.

After the disgrace of his affair (Clive reasoned) Noreen must have put their house on the market. She'd found solace with that local guy and emigrated to Seattle. They must have got around the considerable legal problems. These had surely been complicated and time consuming, unless they had a contact to speed up procedures. He meanwhile was shacking up with Pixie Wright, showing a heedless teenage enthusiasm.

Did he really sacrifice everything for that crusade against corruption in the square mile?

At this point they were startled by the chime of her doorbell.

They exchanged looks, swapped terrible scenarios, until finally she got up to investigate. Pit slipped away to hide in a bedroom, as she silently indicated. But the caller turned out to be a female friend, from the same apartment block, calling around to say hi. As the conversation dragged on she offered Pixie a spare theatre ticket for that very evening, which was accepted.

Clive was troubled, yet remained hidden behind the bedroom door. Finally, after a lengthy chitchat, the girl withdrew. Pitt came back into the living room, struggling not to panic. But he dissembled his objections and presented an ironical front.

"D'you expect me to hang around here all evening?"

"Relax. Shouldn't we behave as normal?" she told him.

"What are you going out for?" he asked, beginning to pace.

"I want to see this play at the Donmar. The last time I saw a production of Pirandello was on a school trip. She would be suspicious if I refused now. She's a trustworthy woman. We have to maintain our safety screen, Clive. I will continue with the story tomorrow."

"I can't believe this," he objected. "Don't you understand the peril we could be in? Are you crazy...thinking about an evening out?" he protested.

"I would advise you to set your alarm for very early tomorrow...when I might continue my account...of your recent past...if you'd like."

"I don't even have an alarm," Clive commented. "Maybe I'll get up when the cock crows, as I did at the weekend."

She sighed and averted her gaze. "You poor man. You've been through a lot. Why don't you take a shower? Change out of those grubby clothes? Read something, watch something," she suggested.

"I guess there's no other prospect," he replied.

"The sun's caught your face," she told him, peering to examine. "There's some special cream in the cabinet. I also have some drops for your eyes."

"Maybe I should tie you up, as they do in the movies," he joked.

"Be a good boy, Clive, won't you?" she urged him.

"You're not going to undo that button in your top lip, are you?" he quipped.

"We need me to sew back a few missing buttons, don't we?"

"Perhaps your father made a wise choice after all," he replied.

"Let's concentrate on *your* painful memories, shall we?" she told him, trailing away.

She'd been packed off to an expensive boarding school at the most tender age available. She was the illegitimate daughter of a Norwegian shipping heiress (she inherited a portion) and an English PhD student, who'd been completing a project on the genome of slugs. The question of illegitimacy and chance shouldn't have mattered.

Her parents had met each other while studying at Leeds University: he was on his first internship project (with his slugs) and she was studying fine arts, infatuated with Edvard Munch and expressionism. She enjoyed her student infatuation, but she was afraid of ruining her future.

Consequently the infant Pixie was parcelled off to relatives of her English father, while her mother's Norwegian family refused any bonds. But they financed a quixotic European education for her that was designed to establish complete independence and self-sufficiency. She grew up privileged and out of the way. She had a relationship with her family that was like an old fashioned relationship with a local bank manager.

In rapid time Pixie was made-up, done-up and out of the apartment.

Pitt meanwhile was left to roam and to brood over his situation. He began to speculate about what other revelations would come, when she resumed her narrative in the morning. But he trusted Pixie already, like an instinct. He felt that he knew her well; although that was mysterious, as his fidelity had no rational basis. She was not deceitful or dishonest; he could vouch for that fact. In his profession he didn't trust to feelings alone, any more than to pure rationality. He had worked closely with Pixie Wright, sharing sensitive information, even before he went rogue against the deal. On that evidence they must have been harmonious as a couple as well, he considered. The only thing was to follow her advice and to wait, even knowing that; meanwhile, their enemies were not standing still.

Clive stood at the long narrow window of her living room, gazing out towards the penumbral city lights. He was offered a familiar metropolitan scene, except that London and all its contents were placed a whole year hence. Or there was a year sized gap in his brain like a financial bubble. His stomach tightened at such a strange and dislocating awareness.

Night time thunderstorms gathered again across the velvety heavy sky, and he noticed a violent drama of a storm, unfolding over the park and adjacent streets.

18

When Pixie returned home she wore a blankly anxious expression. Her mobile rang again and, turning her eyes away from Pitt, she began to chat to the French boyfriend, Bertrand whatever his name was, cupping her hand. She slipped away to take the call privately in her bedroom; her muffled voice sounding dissatisfied and miserable.

When this cross channel contretemps ended she insisted on going to bed straight away. Evidently she'd had a mild lovers' tiff with Bertrand, brought on by the tension no doubt, but also related to her spontaneous outing to the theatre.

"Don't think about disturbing me in the night," Pixie warned him. "I have a double inside lock and a pistol under my bed."

Pitt was taken aback. "What do you take me for?" Clive said. He assumed she was joking about the gun.

"There are unresolved places in your character," she said; signs of strain around her eyes.

"Are there? So that's what you'd call it?" he returned, disconcerted.

"Sleep peacefully, Clive, knowing that you are in the best place."

"I really appreciate it," he admitted. "You've risked a lot for me already. Now it seems I have put you into fresh danger."

"We've got to protect each other, as far as possible," she said, smiling.

"I suspect we are vulnerable even now," Pitt observed.

"Let's not worry about it," she suggested, pulling away.

"You're a really bang up girl, Pixie," he declared.

"You still know how to flatter a girl, with your sweet northern phrases," she teased.

"Always ready to turn on the charm," he replied.

"I note you rediscovered a sharp haircut and a posh outfit."

"Thanks to a friend of mine, not far away from our old house."

"They used to hate you for that. You strayed away from Brooks Brothers," she recalled. "So I assume that the rumours are true...that you were doing consultancy work for a rival."

"I've no idea about that," he said.

"You ought to understand...have no doubt... that Septimus and his new directors will not permit employment to a rival," she argued.

"Just as they disapproved of our relationship."

"Glad you're listening," she remarked.

But he was afraid of what it meant to desire her.

Nervously they went to bed at the same hour, if to different rooms. Clive was quickly conscious of her in the room next door. Pixie could sense him moving about and then his presence in the space as well. She had a pistol under the bed (resulting from their first affair). She was afraid of him, given those events and incidents. She knew how to fire a rifle; in Switzerland she had gone hunting with a group of local men; not just learning how to smile at a future husband or to iron his shirts, but to fully participate in a local culture and society, much to the chagrin of her Swiss guardians.

Pixie's memory showed no flaws; they had been lovers once. Consequently she fretted for hours under soaked cotton sheets. She wasn't just tormented by potential danger, but at the speed of that renewed bond with him. She was kept awake by memories of happy experiences together; as well as the clash between the cruel and the kind. She had tried to eradicate those memories and hardly dared to bring them back; chewing them over in her mind was like taking an emotional cyanide pill.

Intellectually she believed in him, yet in her body she was mistrustful and distressed. She called out from half sleep, suffering nightmares. Clive was awake and heard her, which prompted him to shout back in response, to ask if she was all right. The tension only grew heavier in the air as she refused to answer. Then she couldn't get back to sleep again, as she was conscious of Clive, wide awake, troubled and restless. She listened out acutely, full of desire and fear, stiff and perspiring. She followed his movements in her imagination as he paced about, in the dead small hours of the night, when only urban foxes and service workers were about.

Indeed he suffered a feverishly restless night. He sweltered with the close humidity. At first he pushed his face into the pillow, as if trying to suffocate himself. He was sad and tormented by his actions during the lost year, which had caused him to be a pariah and to lose his wife and son. It was unthinkable that Noreen could have had an affair with that guy in town and then agreed to a new life in Seattle.

Exactly how was he supposed to have attacked Emily Winchurch? What were the circumstances? Pixie might give him the full background in the morning - or later that morning - if he was able to survive this nocturnal hell; an eternal torment of a bad conscience.

Even the brief blackouts had escaped him. He was intensely aware of Pixie in the adjoining room. What was wrong with him? The smooth curves of her creamy body, warmly naked, sleek with perspiration, deranged his imagination. Whether it was misery or lust, he couldn't stifle a desire to find her: a voice that told him "why not?"

This convinced him that they'd been lovers in the past. He felt their relationship in his nerves. There was an intense attraction and sympathy; a friendship that picked up from where they had left off. He gained this insight just as, during their chat, he'd recognised her mannerisms. He sensed a habitual relationship with her, a passionate familiarity, in the recent past. Sleeping apart was mysteriously painful, as if they'd been torn away. He craved her intimacy, to feel her body next to him. Pitt's nerves vibrated through the night like wires in a high wind, protesting against spiritual cold and hunger, after she had abandoned him.

In this manner they endured an interminable night. Not relieved by high humidity, wafting from the ground like acrid incense, which shrouded London outside, as the A/C in his spare room rattled like an old bus on a reduced timetable.

19

When daylight infiltrated the blinds, Pixie chose to escape her nightmares by knocking at his door, most likely to rescue him. She felt safer and justified in the sunshine, knotting a robe around herself.

Her signal stirred him from turbulent last-minute slumbers, which came as a mocking coda of real sleep. In these sweaty phantasmagorical turnings, recent incidents were replayed in an endless loop in his mind; just as the clatter of a novelty alarm clock had earlier shaken Pixie to her senses.

She wanted to discuss those urgent matters, following which she intended to go into the office as normal. Otherwise, there was a danger her boss would grow suspicious; because they already knew Pitt was back in circulation. They must have tracked him through credit card transactions already. She couldn't allow her fears to keep her away from work.

Pitt and she blinked at each other across the breakfast island. They struggled to suppress a percolating feeling of panic. Somehow it was unnatural to have slept in separate rooms, although he couldn't say exactly why. Certainly his nerves, or erotic memories, had recorded things which couldn't be shrugged off. His imagination filled sexual blanks, and he feared this was incriminating. Jangling nerves at breakfast exacerbated such feelings. They certainly didn't enquire how each other had slept.

Yet his nerves were overridden by his need to find out. She knew more about the previous year - as if they'd been to the same movie but he'd fallen asleep half way through. She was cast into the role of a mystic, interpreting, reading his runes. It was like hearing about misdeeds after a drunken night on the tiles; getting all the antics of another guy, who had a dark side to his personality, having to assume that the whole tale was not a vicious fabrication.

Only Pixie was able to brief him. He'd be entirely in the dark if not for her. This was the peculiar dynamic as he leant across the bar and fastened on to her every word.

"I'll try to speak to the boss today," she announced.

"You're piking me, aren't you? Talk to Winchurch about this?" His smarting pink eyes squinted at her, as he nervously scratched up his wavy hair.

"You rented an office of your own. Did you realise that?"

"An office? Are you serious?"

"No, not exactly an office... but you had a room in Clerkenwell. You know... I think it was just off the green somewhere. I never went there. You wouldn't tell me the exact address or location."

"I refused to tell you? Weren't you helping me?" he wondered.

"You had to be secretive. You were trying to protect me. But you had your paperwork, so to speak; conducted your campaign. You considered that it would be dangerous to inform me. Either I could betray you or, more likely, betray both of us."

"There's greater danger now," he observed, playing with the condiments as if they were battleships.

"I realise that," she admitted.

"You're telling me that I was working from there?"

They began to feel the first morning heat, like an angry leather fist behind the kitchen window.

"Apparently you decided to get your own HQ. Where you built a case against Winchurch and his clients. You were communicating to the outside world... and had prepared that dossier of data and statistics on the ZNT case. From time to time you had my help with that."

"Who was I communicating with?" Pitt wondered.

"I don't know," she admitted. "The plan was to get enough evidence, collect enough data to present to the FCA, even the Fraud Squad and, after that, the CPS. You also had a contact in the media. We had developed contacts with the FT and with Robert at the BBC."

133

"All sounds cosy. So why didn't I stick with my plan? I just had to apply myself, put in the homework, as there was evidence... the boss told me to lead on negotiations into the flotation and sale of BIP. I was the guy who made it technically possible," he reminded her. "I was their security."

"While you were one of them, you were not a threat. Later, when you were briefing against ZNT, they got your location, they followed your footprints, both real and virtual. They even managed to locate and raid your private office."

"They did?" he exclaimed. "Did it cause a lot of damage?"

"They removed the files, erased data, and deleted all traces you had captured. They attempted to eliminate you from the virtual world, as far as they could succeed."

"But they didn't, completely, did they! How do you know about this, any road?" he wondered, draining another shot of coffee.

"Sep's people couldn't entirely succeed, because you'd developed a complicated network of proxy servers. They caught glimpses of you, but you sent them along the wrong tunnels, so they lost you."

"In that case I'd use compromised servers," he told her. "I would have built in some redundancies... and piggy backed off other people's servers," he explained.

"You rented a server from a Thai company. The engineers hired by Winchurch were unable to trace you back... because you selected different servers and mechanisms."

"I kept busy, didn't I? Very busy. Some year for me that was, wasn't it," he commented.

"Looks that way Clive," she agreed, trying to discover some appetite.

"No two ways about it," he replied.

"You even adopted categories of porn sites as disguise. So they would be nervous even if they removed your mask."

"But I didn't present any case to the authorities. Assuming that the relevant authorities would have the guts...and take that leap of faith," Clive thought.

"You didn't get the opportunity, or you lost it yourself," she explained.

"So with my lost memory I'd nothing to show?"

"It's the information you have forgotten, or mislaid, that is vital," Pixie told him.

"Can't say that I disagree with you," he said.

"As we speak... the deal went through," she commented. "BIP is no longer British or listed here in London as a British company. It was successfully raided by ZNT, even without your lead, and against your judgement. Behind ZNT stands a consortium of various high value individuals and groups."

"Certainly Pix, because they include mafia figures, many with communist pasts, or involvement in the drugs trade, as well as CIS oligarchs and BRIC entrepreneurs, thirsty for respectability on the global stage," he stated.

"This consortium bought shares, literally using laundered revenue streams. These can be sourced to totalitarian regimes, or criminal groupings in other parts of the world, if anybody is foolish or brave enough to do that," she explained.

"Which is where I came in," he considered, with a grin.

"Also why they forced you to leave the negotiations team early," she said, ironically.

"Winchurch persuaded BIP to float, and then presented an artificially low share offer, way below true market valuation. They took advantage of low stock prices during the recession. His task was to persuade executives, and the workers, at BIP, to accept the offer," Clive concluded. "I can imagine the conversation. ZNT needed Sep and the British establishment to achieve their goals. That was to be listed on the London exchange and to purchase key British assets."

"They are benefiting from previous R and D, drawing on capital assets," Pixie explained.

"I came to my senses too late," Clive observed. "Whatever my strategies, I failed to prevent this business going through."

"It could be possible for us to reverse engineer the ZNT deal... We can do that, if you can literally relocate that missing dossier. Any idea where those files may have gone to?" she pressed.

"That's the fifty million pound bonus question." Pitt exhaled and rubbed his face again. "ZNT is Swiss based; one of the largest global players, since the millennium."

"Not only that, but they are headed up by a guy who already owns key assets, including a bundle of luxury brands names.... fashion, cosmetics and even diamonds."

"Winchurch Brothers provided this character with a global brand in pharmaceuticals, a chain of private hospitals and health care franchises... with a huge R and D investment."

"The company helped with cross border transactions... advised on how to circumvent the regulatory environment here..."

"We, that is Winchurch Brothers, enabled the consortium to offset their debt, initially raised from the banks in order to purchase BIP, to avoid paying British tax on their future profits," Clive calculated. "It's like paying themselves back for getting into debt. Can you think of individuals doing that?" he declared.

"In return Sir Septimus was able to take a huge commission, literally to rescue his own company from liquidation," Pixie considered. "After we'd crystallised our losses."

"The employees at Winchurch's are grateful no doubt, to keep their jobs. They are saved because traders find value in a triple dip recession. But what about the health of the economy as a whole? How about the people at BIP, after ZNT restructure, repatriate and eventually refloat?"

"Sep and the ZNT consortium know you have evidence. They fear being turned into a legal soap opera," Pixie continued.

"That's marvellous, 'cause I don't know where it's stored now...what I might have done with that information."

"You may have forgotten, but are they going to take any risks?" she asked.

"Do they doubt that my memory has blanked?" he replied.

"You knew they might call, while you had that office in Clerkenwell. It was only a matter of time."

"What was I doing there, exactly?" he wondered.

"There were bars on the doors and windows. You installed surveillance devices. Yes, it was an incredible set up. You knew that even security precautions would not stop those guys. If they had access to US and European networks... if they could fight an intelligence war against western information and defence systems... if they can dare to assassinate their opponents in the London streets, then they have the means to track 'Lucifer'."

"Who's Lucifer when he's at home?" Pitt asked, looking horrified.

"You are Clive," Pixie told him. "*You* are Lucifer. You were the errant investment banker, who shaped himself up as the whistle blower."

"So I wanted to frustrate ZNT. I stood in the way of these hyper rich criminals. They're playing the markets now, with all the greedy fervour of the newly converted," he said. "Join the capitalists to beat them at their own game. If your ideology can't deliver prosperity for the people, not even enough rice and potatoes, play the free market instead. Trouble is they got very successful at the grand casino, didn't they. So much so that the casino virtually belongs to them," Pitt commented.

"Yet how can you...how can *we*, hope to frustrate such powerful people Clive? Don't they effectively run the world these days?" she objected.

Clive gazed uncertainly into the deep warmth of her green eyes. "That's a fair point, Pixie, I have to admit! Was I stupid? That was the biggest lot of arrogance I ever attempted. Now we're both in the cooking pot," he agonised.

"They are determined to make you pay the penalty," she agreed.

"There's no doubt they screwed with my head, and with my life!"

"Yet they felt your presence," she told him. "They still regard you as a potentially deal breaking threat."

"Just an annoying nay-sayer at their meetings," Clive said. "They would like to delete me like a negative message on their devices. They extorted the world's resources... fed our addictions... so need to exchange currency surpluses into technological assets...as well as social and political influence," Clive calculated.

"ZNT have powerful friends," she warned.

"But they don't tolerate an enemy like me," Clive observed.

20

Their meeting continued as if they sensed the peril of the outside world and recoiled from it. They understood that the cosiness of sharing breakfast together, as if on any work day morning, was an utter illusion.

"Got any idea where I sent my information?" Pitt asked.

"How can I?" she told him. "You were trying to protect me Clive, don't you...remember?"

"That's a brilliant example of gallantry," he remarked.

The increasing temperature from outside felt like a column against his back.

Pitt aimed another arc of Assam into a square tea cup. His hand was shaking, despite his best efforts. Yet they had to keep calm - both of them. Don't look down at the long drop as you squeeze around the rope bridge.

"We should speak to Emmy Winchurch, don't you think? Or *I* should try to contact her. All I know is that she's recovering in hospital. In England rather than abroad... though there was talk of sending her to Geneva. That was Winchurch's first idea... but the unfortunate girl was spared such a fate. Sep decided on a private clinic here, so that he could visit her more easily," Pixie explained.

"I assume Sep was in touch with his security team, after I was seen on the street last week...back in circulation," Clive said. "Did he want to speak to you?" he asked.

"Well of course. I didn't have the benefit of your supernatural story. There was some reluctance to inform on a former boyfriend. But you were a rapist on the run, as far as I was concerned. After the crime your movements were mysteriously lost. I didn't have your side of the story. I thought it would be a break in their enquiries."

"Sep brought his detectives in to speak to you. Did he want to question you personally?"

His hands still shook. Maybe he should quit on the coffee.

"No. They talked to us again, that's all. You know... you had appeared outside the entrance. Your audacity very much surprised them. But it was a fleeting encounter."

"Your willingness to cooperate makes me feel safer," Clive admitted.

"Oh, but I gave a negative attitude towards you," she replied.

"That will protect you," Clive said. "It may give us a breathing space."

"The security people did a sweep around the City. Where on earth did you get to that evening?"

"Back to my home and family," he told her. "Or so I imagined at the time."

"Did you really believe your life hadn't changed? That your wife would be there waiting for you," she sympathised.

Clive face grew troubled. "I wasn't so well informed," he reminded her.

"You poor man," Pixie sympathised. "You didn't even have any home to go to."

"I've lost my mind. Now you understand what's happened."

She stretched her elegant limbs in the pink satin pyjamas. "Anyway you managed to avoid his security people on the day."

"Pure luck," he commented. "How did Winchurch ever invite a bloke like me, his enemy number one, to his precious garden party?" Clive asked.

She smiled and toasted him ironically with the orange juice. "Of course you were not invited to this event. You gate-crashed the party...after you got the details from me. Naturally I was the person he invited. He's always had a little thing about me. I told you about his celebration plans."

"Since when did he invite employees anyway?" Pitt said.

"It was a victory party," she said. "How do you imagine? Yes, the ZNT deal was a life saver. We were permitted to rub along with the rich and powerful."

"Oh yes, they reward us like Champions League footballers," Clive objected.

"Everyone fully deserved their free drinks in the sunshine... City standard catering, which was a big thank you to Winchurch Brothers' staff for loyalty and, no doubt, professional discretion. It was a lovely party, before you know what...or you know who, came along," she recalled, munching on another triangle of toast.

"Sounds like the office party from hell," Pitt grumbled.

"Quite. But in the spring sunshine, with champagne flowing, excellent catering, first class entertainment... well, it was all quite glorious, actually."

"I'm happy for you," he commented.

"Everybody was, you know, invited; there was a swing band playing, people were thoroughly enjoying themselves," she recalled. "Before Lucifer dropped in. Until you showed up, that is... lurching over the lawn towards us."

"What were the circumstances?" he replied.

"Septimus didn't expect you to turn up," Pixie considered.

"I don't remember anything about his smashing little do."

"As I remember, there was only security at the gates. Minimal security, just to check invitations," she said. She had to squeeze her mind to gain these details.

"This showed his confidence at the time," Clive remarked.

"Perhaps. It must have been simple for you to breach ...to just clamber over the wall around the estate somewhere. I used to do the same at school. After all he's not a Victorian land owner with game keepers. Not this generation of Winchurches," Pixie reminded him.

"He must have known I had information against him. Regardless of the fact I was fired and my face didn't fit any longer."

"Remember you were out of a job. You knew a lot about ZNT, but you didn't possess the evidence. He underestimated your knowledge... your capability. He relaxed too soon. That was his mistake."

"I was toast," he argued. He dropped a slice back on the plate to demonstrate.

"You were just out of a job. Not yet criminalised."

"Really? So they all just looked out and noticed me coming up the lawn," Clive wondered.

"That's right. You looked quite menacing. Literally fired up. I suppose from the effort of finding the house and then getting over the wall. My reaction was embarrassment, to be honest... regret at informing you of the party."

"Do you think that Sep was following my activities?"

"He knew about your campaign... that you had a type of HQ off Clerkenwell Green," she explained. "Sep felt in an insuperable position. Only those guys on the same team understood your intentions; had any idea of your case. To the other Winchurch people you are just an embarrassing loser, or some type of crank, following a personal vendetta."

"What am I supposed to have done at this bloody garden party?" Pitt wondered.

"You confronted Septimus. You challenged him."

"Must have thrown him off balance," he replied, shielding his eyes.

"He heard you out, but more or less laughed in your face. Well, that isn't really his style, but he grinned and bore it."

"What was I really trying to achieve?" he wondered.

"After that you seemed much taken with Emmy. You didn't leave her alone all afternoon, actually. I mean, she literally didn't leave you alone either. I did my best to ignore you, out of pride and disgust, but I was actually furious with you."

"Your reactions would deflect any suspicion," Clive argued.

"That was a natural reaction, which helps us. Sep's false memories of that day will give us some time and cover," she thought.

"Right. Then if I attacked the girl, as they claim, then I must have the cops on my trail?"

"If the police had ever been involved," she commented.

"But if a guy intends to commit a crime, then he doesn't make it so obvious. If he plans to rape a girl then he doesn't advertise the fact. Not by flirting with her and carrying on in front of the guests."

"There was that show down scene with Septimus on the lawn. After that you were upset, agitated... until Emmy came down to see what the kerfuffle was about. You seemed to have a magnetic effect on her. It was one of those disturbing moments in life. That's how it looked."

"That's nonsense, because I'm a dedicated family man. Although by then I didn't have a family," he mused.

"Septimus was livid when he saw you together. You had finally succeeded in getting through to him. You were hurting him, via his daughter. You'd engineered a breach of the family firewall."

"Didn't she want to listen to her father?" Pitt said.

"She literally told him to go throw himself into the lake. You couldn't bring down his business, but you were damaging him as a father."

"Could I be as devious as all that?" Clive mused. "Why didn't I keep my mind on the job at hand? Where was my focus on the details? My reputation in the company?"

"You got drunk and loud with Emmy. That alone wouldn't get people's attention. You were kissing her with your arm around her waist."

"Bloody hell. God spare us. That was enough to get attention," Clive agreed, shamefaced.

"That was as much as I could tolerate. We were supposed to be a couple. When you didn't apologise I literally slapped you across the face."

"That doesn't sound like you, not at all," Clive objected, leaning back.

"I literally lost my cool," she admitted. "I didn't hurt you, because you found my action amusing. The pair of you didn't care about the powerful people there... who witnessed this outrage. Politicians, diplomats and business people. Emmy thought it was a great laugh."

"We were definitely making a bit of a scene," he admitted.

"All the Winchurch employees were looking on. They made a show of trying to ignore you. Sep kept a hawkish eye on you throughout...clutching his flute of *Pol Roger* in cold fury. Before long he mustered security staff to expel you. I can see them squaring up to you," she said, suffering a tremor under her eye. "You managed to beat them back in the wine tent. There was a dreadful rumpus, to be honest. The party didn't go as swimmingly after that."

"No wonder I'm not as popular in the office," Clive remarked.

"Sep was in touch with his ZNT friends. But it wasn't possible to get their thugs over in time. Sep persuaded his guests to go back into the house. Then I noticed you striding away with Emmy... into the trees at the bottom of the garden. I remained standing outside for a while, looking out... because I was concerned, even though nobody else stayed around to witness. I somehow hoped that you would return to your senses," Pixie argued.

"Whatever got into me? I never imagined I was capable of such behaviour," Clive said. He closed his eyes and rubbed his cheeks, as if to erase his shame.

"It was getting dark. I was on the terrace, watching out. Sep went back into the house, reluctantly...he had such an expression on his face... compelled to look after his guests."

"Didn't he want to chase after us?" Pitt wondered. "What was wrong with the bloke? This is his daughter we're talking about!"

"Sep despaired of influencing her. What good would it do him? I told him what I had seen. He contacted the security director, yet again, saying that matters had gone far enough. But we spotted Emmy returning, running up the garden, towards the terrace. She was naked and screaming, with streaks of blood on her chest and stomach....it was just terrible, Clive."

He was stunned and stared at her, almost as chalk faced as she. "You may as well continue, love...give me the whole picture!" he prompted.

"Finally Sep's chaps arrived, carrying weapons, and spread out into the trees... were looking for you. Some of these guys were ZNT personnel. But although they were searching for hours, they couldn't track you. You'd managed to disappear from the scene."

"What happened to Emmy?" Clive agonised. "They reckoned I was a monster? She was put through a sexual attack, at my hands? Why are they sure about the scenario? Maybe she went off into the woods with me, but how can we say what happened then? We don't know that the girl was raped," Pitt argued.

"Don't be ridiculous Clive. How do you think they know?" she replied.

Her assertion threw him. He ran fingernails over his scalp. "True enough," he replied, trying to focus. He tried to fill the bottom corners of his lungs. "But I don't remember these events. I'm totally horrified and confused by what you've described. As if you're describing the antics of some deranged maniac."

She wanted to touch his hand, but drew back. "Don't torture yourself Clive. We can bring back lost memories."

"Some comfort," he said bluntly. "But there's something I need to tell you about. Right, but I don't know how you'll react. Then I'll have to be completely up-front with you, Pix. Not every detail is lost from my mind, as a matter of fact. Strange as it may sound to you... if I ever met Emmy Winchurch again I'd recognise her."

A flutter of confusion passed over her features. "*How exactly* could you recognise her? Would you mind explaining that to me?" she challenged.

"All right, I'll do m' best. I would definitely recognise her. Even though I don't know exactly. I couldn't properly explain it," he admitted.

"You'd better make a start," she suggested.

"I saw her face in my sleep," he admitted. "Flashes."

"How can you be sure? Describe her to me?" Pixie challenged.

"Nice brown eyes, long hair... with a sprinkle of freckles over her cheeks. It's quite specific, wouldn't you say? She looked at me boldly in the dream, and she has a mouth, as they say, made for sex. Does that sound anything like her?"

"That's accurate, but I wouldn't talk about her like that. Do you think it's appropriate? You're not with your friends now. All right?" Pixie said.

"Why am I seeing her in my sleep? Have I seen a photograph of her?"

"Did you ever look at her portrait on Sep's desk?" she speculated.

"That could be it, except I've never really looked around Winchurch's office suite. We always met elsewhere... to accommodate other people. I've no idea if he keeps any photos of his family on his desk."

"You broke into his office," Pixie revealed. "I helped you. You were trying to figure out security codes. In the process, you may have seen a photograph of Emmy."

"A predictable behaviour pattern," he argued. "In the circumstances."

"It makes more sense to think you were not yourself," Pixie said.

"There was definitely something amiss with my life."

"Not a regular day," Pixie agreed.

"Definitely they'd been warping my brain big time," Clive argued. "It's appalling to believe I harmed her. That I may have raped Emmy."

"A girlfriend works in the Royal Westminster Hospital. I've asked her to bring a syringe with her, last night. We are going to take a blood sample from you. Do you agree to that?"

"What will you do with my blood sample?" Clive replied.

"She's the girlfriend I went to the theatre with last night. Yes, it proved to be useful in the end. No I certainly wouldn't talk to her about this. I only talked in an abstract way. From a blood sample she can look for levels of steroids or hormones. These can be used to affect personality and behaviour. After all ZNT have acquired pharmaceutical expertise. My friend works in that area and she'll give us feedback."

"Just go for it," he implored. He leant back and heavily expelled breath.

"She'll get the results back to me, as soon as possible, maybe in a few days," Pixie offered.

"That's a smart option Pix. There's nothing to lose."

"We'll just pop into the bathroom then, to take a blood sample. Then I can make myself up, ready for work."

"I supposed you've got a syringe, do you?" he asked. "Then I assume you want me to roll my shirt sleeves up."

21

Clive took a seat in one of her modernist chrome armchairs. She had a deck view over the park. Hot sunshine gleamed like a hungry tiger's eye.

"Can you explain me to myself?" Clive urged, reeling from her account.

"Would you really want me to do that?"

"Then what else do you have?" he asked.

"You hacked the Winchurch systems. Honestly I knew you were good, but not that good," she admitted. "The other guys hated you, but they began to respect you."

"I wouldn't have to be that good, Pix," he insisted. "I'm not some teen genius in his bedroom! It would only be a matter of tampering with black boxes, or even social engineering. It doesn't take genius to achieve that, I can assure you."

"Not unless you are a specialist," she told him.

"No, you just talk to the engineers. I had access to PENTEST and would just leverage weaknesses in the system," Clive explained.

"So you wouldn't have to use proxy servers?" Pixie asked.

"No, not as such, as I was categorised as code staff. Why would I consider an attack? Not while I had legitimate access. Why position risk? I had a back door into the system, using naming conventions. So presumably I created an account... with elevated rights... leading back to nothing in that case...with a hall of mirrors to hide my tracks," he argued, trying to retrace his steps.

"This came out over dinner one evening," she recalled.

"Well you're the 'head and shoulders' girl. You are the expert on risk. So who better to discuss this with?" Pitt wondered.

"That evening we considered seeing a movie. Taking a walk down to the Everyman. I was scared by the implications."

"No, I don't suppose we were in the mood for a movie," he told her.

He followed a super jumbo, floating like a balloon into Heathrow, crossing from one time zone into another.

"You admitted looking at documents. Septimus moved money around, setting up off shore accounts, inventing revenue streams. You discovered segregated parts of the network. These hadn't been audited, or logged and made non-accountable. "

"Very interesting, because I would be adept at finding misappropriated funds."

"That's what made Sep so incredibly bitter about you."

"Clive Pitt, the grateful Halifax grammar school boy, an inside threat all along," he said.

"You made copies, you indexed and annotated. You siphoned away the evidence... somehow...somewhere. You'd enough to cause an earthquake in the City and beyond. Presuming you could circulate the information - to get the attention of regulatory bodies."

"I was the guy with the capacity to damage him. This strategy was dangerous, but I don't suppose the authorities keep a hot line for whistle blowers," he commented.

"There were names there... important people, some of them had been given state visits here. Literally guards of honour by royalty. They are the sponsors of operas and football clubs of course... they spend their pocket money on these hobbies, speculating on the currency markets, buying up bonds, five year and ten years...and picking up cheap stocks as a sideline."

"These are high value customers... global business people and financiers," Clive agreed. "We fully know who we're dealing with."

"But we were both afraid. It was enough to turn our hair grey," she conceded. "We thought what good can this do for us or anyone? What is the use?" she recalled.

"We can do something," Clive argued. "If we can remember where I've stored this data and information. Where in hell did I put it all? Is it possible to retrieve it?"

"Clive, I keep telling you, that I don't have the least idea," Pixie admitted.

"Or if that info is really lost now forever - in the clouds... if that's the case then so am I. So are we. I've dragged you into this black hole after me," he apologised.

Pixie was suddenly drained of breathe and colour. "Sep's team didn't know you'd hacked his systems. He was back at work, buzzing around the trading floor as usual, hopping from one desk to another. But in the evening, when many of the guys were leaving, he called me back in. He'd started to worry about the deal, because he wanted to ask further questions."

"What did he want? He suspected you?" Pitt asked.

"Hardly. He was trying to confide his troubles."

"Why would he want to do that?" Clive wondered.

"He needed to speak to someone. I'm the daughter he wished to have. Ironic," she said, "as my parents disowned me. Anyway that's how Sep rationalises his fondness for me. That's how he rationalises his wish to be near me," she explained.

"The old bugger. Is that because you are close to me?" he countered.

"I'm literally a canary in the cage. Anyway he adopted a considerate tone with me. Whatever we may think of him he's incredibly driven. Of course he is ruthless. It's ancestral. He had a fixed idea that you want to ruin him. He explained how sensitive, secret files had been copied. This theft had the potential to throw us out of our jobs, he warned."

"He surely knew I was the guy responsible," Pitt argued.

"Obviously Sep had suspicions about you. Your behaviour pattern was irregular. He heard about your ethical objections... rumours and hunches don't remain secret. He doubted that you were to be trusted. On consulting with ZNT he decided to employ heavier tactics."

"Oh right, so exactly what tactics did they employ?" Pitt enquired, trying to get on top of his nerves.

"You may remember the thick necks? The guys who tried to teach you a fatal lesson? They rounded on you, in a toilet at the football ground. They caught up with you just before half time, when you popped down for a wee," she recalled.

"You're pulling my leg?" he said. "They worked me over in the toilets, at a footie match? Definitely qualifies as dirty 'tactics'," Pitt said, disgusted.

"A premier football game, I think you told me. You got a pair of complementary tickets…a seat in their hospitality area. I didn't want to go with you. They kicked and punched you to an inch of your life."

"Bloody hell, as bad as that?" he considered.

"The police and stewards thought you were the random victim of hooligans. You know, rival football fans. If the wrong people found your body, then it could be passed off as murder. But probably your enemies didn't intend anyone to find you."

"This is incredible," he declared. His stomach was in his mouth, just to hear about this afterwards. "That explains the gouge under my eye, do you see?" he demonstrated.

"A couple of fans at the game tried to intervene. They managed to save your life. But they were also beaten up… though not as badly. You were in the general hospital for a month. There were stories on the news about this. Because there isn't mindless thuggery at top games anymore, they argued. But then there aren't any security cameras in the loos," she pointed out.

Clive made an astonished face. "You're confident that Sep knew about this? That he organised this attack?"

"I don't think he organised that. He commented that it was suitable punishment. Probably his powerful friends were behind the assault. He was concerned about media coverage."

"He's a charming old gentleman isn't he!" Pitt said.

"He argued that you required a psychiatrist, not a doctor. They said you'd probably suffered a breakdown. Your colleagues claimed you were paranoid. You had a persecution complex."

"This beating could explain my memory loss," Clive observed.

"That's definitely a good theory," Pixie agreed.

"But there are other theories. Otherwise you wouldn't be taking a blood sample."

"Our colleagues were full of praise for Winchurch... because he agreed to treat you at his private hospital. You were put into the hospital. You stayed there for weeks. Then suddenly you came back to work again."

"You are saying that I didn't lose my job?" Clive asked, amazed.

"Sep gained credit for retaining you."

"I reckon there was already enough scandal... without firing me," he argued.

"Sep wanted to keep an eye on you."

"But how could he tolerate the risk?" Pitt wondered.

"Don't we live with risk... don't we gamble every day? Don't we get a buzz out of it? They didn't want to be another Lehman's. At other times you sat in our area, staring blankly at your monitors, talking to yourself... refusing to speak to anybody."

"You're painting a lovely picture. I had already suffered a terrible alteration of personality."

"One afternoon you got into a heated argument with Spence. Again it was your obsessive hatred for the deal. In the end you put your hands under a desk and threw everything over. There was a terrific rumpus at this stage. A pile of guys jumped on you and tried to restrain you. But you'd somehow got the strength. You were a man possessed... by a sense of outrage I suppose."

"Bloody hell," he murmured. "Just as well I can't remember this."

"Security was called, although you'd fled the building."

"They regarded this as my resignation?" Clive suggested.

"We didn't see you again until the garden party."

"The garden party again," he commented. "Why would he invite his staff to his country estate? Did he ever ask you before?"

"Well he was not thrilled to see you. We all know what took place in the woods after that," Pixie said.

"What is alleged to have happened," Clive reminded her.

"Something happened. Emmy and you are the only people who know the truth...unless there was somebody else lurking about there."

"Right. Is that possible?" he said. "Do you think it was a set up?"

"But I should go into the office as normal. There I will try to meet with Sep about this. Gauge his attitude to the whole affair, at this point," she offered.

"Did you say I was sent to his private hospital?"

"You may have escaped from the hospital, when I saw you last."

"On Friday afternoon, do you mean?" he said.

"But I can visit Emmy and talk to her about you. So that we can get her version of events. It's the only way forward," she argued.

"You can't be late for the office today," he remarked.

"No, but first of all I want some of your blood."

Clive gave a jump. "Now we're talking."

PART TWO

22

Pixie scrutinised her monitors all morning; secretly distracted, edgy; trying to maintain her trained composure. Her nerves flickered and shunted along with the figures across her multiple screens.

The idea of visiting Sep's daughter proved difficult to achieve. She felt intimidated by the usual hustling atmosphere; as if colleagues knew she was back in touch with Pitt.

Septimus Winchurch himself kept secluded in his office suite for much of the morning, which was not typical. She could picture him in conference with managers and shareholders around the world, picking at the details of the takeover again; or the potential evidence. She saw him in efforts to manage the crisis of Pitt's shocking reappearance; as well as to calculate consequences and limit damage. Most likely he glimpsed his own potential financial end game and wanted to freeze Clive in his tracks.

Later the boss resumed his active habits and looked apparently buoyant. Sep dashed across the room, conferring with staff around their work stations, gripping reports (harmless ones) as was his alarming custom. Following the successful issue last year, which had protected the firm's viability, he was freshly enthused by work; the markets were stabilised, liquidity restored. Somehow the year's ugly confrontations with Pitt, and the nasty side-effects on his private life, hadn't interfered with a renewed hunger for professional life. He hadn't lost his appetite for money. The whole point was to make millions in profit, as a pub wishes to sell beer.

Pixie kept a wary eye on him, but it was difficult to find a moment to approach. Wouldn't any leading questions arouse the boss' suspicion? What was her motive for visiting Emmy in hospital now, after weeks had passed? It was common knowledge that Pitt had surfaced again, threatening collateral damage. The man's character had been assassinated, multiple times, yet he came back for more; he was a topic of contempt, ridicule and even fear. Rumours and gossip would start up about her too, Pixie Wright, the head and shoulders girl, even though there was little to go on. Her colleagues would misconstrue the little information they possessed about Pitt and she together, like an unfounded profits warning.

However, it was Sep himself who approached and requested to speak to her confidentially. He came out of his suite and placed himself shiftily at her desk: "Can I ask for a chat with you Miss Wright?" he said. He maintained his paternal smile for everybody, but his eyes dashed around the floor. Sep felt other eyes on him and was concerned about the impression, nothing went unnoticed.

In a shy but peremptory way he gestured her towards his sanctum. Once she'd gathered her bag, a cardigan and even her coat - as if stalling -she followed his portly form and looked about anxiously herself. She told herself not to worry, arguing that it wasn't such a big deal to be invited to the boss' office? She had to consult with him regularly, like everybody else, as this was his style.

Once she turned up at his office, past a high security PA, Sep invited her to sit in front of him. The visitors' couch offered any half recumbent guest impressive, satanic vistas across the city, directly over the boss' shoulder. This put the visitor at a nervous disadvantage, because at this angle Septimus was in partial darkness and silhouette. Such apparent luxury and generosity disadvantaged rivals. Indeed this position had views right across the square mile below, stretching towards Wren's monument, that lofty marker to a re-born London. The impression was that the whole area was largely owned by Sir Septimus and his peers or cronies, yet this was as illusory as a British owned chocolate bar.

"Forgive me for calling you away," he began. "How do the markets look today?" he asked, making small talk. Then a change of tack: "I fear that your sighting of that dreadful Yorkshire man continues to plague my mind. You did, Pixie, didn't you, inform our detectives about everything you learnt that day. You gave them all the information you have about that arrogant chap, when they interviewed you again?"

Septimus rested his emollient, eager brown eyes on her. This zeal reflected in the glass table top, as his diminutive stature produced a low posture in a plump leather swing chair. There was a pair of half-moon spectacles on a pile of paperwork, but he only wore them to read or study. His glance was equal to hers only because of the seating. He resembled a pampered schoolboy with premature ageing, with a wavy silver quiff; in possession of brilliant and tragic talents.

"I informed the team of everything I know," she assured him. "I didn't withhold anything in my knowledge. I was open with them about all available facts. Why should I be secretive? A man like that can mean nothing to me."

The financier leaned short sharp elbows on the expansive glass top. He thought carefully, then compressed his soft skinned, wrinkled face and smiled paternally at the young woman. "Certainly that's good sense. There's no-one who wouldn't strangle Pitt now, to stop him. He can have few hiding places left, I imagine. Nobody is willing to hide that deviant scoundrel, unless they are entirely ignorant of the whole affair."

"Why are you continually obsessing about him?" Pixie remarked.

There was an ironical twinkle as he absorbed her idea. "He's still at large, isn't he? He remains an unpredictable danger."

"Didn't you say that he has nowhere to hide?" She feigned naïve ambiguity.

"We need to draw a line under this affair," he stated. He couldn't avoid a readjustment of his seating position, whenever he raised his tongued brogues from the floor. "We've been complacent."

"Then what have you got to be afraid of?" she replied lightly.

"I want to ensure you aren't omitting something...that you don't think is important... but which may be... in helping us to locate and eliminate... his potential influence," Winchurch argued. Wide lips raised into a dry smile, to reveal blocked teeth for a moment. His large clasped hands knocked the table top in punctuation.

"There are no conscious gaps in *my* account," Pixie insisted. She kept her knees primly crossed and gazed at him with a sweetly neutral expression. She had perfected this with Madame Briest in Geneva, whenever she had slipped out illegally to meet local friends in the old town; including her forbidden lover.

"You're not feeling under any form of pressure are you Miss Wright?"

"Nothing but the tension of sitting in my boss' office," she replied.

"Hah, indeed." Sep relaxed his shoulders and laughed reassuringly. "You sometimes have such a charming way of responding," he said. "But you'll tell me if you feel any danger from Pitt himself?" he pressed. "We shan't let him get at you!"

"Not from Pitt. Absolutely not," she said. "I told your private detectives everything I knew last Friday."

This alerted the shrewd Winchurch and suspicion rippled over his brow. His head was large for his body with a forehead shaped like an anvil. "Who could have imagined Pitt turning up here again last week? Apparently he may have been sneaking about the City for weeks...or months. Where on earth did he disappear to? After he evaded us? Do you have any ideas?"

"I've no idea where he might have been," Pixie replied.

"Do you imagine the scoundrel was doing consultancy work for a rival of ours?" he considered.

The cunning, penetrating eyes settled on her confidingly again, above that violent ripple of curls; the ears pushing through, quite large and fleshy, but trim as pound signs. His gaze was forced on her by his lack of height; there was just a fat knot of silk tie between his chin and the glass top. Yet he had trained himself to look dominantly upwards, rather than to incline backwards, as could be the world view for many shorter men.

"Did you ever expect to see Pitt again? What a nasty surprise for you."

"No. I don't suppose that I did," she admitted.

"You thought he was already dead?" he pressed, as if shocked.

"I thought that, most likely, you would have him arrested. I expected to see a charge, a court appearance and conviction. If we ever saw him again, it would literally be in prison... a secure unit."

"Patience, my dear. Are you saying you'd actually visit him in prison?" he replied.

"But if I was convinced by circumstances, then I would have no motive to see Clive again," she explained. She tried not to be distracted by the outside vistas, which led her eye as far as the Shard.

"Are you certain he didn't betray any clues? About his current activities? Or concerning his present whereabouts?" Sep toyed with an arm of his spectacles.

"Only that he disappeared along the street," she said.

"Thanks for the directions, Miss Wright," he commented. "We first lost him after that atrocity against my family, you understand. Then on Friday he reveals himself, for no apparent reason. He escaped again in the middle of treatment, and then showed right outside this building," he fumed. "We thought we had him safely under lock and key."

A ring of curiosity rippled her tone. "Is that so?"

"Our colleagues at ZNT lost him somewhere on Friday evening apparently. Yes indeed. Try to rack your brains, Miss Wright. What could he be up to? Was there something about his appearance? His look? Any single clue may be vital," Sep told her.

"Clive seemed unaware of taking any risk. He appeared disorientated... or oblivious to past happenings. Literally like an innocent man."

But Pixie took the new information that ZNT agents were trying to find Clive.

"Miss Wright, fanciful speculations are of little value," he objected.

Pixie's eyes narrowed against her will. "Can you dismiss these ideas, after he was beaten to within an inch of his life?"

"What should you care? How do you know?" Sep wondered. "Do you imagine that sanctimonious traitor deserves even an inch of his life?"

Pixie fought to stifle a reaction. "Blows to the head may have affected his judgement, not to mention his behaviour. How can you be sure he was in control of himself?"

"I wouldn't put it past him to deny everything," Sep remarked, shuffling. "He is smart enough to offer us some elaborate plot...to justify himself."

"Even the judge and jury would listen to his side of the story," Pixie said.

"Pitt destroyed the life of a beautiful young girl in the process. My daughter, I mean... that's who we are talking about," he added bitterly. "Emmy had her whole life in front of her. She's missed all her exams this year. He is guilty of the terrible offence we accuse him of... this outrage against my family. You should know better, if you want to let him get away with it. Not even in his own twisted mind."

The financier's cheeks and eyes puffed with rising blood, as he see-sawed on his padded chair.

"That's hardly likely, you know, given all the evidence against him," Pixie commented.

"Quite so. He's had many chances to face up to his own actions. He has to be confronted with the consequences. But you don't sound as certain as you once did Miss Wright, about the evil nature of this rogue... this pit trash hooligan."

"Why should I condemn him, if it could affect my own work?" she wondered.

He studied her intently. "Mm, well, Pitt was Lucifer in the ZNT deal. You understand the subversive role he took. Our partners are concerned to stall his wrecking actions. If we'd listened to him, then you and even I would be living under

160

Waterloo Bridge by now. You'd be selling that magazine for the homeless. By that I mean all the junior staff at this firm. You'd be applying to a housing association in south London, wouldn't you Pixie, for a roof over your head. You'd be turning down the drug dealers on the landings and street corners."

"That would be most unlikely," she informed him.

"Do you really imagine so?" he challenged. "Where else do you hope to sustain your present life? Which business is going to pay you as much as this, Miss Wright, never mind your property and shares portfolios? Are you intending to go off and do some secretarial work for the *NHS*?" he challenged.

"I'm aware of my present conditions...and remunerations," she assured him. "Do we follow this profession entirely for ourselves, Sir Septimus? Clive was adamant that the City has a crucial role... that the financial system shouldn't be bankrolled by criminals, oligarchs and former communists," Pixie stated evenly.

Sep gave a startled and appalled chuckle. "That's his world view? Then where does the value come from? What does Pitt know about the higher echelon of finance? What right does that self-righteous prig have to sit on judgement of a risk taking industry?" he fumed. "Only the loonies and the losers describe this place as a casino," he insisted. "Doesn't stop them drawing on their pension funds, or other investments and stakes," he retorted.

"Are you asking us to lose any ethics, Sir Septimus?" she replied.

He fixed her sternly through his wiry bristling eyebrows. "What would you expect from the money markets? From the global trading of bonds, currencies and commodities? The markets are the province of saints and do-gooders?" Sep wondered. "When did you lose your mental grip on current market conditions, young lady?" he argued, tossing his spectacles back down.

"Clive thought you had lost the plot, in regard to the ZNT deal. He said you had got into bed with those fund managers. In

Clive's view the firm couldn't justify being exposed to such huge risks, as they pushed us into illegality," Pixie reminded him.

"You consider that Pitt wanted to save the world?" he jeered.

"Not exactly the world," she replied. "But everybody here at the firm, including yourself...and even your family."

The financier looked away an instant, to enjoy a bitter, sniggering soliloquy. "We help bankroll UK PLC. That isn't like your grandmother's tea party, I can assure you. You want to play fair, do you; you want to obey all the rules and regulations? The world has changed, the global economy has shifted. You have to deal with the post-crash world and the creatures it has created. It isn't a comfortable place, half the time, but we have to manage the change and, let's be frank, take advantage."

"But Clive raised serious issues about governance at ZNT... relating to the divestiture at BIP. Clive made a strong case against brokering an unsolicited acquisition. He had evidence of insider trading and fraudulent transactions. Why did you attempt to erase his documentation?" Pixie coolly challenged.

"Do you want to transfer City revenues overseas? Lose competiveness abroad? Consolidate the European markets in Frankfurt? We already have to contend with stupid politicians at home and abroad," he pointed out. "We're already locked in an absurd square dance with the Revenue and the Exchequer, without playing social worker to a traitor like Pitt," he complained. "Didn't we offer Clive and his family our international relocation package? Extremely generous terms, including tax and immigration support. Was he prepared to take me up on that?"

"For Clive these were principles. We're literally struggling to keep control of our own economy... to manage UK business and industry, to the interest of its people. That would be his argument, if you asked. Otherwise we may literally lose our political and social freedoms, along the way. Do you want to service these tyrants, Sir Septimus?"

"Tyrants? How are you going to bankroll your liberties? How are you going to maintain our global position? Remain competitive? Retain a first world standard?" the banker argued.

"There surely has to be a sense of due process," she said.

"Pitt breached the trust I placed in him. He would have destroyed this company, for his brass farthing principles. I should have left him with his father in that dusty building society. My family has been in the City for over three hundred years. I know more about sustaining this company and UK plc. This sex criminal was obsessed with destroying my reputation... and I'm determined to take him down, Pixie, before he sets himself up for another pot shot. What the hell is he doing back on the streets, anyway?" He worked up a melodramatic fury.

"Clive understood the risks you were taking with ZNT. He was literally attempting to give you the information," she replied. "He had good reasons to suspect the motives of that fund and he was, you know, trying to save your reputation. He wished to warn you about unnecessary risks."

"How can you be so deluded about this nasty mill boy? This prig, who was motivated by an irrational personal grudge," Winchurch insisted, easing his tall, stiff shirt collar.

"Clive faced personal dangers...to blow the whistle on the flotation. He took on huge risk. Why should he do that? You've gambled all on ZNT. In the short term he was prepared to break rules. You know, to hack your systems, to consolidate in the long term. Clive was desperate to change the culture at this firm," Pixie argued.

The financier was not buying it. "Why listen to this malevolent rogue? I was fully vindicated when he destroyed the virtue of my daughter," he said, angrily.

Pixie's serene expression showed faults, like hairs in face cream. "Did you study his evidence or, you know, take his views seriously...even before that crime?" she wondered.

Sep had a suspicious, stung look. "I didn't need to study his arguments to understand them. But it is a hypothetical conundrum, isn't it? The world has shifted and we must shift too!

Are you certain Pitt hasn't been in contact? He hasn't threatened you?"

"Absolutely not, I can assure you."

"Perhaps he has persuaded you about his case and, who can say, won back your confidence?" he asked tenaciously. He leaned across and studied her with a penetrating sheen to his ruthless, hound dog eyes.

"It's hard to keep a cool head, but I am capable of making my own judgements," Pixie said. She reinforced her detached persona.

"Any idea what he did with that stolen data? He stole very sensitive information from us, don't you know? He had no authority to look at that. Did you forget that? You've nothing to share about our missing files, do you? Didn't you get any insight from Pitt? Has this memory gone to nothing? Or is everything stored beyond our reach?" Sep persisted. He rolled around a paperweight - consciously or not - which contained the image of his wife as a young woman.

"I have to apologise, because I'm also at a loss," she told him. "Clive probably takes all your secrets with him," Pixie argued.

The banker scrutinised her as if scrolling through her HR file. "So he didn't pass anything over to you, for safe keeping? He didn't put you under any pressure like that, to aid and abet?"

"I'm not so easily susceptible to pressure," Pixie assured him.

"Hmm, well, such a man will go to remarkable extremes. You have not been taken in by him like that Miss Wright, have you?" he pressed.

The questioning was disturbingly direct, but her composure was expensively well trained. Her old school in Geneva was down the *Strasse* from ZNT's elegant, if discreet headquarters. "I was merely horrified to see him again, and I rushed away from him," she reported.

The financier's gaze twinkled. "That's a completely understandable reaction. The sight of him alone must be terrifying to any woman. He's a menace to the opposite sex. But it would have been profitable, in retrospect, if you had tried to speak to him...to get some clues about his intentions...his likely movements."

"It was a natural reaction," she said. "But I didn't lose my head."

"No, good for you... you must have been frightened," Sep agreed, reconsidering. "I can only think he was taunting us, because Esmeralda's ordeal was not made public. I refused to offer her to public entertainment in the gutter press. But the faster Pitt runs, the quicker we shall play catch up," Winchurch predicted. "Our partners already warned me and I have a top investigative firm involved. We have every confidence in their detective work. Pitt doesn't understand what he's up against now. We're going to take him out soon. This has gone far beyond a grudge match," he suggested.

Sir Septimus took advantage of his springy chair to relieve tension.

This interview terminated, Pixie returned to her desk. It was a struggle to recompose herself or see any point in her work. Then she was conscious of getting nowhere in her desire to help Clive. She found the courage to call through to her boss and say there was something else on her mind. Her boss was also finding it difficult to concentrate on any other matter and suggested she came back.

"How may I help you? What's concerning you?" Septimus ventured, as she was admitted.

"Excuse me, sir, but I forgot to ask you. What's Emma's condition these days?" Pixie enquired. "Can I ask how your daughter is recovering?"

"Slowly," Sep replied. "Much the same. Why do you ask?"

"Do you mean that she is still traumatised? Not able to speak very well...not willing to mix with others?" Pixie asked.

"She has made some improvement," he added, struggling for a layman's account. "Thanks for asking."

"That's all right, Sep. I'm concerned about her. I was present that day. I was the most reliable witness."

"The doctors are doing their best. She isn't sleeping very well...she still has those bad ideas. I don't know when she can go to university, or meet with her school friends again."

"I would like to visit her. Perhaps it would help. I need your permission and we'd have to arrange a suitable time, if you are in favour."

Pixie was running hot and cold, but she sustained a shiny exterior. The hint of blush on her cheeks looked charming, flattering to her boss, rather than a betraying sign of fear, in recognition of her dissembling tricks.

"You would really like to pay her a call, would you?" Sep's features lightened.

"It plays on my mind, that I haven't visited her in hospital yet."

She felt her breathing constrict, convinced her true interest was transparent.

"That's a touching thought Pixie. I appreciate your offer. You may be the perfect lady to chat to her. You have always been an example to her."

"Is she a patient at one of the new BIP hospitals?" she wondered.

"She's a guest at the Sir Septimus Winchurch ZNT Research Hospital, no less," he stated proudly.

"Quite a name," she agreed, playing him.

"As it has been, rather flatteringly, re-named," he said. His warm eyes glazed with tenderness and he offered a charming smile. "I have to spend our profits on something. I can't dole out big bonuses every quarter to you guys," Sep added. "You get rewarded for closing a deal here, not closing the company. One does like to do some good works. My colleagues and I are determined to use our wealth to help the less fortunate in society. My family has always been involved in charity and philanthropic activity. So don't let anyone tell you otherwise, Miss Wright. I believe we are mending broken lives. You may remember those little infants from Bethnal Green coming to see our offices and learn what we bankers get up to," he recalled warmly.

"Are there official visiting hours at your hospital?" Pixie pressed.

"Not exactly, as it were, but I'm visiting this afternoon, if you'd care to accompany me," Sep offered.

"I would like that very much," Pixie told him, finding a smile.

"You're really very welcome, young lady," he told her, delighted, puffing out his broad chest. "This is a private research hospital, of course, so there are not open wards there, as such. But I'm sure you can visit my daughter, and get a little tour of the place. The executives of this company tell me that much of their work is cutting edge."

"If you don't need me around the office today," Pixie replied.

"Don't worry about that." Sep found such dedication amusing. "What a blessing you are Pixie. As many of our chaps say, you are the "head and shoulders" girl. What would I do without you? You're one of the best traders in town. If only our Esmeralda had taken after you from the beginning," he said, regretfully.

"Is she going to be okay with a visitor?"

"Come and join me this afternoon. Leave work alone for a few hours. We're comparatively quiet this quarter. We've had our big success, so why not enjoy the glow? Perhaps it isn't too late for my daughter either."

"If you are sure about that," Pixie said. She didn't have another plan, but she did have second thoughts.

"Excellent. That's all settled then. I'll have them bring round my car...and I'll call for you," he smiled.

Pitt and she had intended to go to the hospital together. But that could be risky and dangerous to pull off. Pixie realised that her improvised ruse to get access had become more likely. Clive was sometimes over confident and too bold, just like his old self.

Clive would never gain access to the hospital himself, she thought. It was much better and safer this way. To a degree she preferred to speak to Emmy alone. The girl was more likely to open up to her, as a sympathetic female. Then she could get closer to the truth and test Clive's real character.

23

Following lunch Sep summoned her and they left the Winchurch building. His head-of-state BMW was delivered from a parking zone beneath HQ. This vehicle was imposing amidst a fleet of employees' luxury sports cars. The financier had decided to leave his regular chauffeur behind and to drive himself. This decision alarmed Pixie but there was no way to avoid this head to head.

Sep liked big limos as they made his shortness an irrelevant factor; after they had been adjusted to allow him to reach the wheel. Maybe he wanted to be occupied with the road during their trip, to distract himself from internal agitation.

Winchurch's characteristic impulse to take control made Pixie uneasy. Ironically she felt much safer with Pitt. But at this stage she didn't want to give Clive all her capital. They were involved in a dangerous game with Winchurch and his powerful new clients, some of whom had places on the board as part of the deal. Clive had tried to whistleblow, but his arguments had been stifled. They'd knocked the instrument from his hands before he could play. Pixie was put into a difficult position then, exposed to the financier's scrutiny. What if he already understood her deception? Sep had brazened out parliamentary committees in his time. Coping with a disloyal analyst was just like shooting a sluggish grouse.

The pavements around the Old Lady were thronged, presenting a typical view, yet she felt isolated and threatened. Pixie hardly dared to look at her boss; to lock in with his pugnacious profile. Sep occupied the driving seat; fully knowing that she had given assistance to Clive; that she might be willing to help him again. To an extent, since Pitt's re-emergence, she still suffered divided loyalties.

For some while the young woman and her boss didn't speak. But his first remark heightened her fears. The car had wound its way out of London, taking the motorway south. He no doubt felt freer to talk, while she felt more confined.

"Are you afraid Pitt will be back in contact?"

"With me?" she replied. "Clive doesn't know how my life has changed," she insisted.

"There's no need to be afraid of him, you know. Lucifer has already fallen and we'll snuff him. You should contact me immediately, if there's any sign of him. You have all our security contacts, don't you?"

"Certainly," she replied, pretending to follow his surging over-take.

"Good girl," he exclaimed, darting glances at her. "You will be the one he wants to see, if anyone. Pity that he didn't bump into me instead. He wouldn't have got away so easily. We'll break his balls, if you'll excuse the phrase. Typical of him to pick on the ladies," Sep remarked, referring to the previous week's encounter.

"All the same, he's quite a hefty guy," Pixie reminded him, teasingly.

"I can take care of street scum like that," Sep assured her.

"Do you really think so?"

"In actual fact my wife is a little taller than me. She isn't a lot shorter than you. Of course you've met her a few times haven't you? My physical size isn't something that has ever bothered me," he argued, turning to look at her for a few seconds. "I was the nimblest wicket keeper of my year."

"Why should it?" she offered, tensely. "Stature isn't a man's only weapon."

"Exactly so. We'll see Clive Pitt go to the devil and roast yet, have no fear," he remarked, with a certain relish. "For all his scruples he's a big bully of a chap, wouldn't you agree? But have no concern, Pixie, because a strong physique and a determined character isn't going to help him any. If the old school taught me anything it was common sense... as well as self-reliance and respect for others. "

"Don't you see any merits to Pitt? Doesn't he have any positive qualities?" Pixie stated.

"My dear, have you lost your senses?" Sep replied, shocked. "Are you sceptical? Didn't you see him take my child into the woods that evening? Don't begin to doubt the evidence of your own eyes. If we can't trust your own eyes, then what can we trust? Can I ever doubt that he raped my daughter?" he implored.

"That's the crux of the matter," Pixie said. "I saw them vanishing into the trees together, you know, but nobody knows what took place after that."

"Young lady, we have a damn good idea. Are you suggesting somebody else carried out the attack in there?" He was puzzled and considered it for a moment. Then he tried to compose himself, to enjoy their journey and to concentrate on the road ahead.

"You immediately blamed Pitt, but you didn't fully investigate. Sometimes we can't guess the truth. Terrible things are going on, strange events, that need deeper explanation. You looked at the facts," she argued, "and took them at face value."

"Emmy ran back into the garden, screaming and bloody. She was in no doubt about what happened. Meanwhile Pitt had disappeared from the scene," Winchurch reminded her. "Do you need something more specific?"

She registered his paternal sorrow. "I admit that Clive fled the scene, knowing he would be accused... with no way to explain himself. Who wouldn't have run away in those circumstances?" she suggested.

"A man with nothing to hide?" he suggested.

"Or with no-one to hear his version of events," she replied.

"That's an unpleasant and improbable idea. What sort of evidence do you need?" he objected, fidgeting.

"It may have been a trick to remove him from the picture," Pixie argued.

"It was the action of a desperate criminal," Sep insisted.

"The truth is stranger than we can imagine," she argued.

"Really, I'm not a fanciful gentleman," he insisted.

"What if a deception is going on? You are missing that, and accusing him unjustly."

"My daughter is one person who has a clear idea, and I don't tend to contradict her," he insisted, introducing an extra shot of speed.

"How can we peer into that dark scene? Then claim to know what happened?" Pixie said.

"She saw Pitt clearly enough," he replied.

"Are you sure, Sep? It must have been crowded within that copse, by the time they arrived at the centre. Excuse me for reminding you, but wasn't Emmy blindfolded... before she was forced to..."

"She saw him quite well enough!" Sep declared. "Yes, this evil wretch led my girl away from the house and he attacked her in the trees. Why are you employing one detail to exonerate him?"

"Did you think if some other guy, or guys, may have been hiding in the woods... waiting for them in there? Is it too far-fetched?" she suggested, terrified by her boldness.

"Not possible. Who exactly may have been there? Nobody else was with them," he objected, revving unevenly.

"If it was dark and, as you admit, she was forced to wear a blindfold."

"Emmy has told us that Pitt was responsible for this. He bound her, tore off her clothes, hooked her into the tree... my god... how many more times? ...and then he exploited his power over her and committed these evil deeds. She didn't need to confirm that with her eyes!"

"Any accusation of rape kills Pitt's credibility," she reminded him.

"Well, young lady, that's his doing. There are few more terrible crimes," Sep told her.

"Emmy literally says that Pitt was the only guy in there? She didn't feel that something else was wrong?" Pixie pressed.

"For goodness sake, she didn't. Pitt was all over her that afternoon. Wouldn't leave her alone, would he? Twice her age, the man is. You can remember that. He even punched a couple of her uncles... my wife's brothers, back in the house... when they dared to object to this behaviour. We found my wife's brother laid out... flat on his back on the four-poster. No offence, Pixie, but he should have known better to even get involved with my daughter. Why was he messing around with a teenager like that?"

"Not to begin with. He just wanted to speak to you. When he first arrived at your garden party. It was literally only later in the afternoon that this situation developed."

"When they first set eyes on each other? How did he get such an influence over the girl? After they had been drinking and taking highs. Doesn't she have any sense of danger or self-respect?"

"You needn't remind me," she told him.

"All my eminent guests looking on ... them snogging together, laughing and playing around. What a ghastly word 'snogging'. Including a member of the present cabinet, the Chinese ambassador, some directors of the Swiss hedge fund no less... as well as old colleagues and members of the family," Sep recalled, grimacing over the wheel. "What a dreadful scandal. What a shame on the family. How are we going to live that down?"

"Clive was definitely not his usual self that day," Pixie remarked.

A suspicious air developed around the banker. "They found matching strands of his hair. Wool fibres from his golfing pullover, worn on that very afternoon. What more circumstantial or forensic evidence do you require, to convince you?" Sep asked, fighting to keep control, as he caressed his dream machine around another corner.

"I'm sure you have lots of evidence against him," Pixie said.

"We certainly do," he told her. "So I'd keep a lid on that pot of whitewash."

The BMW darted under an archway of trees, which spread across the lane, plunging them into seconds of darkness; before dazzling sunlight burst back.

Pixie began to recognise the route from the notorious garden party, as she edged her neck awkwardly to the side.

"Why is he running then, young lady? If he's the innocent victim of a set up?" Sep added.

"Did you think he was capable of such a terrible deed? You know, before he was working on the BIP negotiation?"

"I trusted him, Pixie. He's responsible for serious theft. Furthermore we want all our intellectual property back. Before he takes his final bow from the markets," Sep vowed.

"I had to stand about sipping my champagne, trying to make small talk, knowing my former boyfriend had humiliated me, you know... in front of everybody at the party, including those important people you referred to," Pixie remembered. "His behaviour was outrageous... I was literally mortified. But I was so shocked because, to tell the truth, this was not typical or predictable."

"He conducted himself sublimely in character," Winchurch insisted.

"How will you know he isn't a 'danger'?" she asked, picking up on his previous remark.

"Pitt has more dangerous enemies than just me. Now we see how this self-appointed saint, this mill trash... the son of a northern building society manager, really enjoys being the quarry of big finance," Sep said, with contempt. "If it hadn't been for me where would he be, anyway? Why he'd be stamping god damned savings books."

"Anyway he's a capable man who would succeed in any career."

"He's a malign and violent criminal," Sep replied. "He'd be running a bloody Christmas club."

"Clive didn't always feel comfortable with his colleagues here...because, you know, most of us come from a very different social, and economic, background," she recalled honestly.

"What about it?" Sep returned. "Didn't we offer him a career?"

"We tend to be a cult unto ourselves, sir. A school away from school. Yet he had a constructive relationship with the team.

After all you made him an associate. His marriage lasted. He was a father," Pixie reminded him.

"With all respect, young lady, are you the best authority on his marriage?"

"He enjoyed my company," she ventured.

"A keen eye for the ladies was all that linked him to the human race," Sep argued.

"Maybe you touched on his weak point," she agreed.

"Pitt has more than one weak spot, I can assure you. He doesn't know who he is up against. He's going to fully re-compensate, as certainly as we retrieved his shares and dividends. I'm sure his true opinion about women was lower than for rest of us."

"He could be moody at times, preoccupied, which is not surprising... but he's no misogynist. You claim that he hates people, but actually he is shy in a group. He was most happy concentrating on his job, to be honest. And he excelled in his work...he was literally one of our most outstanding people."

"You're sadly deluded. Don't try to make me laugh Pixie. It is painful for me to laugh these days."

"When we were together he became more unpredictable. He was under strain...isolated. But I was never afraid of him. Clive never resorted to violence, or the threat of being violent... never mind *sexual* violence," she argued.

"What do you think that proves?" he wondered.

"How can such a charming and attractive guy turn into a rapist? How can you say he hated women? He was always caring towards me."

"Is that so? If you aren't his greatest love, you are certainly his best apologist," Sep replied. "How does my daughter feel about his charming ways? Perhaps you are going to ask her later. Assuming she is in any fit condition to talk to you."

Pixie's blood froze: she stared rigidly into the congested exit lane.

Sep's shrewd eyes sought hers. "How can you be so misled about this guy?"

175

"Nobody will offer a positive opinion about Clive," Pixie argued.

"You want to identity with this king snake, do you?" he hissed.

"I dare say he would like to come forward...to volunteer the truth."

"You at least would be one girl to speak up for him," he suggested.

"I'm trying to think why Clive resorted to violence with Emmy. She gave every indication of consenting, if that was on his mind."

"A girl has the right to refuse at the last moment, doesn't she?" he retorted.

"But it doesn't make any sense to me," she said.

"No sense? Pitt told Emmy that he was seducing her to get revenge against me. On hearing this she refused and then he attacked her. That is precisely how it came about, if you really want to know. He cynically used my daughter in that way."

"That's what she told you?" Pixie asked, shaken.

"Precisely what she told me," he insisted. "Do you need to listen to the recording?"

"Well, after all it's her word against his. There's a recording? Emmy had a string of aggressive boyfriends, an abortion that was in the media... involved in a brawl in a night club. The latter incident was trivial I appreciate and exaggerated out of all proportion to..."

"Nobody has ever claimed that Esmeralda is a good girl," Sep interrupted. "We know she isn't her mother's pride and joy. But even bad girls shouldn't be attacked by a brute like Pitt... deliberately harming and manipulating her to damage her father."

"Rather crude when he had more sophisticated means. That doesn't sound like the caring man I knew, not in the least."

"What do I care about that? His crime has more than washed away our girl's little sins. Her previous conduct will never detract from the contemptible treatment she suffered."

"Agreed. But after this sex attack Pitt's campaign against the deal was nullified. Are you entirely confident about your new friends?" she asked. "Are the guys with the billions necessarily your best allies?"

Winchurch continued to glare ahead, while roaring along a high-hedged lane, going much too fast. The freshly raked past made him wrathful against the accused and the woman who defended him.

"Even if he was put up to this, I could never forgive him," the banker admitted. "Not that I believe for a minute that he was."

Sep had to constantly adjust his seating position. These luxury end German saloons were not meant for physically smaller people, he considered. He had a tartan cushion under his rump, which he used during shooting breaks in Scotland. Winchurch felt uncomfortable in his Piccadilly hunting tweed jacket, which was meant to denote leisure time.

"Emmy also dabbled in drugs. You may as well know that. Often she got them through my own employees," he admitted. "I would sack them all, if I could catch them all. You know that it goes on. That was another scandal that I had to deal with."

"Clive objected to drug abuse, and any other form of abuse... you know, which had corrupted our corporate culture here," she said.

"My daughter enjoyed shocking people. He probably noted the discotheque business, but did he know about her other activities? He obviously didn't know the damaging effects of rape, any more than we, her parents, before this hateful deed."

"Why didn't you contact the police?" Pixie suggested. She was tense even as she tried to float into the soft seat.

"To be dragged through the media and legal system again? Put Emmy at the centre of another lurid scandal? To become the salacious subject of a yellow press splash?" Winchurch replied. "No thank you, my dear." He bounced somewhat from his seat - over the country bumps - but kept a grip on the wheel, and the BMW was automatic.

"Don't you have full confidence in the police?"

"To a degree, but I love my daughter, and I want Pitt apprehended quickly. He badly let me down and I'm going to have his guts," he pledged coldly.

"The ZNT security people are more or less assassins. You must realise that," Pixie told him. "Doesn't Clive have the right to due legal process? Anyway these security companies have not been successful so far," she pointed out.

"More time for Pitt to recover his memory," Winchurch suggested.

"Undoubtedly he must have suffered a trauma."

"Can Pitt exercise such influence over you, after so much time, in his absence?" he asked.

"If you're hunting him out of revenge then you've, literally, lost your power of reasoning," Pixie warned.

"Is that a warning? I remember how he treated you. *Atrociously.* A typical chauvinist. During your affair. *Misguided* as you must have been. I could almost *blame* you as well. But anyway we've arrived now."

"Oh yes, is this the place?"

24

There was a signboard at the perimeter, spelling a legend of *The Septimus Winchurch ZNT Research Hospital*, half hidden along an otherwise obscure and bumpy lane. He threw the car up a sloping access road, where singed hedgerows were superseded by irrigated exotic shrubs. The financier drove up the gravel entranceway into landscaped territory, where the rough surface transformed into melted liquorice tarmac. Some four hundred metres further along they approached a security building, complete with barrier and uniformed guard.

"You have security at a hospital?" Pixie asked.

"There's security at any hospital, my dear, if you'd care to check," Sep explained.

Pixie was mortified at the stupidity of her misplaced question.

A youthful guard brought his fluffy face to the driver's open window, nodding dutifully at Winchurch and casting an admiring glance over Pixie. Friendly greetings were exchanged before the guard raised a striped pole and waved them through.

"A good job well done, young man," Sep praised, with a royal wave. "We shall see you again!"

At which he fulfilled a showy skid and powered ahead into the visitors' car park. He was known for his gallantry to new and youthful members of staff at all levels of the organisation.

"Why did you want to rebuild and sponsor a whole hospital?" she asked.

"You consider me vainglorious? Doing my Napoleon routine? Short men, you understand," he jested.

"Surely you were taking on a lot, with your holding in BIP... combined with your day job, as it were," Pixie said.

"Not for me," he replied, knowingly.

There was no shortage of parking space, and he skewed the BMW carelessly around. In a sense he didn't own the car, but the taxman would never enjoy it.

"The original hospital building was here. Crumbling since the days of Gladstone and Disraeli. We established a charitable trust. How could I sit out in my garden with an easy conscience?"

Winchurch killed the engine softly, with his senatorial thumb. They sat in deep rural silence; interrupted only by gurgling hosepipes and an alarming peacock screech.

"Yes, this hospital received generous support from our talented fashion designer. Did you ever meet, Victor at ZNT? He makes quite an impression. Then we were able to build two new wings. Yes, following complete restoration, using old outbuildings for storage and supplies. If you ever go to Moscow or Budapest you can visit his shops, or his factories. The new board has a strategy to take over the NHS. At least the more profitable departments," Winchurch argued. "They will be grateful to get universal health care off their backs."

Clive had been admitted as a patient at the hospital. He was sent there after his criminal activity was first detected, following his "delusional mental dysfunction". This took place exactly after he counter-argued the deal, and then was found hacking in to Winchurch's encrypted files.

The company tried to nullify him in a show of forgiving and understanding. So Clive was admitted to this very institution for unspecified treatment and rest. Pitt's criminal behaviour had removed him from the fire sale of British Imperial Pharmaceuticals, along with its numerous brand names, products, knowledge, investments, scientific research, not to mention workforce.

Pitt had been kept in this renovated hospital complex while business had been concluded without him between the buy and sell sides.

"Which medical conditions are treated here, exactly?" Pixie wondered.

They stepped out into the burning breeze, and began to traverse the parking lot.

"People in distress...as it were, suffering from nervous disorders... severe shock and trauma. Patients may be the victims of serious crime, like Emmy, suffering psychological damage. Or they could also even be criminals...yes, certainly, with mental or behavioural disorders, from home or abroad. Never thought I'd be supporting a hospital that would one day treat my own daughter," Sep observed.

"Do you mean that it's a kind of sanatorium?" she suggested.

"You mean, as they have in Switzerland? No, nothing like that. Not in the old fashioned sense," he explained testily. He got into his rapid energetic stride, while Pixie politely constrained her step. But he wasn't his typical cheerful, optimistic and energised self.

They cut between velvety green lawns, beds of fleshy roses and clouds of late summer flowers. The farm lands and fields were blanched under a shimmering haze. Rows of horse chestnut trees - once a splendid guard to the driveway - were now leafless, as if in the depths of winter. Lines of oak trees were like burnt corpses at the sides of the road.

A cinder path took the oddly matched pair along a modern outbuilding, housing two new units. These wooden constructions resembled an extended chalet, very much influenced by the Swiss style. She wondered if the architecture was influenced by members of the Geneva based hedge fund.

They came into a similarly styled reception area, where a group of medical personnel were already waiting for them in a huddle. They immediately recognised Sir Septimus, as their friendly and excited faces exhibited.

"Good afternoon to you all. Such a pleasure again! This is my visitor, Pixie Wright. This talented young lady is a trader for me, a superb analyst... in market risk and credit...formerly on our China desk. Yes, she's on a visit this afternoon. Doctor Morran suggested that it would be therapeutic for Emmy to see another girl. So where is the good doctor presently? Attending his daily round?"

"I paged him," replied a male nurse. The guy shuffled, coloured and stared at the floor.

"Then page him again," Winchurch remarked. He gazed evenly at Pixie as if he found her pleasantly distracting.

Pixie stood still, statuesque, hiding her nerves, as the situation required. Her loyalties were as divided as chopped wood. She hid her thoughts by fiddling with her *Jaeger* suit buttons and nudging her lozenge of ash blonde hair. Somehow the ceiling felt oppressively low, the entrance too narrow and out of reach, although objectively the space was proportionate.

This tense mood was broken when the doctor arrived. This was Doctor Morran, a stork-tall, stooping man, with lank sandy hair to rounded shoulders. His eyes were magnified behind heavy glasses and as melancholy as a hangman's. He kept his counsel, pink fingers tucked into a regulation white coat. A theatrical stethoscope dangled pink and rubbery from his neck.

"Doctor! How is my little girl today?" Winchurch enquired.

"Very much making excellent progress, sir," Dr Morran answered.

"Good news. Good news. Is she still in the mood for a visitor? You think she will be able to cope with a new face?"

The doctor's lugubrious eyes sharpened with interest as he noticed Pixie. "Charmed! Very charmed to see you, I'm sure. Is this a young lady friend of yours, Sir Septimus?" he leered, with a lick across is long top lip.

Winchurch was taken aback. "Miss Wright works for me in the City. Do you suspect me of taking out beautiful young ladies? Only once, Morran," he qualified, "and she became my good lady wife. Oh yes, she and I met as undergraduates at St Andrews in Edinburgh. Did you know that, Pixie?"

Pixie gripped her favourite handbag and offered a smile at the correct intensity.

Doctor Morran coughed awkwardly and, painfully, extracted his gaze from the figure of Pixie. "Shall we proceed then, Sir Septimus, and make enquiries as to whether your daughter, and *our patient*, little Emmy, is ready to converse with this lovely interlocutor?"

"Why certainly doctor, lead the way... whatever you say," the banker offered, spreading his arms.

"Your daughter has been put under gentle sedation. For her own benefit you should understand," Morran said, heading towards an initial corridor. "Her standard nightmares persist as she continues to relive bad experiences. These nightmares happen, and her psyche then attempts to process negative images. To assimilate these traumas within her socialised ego, as well as to reconstruct a stable idea of selfhood."

"For sure, your work is most impressive. You are the master of your specialism. I'm very proud to lend my name here. A close relationship with this hospital is one positive outcome from my daughter's ordeal. I have full confidence that you will mend her, and she'll come out like a new girl."

"Indeed, that's positive, because after her ordeal, shock and negative consequences were to be expected," Morran said. He carefully led the way, picking off the antiseptic tiles with his grasshopper legs. "There are malign, negative and unhelpful thought patterns in this child, which we see through the scanner, lighting up those affected areas of her neo cortex."

"Impressive, although I don't think these effects are going to wear off quickly," said Winchurch, almost skipping along between them.

"Anger, recrimination, hostility, upset. Mental disturbances of the frontal lobes, yes indeed, difficult to expunge. At this clinic we offer radical therapies, revolutionary treatments."

"All very impressive research. These breakthroughs are exactly what we fund you... to achieve," Sep replied.

"Yet conversely we do not shy away from pharmaceutical intervention. Especially as BIP is the world's leading producer of psychiatric drugs. We possess a growing chemical arsenal in fact, to combat the range of traumas and mental conflicts... yes, suffered either personally or socially," he explained, monotonously.

"Quite so, very interesting doctor. Follow along, Pixie."

"At the *Sir Septimus Winchurch* we are able to test many of the new products that come from BIP laboratories. Nature's healing has never been so enhanced... or so revolutionised. Without these radical innovations, as one can say, in mental health care... well, then your daughter, for instance, would not, I stress *not*, recover as you should expect ...or as efficaciously," Dr Morran insisted.

"No doubt you are performing miracles, doctor," the banker concurred.

"We have the resources to discover the human brain, as explorers of past centuries discovered continents and then planets," Dr Morran explained.

"I notice that the majority of your patients are young. And there seem to be a number of women," Pixie remarked.

"How did you notice this?" Winchurch replied, not suspiciously.

"In passing I looked into rooms and wards," she admitted. "Don't you care for any older people at the institution?"

"Your observation is perfect, Miss," responded the doctor. "But it is pure coincidence."

"Indeed Pixie is a very perceptive young lady," Winchurch agreed, keeping up.

"The majority of our guests are indeed young. They are also living, which is no more relevant. Many of them by chance are female. We don't treat inmates differently according to age or gender. Only conditions or syndromes vary. It follows rationally that categories are admitted for treatment, according to procedures conducted here... at the *ZNT* Sir *Septimus Winchurch* Hospital," he said proudly.

"So older people don't suffer from mental illness, according to this logic?" Pixie guessed.

"Well, we do not age select, young woman. There are men of all ages in L Section. Or the subject of mental conditions, as a result of damaging experiences, leading into criminal, deviant or degenerate behaviour... or actions," he explained.

"That description covers your former boyfriend," Sep remarked.

"You once had him here as a patient, didn't you? Don't you remember that name? A certain Mr Pitt, you surely know," she persisted.

"Pixie, my dear girl, this is hardly the time. Dr Morran would not remember Pitt," insisted her boss. "He was quickly patched up and sent off again. Why should my doctors waste treatment on that clog-town radical?"

"What sort of patch do they apply at this hospital?" Pixie dared.

"What exactly are you referring to?" the banker returned, turning up his eyes challengingly.

"No, indeed we would *not* remember him," said Dr Morran.

"There you are Pixie, this guy was nothing out of the usual."

"We focus on self-victims and international volunteers. Anyway I am a psychiatrist and neurologist, not an admissions assistant, Miss."

"You promote yourselves as a psychiatric hospital, even as a research institute. You told me that you're at the edge of medical research. Yet you seriously claim that you don't keep full patient records," concluded Pixie. "You erase them from your database as soon as they depart?"

Her legs wobbled as she risked these questions. The momentum of their bustling group helped to keep her upright. They reached the end of one corridor and turned into yet another.

"We maintain a comprehensive individual record on every patient checked in," the doctor retorted. "They are accessible to all senior staff here."

"Pitt was never a patient here in the conventional sense," Sep argued.

"Really? But he was subjected to treatment," she replied. "Were you trying to help him? What exactly did you do to him?"

"What do you care?" Sep shot back.

"I care about what really happened to him here."

185

The financier was not willing to answer her questions. "May I remind you about the purpose of today's visit?" he told her.

"Your daughter has always been a troublesome patient, sir," Morran commented. "We shall need your signature again before you leave."

"Trouble has been my daughter's middle name," Sep remarked.

"Emmy has problems of control, in the private and public spheres, especially when she isn't medicated. She definitely has a mind of her own. For instance she continually enquires about all medicines and treatments, that she receives here. So there are issues of trust and obedience. She's a bit of a tomboy, if I may say so, as a matter of fact," Morran argued.

"All right, but a tough and resilient personality will help her to recover," Pixie argued.

"Let's hope that you are right," said her father. "She needs to wake up her ideas, if she wants a happy and successful future."

Pixie was unimpressed. "Wouldn't she be better off at home with family and friends?"

"She deserves special treatment," the financier argued.

"Maybe you should have second thoughts then, for her sake."

"Young lady let's pause here for a while. Let's sit on the couch here, shall we? That's right, make yourself comfortable. Be my guest. Stay here with us, Doctor Morran. Let us explain and go through a few points, with Pixie here."

"I prefer a vigilant and considered posture," the doctor replied.

"As you will, my brilliant friend... but simply listen to my analysis."

"All right, Pixie, let's cast our minds back, shall we? Don't you remember that fateful evening clearly?" Sep asked, settling on the seat next to her.

She was huddled, with hands on her knees. "But it would depend on what you mean by 'clearly'," Pixie replied.

186

The doctor stood about, icy and gloating, flanked by two impatient psychiatric nurses.

"What were your feelings or impressions of that day?" Sep persisted.

"I was shocked. I remember Emmy running back to the house. After that my memory is hazy. My thoughts were shooting in every direction."

"That's understandable, Pix," Sep commented. He patted her arm reassuringly. "All my guests had gone back into the house. Best place for them. We were missing my daughter. Then you returned distraught and explained how you'd seen Pitt going off with her. I should have sent out an alert immediately. I didn't expect Pitt to show up at our party and behave like that?"

"Security was light. Why was that?" she replied.

"But it was too late. Pitt had apparently vanished. The only other guy in the vicinity was my head gardener. He'd be too occupied with horse manure to intervene. We could only sip our drinks politely, knowing something dreadful had happened, yet hoping for the best. Then, as we gazed out over the patio, my wife and I noticed a naked figure running across the lawn... tripping over the knot garden...and gradually we recognised our Emmy. She was crying, her hair wild, and her torso bloody... she was like some horrible ghost, some dread come back to haunt me. Imagine my horror at seeing our child in that state. How do you feel about Clive Pitt in that regard?" he wondered.

Pixie was disconcerted. "It's a painful memory." She kept her gaze on the blankness of that highly fired floor surface.

"When the ambulance finally arrived I directed the medics to take her here, to the ZNT hospital, named after me," Sep explained.

"The perfect institution," Dr Morran remarked, with a modest smirk.

"The worst night of my life," Winchurch insisted.

"You plan to keep Emmy here indefinitely?" Pixie interjected.

"Only until she feels much better."

"As soon as intervention records a measurable improvement," Morran confirmed.

"When she's able to resume her normal life," her father clarified.

"You are not going to talk to the police... even now?" Pixie concluded.

"I have explained my reasons, for not involving the police," Sep reminded her.

"Isn't that irregular?" she asked. She heard the echo of her voice stifled along the long brittle corridor.

"Do you think your old love, Mr Pitt, always sticks to the rules?"

"All right, but I'm surprised that you trust so much in private security companies," she replied.

"Why? I've got the very best people for the job," he insisted. "Even our friend Viktor needs to protect himself. He's a high profile figure, not least in the world of fashion. He's terrified of meeting the same end as Versace, you know. He may be well connected... informed about personal security...but he's still a bit paranoid. Don't tell him that I said that. He's a rather strange fellow, all round, but these artistic guys are different to us, you know." The banker entwined his large hands.

"This ZNT manager is telling you not to involve the authorities?" she said.

"No, but I've told you... my reasons for protecting my daughter and our family."

"Maybe secrecy isn't the best option," she persisted gently.

"You remind me of my wife's logic, in so many ways... particularly when she was younger. In some regards you do. But that doesn't mean I'm going to follow your advice either," Sep quipped.

"I don't want to add another level of deception to this affair," Pixie said. "How much longer are we going to sit here?"

"We'll go then... if you're restless... and finally say hello to my daughter. I assume you are still interested to see her?"

"I would be delighted," she said.

"Off we go then."

Pixie was busy with the sequence of past events, as they rose again and clipped off the corridor. Clive was admitted after he was nearly beaten to death at a football match. This assault had come immediately following his hacking activities. Clive had been incarcerated until ZNT completed their acquisition of BIP. Then Clive had been put back into circulation again. His head wasn't in the same place.

Pitt was team leader on the valuation and flotation of BIP. He'd also been in close consultation with ZNT throughout, sometimes face to face. He'd also been in there alongside Sir Septimus, when the financier presented, in person, a fraudulent valuation and share offer to a conference of BIP shareholders in Birmingham. They travelled up to 'Brum' together, to address investors, as well as to speak at a mass meeting of workers and officials.

Therefore when Pitt was let out, he was powerless. He only had the strength to turn whistleblower. Despite suicidal implications, Pitt, at some point, had decided to pull the pin. At this stage he retained his faculties, although he had suffered head injuries at the match; as well as unknown treatment afterwards.

Pixie was taken deeper into the hospital complex. She struggled to get her own confused thoughts into shape.

Emmy went off freely with Clive that day, she considered. What if Emmy had gone with him intending to have sex? Of course she was entitled to change her mind. Or maybe she had sex with him and then had regrets. She wanted to shock her father, but she was afraid of his possible reaction. That wouldn't be a unique scenario. Emmy risked adding a new scandal to the old. She knew that there was quite an assembly of VIPs, corporate heads, diplomats and politicians.

Her father had initiated a man-hunt for Pitt, orchestrated by his own security staff, then joined by ZNT agents and, plainly speaking, their corporate thugs.

Sep couldn't accept the idea of Clive, that company traitor, seducing his daughter. The biggest consequence of that alleged sex attack was to destroy Clive's case against the takeover. Therefore it was crucial that Pitt rediscovered his memory - lost in the cloud.

"Here we are," Doctor Morran announced. "This is Esmeralda's deluxe room. She was browsing a learned book when I left her. I am sure she will enjoy this charming visitor. But may I remind you that her medication leaves her under partial sedation. You may find her subdued and not especially talkative."

There was then a terrible scream from within the room. This was at such a pitch that it even startled Doctor Morran, gluing him to the wall for some moments. Pixie gasped as the tension burst around her.

Not so much a scream, as a terrified roar, interspersed with shouts. Yet these were muffled and indecipherable through sound proofed walls. They all jumped at the noise within and stared at each other in amazement

Finally Doctor Morran gathered himself, retook the initiative and burst in to investigate.

25

Clive's hearing was sharp as Pixie picked up her jacket in the hallway and left for work. He was relieved that she'd allowed him to sleep over; discussed the present situation and agreed to follow up their information. The hope that she would brief him on the events of those missing months had been a perilous adventure. Or anyway she agreed to give him the benefit of the doubt. Or she's refusing to think the worst, even while she didn't restore him to his previous status.

Miss Wright still had personal capital, not least the trust of her boss. Sir Septimus refused to believe the worst about *her*, contrary to evidence. Pixie had the poise to look after herself, Clive thought. She'd constantly proved that in her job and when helping Clive to gather intelligence against the deal. Pixie had taken risks by resorting to soft engineering techniques, simply by finding pin codes and passwords, transferring them over.

However, even if he had lost the specific details, Clive couldn't help being concerned. Was she brave enough to face ruthless business interests? These guys were the true power brokers. ZNT had all means at their disposal, yet no business ethics or respect for law or rights. Clive had gate-crashed their digital operation and they were not thrilled to share virtual space. Pixie's profile was vulnerable simply by being associated with him; and she didn't have any sentimental log out with these brokers.

Meanwhile Pitt searched Pixie's flat. In part he was doing this for her benefit, yet on another level he wanted to check her reliability. There had been many twists since they first became friends. He had developed suspicious instincts during that missing year, not only techniques of corporate espionage and surveillance. He didn't exactly ransack her apartment but he did search thoroughly; pulling out drawers, rummaging cabinets and storage spaces, checking for evidence and hidden compartments.

"Do I question her honesty?" Clive asked himself. "Isn't this a sign of my paranoia these days? Or am I behaving like this because I don't expect her to come back? Or maybe I don't expect to survive myself. So what was I up to?"

Due to the big clean spaces of minimalist design, his search didn't take long. When the physical search was complete, Pitt went through her electronic accounts and digital traces. He was able to second guess text speak, passwords, because the system didn't lock him out. Her on-line presence was predictable, with no references or links to him. To an extent she'd taken precautions to remove him, he suspected.

Among her voice mail he discovered friendly messages from Winchurch. These were not entirely compromising yet Pitt was amazed to hear them, to find the financier's voice converted there. While this was not incriminating, such contact was irregular; not entirely professional. The emotional import of these messages was coded, so that Pixie might miss the significance or nuance. But Pitt was able to decipher the inference.

> *"Oh, hi, my dear young lady, how are you feeling? You were a marvel this afternoon* (nervous cough/ drawing of breathe/ indecision*) you're a clever and delightful girl. Do you mind me saying so? Would have fallen apart without you... your input.* (Begins to speak, reconsiders his thoughts*) Look forward to picking it up at tomorrow's meeting and thereafter...yes...so... sleep tight."*

Digging deeper Clive located an encrypted address book and in this he discovered his old telephone numbers (professional and domestic), as well as a Hampstead address. Careless of her, he considered, not to permanently erase this evidence. Presumably the place in north London was where Pixie and he lived together. Was she clinging on to these memories, despite events of evil portent? It matched the concept of an apartment above shops.

Clive found old photographs of himself. He took time to install software to isolate and retrieve these files. In a high cupboard in the guest room he found an external hard drive. She must have forgotten about this because the box was covered in dust. Pixie had consigned him to the dump bin but she hadn't entirely deleted him.

Taking a further search of her bedroom he located images of them together: a slide show of their adventures, their memories as a couple. This was an extraordinary find, as he retained no memory of even dating her. Pixie forgot to erase the memory of a neglected digital photo frame; some antique device that she kept at the bottom of the bedside cabinet. Pitt was startled, as well as fascinated, to look at these pictures. A few presented him alone, usually in a flattering or humorous light, yet a majority of these images captured them together, on time lapse. "My god," he told himself, "she was right fond of me."

There was a great shot of him in a fishing boat off Cuba (as she had tagged it). But that had been a family holiday. He had normal recollection in regard to that vacation. Noreen and he went off to the Caribbean to celebrate a successful float, as it were, by snagging barracudas, in a Hemingway style.

In that image he was happy and tanned, strong and golden haired; he was toasting his wife in rum, jokily but deeply, and posing at the wheel of that tough little round bellied boat. He was portrayed at the height of his success and power; caught at the peak of his earning potential. He radiated confidence and optimism, like a colossus.

Then he located another image of Pixie and he together. It was dated later he realised, with the more mundane setting of a canal barge, possibly near to Camden Lock, was it? A bit more mundane than shark fishing in the Caribbean, he considered, but then, he assumed, it was dangerous for them to be spotted together.

A sun set behind, putting their smiling features into shadows: Some place where a genuine bond was more powerful than a fat annual bonus.

He didn't look wired-up, or disjointed, in this picture. It didn't seem unreal. Rather there was an extra alert quality to him. He was wearing a loose necked Irish fisherman's sweater that Noreen bought for him on another holiday, around the Dingle peninsular. He was disgusted by the treachery he'd displayed towards his family. How shameful, he thought, to betray Noreen by having an affair with Pixie. But would he have worn that jumper with Pixie, knowing that it had special significance to his wife? Perhaps he was wearing that sweater as a signal to his wife, of his intentions or true feelings. Or wearing this garment may have been a sign of his damaged mind at that stage. It could be seen then as a warning that he'd become a type of clone in a blank dimension.

But it was weird to him to go through these pictures. They informed him that he'd enjoyed a regular surface existence during that lost year; assuming that infidelity or espionage was at all regular. During that shadowy period he had conformed to his routine, even while he undertook incredible deeds, made dangerous moves to expose his employer. Yet these actions stayed beneath his surface awareness, like a microchip beneath the skin.

Even to recreate his routine during that hidden, sinister period felt strange. It was disconcerting to think about himself living and breathing during that hazy year: To have selected his clothes each morning, to have washed and shaved, with Pixie in bed in the next room, not his wife. This was unnerving enough. Indeed to imagine fulfilling the duties and chores of an average day. To imagine waking up in the morning and falling asleep again at night - this was strange enough.

Pitt was surprised that Pixie had neglected to destroy these images. Had sentimental regret made her so careless? She could have erased them if she had thought to. Despite himself Clive experienced fresh feelings towards her. His mind made contact with the sensual memories, imprinted by his nervous system. Not only was she breathtakingly lovely, but she was remarkably brave and smart. Too smart to forget to eradicate those dangerous images, if she chose, linking her conclusively with Pitt. He'd been so much obsessed with his own fate, that he'd overlooked the dangerous choices she was pressed into making.

Pitt was sorry to lose the evidence of their relationship. He was tempted to save everything too. But he instantaneously overruled the impulse, to protect them both from risk. Pixie didn't realise the protective value of her boss' inappropriate tenderness. But to those hedge fund guys her mementos were like a batch of useless junk bonds. Her keepsake pictures might land her at the arbitrage desk from hell. She would be de-installed from the financial system, despite her impressive capacity in the job, like an obsolete network. So he eradicated all these ghostly traces left behind. He hoped it wasn't a premonition of their fate or an expression of their fragility.

Could he really be falling for Pixie again? He was no less a family man than before; or maybe no more of a married guy? Would he be in a position to forget about their affair, and his infidelity, the second time around? Desire for the girl flared up from the bottom of his soul like heat from hard discs.

26

Restlessly, finishing up his electronic housekeeping, Pitt took up her car keys and let himself back out. Crossing the threshold, he had to overcome his own dread of what could be waiting. In the outside corridor he encountered a woman in her night dress, in ridiculously fluffy slippers like pink porcupines, who was taking a little handbag doggie for a trot. He guessed that the animal was an illegal resident, as she hustled the creature back inside with guilty looks. However she seemed to recognise him and gave a half smile. Of course he had never seen this lady before in his life. Otherwise his progress downstairs was undisturbed. Pitt took the lift alone and passed through the lobby unchallenged.

Pixie owned a car but, on a typical day, didn't like to drive to the office. Not to possess an expensive sports car would be seen as an aberration in their work. You had to spend that part of your bonus that was not placed into shares, or some other tax avoidance gyration. Pixie was the owner of a car but opted for public transport. In fact she was a bit of a Sunday driver, with light dresses and soft leather gloves. As a tenant of this apartment block she could use its underground car park.

Clive guessed that she would have such a perk. So he went down to find her car, holding the swab that informed him of the marque. On a typical day he would use the Tube and buses to get around town, or sometimes flag down a taxi when in a special hurry, but on this occasion he wanted mobility; not to mention independence of action.

To complicate things there were a number of cars the same as hers. So he was forced to shift between the rows of vehicles, checking off number plates, as if stealing to order. Fortunately there was not another soul about, in the fumy subterranean area. After a few frustrated attempts to break in to a vehicle he had success; but realised he was about to drive around in a pink

Porsche Carrera. To define the colour precisely, it was champagne pink; a highly personalised car that belonged to Pixie Wright. Now he'd draw attention to himself - be highly visible around London - by borrowing this sweet machine for a few hours.

Pixie enjoyed the material benefits of working at Winchurch Brothers, as did they all. The luxurious life style was lately a symbol of everything she stood to lose. Apart from her life itself that was, because she couldn't take it all with her. The ideal girl - who often out performed her male colleagues - had become a rogue element too - if only they would notice. But who'd asked her to undermine the deal? Who was the guy who persuaded her to ruin her life?

Pitt settled his posterior into the soft sculpted seat. He quickly familiarised himself with the Carrera's busy controls. He was confronted with a crowd of unfamiliar dials, like a lot of round competitive faces through the wheel, silently expressing complicated ideas to him. Yet he was an experienced driver. He worked up ferocity and unleashed a torque of acceleration. This was no particular problem - just the colour.

Without a second of hesitation he smashed through a security barrier, emerging at the top of an exit slope. The parking attendant barely had time to wipe condensation from the glass of his booth. Pitt was out on to the streets of west London, which were eternally busy. Yet he had to sit and sweat through numerous sets of lights. The jams became frequent as he drove deeper into central London; Notting Hill, Marble Arch, Oxford Circus and beyond. All signs of that flash flood in the night had disappeared. Sunshine burnt through mist; fumes danced agitatedly in the air.

At this point an imposing limousine pulled out in front of him, like a reflexion across a convex mirror. He was startled to be reminded of the car that took him virtual hostage in the City that day. Somehow this spooked him, this was *deja vu*. Didn't he recognise that stretch limo? There surely couldn't be two the same.

He couldn't be completely certain though. Not when there was a fleet of those vehicles working the city twenty four seven. Clive was piqued with himself because again he wasn't able to memorise number plates.

"You crafty devil, you're not making my life easy!" Clive declared. He enforced a radical shift and turn.

The only way to trace the limo was to give chase. But, even though he took risks and sharp turnings, this proved difficult in the confusion of West End streets. The Porsche got trapped alongside a theatre delivery van, turning down a one way street; and it was near impossible to turn back. There was even a fracas with a team of delivery guys, who were taking scenery into the Duke of York's theatre. Clive was asking them to wait with a substantial piece of the forest, while they told him exactly where to go. This was terrible luck because the theatre didn't change productions that regularly.

The limousine meanwhile had slipped back in to the radiation, as if it had never been, like a cat under a fence. Clive shouldn't try to give chase to every long car in London. Either he was mistaken about the vehicle, or they had provoked him into a futile pursuit. If they were playing games, then he had to keep control of his nerves. He couldn't afford to panic; he had to keep a lid on that boiling milk sensation within, if he was going to extricate himself from such a dead end.

Shaken, adrenaline pumped, he edged back to the Charing Cross Road, struggling to tame the effete beast of a car, hampered by a line of buses and crossing pedestrians. But he was determined to keep a clear head above the darkness.

27

Pitt became lost in Hampstead, when he came into the area. He had no satnav gizmos to navigate by. Impatient with himself and his directional skills, forever a perfectionist and his own worst critic, he tried to find his way around that warren of narrow streets and alleys. The imposing Victorian suburb was a maze of anonymous avenues, dead ends and misleads. For him it was easier to get from one side of Leeds to the other on the final shopping day before Christmas.

Pitt didn't remember living in the borough; there were no flashbacks, no images of the past. His heart thudded now, his stomach turned to an acid bath, like a foreigner on an expired visa. He suffered these episodes, in which hieroglyphs passed across his mind: the street scene went hazy, the ground swayed, and he was afraid of passing out.

"This place is a bloody nightmare," he complained, to himself. "It's sending me crazy."

Finally he decided to park her car and to go by foot, as if setting the difficult game to one side. At least he'd obtained the address of the flat, where Pixie and he had supposedly lived together. He intended to track down this place, take a look at the property, to get a feel for their old life, as he had to begin from somewhere.

Still, he had to ask frequently for directions; from a grandma with half term charges, a furtive chap carrying his newspaper back home. That wasn't enough, so he turned to an African nanny and a group of Japanese youngsters who only had enough English to say they were tourists. Clive suspected that he enjoyed asking directions merely to feel back in touch with ordinary life and regular people.

"Now I am a tourist in my own life," Pitt told himself bitterly.

The Nigerian lady pointed him eagerly towards a stairway, and instructed him to continue down. There he reached another steeply inclined street of huge, austere Victorian mansions. Hampstead wasn't dissimilar from districts of Manchester or Leeds, he realised, except its features were placed back in a different order.

Pitt rolled his sleeves fully past his elbows and surveyed the landscape. He set off again and cut along a little footpath. This route had a rural quality, and he found himself looking over a series of cottage-like residences. Reaching the end of the lane he emerged on to a wider street, a busier thoroughfare, showing a row of boutique style shops. When he went down to investigate, checking off his scrawled address, Pitt realised it was there, in one of those flats above the shops, he'd been living with Pixie Wright. She'd bought the property as an investment. She'd been keeping up a second home - her love nest. Actually he'd been living with her only months previously.

Approaching the line of shops Clive looked about, trying to pick up his bearings from the past, yet he couldn't find the antiques shop. The address seemed to match his notes, but he only noticed a florists', a wine shop and a furniture shop with apparently new stock. Heat and frustration was starting to get to him. Why did he want to return here anyway? It was out of morbid curiosity and a need to authenticate her story.

A small dark man rushed from the interior of the florists'. He approached Pitt smiling broadly, extending arms towards him and looking extremely pleased - as if the prodigal son had returned.

"Hey there! Mr Pitt, are you back?" he called.

Clive stiffened, staring down with apprehension.

"What's wrong Clive? Are you all right, boss?"

If he truly knew the man, why didn't he recognise him?

"Coming back to pay us your visit?" he beamed, getting in close.

"Do we know each other?" Clive wondered, drawing back.

He assumed a default stance and pushed his fringe from his eyes.

The little man laughed; long stained teeth, enormous shining black eyes, probably Middle Eastern in origin. "'Course I know you Mr Pitt! Would I forget? I have a very good memory, a very good memory," he said, knocking the top of Clive's arm. "So did you move back into the area? Or you just enjoying old times?" he asked.

"Trying to remember what it was like," Clive agreed.

"Anything the matter?" asked the man. "You look stressed, boss."

"What's your name again, sir? Excuse me, because my memory is appalling these days."

"Anwar Ahmed. You forget my name?"

"I'm sorry, Mr Ahmed. That's really rude of me. What happened to the antiques shop?"

The man's face crumpled in anguish. "Oh, God save us, some guys came here...two months... and they smash the place to pieces. They destroy all the stock."

"They did? Why would they want to do that?" Clive replied.

"Thousands of pounds of damage. I don't know. The lady had to move out. She was insure', but decided not to open again. And they even destroy your place as well. Your nice flat upstairs. I came home and found that wrecked. When you had it so nice. Though you were not living there at the time. Very lucky, eh?"

It made simple sense now. "You and I used to speak to each other?" Clive asked.

"That's right. Sure we did, Mr Pitt," said Mr Ahmed, giving Clive's chest a little enthusiastic chop. "How you keeping, boss? Always a pleasure to talk to you, Clive."

"I assume that I was buying a lot of flowers from you," Clive remarked, recalling Pixie's descriptions of his conjugal behaviour.

"Every evening when you come back from work? Lots of blooms for Mrs Pitt."

"Pixie?" he wondered.

"Pixie. Lovely lady. How is your wife?"

Pitt considered himself a foolish hypocrite. "She's very well, thanks very much. But I have to tell you, we were not married."

"Your secret is safe with me," replied Mr Ahmed. Yet his smile had turned uneasy.

"Pixie and I were really happy together, but we were not married," Pitt confirmed. "We were definitely living in sin."

Mr Ahmed's face compressed with sincere sorrow. "Are you sure? That is a pity, Mr Pitt. Such a shame. But you sound as if you are married. Shada and me could hear you two frequently fight. I would listen to your shouting at each other and she was crying, some time," he recalled. His face held an expression of melancholy resignation. "Just like married."

"Really? Pix and I fighting? Right, well, I suppose we were under a lot of strain," Clive said, trying to recreate the scene.

"Lucky for you there was a florists' nearby, eh? So you can make peace with her. So I'm sorry to hear your marriage ended."

"Our relationship ended," Pitt confirmed. "But lately I've been seeing her again."

"Good for you, eh? Really lovely lady, Pixie."

"What did we talk about? You and I? When we got together?"

"Everything. Money, football, politics. Women! You come into my shop, buy flowers, we drink coffee and have a little talk. Happy days. You must remember?"

"Not so well, Mr Ahmed. I suffered a bit of a trauma."

"Something bad?" he wondered.

"A knock on the head, at least," Clive told him.

The florist considered. "You think connected to them destroying your flat?"

"Who's running the shop these days?"

"A new couple there now. They don't like flowers, they sniff coke. That's right, in the flat above the new business. A boring pair of bastards. They own that furniture shop there. And they don't speak to me. Why don't you come in for a while Clive? Like we used to do. I'll make us some coffee and we'll catch up. How's your work these days? Going better?"

"Take my apologies, Mr Ahmed. I'm forced to let you down. Let's make it another time, shall we?"

"Sounds as if you still face terrible problems, Clive? Have trust, everything shall be well in your life and business. Have trust in God. You are always welcome here."

"Cheers, Mr Ahmed, but I should be moving away from here," Clive told him. "Maybe for your good too."

Pitt left Mr Ahmed smiling but a little puzzled, and wandered confused along the street himself. He was absorbing the information that their apartment had been ransacked by intruders.

The Hampstead prospect was generally quiet and reassuring. A distressing sense told him he shouldn't hang about. He wanted to find her pink Porsche and get out of there. He must have strolled around these very streets with her, hand in hand (?), sharing a balmy evening after work - not that long ago. What did they say to each other, between patching up arguments and admiring floral arrangements that is?

There was love between them, going by the evidence so far. They had rediscovered the spark. There was also conflict in their relationship, if Mr Ahmed was to be believed. Did this come from their personalities, or was it triggered by conflict and conspiracy at the office? If they'd had an affair, cared about one another, then should he ask Pixie to stay with him in future? That would be possible if his marriage had been terminated, as it had been, after his wife had cleared off to America. Should he persuade Pixie to pick up where they had left off? Or was their relationship merely an office affair or - not even a fling - but simply an illusion? A flirtation that had transgressed?

Noreen had her reasons to leave and, if he discovered them, he might be able to repair his marriage. How could he resume communication with Noreen, and hear her side of the story? That felt quite improbable and difficult. The situation at work was exceptional; it had pushed them to the limits, their marriage under pressure, Clive considered, not just Pixie and he.

Clive was disturbed by the idea of setting up home with Pixie, or any other girl for that matter. He had indulged in fantasies about Pixie, but these were merely an escape route in times of stress. There's an inner voice, a wiser counsel, isn't there, reminding us about what is right. Apparently this wiser voice had been ignored in regard to Pixie, at some stage. However he still couldn't remember the specifics. What he recognised came through his fingertips and nerve ends; or at best insights and impressions, bypassing memory and wisdom. Pitt was somehow able to vouch for her past support, even though he couldn't exactly say why.

He hadn't so much lost memories as failed to retrieve them. Now he was washed up in his own life; stumbling about London, trying to gain clues about his position, while fearing that he was already caught in his enemies' net.

28

In the course of tackling another Hampstead hill, Clive became aware of footfalls behind.

The thought of being followed caused instant GBH against his coronary muscles. He was trying to keep a regular heartbeat, to measure his paces, to regulate breathing, as if taking on a challenge. He prided himself on dangerous sports, risky adventure, walking and running challenges. But that wouldn't hold; he was not doing this for self-satisfaction or leisure, or bonding with friends. He was not even battling with competitors in cyber space. *These guys mean business*, he told himself, almost as a joke.

Probably he was being naïve by looking back over his shoulder. But he wanted to get some idea who was tracking him. In fact there seemed to be more than one guy following; perhaps there were as many as three.

Absurdly the burly trio were wearing bowler hats. Blokes didn't wear bowler hats any more, he argued, other than a few club door men trying to impress. They were intent on their prey (the time of watching and waiting had expired). Possibly his enemies judged that a corner of Hampstead was an ideal hunting environment.

Despite a quaint dress sense, his pursuers looked like standard thick necks. Pitt wasn't used to playing the quarry, but he felt that these attack dogs were closing in. When Clive looked behind and began to jog, they made no attempt to disguise their intentions. Unlike Mr Ahmed at the florists, they were not in a mood to chat about the affairs of the world. Rather, with the brutality of a Victorian publican along the Mile End, they were determined to call time.

Pitt had nearly killed one of them already, after the vicious attack near to his former home. Or maybe he'd really snuffed that guy out by accident. The memory of the man's destroyed bloody features haunted him still. They wouldn't be pleased by the shock result of that violent episode. That would have frustrated his enemies - whoever they were - but it would have strengthened their resolve. Equally their urgency made him wonder if he could potentially nullify them.

Pitt took flight through the red hot afternoon, bolting for his life from one turning to the next, in the way they expected.

Yet he wasn't exactly sure who 'they' were. Who really ran the world? If you made enemies in the City as a high ranking figure, then the outcomes were serious. There were a number of candidates, including his former boss. Who was responsible for setting these wild dogs on him? Right then it was not so urgent to hear the name of their employer.

How could he shake their fangs from his trouser seat? The thugs would catch him eventually, unless he found more cunning. Pitt knew instinctively that his flight was too direct and visible to his chasers; as they strode out and held him in their sight. Therefore he began to be more erratic, unpredictable, as he'd seen in war movies. Soon he dashed suddenly to one side, when an opportunity arose; running at full tilt down a pathway. The tactic worked to a degree, as there was a delay before they picked him up again; the trio of bowler hats bobbed along in his direction across the top of a hedge.

Perspiration flooded his new shirt, which still retained showroom creases. Nobody had the time to iron his shirts at the moment, least of all himself. He was glad to be in physical shape, even though he was pushing the limits. But he didn't consider himself to be any kind of secret agent or hero, just a mathematician turned City banker, who had upset a few powerful guys by saying the truth.

As a youth he was an idealist using technology to make a name and possibly his first billions. His father was dismayed at that time. He considered Clive a bedroom fantasist and tried to persuade him to start at the building society.

Clive remembered his first introduction to Sir Septimus. The banker had been impressed, warmly welcoming, fizzing with enthusiasm. It always helped your negotiating position Sep argued, if you could produce a particularly beefy, confident guy, with a brilliant mind into the bargain. That had been a successful strategy. Not only on the trading floor, to strut along peacock walk; but in meetings with clients and rivals; to gain business, to consolidate agreements, as well as, of course, to intimidate any competitors or naysayers.

Nobody knew what made Pitt tick back then - including himself. Clive wasn't aware of any particular business ethics. At first he didn't know where the moral line could be. But at a late stage of the ZNT deal Pitt got a feel for that moral line. Like a ballerina who refuses to sweat off extra pounds, he refused to cross that border.

How could he have suspected - either as an intern or as an associate - that his exciting career at Winchurch Brothers would, one day, push him out and force him to run for his life?

Clive became aware that one of the guys split off. The suit separated from his cohorts, no doubt thinking to double back and cut Clive off. They probably had a navigation device to orientate them. They found their way with ease around the complex plot of Hampstead paths and lanes. Pitt had broken his sophisticated wristwatch days ago, so couldn't take that aid. The watch had been a gift from the director of a Bavarian forestry company. It was thanks for helping him secure the timber from Hungarian woodland.

At some point the bowler hats would intercept him. Then it would be check-mate in their favour. From Clive's point of view the business couldn't be allowed to end there. The details of this hidden scandal would stay secret and be buried with him. But he'd be damned if he allowed them to win out. How could he keep ahead of three of them? He could try to keep them separated, baffled between each other, like a careless group in a hall of mirrors.

Soon he would be sandwiched between them, a bowler hat at each end of the lane. Pitt clambered over a brick wall, rolling over pieces of glass at the top. With an effort he got over the top and fell over to the other side. He crashed down with an inelegant thump into someone's back garden. He'd fallen awkwardly, as pain shot through his right knee and thigh. But he got to his feet, and judged the demands of the terrain ahead as it swam about his vision.

Fortunately the pain was instantaneous. He strode out across a spongy green lawn, which was basking under sprinklers. He enjoyed a few moments to cool down. But he couldn't waste another second. This was the complex territory of a classic English garden. Not every day did you flee for your life in someone's back garden, he thought.

Seconds later, he watched the two suited thick-necks follow in the same direction. They tumbled awkwardly over the wall, like poor nags taking a lunge at Beecher's Brook. They suffered an equally rough landing, with the extra point of a trellis. All the air was smacked out of one of the guys. The character emitted indignant grunts of complaint, face shoved into the dirt. They were soon on their feet however. They didn't even brush down before picking up the chase. Obviously they enjoyed the rough British sporting culture. Pitt had never enjoyed it exactly but he'd learnt to survive from an early age.

Pitt found himself under tree cover, darting between intense light and shade. He took a swift course among shrubberies, crumbling walls and hidden nooks. At the top of the garden he noted a glowering gothic mansion. Some fantasy castle for a Victorian banker or lawyer. Yet the thugs were rapidly following, even closing on him, running not far behind. Pitt could only sprint as hard as he knew, praying that he was the strongest and fastest of four men. How likely was this? Perhaps people somewhere in the world were gambling on-line for and against him. It was down to physical competition for survival. It wasn't about cleverness, or challenging unseen opponents with your gaming knowledge.

He confronted the limits of the garden, with no place left to turn. He was forced to scramble over the next dividing wall into the adjoining garden. In the struggle he dragged down honeysuckle and pulled out lumps of old brickwork. His lungs reached a burning limit, and lactic acid took bites out of his muscles. He dragged himself up on his deeply scratched leather soles, as if he was being whipped through an alternative London marathon.

There were indignities to endure as he jumped at the next wall. His new chalk-stripe pants were rent on a thorny trellis, his shirt patterned by chlorophyll. Yet he still had the will to escape.

His pursuers vaulted down again, missing only their bowler hats (left to confound someone's deductive thinking). Indeed they were suffering, judging by the anguished snarls; which didn't sound in English, although that was hard to tell. One of the thugs proved fitter, as he was pulling away from his comrade, Clive realised, dashing a concerned look around.

Pitt began to sense that he was not the fittest and strongest. One of these thick-necks had apparently given up the ghost, but his mate kept running hard and, within minutes, he caught up with Pitt. Luckily there didn't seem to be firearms or any lethal weapons involved, at this stage. Why didn't they try to kill him immediately and be done? They wanted something from him first. He was surprised that they didn't try to take aim.

Losing stamina Pitt decided to stop, to set out his stall and fight the guy. He'd run out of strategies and had nowhere to turn. This one was huge; by then drenched in sour sweat, with a reek of spirit and spices. Bowler hat missing, he presented an entirely shaven head, top skin peeling and slick with sweat. His eyes popped with effort, showing little sense, beneath a burnt bullish neck, snorting like a bull too, as the fellow summoned remaining strength; lifting his head he put up fists as massive as limestone lumps on the moor.

The guy took a wild swing around the block, nearly lost his footing, and a struggle commenced. They each landed blows to the body, then fell on each other wearily, straining for a dominant grip. Pitt felt like one of those daring athletes that used to ride bulls in ancient Crete. He was oddly filled with strength and resolve, as his blood surged powerfully.

"Give it up Mr Pitt," the guy urged.

"Never," Clive returned.

"Hand back all what you stole."

"After you!" Pitt urged.

"You're finished."

"Who wants me?"

"You're done," the guy grunted.

"What do you think I am?"

"You are Lucifer," the guy insisted.

Clive noticed - peripherally - that somebody else was approaching, across that stretch of lawn. Neither the hoodlum nor he was in a position to identify this other individual. The thug assumed his colleague had caught up and he gained a definite surge of confidence. Clive lost spirit because he also expected the other thick-neck to come and finish him off. Pitt experienced some despair, he felt weak and doomed, unable to resist any further.

"*We got Lucifer*," the guy declared. He had Clive in a strangle hold and was grinding his short teeth in appreciation.

But at this the villain was given a hefty blow to the head. An instant later he folded. He was a pile of unsavoury sausage meat on the turf; all mince and gristle. Pitt staggered, in and out of the dark, astonished by the sudden release. Then there were stars, even in a deep blue afternoon sky, and he suffered a blackout.

The next thing he knew:

"Are you all right, my dear chap," he heard. "Do you require any medical attention? Should I telephone for an ambulance?"

A quite elderly gentleman, in Bermuda shorts and a flowery shirt, came into his vision. The chap was still brandishing a croquet mallet. This was the instrument which had been brought down on the thug's skull. Further up the lawn was a young lady, in lime green spandex shorts, who was also holding a croquet mallet. She was gazing down at them with anxious curiosity, as if her father had pulled off an unconventional shot, which involved a criminal's cranium.

"No, I should be good," Pitt assured him.

"Why don't you have a nip of gin? To make you feel better?" he volunteered.

"You haven't killed him, I hope?" Clive asked ironically. He examined the lumpy suit spread over the grass, as if training to be a door mat.

"He'll pull through."

"I'm not so sure about that," Pitt said, looking the guy over.

"We were having our little game... when we noticed you running across the garden...and this brute of a chap bounding after you... what did he want you for, huh?"

"A loan shark," Clive declared. "Yes, that's what he is. I already made a full payment, but it wasn't enough. No, they intended to make me pay up. There are two other guys around this area. So best be careful, mate."

"We'll notify the police before he comes around."

"That's up to you," Pitt informed them, recomposing himself.

"You advise not to involve them?"

"Let him dream about his motherland," Pitt replied.

As an accused rapist he was in no hurry to be interviewed by the police force. There was a heap of circumstantial evidence ready to be accessed.

"If that's what you advise. Don't want to be nosey!" the chap said, jauntily.

"Be careful to lock your windows this evening...as a precaution."

"Rather over-dressed for a day like today," observed the gentleman.

"Yes they can be bloody formal. Although I definitely tried to loosen his collar," he said bitterly.

"Shark is the right name for these chaps," the gentleman judged. "They're all in bed with the tax man, you know."

"There's something to be said for the tax man," Clive replied. "Can I leave by the side gate?"

He began to stagger up the slope of their extensive garden, trying to shake off thick mental cobwebs after that involuntary cat nap.

"What happens if this brute begins to revive?" asked the young woman, as he went by on wobbly legs.

"Take another free shot," Clive suggested.

He escaped back into a gravelly private road outside. He gave an exhausted laugh at his luck, while trying to navigate back to his parking spot.

To find her *Carrera* Pitt had to fathom a maze of streets, wary of the other two suits in circulation and tracking him like drones. In the brightness he buckled at the knees, mentally faltered, as if he required a power source. He finally got back to the car - at least it stood out - trying to beat down his rampaging heart. Pitt let himself back in, relieved that it hadn't been vandalised. He composed himself and began to re-familiarise the dials. After all, like many aspects of his life, it didn't belong to him.

While doing this he took note of a black Humber down the road, like a massive safe box, parked ominously half over the pavement. This was their style in edgy capital cities the world over, as if the rules didn't apply to them because they were special. They would park where they pleased, even to get a quick bite to eat. Such a casual style was a calling card to the masses and a reminder of their contempt for any official rule or retribution. Anyway paying a parking fine around their London playground was a mere nuisance.

As he hit the ignition and pulled away smoothly, Pitt had an opportunity to get ahead of them, assuming they hadn't already guessed his next move. Clive had done well but he still felt traces of sticky fibres against his skin.

He continued through these north London suburbs until forking off to the motorway. After a ninety degree circulation he emerged at the southern end, venturing towards Winchurch's country retreat.

He was keeping ahead of his enemies. But for how long?

29

Going by Pixie's descriptions the house was near a Buckinghamshire village called Featherington. She explained that Sep's country estate had been purchased by an ancestor during Jane Austen's day. This banker raised bonds for Spencer Perceval to finance war against Bonaparte in Spain.

As a leading financier of his day, and a Treasury advisor, Joseph Arthur Winchurch purchased a rundown Jacobean farmhouse, as well as the land attached and several large houses besides, using his handsome profits after the Peninsula War had been won. A new hunting lodge had been built over the original foundations. During the following century Joe Winchurch, and his sons and grandsons in turn, expanded and improved the property further. It became an impressive family home, right until the twenty first century, as Lady and Sir Septimus Winchurch, with their only child Esmeralda, continued to reside there, at least at weekends and during school holidays.

Clive undertook a lengthy drive into the green belt. Or so it felt to him, as the effects of extreme exertion set in, putting him into shock; something like physical shut down, following that brawl on the grass; with cortisol spreading numbness around his body. Psychologically he was feeling isolated and under severe pressure. Where was the escape key in his mind? Mentally he was groping in the dark with his face shoved into a concrete wall. Was there a concealed catch or number pad? Would the combination ever come back? Or was he just a rogue banker waiting to be deleted from the system?

In Clive's job he was used to a crowded agenda, a packed diary, bustling with people, activity and communication, meetings scheduled and unscheduled; leaps around town on a hunch, last ditch video conferences with clients around the world. Not only had his enemies locked him into the dark, he had lost connectivity or even simple *human* connection. This was unnerving, isolating. What's more at this stage he couldn't allow himself to fully trust Pixie. If he was being honest he couldn't entirely trust *himself* either.

They were both; Pixie and he; trained as double dealers on the markets. For all its excitement and rewards his job was a game of bluff and trumps. Arguably it was trained into their genes to trick competitors, to best their rivals in other firms, to dissemble and distract; despite team cooperation. That was exactly the point; did she regard him as the team leader any longer? She'd been schooled from infancy to conceal her true intentions, to guard her best interests, not just vulnerable feelings. She was a player in the City too, a leading risk management/ quantitative analyst. Therefore she'd be keeping her true opinion - her final verdict - tightly to her chest.

Pitt was cut off from his wife, family and friends as well. He was receiving contradictory, negative information about his own personality. This was the strategy of his enemies at the company and at the hedge fund. They were leading him to assassinate his own character, to lose faith with himself. How much longer could he endure the assault? The vicious internal assault on his identity? His thoughts drifted back to that lost period, as if he might fall asleep at the wheel. The experience was like speeding along a dangerous auto-route at night, with an unmarked surface and blankness on all sides; his obsessed concentration an unbroken beam of headlight.

Clive scrunched over the wheel, eyes burning as he was without shades. He was trying to recognise features of the passing landscape. He must have taken this route on the day of the fateful garden party. Presumably he must have driven himself to the area. He mourned the disappearance of his own lost car. Or had he hired or stolen a different car, or had someone given him a lift? Not Pixie. The bulk of his memories had been liquidated, yet he was forced to live with the consequences.

A view of the scorched countryside didn't revive his mind. Only the memory of a trip to the south coast with his wife and son - a few years back. There was no problem at retrieving those memories, beyond the missing year. Doreen had an aunt in Dover, and they'd come down from London, went to stay with this spinster aunt over the summer, rather like David Copperfield. Yes indeed, he had now taken to fighting butcher boys, like David Copperfield on his journey. He'd no doubt that the mafia butcher boys would have climbed back into their Humber. At least there was some advantage in taking Pixie's car.

The hilly fields and meadows looked familiar, vaguely, as he considered (trying to get a spark of memory) although tinder dry and straw brown. Only wild flowers were winners this summer; pointillist explosions against the baked fields. They were casting their seeds, their ancient genetic codes - memory chips of infinite space. Simplicity and complexity combined, if only humans could design something like that.

Why hadn't they killed him back there? They had a clear sight to eliminate him, without fuss. Taken him out. Of course they required his memory. That was it, he told himself, because he'd put his memory somewhere for safe keeping. The problem was that the hiding place was too safe, of course. Yes it was just like losing your damn car keys somewhere around the house. When he used to own a house that was. His enemies must still believe that he, Pitt, knew where he'd put his evidence. Was it transferred to a mass storage device?

Pitt got this vital point, while he was speeding down the motorway. Powerful players urgently required his memory back.

That was the end game for the deal. Those ZNT guys and Sep needed his dossier intact, which didn't stop them from screwing with his head; or treating his body like a paper bin in their way. He wasn't sure that anyone knew or if the data survived. They were concerned that his evidence was accessible in some form, if it fell under the wrong eyes, perhaps to the authorities. This was despite the fact that Pitt couldn't remember exactly how he had gathered the information. How effective were the regulatory bodies, even if he was able to hand over the evidence? What other option was there, if he could save himself?

His enemies would try to extract the information by force. After that they would dispose of him. Sep and friends were confident that they had destroyed him, professionally and personally. Somebody in ZNT was counter-plotting against Sep. But the snag was that all the evidence was replicated. Clive's case had vanished from his mind, but it was stored safely elsewhere; his dossier was in a virtual hiding place, waiting for the right moment to destroy both Sep and ZNT, like a killer drone ready for an order to take off. Great, he was thinking, but who will give the order for the attack?

They knew his dossier contained incriminating data, copies of documents and letters, electronic trails and other evidence of fraud and theft. Their ruthless pursuit proved to Clive that they were afraid of this scenario. Clive too had to hunt down and locate his lost dossier. How was that going to be achievable? His brain had been sent back to a pre-technological condition.

There was just one accessible road into Featherington village.

Pitt had grown so hungry and thirsty that he decided to call into a local pub. He swung her pink Porsche into the rear car park. From there he gingerly locked up and walked stiffly around the side of the building, looking around warily, into the porch and then into the lounge bar.

His exertions in Hampstead had shaken him to the core. Pitt decided to take a risk to get a pub meal and a pint at last, before his adventures continued. He struggled to keep on top of his shaking and trembling. He decided to call into the Gents' to repair his appearance somewhat. There was only so much he could do. When he came out and approached the bar, staff and patrons made concerned enquiries about his well-being.

"Are you a'right, sir? Anything bad happen to you?" said the male publican.

This guy surely knew Septimus, in name and person; but Clive wasn't going to mention him. He already guessed that his own torn appearance would stick in their minds. But he was grateful for their concern, their lack of suspicion. Pitt took a shadowy table at the back, trying to avoid curiosity in a friendly way. Although when a lady - the female publican - discussed her problems with putting young children to bed, he added his pennyworth, as a father, sardonic and knowing. Then he tucked into his locally produced gammon steak and a pint of Red Kite bitter; almost ferociously. Part of him wanted to stay in that bar all day and get properly juiced. Unfortunately, however big the temptation, that was a fool's paradise.

Later, returning outside, replete, the world seemed back in focus. But he knew there was still a job to be done. From here he had no need to ask directions to Winchurch's estate. As he stood in the pub's front garden, admiring the quaint houses and lanes nearby, he could see the upper gables of the financier's substantial house. The property was perched on a hill, maybe an artificial landmark, albeit half concealed behind cypress trees and Lebanese pine trees. The tended gardens stood out on one side of the acclivity, for miles around, like a painted oasis. Still, even as Clive gazed towards the almost fantasy residence, no fragment of his original visit came back into his thoughts.

A short drive into the village revealed an oak sign reading "Close Copse House - Traders' Gate: 10am - 4.30pm. Announce Yourself". This afternoon Septimus or his family was unlikely to be at home. The financier would be at work as usual, and the family would be residing at their London house. But the banker would keep some staff at his country estate to keep an eye on things.

Pitt understood that Emmy and her friends would hang-out during holidays. As well they might, when they could enjoy a swimming pool, tennis courts, a gym and other facilities. Clive was careful in leaving Pixie's chichi 4S parked up a quiet lane for safekeeping. As he looked back it resembled a rocket powered lipstick. He didn't want to lose her car into the bargain. It was better to explore by foot - while keeping her wheels and his return journey in the bag.

As he began to prowl around, Pitt knew that estate stewards would not hail his arrival like an unexpected royal visitor. He hoped to get some ideas and clues, to restore familiarity. If he could achieve those reboots he could join again with Pixie. Together they could go on a fact-finding visit to the financier's hospital.

Pitt discovered a set of neglected iron side gates. These had been kept locked and tethered with wire for ages, apparently, but he had no problems getting over the spikes. This gave him an unconventional path into the estate; which would help to cover his steps. Even from this distance he noticed drawn drapes and shutters over upstairs and downstairs windows of the great house, as well as numerous fat padlocks. At the entrance to the estate's gardens and attached farmland, he came across prolific "No Trespassers!" signs, hammered into the ground.

There was an aura of violence and tragedy about the place, Clive felt. There had been a dreadful event here (he could pick this up) that had ripped the spirit out of a beautiful place, as it had destroyed the unity and feeling of a particular family. The modified façade of the house revealed this as subtly, but as unmistakeably, as a human face. Pitt slinked watchfully around the perimeter, which was wide and eccentric in shape. The house showed traces of numerous historical periods: fortunes gained, and sometimes lost; gambles bringing profits, allegiances rewarded, fortunes made or lives quietly lost. The rear had pretentious porticos and Greek style columns. Despite Sep's colourful historical pedigree there was a parvenu quality to his recent additions.

Still, the grounds were beautiful, despite the apparent grief of the house; such an expansive and venerable house. Clive found a rear terrace, from where Septimus held his party to celebrate the completion of the deal; as well as to welcome ZNT members on to his board. It must have been a huge and landmark transaction, because it ensured his personal survival as a big beast in the City, not only his employees' positions.

Clive fought to gain purchase on his personal involvement, some flash or detail of memory, now that he'd arrived on the scene, to unlock a few of those secrets in his mind. To this point his mind refused to yield. He just felt like a ghost returning to the scene of its colourful life.

He wondered if Winchurch had abandoned the place entirely. Or was he keeping away temporarily, allowing those terrible memories and consequences to settle. The banker wanted to concentrate on his struggle to regain Pitt; to regain not merely profitability but his peace of mind. During her summer break Emmy had enjoyed a run of the house and gardens. In addition to those other facilities, there were stables, containing a group of white horses as pretty as a singing group. There was even a bar and of course servants at hand. Quite a place to bring your college mates back to.

But Clive had to remain vigilant as he poked around, because he spotted a trio of black suited stewards. One of them had a shotgun slung across his shoulders. Fortunately he was then warned about their presence and they were in the distance. But he knew this wasn't a stroll around the park with them patrolling around. Maybe those guys didn't expect him to be there. Maybe they were not in a suspicious frame of mind this afternoon. Yet he couldn't be absolutely certain about that. The security people must be in communication with each other. They knew that 'Lucifer' was free and they needed to be alert.

Keeping eyes in the back of his head Pitt walked across the patio (imagining the busy scene earlier in the summer). He walked around the rim of the now empty swimming pool, intended for Emmy's enjoyment alone, until tragic events had intervened. A huge kidney shaped hole.

Pitt moved away from those shuttered windows, tricked off a set of limestone steps. He walked in to another flower garden and to a stagnant carp pond at the next level. It contained a Neptune statue which, he thought, resembled Sep himself. From there he waited, still and anxious, as he'd watched a second group of stewards - or were they security people? - wandering around greenhouses. Able to breathe again, Clive pressed on around beds of succulents. Further from the house flowers were allowed to grow somewhat wildly. Lush, spoilt vegetation ruffled in the hot breeze. There were signs of recent gardening, with a wheel-barrow and split compost bags at the ready.

His eyes followed the tops of Cypress trees, lining the house's driveway. They were considered to be holy trees. The groves had developed impressively over the centuries. They were suffering in the drought that summer. Beyond the welcoming guard (planted perhaps in the Regency period) there were gnarled old oaks, marking off the fields.

Clive was aware of being conspicuous at this point. He was in easy observation for anybody watching from the house. He felt that it was very unlikely that there was an observer at the window. No doubt the interior was an even lonelier place. But he was a field day for the stewards, like a naïve poacher.

"I need to get some cover," he warned himself. "How many hounds does he need to catch this bloody fox!"

Soon the manicured lawns came to a dignified halt. Horticultural civilisation ended at a wild tangle. There was a bigger pond, stagnant and drained, where land led away from the house in graded steps. His every footfall disturbed crowds of pheasants that were hiding and scratching around the earth among burnt corn stalks. The startled creatures scuttled away in blind panic, uttering alarm cries like hordes of panicked Orks. Their sudden noise and movement set Pitt's pulse jumping. In a normal year the pheasants were nurtured for shooting. It was unlikely that Septimus and his cronies would aim any barrels at the birds this year. Clive would do his best to prevent those guys turning their guns on him instead. He might persuade those managers in Geneva to break cover. They were betting on his demise, but they should place some hedges against his escape.

Beyond the pond was a face of woodland. Pitt stood about for a while, considering the situation, with the searing sun beating the top of his head. The trees formed a dark and imposing wall ahead. The dreadful scenes that Pixie had described, involving the party, assumed some edges of reality in his mind. This was the scene of the crime, whatever the truth of the allegations. However he still didn't recall any facet of that terrible day, other than a restored portrait of Emmy's face, which he must have noticed in the boss' office.

He walked through tough vegetation, ignoring hooked teeth of nettles and thistles. He was already showing the effects of those sauna-like conditions. The hair on the top of his head was scorched, as the skin of his face was taut and tender. The undergrowth was so dry he was afraid a fire could start up with every step. Yet he plunged through the tangled area, and reached the edge of a copse. Clive dived ahead. He staggered through this tangle of trees, with thorny limbs clutching and panicking. He continually snagged, as thorny trees gouged at flesh and tore a strip from his Bond Street shirt.

It would be difficult to drag someone into these trees, against their will, he calculated. The tree canopy was complete and undamaged in this area, sheltered from direct sun. Shafts of light broke through, looking as solid as steel lances to the eye, but the atmosphere was of woody blackness and decay.

Either these woods were a place of refuge, or they were a trap. Now he was putting himself back into the trap that someone had set for the girl - not to mention himself. A place from where nobody was likely to locate your struggle, even if they heard any cries for help. Pitt felt the sweat on his face turn cold, as he recreated the assault that had taken place; according to Pixie's account.

Pixie would have been too far away and too distracted, to have heard any screams. She would have lingered anxiously on the terrace, looking out over the gardens. Meanwhile all other guests had been ushered away and hurried back into the house, as if from a violent downpour. Clive wondered how Emmy had been crazy enough to go off with him. Clive had been completely unknown to her, except as a business enemy of her father's. What had he been thinking of himself? Some evil spell of sexual attraction had come upon them. Didn't she have any idea of appropriate risk? Then again he couldn't judge her character, any more than he could turn back the clock.

Emmy's portrait photograph - as he recalled - depicted a very sexy nubile girl; with streaks and panels of blonde hair in her otherwise dark mop. He remembered her facial features and style quite vividly. She painted a lovely portrait all right, with those large honey-brown eyes and a made-for-sex mouth.

On a fantasy level he liked the idea of having sex in the woods. Emmy was gorgeous and, if she was up for it, they may have disappeared together. But many guys would have had such libidinous thoughts, he realised. Particularly if they were spiked up on a bull market or a hectic trade. They could be awash with testosterone. To be exact it was the rape that was not acceptable. At the office this was the necessary hormonal cocktail, he suspected, in the struggle to keep ahead. Not to mention those steamy nights with a definite lack of sexual encounters. He hadn't made love to any woman since losing everything. But while in immediate physical danger you didn't think about making love, not even with Pixie: survival was the priority.

Noreen and he enjoyed sex in a variety of positions and flavours. They had a licence from the vicar, but they tried to ignore that calming factor. They liked to make love in different locations and places, including romantic situations, such as in the back of their car above the beach at Cannes. How could he ever forget that? Yet they were limited by the constraints of caring for a young child. Of course even unconventional or risky sexual adventures have to be consensual, don't they? When you are experimenting with your boss' teenage daughter, for sure.

He was plunged into complete darkness. He felt his face scratched, as if by long clawing fingernails. Now and again, in contrast, he picked out perfect shafts of clear light. He put his foot into a foxhole, or whatever animal had dug these tunnels, and stumbled to his knees, as if he'd fallen down before a church altar.

In front of him, a vision of light remained pristinely untouched. Clive tore himself free; he stumbled out into a clear area at the centre. The place was illuminated by a column of sunshine, he noticed. Hot natural shafts cut through a gap in the tree canopy, smouldering in the dusty air, striking against a dark and crowded backdrop. As he scrambled back up and picked around, there was evidence of fires. He saw that old fallen tree trunks were used as seats. People could gather to socialise at this spot, or even to have a smoke. He got a mental picture of Emmy and her group of student guests. The estate gardeners were probably the most regular visitors to this hidden communal area.

If he had gone anywhere with Emmy that evening, then this would have been the spot. Or more likely she would have taken *him*? How could he have known his way around the area? She knew the estate; it was her playground; so she also knew the route to a secluded meeting place among the trees. Did she invite him with the idea to take things a few steps further? After they had been seen kissing at the garden party? Did their sexual encounter get out of hand, or were there other factors involved? Other men?

Pitt sat where the girl and her friends must have regularly gathered; on a fallen tree trunk; and he thought back. But he only had the general outline and suppositions to go on, as if confined to wandering the perimeter. His mind couldn't reach for a full reconstruction. There was Pixie's, other peoples' account of what had taken place, and then there was a cognitive gap.

His whole situation felt as enigmatical as the darkness. Clues? What clues? Pitt gazed helplessly ahead into the imperceptible shifts and changes of the columnar sunshine. His current situation was a parody of his job, as he stayed late into the night, into the morning. Going over the general outlines, examining the small print, trying to rack his brains to make any sense of the BIP flotation and understand how ZNT could meet the acceptable standards of probity and governance.

30

Pitt considered the credit and debit sides of retracing his steps to the house. Those black shirted stewards patrolled the gardens with determined menace. He didn't plan to try those weighty yokels with a friendly hand shake. 'Rent a Mob' could have been tipped off about his drive into the countryside. They were conducting a search and had become extra vigilant. As soon as his route was tracked it was even simpler to receive updated, find-and-destroy instructions from London.

Instead of wandering back up the garden path, Pitt pressed on through the back of the estate, beyond the copse, to discover what may lie beyond. And he was wiser to exit altogether that way; to reach the car by doubling back around the perimeter. He suspected there was a simpler path, known only to the gardeners, or perhaps to Emmy and her family, but hidden to him. On the day of the garden party, that previous summer, Clive had followed a similar route. On that occasion he was trying to break in to the estate. He must have circled the outer brick wall, searching for any hole, created by vandals or crashes, or even a remote gate by which to enter. Did he know that there was no wall at this point, but a secret path? He speculated if he had really trespassed alone that afternoon, or been accompanied, or led, by others; by whom?

Clive emerged at the top of another meadow, which was also filled with a dancing riot of flowers; a beautiful side effect of those arid summer months. The hot sun cut into his vision like a molten sword. Like fire running along a fuse this cascade singed his optical nerve for some minutes. The icy mask of his face, formed in the cool of the woods, evaporated in a moment, with a tautening of his burnt skin. As the black smoke cleared from his vision, gradually, Clive started to pick out features of the landscape. These notably included, at the foot of the fields, another road. This was more than just a country lane, most likely branched back to the major road, significant enough to feature on a map.

This discovery was interesting to him. He assumed the estate would be inaccessible from the rear, other than by specialised vehicles. You could make an escape this way, he realised, as he hiked down the meadow to investigate. You could arrive at the back of the estate, and find your way inside through the trees, if you knew the way and had it properly planned. Of course on this occasion he'd stumbled on this strategy by accident. There it was, a significant road, allowing a getaway, if it was required, assuming a car was parked nearby, engine ticking over, ready to drive off again. Was he really capable of plotting the whole crazy stunt by himself and carrying out a cruel attack on Emmy and her family? They claimed that he was so embittered, so angry and vengeful, as to behave in that extreme way, to act without any constraint, but Pitt refused to believe it - their propaganda and dark arts.

He poked around at the bottom of the field, thinking if he was going astray. But when he ducked through a gap in the hedge, this immediately gave access to a sandy layby. A few cars swished by even as he stood about, considering the implications. He didn't even notice the astonished looks of passing motorists, or respond to the occasional ironic hoot or juvenile gesture. Just as long as a Humber or limo didn't arrive, to disgorge a bunch of thugs, then he wouldn't take any notice.

Close Copse House was not fortified from the outside world. He, or whoever might have been around on that evening, could make their entrance; and their getaway. He, they or whoever, could arrange for a car to be waiting in the layby, while you ran back down here... and then the car could speed off, and then it could join the motorway back to London, as there was a junction just a few miles away. You could complete your malign deeds at Close Copse House and depart in haste, Pitt considered, like a gang of petty burglars.

Hadn't this been his approach that day? He forced his way into Sep's celebratory garden party; he must have alighted here and made his way through woods and gardens, until joining guests on the patio. Alone? Pixie reported that he had showed up there alone, a written-down debt somehow bouncing back.

The house was like an ancestral home for the Winchurch family, so why not make the property more secure? Sir Septimus obviously didn't expect intruders or that anyone could discover the hidden path. He knew the lay of his own land. The woods formed a natural barrier at this position. He wouldn't want to cut them down to extend a wall.

He didn't believe that Sep would offer his own daughter as bait. Winchurch clearly had nothing to gain from that outrage. But could he make the same argument about members of the ZNT group? They were capable of destroying the life of a young girl to protect themselves, and their investments and reputation. They would arrange this to erase the whistle-blower and dissuade the boss from taking his call.

Clive picked up a track on the other side of the road. This went through dusty trees and, with pieces of machinery and discarded objects on both sides, suggested a nearby settlement. Before long an ancient piebald dog picked up his scent, toddled towards him and began to bark; this in turn provoked a kerfuffle of chickens and geese.

Rounding the next corner Clive discerned the brick work of a cottage, but not picturesque, with its slate roof, rotten carpentry and tumbled down garage or workshop. Maybe the proximity of a dwelling so near to the road, and to Close Copse House, wasn't important, yet this discovery required further investigation.

A short distance further, as Pitt sought a closer view, he stumbled across an elderly man. The old chap was short and very solidly set, with craggy red features, in dusty old clothing.

Clive must have been intimidating for the man. However the other continued walking towards him, as if he was too old and humble to harm anyone. Yet he was quite a strong guy, with big working hands, for all that.

"All right, mate?"

"Where are you heading?" the old chap asked, in a friendly fashion.

"Nowhere in particular," replied Clive. "This is your place, mate?"

"Certainly. I live there," he confirmed, gesturing behind.

"Then I'd like to have a chat with you, if that's okay?

"All you got here is a dead end," he declared.

"Just a few minutes of your time? I'd appreciate it."

"You want to chat with me, do you?" Suspicion came into his reddened and cheerful face. "What about?"

Despite the temperature he was wearing a thick sweater, rubber boots, although topped off with a floppy hat.

"I want to speak to you about some events at the house...the Winchurch estate..."

"Oh yes, do you? About Sir Septimus?"

"In regard to his daughter Emmy, some months ago, I think..."

"Doesn't have much to do with me," he replied bluntly.

"Hi, my name's Clive Pitt!" He offered his hand.

"Fred Chippendon." The old chap brightened gratefully and proffered his own bulky hand.

"Hi'ya Fred. What do you work at around here? Are you retired?"

"No, I'm not retired. I'm still working; fit and active!"

"Good for you."

"I'm one of the gardeners on Sir Septimus' grounds. I use my hands."

"Do you remember Septimus holding a garden party?"

"Do I? We did extra work. Preparation. On very little pay."

"You know that his daughter was attacked that day?" Clive risked.

"The squire kept it pretty much hushed up. They didn't want her to be dragged through the mud any more. They said she was molested, but goodness knows what really happened. What's your interest then? Are you a policeman?"

"No, not a policeman, but an investigator... I was hired by the man who was accused of raping her," Clive stated boldly.

"Is that right?" considered the old man.

"If I can't get enough evidence to show he is wrongly accused, then this guy could be banged up in the slammer forever!"

"If he's innocent then I oughta speak up," said Chippendon, rubbing his big sore nose. "Such mistakes can happen. I've read about that. Why do they accuse him of attacking her?"

"He was seen walking away with the girl. But he doesn't remember anything about the incident. Now they say this is amnesia for a guilty conscience!"

"They got all sorts of cures for ailments. Then why don't you come inside for a while, to talk this over?"

"Thanks Mr Chippendon, that would be great!"

"There's not much to tell," said the old chap. "Not much better 'n nothing."

"I should hear what you have to say," Clive replied, wiping his face again.

"Might be significant to you, who can tell? I would tell my story to Sir Septimus, but he never comes down here these days. Maybe he's got too much on his plate... and with his fancy business in London."

Fred showed the way towards his home, with a bow-legged gait. In the yard of the house they were greeted by another large, aged dog; a wall-eyed cross breed, mostly collie. It sniffed around Clive's scuffed shoes and trousers with a guarded growling - although its tail kept wagging. Chickens flurried in numbers about the dust and gravel, and there was a huge black goat tethered to a fence post. Clive flinched as he was caught in the detached black slots of its lemon-coloured eyes.

There were heaps of broken pots, bundles of canes and vital accessories to the old man's work, cluttering up the yard but making it characterful.

"Do you live alone?" Clive asked.

"Quite alone," Fred answered. "My dearly beloved wife has been dead for these past twelve years."

"Oh. I'm sorry. Do you not heal after all that time?" Clive wondered.

"Not really. You just put it to the back of your head."

"Is that so? Yes, I know where you're coming from," Pitt replied, thinking of his own family. "You lose somebody into the shadows."

"Yes, yes. You've certainly got a point there, young man."

31

Chippendon yanked at a weather beaten oak door, virtually hanging off its hinges, and clumped inside. He groaned and gestured for Clive to enter the tiny room; his kitchen. He fumbled for an electric switch, but it was still almost dark. There was one small window over a crowded draining-board, but natural light was masked by grime and hanging branches. There was the twitchy noise of an intrepid chicken, stalking about somewhere in the homely gloom.

"It's quite cosy in here," Clive remarked. "Good to get away from the madness of this world...the speed and stress of contemporary life."

"Feels like a bit of a refuge does it? Tho' I need to see a bit of life, I like to see a movie up in town, from time to time. Then there's m'football," he added enthusiastically. "Do you enjoy football?"

"Not for a while," Pitt replied.

Gradually Clive's eyes adjusted to the surroundings. He sat at a heavy oak table, showing rings of centuries. In fact the kitchen was rudimentary; with its squashed stove, various dented pots and pans and an arrangement of tin cans and jars: the place of a solitary old man; with dangling bulbs and stains of winter damp. The only freshness and savour came from boxes of fruit and vegetables. Yet to Clive's eyes the place was endearing, peaceful, even safe. He could almost live his own life in this style, but knew that was an illusion.

Mr Chippendon boiled a kettle, whistled and began to prepare tea. The brew was served up exceedingly hot and sweet. Then Fred took a gasping intake of breath, pulled up the waist of his trousers and slumped happily on the cushioned seat. He revealed a glistening vermillion pate when he scrunched up his floppy hat in a solid brown fist. He was squeezing his own teabag in the mug and sitting across from his visitor.

"Oh, I expect he'll settle up when he's ready," the man insisted cheerfully.

"Winchurch, do you mean? He owes you some wages?" Clive replied.

Chippendon drew on the rim of his tea mug; supping noisily; sighing heavily. "Know the squire, do you?"

"Professionally."

"You're a City gent too?"

"Used to be," Clive replied. "Seen Winchurch about the estate recently?"

"What're you after 'im for?" the gardener asked.

Pitt considered. "Got one or two matters to sort with him."

"Oh? Not seen the squire... not after what happened to his daughter."

"So he's more or less stayed in London?"

"Just once I saw him with some fellas... came down from London...maybe with his partners. Some security people and business men, I'd say."

"They didn't come to visit you?" Clive wondered.

"You must be joking," he guffawed. "No, they was walking about the estate, and then they was down in the trees here."

"I noticed there's a clearing in the copse. Do you go there often?"

"I go in there sometimes. Tidying up the loose wood and looking after the place. The young lady used to go in there a great deal. It was about her favourite spot, I'd say."

"They would kind of hang out there?" Pitt assumed.

"I don't rightly know. But in the summer she was on holidays," he explained. "I would be bending doing something, and there *she* would be. I can tell you she was sometimes with boyfriends. I don't know what they got up to in there," Fred said, "but I've got a good idea. I'm old, but I'm not stupid."

"Did you notice her on the afternoon of Winchurch's garden party?"

"When he had all those important people visiting, do you mean?"

"On the day she was molested, to use your words."

The man struggled to search back. "No I didn't actually set eyes on Emmy that particular afternoon. Poor creature. I kept to this side of the house and gardens on that day...once my work had been done."

Pitt tried to keep the exhaustion and anguish out of his face.

"Sir Septimus required me to do a bit of watering... to smarten up the gardens before his guests arrived. Then he gave me the rest of the day off. He wasn't going to invite a scruffy article like me, when he had all those diplomats and politicians there!"

"He definitely wouldn't!" Clive agreed. He was enjoying the tea, which was strong enough to cure many animal diseases. "Not that I had an official invitation myself," he said.

It was comfortable to be with Mr Chippendon, who was an advert for the sanctuary of old age perhaps. Cheery Fred with his faithful collie, a quaint old cottage and a bit of a garden; as if the subtle methods of the professional killers of ZNT could not reach them.

"Except some evenings I take a walk up to the village. I have a couple of pints in the 'Grenadier'... before I come back home again. They always have the match showing there. I always catch up with my football. I keeps myself to myself in there. But I've got a few friends up there. A couple of ancient fellas like myself," Fred explained, in his dry low voice. "Among the lager drinkin' youngsters."

"So did you notice anything different that evening?" Clive wondered.

"Help yourself to one of those oatie biscuits. That's right," he offered. "Well, poor old Snow here, my collie dog, wouldn't stop snarling and snapping." The canine in question had insinuated itself around the old man's chair, and now cast up a baleful expression.

"Your dog was upset by something?" Clive asked.

"He wouldn't quieten down! Even gave him a tap on the nose, and I haven't done that since he was a puppy... small enough

232

to put in my coat pocket... there was something eerie about it, out of the ordinary. Not long after there was a tapping at the door. Yes that's what happened. Very soft, hardly *hearable*," Fred recalled.

"That's useful. Will you continue?" Clive urged.

"I was sitting in my armchair by the fireplace, when there was this gentle knocking sound. I was startled and Snow began to shrink and whine again. When I finally got to the front door to see, well I found some fella asking me for directions, who wanted to find Close Copse House."

"Did you recognise him? Do you?"

"Some fella looking for Winchurch's garden party, that's who."

"Did this man look anything like me?" Pitt wondered.

"You? Why would I say that?" Fred replied, looking bewildered.

Clive felt his limbs instantly unthaw; his heart retracted. "That's good, that's... a relief."

"Is it? Well, I said that he would need to drive back towards the village...find the front entrance. He couldn't rightly get access to the back of the estate...not by car!"

"I see. So was this bloke a guest at the party? This guy had lost his way?"

"Easy to lose your way around here!"

"What did this bloke look like? Can't you remember?"

"Didn't see him too clearly... my eyes aren't too good. But I did get a glimpse. Yes, I got a look at him all right."

"Can you describe him to me?" Clive persisted, spreading his big aching legs.

"Tall fella. Very tall. Unhealthy."

"Unhealthy? Can you be more precise?"

"Is it important then?" Fred complained.

"It could be," Pitt confirmed. "Sorry to push you like this."

Mr Chippendon reinforced his recollection with another swig of tea, as sludgy as wood water. "In a beautiful silk suit, he was. High heeled boots. Fashionable. A rich looking fella, with a pony tail. Must have been an associate of Sir Septimus." The old chap took another slug of tea as if fully satisfied.

"Can you tell me anything more about him?"

"Those shiny type of sunglasses. But he'd got a nicely trimmed beard, just on the point of his chin it was," Fred remembered. "Very striking."

"Anything else?" Pitt asked.

"Well, he also had a bit of an accent," he added. "So he must have been foreign."

"Right, so he wasn't British. Were you able to locate his accent? Any ideas?"

"Sorry, I can't say what country he came from."

Pitt scraped at the bottom of his jaw. "How old was this guy?"

"Middle aged. A bit eccentric. Creepy. I would certainly say he knew the squire, because he called him Sep and said he was a long-time admirer."

"Did he?" said Pitt. "This bloke wanted to know how to reach the house?"

"That's right. Then later in the afternoon I decided to walk up to the village to see the football... and afterwards to visit my sister in law."

"You're implying that you bumped into this character again?"

"At dusk I left Joan's, my sister in law's place, to return home. It's not safe to walk down the road after dark... after a few glasses. Not so many cars go along there, but it only takes one to knock you over, doesn't it?"

Pitt nodded and sank the remainder of his warm ditch water.

"It was a clear humid evening, as it's been most of this summer. Difficult to walk far in that heat. Then, when I got to the bottom of the hill... I was about to turn up into my lane for a night cap... when I noticed a car parked in the lay-by. An enormous long black motor," he remarked, spreading his thick arms.

"Really, a black limo. You saw this car then, did you?" Clive returned.

"Never seen a car like that before in my life. A beautiful and frightening machine," Fred judged.

"The limousine," Clive breathed to himself.

"Yes, a limousine, that's what you'd call it... so long 'n' sleek you'd think your eyes are deceiving you. Not even Sir Sep'imus has a motor car quite like that one," he grinned.

"Was there anybody in the car? Waiting outside? A chauffeur?"

"A fella in a uniform was standing about," he said, thrashing the old rug of his memory. "A large fella, smoking a cigarette, leaning his elbows on the roof and waiting."

Not often was Fred required to summon up a recent experience as a significant memory.

"Did you approach him? Any idea what he was waiting for?"

"Something warned me off. This chauffeur fella was waiting for something...for somebody. He didn't look as if he wanted to be interrupted... or asked any questions."

"You were a bit alarmed?" Clive said.

"Yes, I was," Fred admitted. "You hardly get anybody stopping here, unless they've got mechanical problems."

"Did the limo have a mechanical problem?" Pitt wondered.

"No, the motor was running!"

"As if they were waiting for something, or somebody?" Clive pressed.

"He was very alert this fella... Resting his elbow, dragging on his ciggie... staring up over the meadow towards Close Copse at the top. Where you came from today," Fred recalled.

"Obviously this wasn't the same guy who knocked at your door."

"No, not the big creepy one, it wasn't. Not the one with the funny beard and accent."

"I met the guy once, but not face to face," Clive said. "What happened after that?"

"I remained hidden at the top of the lane. There was a flaming sunset, a real shepherd's delight. I had a good view where I was... and I was interested to know what that fella was waiting for. Then all of a sudden," Fred exclaimed, mimicking his astonished reaction of the time, "I see'd some shapes running down the meadow. After a while I realised it was that eccentric fella who'd called on me earlier. That's it. Running he was; running like the devil down that field, towards the limousine. That was obviously his car. The chauffeur was waiting for him with the motor turning over."

"You're implying the strange looking guy was not alone," Pitt suggested.

"No, there was another fella with him. It was growing dark by then. I couldn't see their faces clearly... wouldn't in the best of light, at that distance... just their outlines against the sky."

"Was the other guy about my height and build?"

"Couldn't rightly say!" the gardener told him.

"You couldn't identify him?" Pitt declared.

"But I know it was the same eccentric fella."

"Right, the one who knocked at your door... the tall guy, with a pony tail hair style and a bit of a beard on his chin," Pitt summarised.

"It wasn't possible to forget him," Fred remarked, casting a menaced look.

"But you certainly didn't know his companion?"

"Except he kept stumbling and falling to the ground. Looked at the end of his tether and couldn't run much further. Then the creepy fella would go back and drag him up by the arm, and they'd start running again. Must have been running away from something!"

"They both jumped into the car?" Clive persisted.

"Then the chauffeur ran around and they drove away. I fell back into the hedge to hide myself. Lord knows what they would have said or done with me. I just sensed danger," Fred told him.

"Yes, it must have been terrifying."

Mr Chippendon studied his visitor's look, impressed with the impact his story had made, even while shivers still ran down his own aching spine.

"When I see'd those fellas scarpering like that," Fred continued, "I knew that something dreadful or criminal must've happened. Fortunately they drove away too quick to notice me. Then I picked myself out of the hedge... and walked back home again."

"It's the third man who interests me," Clive said. "The one who was being dragged behind."

"I wish I could be more 'elpful to you in your inves'igations," Fred offered.

"That's a pity," Clive said, "but you've been really helpful."

"Do you think that strange fella had anything to do with the attack on Miss Winchurch?" Fred asked.

"Probably," Clive admitted. "Did you speak to anyone about this? The police? Not even Septimus Winchurch?"

"Nobody's been down here. Sir Septimus doesn't have much to do with me anymore," the old man complained.

"You should have told the police," Clive said.

"Just so long as I keep his borders trimmed! Do you think any of 'em listens to me in this village?"

"They had to escape as they entered, at the rear. Where they had their car turning over, ready and waiting. In the limousine, the limousine," he repeated. "With the same chauffeur who stopped me in the City."

A chill passed into his blood and seemed to circulate. His feet, his hands and even his mouth went numb. Why should he suddenly feel so cold on such a hot day? This frightened and perturbed him. He adjusted and shook the sensation away.

"You're a clever detective," Mr Chippendon said.

"Not really," Clive told him. "I don't even have any powers of arrest."

"High powered gentleman is he?" Mr Chippendon wondered.

"Your visitor? Our fella with the winning smile? Most likely," Clive replied.

"I wonder how he makes a living?"

"He makes more than a living," Clive informed him, expelling a long breath.

"One of those types, is he?"

"Are you still employed as a gardener?" Clive asked.

"Haven't been paid in ages... but I keep an eye on it. A married couple from the village is keeping the house clean and tidy."

"The house seems to be closed up today," Clive said.

"Yesterday they were scrubbing the kitchen and shaking off dust sheets. I was by the small pond and they told me to cut some flowers. Sir Septimus is visiting later this evening."

Pitt surprised. "Is he?"

"That's right sir. He's coming to the area again. I believe he's visiting his daughter in hospital today."

"Where's the hospital?" Clive replied.

"The hospital's named after him. Sir Septimus does marvellous things for charity. Paid for that hospital all by himself... so they say. Very generous and warm hearted gentleman, when he's in the right mood, sir."

"He's one charity I would avoid in the street," Clive remarked.

"Wishing you the best of, sir, in your inves'igations."

"Cheers, mate."

"You're welcome, m'friend!"

32

Pitt emerged from Fred's buckling cottage. He followed back along the dry tree-lined path to the road. He experienced a new bloom of cold sweat, while considering Mr Chippendon's account; that evening following the party, after the attack on Emmy Winchurch; with the flaming sunset and a sky striped with hot reds and oranges.

Pitt thought of that sinister guy, running from the scene, dragging along an accomplice. He could be a hedge fund manager, or attached to the deal in some capacity. Pitt couldn't remember such a bearded figure, during the negotiations over the flotation. While he'd been meeting with members of ZNT the most senior figures stayed away, restricting their face to face meetings to Sep.

Clive doubted that Sep could harm Emmy, his own daughter. After all he was his only child and heir. She may have been a bad egg, a 'wild child' to the media, but she was precious to him. One day she would become more like Pixie. Sep doted on Emmy and that was half the problem. Clive knew Emmy had slipped away into the trees with him, Pitt. Something bad had got into them that day, to stir passions. Perhaps the blood test would prove vital, in unmasking some chemical agent or influence on his thoughts and actions.

This foreign accented guy was obviously as mysterious and obscure as wealth and power can be. His actions, and his influence, were as obscure as corporate and non-dom taxing registration loopholes; as tricky as stolen wealth bouncing around in off-shore accounts. He could be as mysterious and out of contact as any private ocean going yacht, when he chose.

Yet this guy, this supra-high-worth-individual, was interfacing with the City to conduct his affairs; as he needed the services of bankers, brokers, lawyers and advisors, while the wealth and influence of this new elite was shaping the world's destiny, as the masters of The New Light Age.

Clive had returned to the village the long way. He sat in the capsule of her pink 911 4S, ignoring the eager faces of the car's controls, thinking things over for a moment.

The sun beat down like a bruised heart, with an insect orchestra at an equal pitch, playing havoc with the A/C. After an elapse he provoked the engine again and snarled away, leaving a small puff of smoke hanging in the dead air.

Pitt had learnt from the gardener that Septimus planned to visit his daughter that very day. But Clive didn't know where the hospital was and assumed that it would be a private establishment anyway. He didn't expect the place to have an accident and emergency division; and he wasn't going to invite himself to another Winchurch tea party either.

Facing uncertain options, other than to remain a scarce commodity, he decided to return to London to await Pixie's return, to get her risky progress report. If Pitt didn't have the location, she might have prised the information from her boss. They already planned to visit the hospital together. Any prying was likely to be dangerous, after Pitt had made himself known again. But he couldn't assume that she had succeeded, or even that she was a free woman.

But then Pitt had some luck when, after getting lost for a while in the lanes and roads, he flashed past an unexpected mansion to the side. His primitive brain registered recognisable shapes, flashing to the side. Then the recent brain was able to form the syllables of *Septimus Winchurch* as if painted across the air. Surely his tired mind was beginning to suffer hallucinations! Pitt turned around, filled his lungs with fresh gas and drove back past to investigate.

Sure enough, his senses were not deceiving him, this was the hospital named in honour of his previous boss. As he cruised by he was able to read the entrance board clearly, which stated the legend of *The Sir Septimus Winchurch ZNT Research Hospital* .

Quite a mouthful; quite a lot to swallow. The building complex had been the original Imperial British Pharmaceuticals research centre, as well as being a private hospital. The fabric here had fallen into disrepair after decades of disuse. Newly acquired by the financier for his ZNT clients, the building had obviously received investment, been restored and improved, was newly equipped and operational. Why had the place received a cash injection when the group's old properties had been almost derelict? Pitt would have advised them to sell the land and capitalise on remaining assets, as part of reconsolidation and rationalisation of the group. He couldn't guess the type of research conducted at the establishment now, or how it was being administered, or the type of 'patients' that were admitted.

Why was a hedge fund like ZNT, with a registered HQ in Geneva, prepared to invest money into a research hospital in southern England? Why not stick to the treasure of intellectual property that they had acquired? They profited hugely from patents and products, without putting money into bricks and mortar or getting involved in actual medicine. What was their thinking?

Even looking from the fence, he observed new fabric, modifications; a complete transformation of the site. The shell of an old industrial unit and medical test centre had been recently upgraded into a contemporary high-tech centre. Clive was surprised by the investment strategy. He had assumed that the acquisition of BIP was related to asset stripping and resale.

Clive wanted to know their areas of research or innovation. Was the place a five star clinic for the hyper rich? A ritzy hotel-hospital offering state of the art cures, amidst the leafy privacy of the English countryside? Then what sort of diseases, illnesses or maladies did they treat? Winchurch himself was an outspoken public critic of public health, so it was unlikely that NHS patients were treated. Clive was confident that Emmy must be registered as a patient and be staying there. They had taken him to this hospital in the recent past, he assumed, following a beating in the toilets of a football stadium. They caught up with him after they had disturbed him hacking into the firm's computer systems. He couldn't remember anything about those experiences, but he might owe his freedom - his present precarious liberty - to an escape from the institution. Clive didn't believe that the new hospital had been established to benefit 'ordinary patients', so to speak, or even the NHS (of which the financier was an outspoken and public critic). He might unwittingly be making their task of finding him easier. Maybe they intended to put him back into a secure unit.

Yet there was a definite prestige attached to this project for Sep. The idea of putting his name to the hospital - acting as its benefactor or sponsor - would very much appeal to the egotistic philanthropist, as glucose to a wasp.

Emmy was stashed away in a safe ward, as hidden from danger and the media eye as his own recent memory. She wasn't staying here for rest and recovery. Pitt didn't believe any such idea. Why not allow her to go off on another backpacking adventure around Asia or South America? Why file her away in this Las Vegas style hospital? Sep didn't want to attract any media or police investigation into the crime, that heinous attack. He rightly feared that prying questions would eventually centre on the deal. The deal was in the background, even if the financier sought to deny that. He feared that the press would show its good campaigning face, rather than its ugly ruthless side. And his new found allies at ZNT, snapping up BIP, as well as several seats on the Winchurch Brothers' board, would also want to avoid media exposure. The aim was to protect his family and professional reputation at all costs, and Sep would be desperate to keep his secret; he bizarrely regarded the rape of his own daughter as a shameful and dangerous secret.

Winchurch would argue that he was doing the child some good. He wouldn't wish to deliberately harm her. His aim was to help her to be happy and successful in life. He wanted the whole family to be proud of Esmeralda, maybe in the mould of a Pixie Wright, as everybody at the firm knew. His paternal devotion took a misguided form perhaps, when he talking about employing her, after she'd been moulded through education. Unfortunately the expensive Swiss finishing schools had been judged anachronistic and mostly closed. But while Sep pushed her towards the LSE or even to Maastricht, the girl was more inclined towards social sciences, according to Pixie. He was terrified of producing a social worker, or even a socialist teacher, even though that was better than a type of hippie drop-out, Occupy character.

Pitt felt he had been incarcerated. He had no specific recollection of any treatment or programme, or interior impressions of the hospital or staff. They moved to plug the leaks, when they began to feel his presence around their systems. They wanted to eliminate 'Lucifer' before shock and embarrassment turned to actual disaster, and the key facts of the BIP flotation began to stick to the media wall.

Even for Clive, when he moved down to London, Sep posed as his benefactor, even surrogate father or older brother; rescuing him from the narrow prospects of that gloomy old mill town, as the financier regarded it. Initially he attempted to forgive Pitt's capital sins, as it were, when the young man first turned against him. Forgiveness of misconduct, obscurity for the miscreant, was the banker's effective response. Sep wanted to avoid any such messy scandal in the City and the financial world beyond, that posed terminal, hard-to-predict risks for his historic family company. He would go to great lengths to protect the reputation of his ancestors, as well as his family's future and inheritance. Pitt's arguments were a snake bite.

33

Once again Clive left the car behind - glinting in a concealed spot - so he might explore on foot. He froze in his tracks at the sight of a security post, complete with barber's pole and uniformed guard. To avoid a direct encounter he cut away to the side, across the grounds, taking care to negotiate electrified fences. He didn't try any experimental touches, as he noticed the carcass of a horse nearby.

It was a no-brainer that security officers would be patrolling the site. So he had to remain vigilant and as concealed as possible. For a well-heeled young investment banker in the middle of a field this was quite difficult. Any feeling of personal security was as elusive as a cool breeze in these parts. The grounds of the hospital were extensive, somewhat wild in places, which allowed him to move about; at least as soon as he kangaroo-kicked over that charged wire.

At the back of the main building he found an orchard and a garden. As he pushed through tall dry grass he saw a crowd of people, about twenty of them, assembled there. Even from that distance he could see they were a variegated crowd. Light music wafted on the air, as if surfing heat waves. The soporific patients were set out on cane furniture, taking shade under stiff canvas and enjoying rounds of cool drinks. They were attended by men and women in green uniforms - nurses? - as well as by occasional white coated figures. The assemblage formed a serene if unsettling picture, as he noticed that only staff were mobile or able to communicate; the 'patients' were catatonic or sedated.

Clive understood that his sudden appearance would have a startling effect. The doctors would be surprised to see him again perhaps. His dress sense would stand out too, even if he breached Winchurch Brothers' dress code; which was traditional down to the black socks; even a pair of smudged spectacles would draw a reprimand. His shoe leather survived, but his trousers and shirt were in stained strips (despite some shop creases). His rag of thick blonde hair was up in a mess - and not that cute 'just out of bed' look either. No wonder Mr Chippendon had felt relaxed with him. Pitt didn't quite blend into the City jungle any more. They had definitely subjected him to a bit of a ragging, trying to put him back into his place.

Nevertheless he strode across the grounds, that coarse brown pampas grass, aiming towards the central hospital building. If not for his costume they would take him as another patient; a mental patient most likely, with his wild hair and manic expression. Yet could he really describe the inmates as "patients"? Taking Emmy and himself as examples? However, one person's brilliant thought could be an insane notion to somebody else.

He was an impetuous, bold, maybe recklessly self-convinced character. A feeling of injustice put a tight fire in his chest, provoked brief blackouts and formed hot and cold sensations. Yet he was anxious about approaching the staff and patients directly. It was a potential minefield of nervous detection, which could lead to his incarceration. He was daunted by the slim odds of encountering Emmy here. Thus for all his fixated energy, Pitt knew it would be difficult to interview her and even more difficult to approach the truth.

As he sidled along an ivy covered wall, he bumped in to a white coated figure. The guy came towards him, moving rapidly, absent minded, when he collided into Pitt. The doctor's face went through many shocked emotional reactions. Until Clive sensed the danger, lifted the guy up by his lapels and plugged him. The doctor was projected backward on to the ground. He wouldn't have suffered too badly if not for the edge of a paving stone. The medic groaned and rolled about and shortly dropped into unconsciousness.

Clive was hampered because the white coat was too small for him. Sleeves drew tightly up his arms, he couldn't do up the buttons. His appearance was even more alarming; he resembled a lunatic in charge of the asylum. Yet it was a credible disguise, he calculated, which could give him access to wards; he didn't have any other options. Pitt lifted the guy up, dragged him along and pushed him into an opened waste bin, ensuring the lid was wedged shut afterwards.

Fifty metres ahead he noticed a wicker gate that lead into the orchard. Pitt reached this feature, unfastened a mechanism and secured it again, in the genteel fashion of a caring white-coated medic. But he was disconcerted to hear the dim moans of his victim in the rubbish bin - the true medic. Strains of musak piped and drifted eerily around the trunks of fruit trees. He convinced himself that any groans of misery would pass unnoticed on the atmosphere; or merely blend into the other vocal complaints.

Pitt strolled watchfully under and between limbs of apple, cherry and pear trees. He progressed with hands professionally behind his back (if only to keep the XS coat in place). He inspected that cosmopolitan group of patients. These people were extremely varied he noted, in terms of ethnicity and nationality. The unfortunates were scattered under the branches, enjoying any cool thread or movement of air. They whiled away the endless hot hours in a narcotic daze. Despite the white coat he adroitly avoided members of staff.

Unable to find a suitably reassuring word for these people Clive moved on a pace. He could only hope to recognise Emmy by his memory of her photograph; the luminous close up portrait. But despite a number of circles around the orchard he couldn't find her among this group. Maybe she didn't want to mix with the others, due either to her treatment or to her temperament. No doubt she would rebel against her loss of control, and the idea of being incarcerated. He didn't want to draw attention to himself and so decided to leave them all in peace.

Pitt left that curiously global collection of souls. Even if there had been a chance to speak, many of them were probably not native or fluent English speakers. He couldn't speak other languages, like Pixie, unfortunately. Why did the medical company wish to gather them together? Business has become entirely globalised, so why not the medical industry - was this their thinking? Only the nomination of a corporate HQ linked them to any specific place.

A set of large French windows was opened, allowing air to circulate around a recreation and television room within. Clive slipped inside and headed across the wooden boarded room, pushed through swinging doors and emerged into a regular hospital corridor. Pitt struggled to adjust to a radical change in temperature and lighting. The rooms along the corridor varied; some were private wards or rooms, he supposed. With a quick investigation he realised that other doors led into laboratories, or anyway rooms that contained much equipment, including imaging brain scanners. There were many of these iconic machines. The facilities came as a surprise. He understood that the focus of research was on human beings. He'd presumed a focus on the development of drugs. British Imperial Pharmaceuticals had produced numerous leading brands of medical products. All these copyrights were now owned by ZNT.

Shortly a young guy in a grey coat, a porter, rushed towards him in the corridor, in a panic. "Can you get over to B Ward doc? It's Protocol C. There's a chinky lady throwing a fit down there... screaming, throwing up; you name it! She's been jacketed as well. I've been told to get some help... and there's nobody around the place!"

"All right, so what's the matter with her?" Pitt tossed back.

"Just part of her programme, doc. She doesn't bloody like it though, that's all. I don't ask any questions. Should you give her a jab up the fucking arse?"

"No, no, don't give her any more jabs!"

"They need you over there..." the porter read off a name badge on Clive's bursting white coat. "Doctor McGregor!"

"No, not now mate. I'm taking a break. Why don't you find another doctor outside?" Pitt began to move off furtively.

"What's the fucking matter? Nice life for some of us, isn't it, eh doc?" he protested.

"I can get over to B Ward...as soon as I deliver a message to Emmy Winchurch. Can you remind me where to find her room? What number is she in?"

"You're going to have to move quickly, Dr McGregor. Patient 305 is throwing a bloody fit, refusing to take anything orally, shouting at us...in her own language...it's a slaughter house. They've got a tube down her throat, necklace and wristlets, the lot...but she still won't fucking quieten down... not for all the tea in China."

"I promise to get over there when I can. I'll even give her another jab, if they want. Just tell me where to find Esmeralda Winchurch. I've got a message from her father."

"250's in C Ward, B43. Beg your pardon Doctor, but don't bloody hang around, will you?"

"Go and find yourself another doctor," Pitt suggested.

"Fuck off," he called back.

Pitt was grateful to see the panicked employee depart - sucked into the vortex of a long corridor. What sort of hospital presented this carnival of horrors? Or was it merely a harrowing image of a disturbed patient? Clive was no psychiatrist, despite his bursting white coat, but he doubted the second prognosis.

To find Emmy's room by those internal numbers and codes was difficult. Any calmer member of staff would spot him as an imposter. He couldn't afford to stand about and scratch his head. But it was while he paced ahead, shoving through sets of fire doors, that Pitt got a nasty shock, as he recognised the shape, the approaching form of Sir Septimus Winchurch.

Unknown to Clive of course, the financier had already arrived at the institution with Pixie Wright. The pair were being guided to the girl's room by a senior doctor and support staff. At this stage Clive didn't know that Pixie was also with the party. Fortunately his old boss was separated by layers of glass and timber. The financier was yet too distant and absorbed in conversation to be aware of uninvited guests. Yet his approach - or their potential reunion - felt distressingly imminent.

Pitt was frozen in amazement for a while, wondering what to do. Sep bore down on him, eating up the corridors with insufferable under-sized jauntiness.

Clive's wherewithal returned and, instinctively, he tried to hide. He slipped into a further side room, out of view, to allow that hostile visiting party to go safely by. Through the last inch of an opening, clicking the door shut behind him, Pitt stole a glimpse of Winchurch. He took an instant image of the financier's darting, skipping gait. Luckily Sep was preoccupied with the occasion.

Clive turned about to investigate this new space; took a breath. The room was west facing and sunlit. There was a breeze from large windows thrown wide. As his sight adjusted to intense natural light, he slowly distinguished the shape and the presence of a girl. She was wearing torn jeans and a *Nirvana* tee-shirt, while she was sitting up on a tall chair by the side of a metal frame bed. She seemed to be alert and relaxed, propped against several pillows, reading a manga book.

She gave the idea of sensing a new visitor, but didn't turn her eyes up to investigate. She presumed he was another member of staff, as he'd entered discreetly and was wearing a white coat. There was a feeling that she was dressed and ready to receive guests.

Could this be Emmy Winchurch? There was a strong resemblance. Had he really blundered into her space? If so then Winchurch and his guests would be heading exactly in this direction. They would catch him in the room with her. There couldn't be a more disastrous outcome. Did he have enough time now to slip back outside?

Yet, for the present moment, the girl accepted his presence without moving or without looking up. There was a suspended peaceful atmosphere. She was too caught up in her book to take notice of interruptions. They were joined together anonymously by a moment of unreality; locked and detached.

There was a chance he was jumping to alarming conclusions. There was no solid proof that the girl was she. Sunlight had dazzled him. For days his vision had been under an assault course. He struggled with the light, as if with the blinding spray of surf. But in this perilous situation he just felt dread, no mix of exhilaration.

He listened to the pattern of her soft relaxed breathing, as his heart rate accelerated. He seemed to be stuck in a wait and see mode. There was a sense that she refused to look at him. It was a sign of her rebellion, her hostility or indifference towards staff, or the type of treatment she was receiving. If only he could ask her. Clive shifted position in an attempt to gain her attention and to finally identify her. Even though it was a nervous situation, he had broken into the hospital with an intention to find her and to talk. Here was an opportunity to question her about the events of the garden party; about his role in that dreadful crime, not only about her course of treatment or therapy.

Minutes later (it felt like hours) the girl turned her eyes up from the page. Her gaze began to wander about the room and to explore. Finally her attention was drawn to that member of staff, a dishevelled blonde doctor in a white coat several sizes too small. The guy was leaning against the wall, staring at her without speaking and giving off a panicky feeling.

The ideas and treatments at this place often frightened her. She wasn't sure if the proposed operations were such a great idea or, as they all claimed, in her best future interests (whatever those were). She wasn't thrilled to let them mess with her head. But the staff here would greet her when they came into the room. Nobody listened to her views, but they were polite and professional. They wouldn't inject you and put you through a scanner, or any of the other stuff, without at least using your name. Just from loneliness or boredom, even isolation, she might return their empty sentiments.

But when she set eyes on this doctor, she made a horrible recognition. She recognised this guy and she was completely alone with him. His presence caused a paroxysm of terror, hysteria, as if the most poisonous spider in the world was dancing on a string in front of her nose.

She stood up and backed her chair noisily into the wall. Head splitting noises came out of a pouty mouth. The terrifying reality of Pitt's presence cut into her memories. Clive gazed intensely at the oval of her freckled face, with the patched blonde/black hair, the large golden brown eyes. These were no doubt beautiful eyes, now wide in terror - just at the sight of him.

There was not chance to speak to her. She was so frightened he wouldn't be able to even calm her. Pitt shrank away beneath her screams, holding up his palms. All the time she fixed him with huge terrified eyes. Her gaze slid around with him. She emitted a shrill cry with every new step. He backed off blindly, circled the walls, bumping into a trolley and spilling glass instruments. These objects shattered on a hard floor, as if disintegrated into dust, with his thoughts and nerves.

Pitt knew he'd seen her face before, not only in a photograph, if at all. His recognition was as unmistakable as hers. Her lovely face was not far away, suffused by the beams of sunshine. Suddenly he had an image of her, a terrible image, of her hanging from a low branch, twining about. Grotesquely somebody - Pitt didn't remember who, perhaps himself! - covering her eyes, with a bag or a cloth or a garment.

But he was shaken back to his senses; her piercing disgust placing him back into her hospital room. She had moved from the chair and pressed herself into a corner of the room; scrunched into the tiniest space, while pushing a fist into her mouth. Pitt forced himself to snatch back his gaze as if to keep his sanity.

Fight or flight took over for him, as he sensed Winchurch charging towards them and standing behind the door. The medical group had surely heard her screaming, even through thick divisions. Inevitably they'd been alerted and would soon burst inside. Of course there was no inside lock to the room. It was a no-win siege situation even if he had time to block the door. Pitt saw that his only escape was through the open outside windows.

There were voices from the corridor. They were gathering outside, because he picked up their concerned and shocked voices. What a nasty surprise the banker was going to suffer. Clive plunged across the room, by the girl's shoulder - she raised her arms around her face - and he jumped out through the window frame. It should have been easy, but in panic he didn't get a good take off step. One time he made a charity sky dive with Noreen. That had required a short countdown and a quick prayer.

He landed in an undignified heap outside, eating gravel off the path. Wincing at the pain he hobbled away, but with increasing momentum. He felt the brutal thump of his heart muscle, like a misshapen foetus. He battled for momentum, to push his legs into movement. In his imagination, somehow, he was running towards his guilt, not so much escaping from his enemies.

When he was confident of being safe (most staff remained in the orchard) he looked back around. The group must have entered to rescue or comfort the girl. He picked out the diminutive outline of Winchurch within. Even from there Clive noticed the frantic body language, as the banker moved about the space, apparently trying to comfort his daughter. Then another white coated figure joined him.

Gazing out towards Clive from the open window, was the unmistakable figure of Pixie Wright. As soon as she distinguished Pitt in the near distance, she was stared out in an expression of frozen amazement.

This was a bad outcome. She already had doubts. Whatever her feelings for him, she would think he was a liar. She'd almost been ready to join his team again, to accept him as her mentor, but she hadn't fully signed up. Now she would adopt the official Winchurch line about his conduct. This wouldn't make a good impression.

But the lost year had not been revealed so clearly. There were many remaining shadows and pockets of darkness. He was linked to the crime and to harming the girl. The most favourable interpretation he could draw was that he'd been forced to participate.

34

Clive was shaken. His resolve was severely tested. He fitted a description of the odious guy they claimed him to be.

His accidental encounter with the Winchurch girl had been a catastrophe. Not only did it plunge her back into a nightmare experience, it put him into the situation as well. But not clearly enough to know the exact circumstances.

Should he continue to investigate the deal? Could he believe in himself, enough to exonerate himself? Did his bad or weak character undermine his case against the firm? Could principles be obliterated by emotional flaws and monstrous behaviour?

He was tempted to share the view of his enemies.

Pitt imagined that he understood himself fairly well; at least as well as anybody does. But was that self-knowledge no more than a false belief system? Did he really know himself at all? This was the crux of it.

He felt intensely ashamed of running away. He was conscious of his renegade isolation. Every breath oppressed him, through the cage of his chest. Apparently he didn't have an emotional support system; any true friends or family. This was not self-pity, but a glance at shattered pieces left on the hard floor.

Pixie would have to abandon him, delete her links to him, before it was too late. She was already leading a charmed life at the company. Clive had objected to cheating in the global casino, but he was a criminal himself. Her previous sympathy towards Clive had been dangerous. Any loyalty at this stage would be lethal, not simply hard to justify or explain.

Was there any belief in his innocence, or any hope he was not culpable? If he was just running to save his own skin, there was no point. Maybe he should be done with everything by handing himself over at a police station in London. He could present himself and explain his involvement with the rape of Emmy.

However this would only work if the police believed his story. They didn't have any record of such a crime taking place. Septimus chose not notify them to start an investigation. His attitude was not going to change, as he still had the same motives. So what was Pitt's incentive to talk to the police, or even to remain within the law? He didn't think handing himself to the authorities would progress his case. Clive preferred to remain elusive rather than to surrender to private security firms or psychopaths with air miles.

Was this the moment to relocate internationally? Why insist on his British life when powerful figures were hunting him down? He potentially had the information to destroy them, but where had he placed it? Apparently his files were lost, yet his enemies didn't understand or wish to understand. But as soon as they tested this fact, they would dispense with his services altogether. It was much more difficult as a fugitive. They were surely alert to any move to the ports. Did he have any ideas? Any contacts?

Pitt reached the edge of the grounds again and found a gap in the perimeter fence, as he read that dark legend again, *The Sir Septimus Winchurch ZNT Research Hospital.*

What if his extreme behaviour was induced by drugs or hormonal injections? His mind was troubled, confused and under duress. He had absorbed information about his character and investigation. Amnesia made him biddable. As ZNT marked his cards his mental images and ideas had shuffled into a confusing sequence. If Emmy had been calmer she may have explained more. The picture was more complicated. Could she recognise other men who may also have been present?

It was hard to contradict the firm opinion of other people. They formed convincing views about his character. Was it worth struggling to prove them wrong? Trying to roll back all those events?

His enemies had induced this flaw. But unwittingly he had been participating. This began when he considered pulling the pin on ZNT. They had recognised the immediate danger of his insider subordination. They calculated his toxicity and decided he must be dumped, as if for drums of cyanide in an African landfill. He had to be quietly rendered harmless, through disgrace at home and work. They were skilled at removing executives who proved incompetent or undependable. It was better to expose a traitor than to contest openly with him (or her).

But those guys in Geneva wouldn't have tried this without good material to go on. They must have probed for his flaws, in order to reveal them, just as you can't buy out a company that hasn't a viable product or service, even if you are going to break them apart as soon as you acquire a majority holding.

He could be the victim of brain washing here, or an equivalent intervention. They had messed with his head, just as they were doing with Emmy. They wanted to put him out into the dark, by persuading him to act against his own interests to undermine his own case. Unfortunately the case had vanished into hyperspace.

Septimus and his clients needed to erase all evidence and protect themselves fully.

Until then it was just one man and his missing memory.

Returning to Pixie's wheels Pitt was astonished to notice somebody waiting on the passenger side. Drawing nearer Clive noted a handsome young guy. This character was looking sharp and relaxed. The dapper character reclined in the soft white leather, laughing crookedly through the windscreen. It seemed as if he was expecting Pitt, or even knew him. Far from looking nervous the character was super confident and mocking. He resembled a preening fashion gigolo.

Clive pounced on the driver's door - the security was disabled - tearing it back to reach inside and try to pull this fellow out of the car.

"Hey, Clive! What kept you? Don't mind me dropping in, d'you?"

Pitt intended to get into the guy's face, but instantly regretted it. He knew at once that he wouldn't succeed. Like eyeballing a psycho in the rugby scrum, Clive felt that it would be a mistake to attack. Pitt wouldn't come off best in such a tussle.

"Calm down Clive!" the guy urged. "You intolerant sonovabitch! Your anger gets the better of you." His swarthy handsome face creased into a sarcastic smile. "You'd better get out of here. Let's burn some rubber, man. You can ask questions later!"

"You're coming with me?" Clive challenged. He leant into the ergonomic shell of the driver's seat.

"Here for the ride!" the guy jeered; twinkly eyes narrowed sarcastically.

"Did you see security guards around here?" Pitt enquired.

"Don't take any chances."

Pitt's metabolism was hammering. He was drenched in adrenaline. It was painful to remain still. He slammed the door, belted up and ignited the car impetuously. The Porsche's back wheels screamed under stress and tossed up a plume of suffocating dust into the baked air behind.

"Fucking way to go!" the intruder shouted.

In no time the hospital site was behind them and he was snaking the lanes, sliding on gravelly corners.

"Trying to frighten me? How fucking pathetic."

"Are you enjoying yourself? Who are you?" Pitt challenged.

"I enjoy sharing the fast lane with you banker boys. You know how to live fast and retire early. I'm getting a kick out of this," he said, punching Pitt's arm.

"What do you want?" Clive returned.

"You know what we want, Clive," he leered. He gazed into the driver's mirror and perfected his quiff of jet black hair.

"You belong to the ZNT board? Your face is somehow familiar."

"That's excellent Clive," he exclaimed, laughing disproportionately. "You gotta head for faces after all!"

Pitt tried to concentrate on the road and also to observe his unique passenger.

"How did you manage to get in here? Into the car?" he pressed, darting his glance across.

"Are you for real?" the man scoffed.

"You think you're God's gift, is that it?" Pitt scoffed.

"Get back on the motorway," he suggested.

"You're too big for your short breeches, mate," Clive retorted.

"Last time I was with Mr Di Visu. You lost track?"

"You'd better start explaining yourself, pretty boy."

"That's right, you're not really handsome yourself." At this the young guy thrust forward his jaw. "Go on then, Clive. Don't like it? Be my guest! Violence brings strangers together. So let's get close."

"Okay... don't want to be unsociable," Clive retorted, gathering his energy.

Clive took a hand from the wheel forming a fist. But the guy grasped his wrist. Pitt suffered excruciating pain, as if all the nerves up his arm had been ripped. He was suddenly unable to do anything, other than wait for the agonising pressure to stop and to try to avoid crashing his girlfriend's Porsche.

"Got that shit out of your system? You won't pull any chicks with that face."

"Did you just give me an electric shock?" Clive asked, panicked.

"I'm wired up," the young guy explained.

Clive threw a throbbing hand back on the wheel, to avoid slamming into an approaching bridge.

"You want to get us both killed?" he demanded.

"Who paid your fat salary and fatter bonuses? If you're such a virtuous shit, me old marrow, why enjoy the rewards so much? Why wine and dine, travel and have fun?"

As Clive was provoked a rough electrical current shot along his arm and gripped his entire body.

"Give this shit a break!" Clive urged.

"I think you're going to come!" the man exclaimed. "Hey, look at you, you're orgasmic!"

The Porsche lurched; swerved, careened across lanes, ending up bumping along the slipway. Pitt was going into hyper panic, while his passenger laughed and had fun.

Then the car practically stopped in the first lane. Effectively they were parked on the motorway, with HGVs bearing down on them from behind. Trucks screeched and snaked, loads slamming and sliding inside containers; drivers going apoplectic; blasting their sirens, shouting through windows. Until Pitt was shocked back to the present moment, scurried to fire the engine and gain speed.

"Trying to take *yourself* out, Clive?" The guy rested his head and chuckled, as if he reminiscing on a sun lounger.

"What the hell, why don't you end this?" Clive said.

"You've lost your memory. Don't you remember?"

"You were with me that evening? When we attacked Emmy? Is that it?" Clive accused. "I have a witness account."

"We have shared memories! How romantic."

"You are going to pay for this," Clive replied.

"You think driving fast can frighten me? In your girlfriend's pink Porsche?" he mocked, with contempt in his voice.

"This is how I normally drive," Clive said.

"Then you need fucking lessons. You need a fucking refresher course, Clive."

"You can say that again," Pitt replied.

"Viktor wants to help. We mean to help you get your memory back. We buy you a nice meal, you see that, and that don't mean you own the restaurant. Do you understand the principle?" he sneered.

"Who's Viktor when he's *dining*?" Pitt asked.

"Mr Di Visu wants the files back... or the copies that you made of his information... which you stole from your employer. He likes you...or he used to."

"He sounds barmy. You're a friend of his, are you?"

"I'm who you want to be," he said.

"A narcissistic poser like you?" Clive scoffed.

"Yes, come on, Clive!" he said, gesturing.

"Come on, what?" he declared.

"Aren't I everything you despise in a man? When women look at me they swoon. You're fucking envious. You want to smash my face in."

"Don't flatter yourself, mate," Clive replied.

"My looks, my charm, my wealth, my power. I've got everything you ever dreamed about."

"My whole life was on credit," Clive noted.

"Admit it. You think I need a pussy pink car like this one? We drink champagne out of a car like this," he said.

"Be my guest," Clive said.

"What chance do you stand with the pretty women, when I'm around?"

"My aim is to end ZNT. I'm not competing. I'm going to get you kicked off the FTSE."

"Nobody is going to listen to a deviant like you, Clive," he insisted.

"That's your idea?"

The guy laughed loudly and exorbitantly. "We understand you better than you ever understood yourself. We have you by the short and Achilles heel."

"How can you know me like that?" Clive asked.

"What a loser you are!" he growled.

"But I'm the bloke who has the evidence. It can be retrieved," Pitt warned.

"Just couldn't keep your hands off that lovely young girl, could you? Shame on you, Clive," he jeered. "You wanted revenge, but your throbbing dick got in the way. Big tits and a come-hitcher look, that's all it took to sink you and your campaign. What a disgrace, you fucking weak minded little cunt hound."

Every word reverberated in Pitt's left ear. "I just want to find my wife again," Clive insisted.

"A woman? Your wife? How are these going to help you? The world's most untrustworthy banker?"

"She's my strength," Pitt argued.

"Huh, don't make me laugh. You dropped her for that secretary in the office."

"She isn't a secretary," Clive insisted. "She's a respected professional."

"You couldn't wait to rip through her underwear and have sex with her."

"That only happened because my wife left me. Don't ask me why that happened. She went off to America... with some guy."

"Your pretty girl secretary doesn't have the full picture. Not like Emmy Winchurch."

"What are you trying to say?" Clive replied, glaring and squeezing the wheel.

"What I'm trying to say is that you hate women too. That's right, you hear correctly. No need to get upset. You think women are another race! Another species! "

"That's utter crap, mate. There are some women who wouldn't agree," Pitt retorted.

"Maybe you don't understand how much."

"You're talking bollocks," Clive said.

"Shall we ask Emmy Winchurch?" the guy laughed.

"I think women love me," Clive argued.

"You fuck them, all right, but you don't love them," he grinned.

"What do you know about it? About me?" Clive shuffled uneasily, shifted his slick hands and stared towards the crest of the road.

"Come on, you're a City boy. Testosterone makes you boys tick. Big decisions and big bucks give you a big erection. You went to after-hours parties where the lovely girls were drunk and drugged up? They'd do anything, everything for a rich banker... and not remember a thing. You've partaken in illegal games and adventures, with all those other guys, haven't you?"

"That's never really been my scene," Pitt insisted.

"You have to let off steam. With an unlimited bank account the imagination is no limit. Wealth fires your lust. The adrenaline of the floor. It's an aphrodisiac for the lovely girls. Why have riches when you can't satisfy your lust? Pretty girls wanting a handsome pay out. What female resources available! After you've finally left the office at night," he remarked.

The youngster revealed perfect squared teeth in a ridiculing smile.

"I'm a married man...was a married man...."

"There was a lot of fun around the East End," he recalled.

"Girls are another commodity to be traded?" Clive said. "You'd give them a share price if that was possible," he remarked.

"Rather, as you might say, you don't have your third leg to stand on!"

"You remind me of a woman yourself," Clive remarked.

"Yes, yes, and do you like me?" he asked, beaming victoriously.

"Not very much," Clive admitted.

"Way to fucking go. But don't worry because we're guys together. We're fucking drunk and out of control, sticking notes into the girls' g strings. Don't be one of these ridiculous hypocrites."

"I guess there's a certain truth in that," Clive admitted.

"We are the perfect companions of beautiful young women.... of any nationality," the man argued. "We are what they want!"

"I don't want to be like you guys," Clive told him.

"Oh no!?"

"You only have your fun because... you fear you may be dead in the morning."

"Life is killing you now, in your boring existences... sweating to cover your heating bills. You have your mouth on the tit of our oil and gas."

"Not until the fat lady sings," Clive said.

"Oh God, the fat lady just had her last orgasm. Now she's on dying on her back," he joked. "How shall I put this?" the young guy considered. "Mm, let me see... you are properly fucked, Clive, my man."

Pitt was silent. He tried to focus on driving, keeping to the lane, as normality slipped by at regular speeds.

"We liked you at first. We had respect for your abilities. You were, y'know, almost a brother to us," he mocked.

"How exactly?" Pitt wanted to know.

"Just don't go around boasting of being such a lady killer."

"I lost more than my inhibitions," Clive reminded him.

"If you turn traitor, City boy, then you have to pay a surcharge."

"You failed to cover your tracks, mate."

The guy leant closer to the driver's side. "You're speaking total bullshit," he shouted. Saliva flicked off his tongue, burning Pitt's dry cheek. "We wanna bring a little sadness and confusion into your life... and to the Winchurch girl."

"You've succeeded," Clive observed.

"Didn't we! Didn't we, just." He nodded as if to salute himself.

"You are the experts."

"As for the rape of that girl," he said, shrugging his shoulders. Then he chuckled.

"What are you implying?"

"She was a real little slut," he snarled. "We wouldn't fuck with your life, without a reason. Why does that old man think so much of her? Well, that's all right with us, if he wants to be the sentimental father. You broke our security and stole our thoughts, okay. We didn't know your secrets until you had ours. Isn't that true?"

They came into London. Pitt didn't know how much longer this guy was going to stick around. Clive wanted to know if the missing year could be restored, or at least if his life could be repaired.

"It's time for me to go! ... I'm sure you have your plans."

"You are going to leave me here?" Clive was incredulous.

"You have a job to do. Didn't you realise that?" the guy told him.

"You're using me to damage Winchurch?"

"You're still an employee? Why did you decide to duplicate your memory, anyhow?" he demanded.

"I'll get my memory back," Clive promised.

"We will help you," promised the sharp young man.

"You intend to catch up with me again?"

"We shall meet again...wasn't that a little war time song of the Brits? Blue bird over the white cliffs of Dover. *Is* there even a fuckin' blue bird in this country?"

"When exactly are we supposed to meet again?"

"Dig a bit deeper my friend," he said.

"You're not taking me out?"

"Won't you play like a gentleman, Clive?"

"You don't think I can invalidate your UK assets? If I can turn my dossier over to the relevant authorities?"

"Who's listening? Go watch another football match. Think hard about your memory. Then we'll ask you for our stolen property."

Traffic streamed and shoppers went about their business along the high-street, just as normal.

"What if I refused to let you?" Clive suggested. "Maybe I should drive you directly to the police station."

The guy found this threat most hilarious.

"So long Clive. We'll meet again!"

35

Pitt decided to return to Pixie's apartment, merely to return her car - which certainly had extra miles and adventures on the clock.

He began to reconstruct her probable movements. She must have returned to London by now. Surely she didn't believe in his innocence any longer.

So he slipped back her pink Porsche and returned to the west London street. Fragments of the barrier, smashed when he'd roared through, were still scattered and brushed into the gutter. After telling a right story to a passer-by he managed to borrow a phone and attempted to call her. Ironically he could only be regarded as a normal citizen by complete strangers, if they had a relaxed attitude to clothing.

Clive learned how she'd visited the hospital with Winchurch, as he had glimpsed. Pixie was the only link to the real world, he realised, or to his old normal life or however that could be described. She might lead him to the truth and help him to escape this nightmare. Or he could put her back into harm's way too, as he feared. In the world of international politics and business there was near gender equality in assassination risk. Pixie Wright was in danger of getting a return visit by those brutal investigators, tipped off by recent events.

Pitt got a connection and she picked up. He was relieved, but not surprised, as she wouldn't recognise the source of this call. To his surprise she didn't hang up at first recognition of his voice, while he awkwardly reintroduced himself. There wasn't the dead flat tone as expected. To his surprise she listened and even made sympathetic noises.

Pitt stood around the side of her apartment block, like a street criminal, trying to make sure that the owner of the phone couldn't overhear. It was unlikely that the guy would make any sense of his account. He struggled to make himself heard above evening traffic. A hot wind swirled litter, dust and leaves around him.

Clive got the sense that she had moved on in the story. There was a fresh note of sympathetic anxiety in her voice. She was already at a more advanced place, where he needed to catch up. Pitt didn't know how she had achieved this advance, but he would like to hear how.

"No, I can't let you upstairs this evening. Not back into my apartment. No, it's literally too dangerous," she confirmed. "What I mean is… that they are suspicious about me. I defended you this afternoon with Sep. He's suspicious definitely suspicious. They made sure I returned home alone. You know, perhaps they are watching me," Pixie told him.

"What do you suggest? Any idea?" he declared, trying to avoid interference.

"You spend the rest of your money, literally check into a hotel and get yourself a hot shower, all right?"

"Are you serious? Pixie you're making this sound like a date," he objected.

"Why not think about this as a date?" she replied.

He considered. "Let's hope that those bloody gooseberries don't try to join our party. Otherwise we might be caviar and toast," he commented.

"Certainly, Clive. If we meet again, you shouldn't stand out. So look nice on our date, will you?"

"All right Pixie, I get you. I can't talk too much longer here. This poor guy thinks I'm going to pinch his device."

"Why should you do that?" she replied. "Then Clive, you should hang up. Give them my contact details, when you arrive. That's if you don't have enough money to pay?"

"Give your money to whom?"

There was a gentle noise of frustration. "The hotel. You know, when you get to reception."

"Right…thanks…where should we meet then? Can I suggest the American bar at the Savoy. Do you know it?"

"Yes, why shouldn't I, Clive? But that isn't the cleverest idea... don't you feel we would be conspicuous at the Savoy?" she argued.

"What about the public bar at Claridge's then?"

There was some restrained laughter. "Clive! That's not a clever idea either."

"You said this was a date," he objected. He checked on the guy waiting for his phone back; looking increasingly grumpy.

"We shouldn't go to those smart places... where our enemies sometimes go...or their friends... thinking they belong there. Are you prepared to bump into them by mistake?"

"Right, I hear you... it's a fair point, Pix," he admitted. "They aren't famous for keeping to a strict budget." Their preference was for high class hookers at the bar, not potential murder victims.

"We'll meet in Leicester Square," she decided.

"You're joking aren't, aren't you?" he complained. "Why d'you want to meet there?"

"It's the safest location, Clive... if we really have to meet in person. Now please give the gentleman his phone back."

The guy was already standing impatiently and expectantly beside him.

Pitt found a chic hotel in the West End - a boutique hotel - to compensate for his abandoned drink at the Savoy. As a matter of fact they had a decent bar at this place. However it was safer for him to drink there than in ritzier places. He was still able to pay for a room in cash. He still had a bundle of Breadham's notes, crisp as a pressed cravat.

On the way to the hotel he bought new clothes, as Pixie suggested. This time the style was smart casual, as if preparing for golf and cocktails on a business trip. This was funny, but not as amusing as turning up along New Bond Street; cutting a dash through the well-heeled promenade in filthy shreds. He resembled a scarecrow, an expensive one, and drew startled looks from shopping tourists; he was either derelict or an eccentric billionaire.

Let inside his hotel room, Pitt looked around, acclimatised, and tried to enjoy the tranquillity. He ran a hot bath in a torrent, stuffed his rags into the basket, took his fresh outfit from the wrappers, and sprawled over a feathery bed. Yet he couldn't switch off and be still; he couldn't clear his mind, as he stared up into a rococo ceiling. All the while his heart bounced and vibrated, as if an earthquake was building. Any step or voice in the corridor outside made him jump. Even as he stretched in the bath, hidden by the steamy atmosphere, his muscles tensed as if expecting to be interrupted.

36

Clive approached the centre of Leicester Square. His wavy hair licked into obedience, burnt skin soothed, trying out a new set of clothes, with his old reliable shoes freshly cleaned and polished.

He envied that carefree attitude in the West End, as he gave the appearance of stepping out. People milled around garish souvenir shops, eateries and showpiece cinemas. Pixie had shown logic in choosing to meet in a humdrum and commercial district. Knighted financiers, such as Sir Septimus, as well as sophisticated hedge fund managers, would not want to be seen dead there. Only a red carpet for a film premier would persuade them to visit; even if they might shun cameras or any publicity. They wouldn't imagine Pixie and Clive arranging a rendezvous at such a grimy location. Even if they knew about the ruse it would be easier amidst hustle and bustle to evade security.

The problem was in finding her, when he began to press into a thronging Leicester Square; as they had stripped him naked in the world of communication. The sheer numbers and bulk of humanity was disconcerting, while he missed her. Although this didn't compare to areas of say Beijing or Mumbai, it was still bewildering. In those cities he could take more time, as his life had not been threatened. There were just the normal risks of a megalopolis; taking a wrong turn from the bar or climbing into an unknown taxi cab, or responding to the wrong group of guys, or girls, and accepting a drink or something worse.

Pitt was growing concerned, wishing they had made precise arrangements. The square was a global meeting place, yet he was lost in the world's swelling population. Fortunately he recognised Pixie at last, as she perched on a bench within the park area. She was wearing a tightly cut pink dress suit. Somehow she had a passing through look. He knew her well enough to understand that she was nervous. This was despite her poise, her projected confidence, as she lifted her chin, emphasising the silver slipper, quarter-moon curve of her jaw.

But she managed a smile and, as he approached, looked him up and down appreciatively. She was glad to see him. Her gaze had a way of flickering obtusely to one side. No doubt they had been on numerous dates before, assuming her version was correct. Still their meeting felt strangely like a first date, even while it was not really a "date" at all.

"Hi," she smiled sweetly. "You're looking nice," she told him, peering up.

"I did a bit of clothes shopping," he explained dryly.

"Really, you made good choices."

"I'm glad that you approve, Pixie," he replied.

"How's the hotel?"

"Why are you bothered?" Clive said. "I'm surprised you want to see me again. Considering what you found out."

"Do you have any idea what I found out?" she returned.

They settled together on the bench. They looked out over that variegated crowd, which was constantly moving, and surrounding them, noisy and unruly, amidst overflowing fast food garbage, pigeons and pigeon mess.

"You watched me running away, didn't you? You probably assumed the worst too. I assume Sep invited you to look around the hospital."

"He literally invited me to visit Emmy. Did you know the hospital is actually named after him?" she explained.

"Well, yes, I thought you had to be a singer, or an astronaut, or even the wife of a president, for that," Clive remarked.

"You're not the only one who can trawl through a hard drive," she told him.

"What are you getting at? Whose hard drive?" he wondered.

"Nothing as dangerous as you attempted. I just took a quick look at the hospital's records."

"Did you really?" he marvelled, perking up.

"Sep was occupied... and the staff too. Meanwhile he wasn't keeping an eye on me. They were too busy chasing after you."

"Well, they didn't catch up with me," he said, clasping his hands between his knees, as if steadying himself.

"I asked to sit down and have a cup of tea...the nerves of young ladies can be fragile," she joked. "I was terribly flustered and nervous. And then I wandered by accident into the manager's office, just off reception. While I was there I had a look through the hospital records, and patient files. You see I'm no slouch at this either Clive. I know how to turn the thing on you know."

"That's clever of you, Pixie. So did you find anything?"

Pitt raised his voice above the antics of excited teenagers on the next bench.

"Emmy isn't just staying there to recuperate," she said. "This place is a type of psychiatric hospital. It's a leading research facility into brain function."

Pitt's face showed surprise. "I noticed the labs and equipment," he added.

"They don't simply develop and test new drugs, but literally conduct interventions and mind experiments."

"Does that have to be sinister? They're the research arm of a multinational pharmaceutical company."

"Listen to me, Emmy has been put there to change her character. Their idea is literally to turn her into a good girl. They don't want to do her any physical harm, as such. Only to lose her appetite for bad boys and their edgy lifestyle," Pixie said.

"Are you sure? That sounds radical. You got all this from hacking the hospital records?" he asked.

"Sep doesn't want this kind of scandal to repeat. What's more, he wants an ideal daughter. He wants her to forget the fact that she was raped. Any father would wish his daughter to get over those traumas. But can that be possible?"

"I don't know about that," he agreed. "But I should tell you that I was not alone that day. If I was really present during the crime, as they claim, then I had an accomplice."

"So how did you find this out?" she replied, echoing his approach.

"Well, I bumped into this old bloke... a gardener at Sep's estate. He gave me an account of another guy...and this guy was dragging me along after him...away from the woods where the crime took place. And then he, and most probably a few accomplices, shoved me into the back of a car. And then they took me back to London."

"All right, so who might they have been?" Pixie asked.

"They were criminal figures... most likely mafia. I don't think that Sep knows about their motives... not fully. Other details are still shady...I can't bring them back... maybe you can inform me."

"I see," Pixie said. "We know that you were taken to that hospital. You were admitted to the institution. You literally broke out of the hospital at some stage...or maybe people enabled you to escape."

"The implication is that Sep didn't know," Clive deduced.

"There was literally only light security at the party. Only personal body guards for some important people. There must have been a reason for that. Sep believed you to be tucked up in a hospital bed, so to speak."

"One of his partners at the fund was trying to hurt him. Even body guards might have done more to protect the girl. Though Sep would never admit this, as it would tend to exonerate me, to a degree," Clive considered.

"He's determined to literally pin everything on you. He cannot see through his blind hatred of you, as he's convinced you're the man who harmed his daughter."

"Those ZNT guys are plotting against him. Maybe he can find the rogue element in Geneva. Can't he understand? Just because, in his opinion, they helped to save his firm? At what cost to his reputation? Or his conscience?"

"Is he that naïve?" Pixie wondered. "I believe that Sep is fully aware of the fraud that has occurred. I'm afraid so, Clive. It was, you know...when those transactions and agreements were finalised."

Clive was trying to think straight, amidst all the typical good-time chaos of the West End; trying to steady his mind amidst the background storm of voices. "I was admitted to the hospital, right? They must have done something to me. Some treatment or procedures, wouldn't you say? Did you find out anything at all there... about what they did to me?"

"I'm afraid that I couldn't find your record. I think they literally threw it away. They are thorough in destroying any evidence... removing any records or traces. Or I just didn't have enough time to find out? Or I'm really not as clever as I like to think?" she commented.

He grinned appreciatively. "Believe me, there has to be a print there. There are always traces of information, if you know how," he argued.

"Sorry, I couldn't pull anything out. You can imagine how my fingers were shaking...or how I was stopping them from shaking," she said.

"Well, I appreciate what you've done, Pix," he told her, rubbing his face.

"We are both mathematicians, but we understand that we are delicate creatures... you know, chemical beings... infinitely suggestible and changeable...however much we may deal with hard numbers."

"Turning a man in to a rapist is simple technology, comparatively speaking," Clive argued.

"The effects of extra testosterone or adrenaline?" Pixie said. "After all they inherited the experts from BIP. They have those resources, you know, literally at their disposal."

"Just simple injections, equivalent to sporting cheats... which can do tremendous damage...certainly produce extreme behaviour, if not alter my character."

"But in terms of procedures to wipe your memory, that is much more complex," Pixie considered.

"What if they damaged my brain by accident, almost... when I took that complimentary ticket to a football game...then had my head kicked in during a break to the gents'," he argued, bitterly. "None of which, incidentally, I can remember either."

"Short of questioning doctors and researchers," Pixie thought. "We can only imagine such interventions, to change neurological or cerebral balance. Who knows if they didn't cut something out of your brain," she declared.

Pitt gave a desolate look and felt his temples again. "Oh God, don't say that."

"My friend should feedback the results of your blood test."

"Ask them to report back as soon as possible, will you?" he replied.

"Clive, you don't have any marks on your scalp. No cuts, anything like that," she reminded him.

"Only the cut under my eye," he agreed, prodding the place.

There was tenderness in her eyes as her gaze followed his cicatrise.

"And that happened a while back," he commented. "If they had left evidence... we could take everything to the authorities," Clive argued.

"They are more subtle than to leave scars on your skull," Pixie argued.

"If you didn't find marks on me, you turned up other evidence."

"They are literally receiving patients from all over the world. When I was going through their database, I noticed this factor. You are thinking that there is nothing unusual there. I can see from your reaction. You are thinking that this is a global corporation? Naturally taking on an international group of patients?"

"It is surprising that people would travel so far, even if it is a leading hospital for brain research. Can they be such a special institution?" Pitt questioned.

"What surprised me is that the patient list is extraordinarily cosmopolitan. The guest list resembles a shadow United Nations."

"How do you know that?" he replied. "Are you claiming these guys have been rendered?"

"I found a list of people who are political dissidents. If you made a list of rogue states, then you would be able to locate them. Initial notes about these people list professions... social position... or status. But also descriptions of undesirable character traits. Their activities and attitudes that posed difficulties for their governments... or in some cases, the organisations employing them."

"Remarkable stuff," he declared.

"They never expect these notes to be read by outsiders."

"What about the background of the patients?" Pitt asked.

"I have never been an Amnesty International member, or any other type of campaigner," Pixie admitted. "But these people could have been on their guest list."

"What kind of people are we talking about here?" he asked.

"So this would include lecturers, doctors, artists and poets.... in fact many of them were from highly cultural or intellectual backgrounds."

Pixie scanned the crowds in Leicester Square as a representative slice.

"This information was stated on the records you hacked?"

"But I was scanning through quickly. It was risky because a member of staff could have walked in. I was literally up against the clock and didn't have time...to make a detailed analysis."

"You did well, Pix, to interpret the pattern... and to understand the significance of..."

"Patients are not precisely diagnosed. They are not treated in recognisable ways. They are put into a negative description of personality type."

"What are you saying, Pix? That these are bogus assessments?" Pitt said.

"In some cases the doctor lists patients as suffering from paranoia, or depression or psychosis, but these are used as general insults, not clinical descriptions."

"The terminology attempts to legitimise their procedures."

"I'm sorry?"

"If they are using psychiatric treatments and techniques for political purposes... as a weapon against political objectors and dissidents. Apparently they misused medicine during the Cold War, before the communist system collapsed, merely to silence opponents. It's kind of shocking that they are resorting to these tactics again...though maybe not such a big surprise."

"Given what we already know about them," Pixie remarked. "I never studied history or politics. I didn't like it," she admitted. "But I'm not mistaken about those hospital records," she told him.

"Highly suspicious and irregular," he considered.

"I have to agree... from what I saw."

"What have we stumbled on now?" Clive remarked.

"Exactly," she agreed, sharing the mood of ominous surprise.

"If this is true, then foreign governments, and companies, are sending their opponents here... to this country... to Sep's newly acquired research hospital, in the English countryside. These unfortunate dissidents are sent here for treatments, punishment, after upsetting their government or even just powerful interests... to be neutralised or rendered harmless."

"In some cases they are being used as guinea pigs... literally to test new drugs, for treating mental illnesses. I assume that ZNT would want to eventually market those new drugs and treatments," she said.

"There's a type of psychological warfare going on," Clive argued.

"I do find this shocking," she told him.

"Most likely this is growing into a lucrative trade in extra-rendition. Wouldn't you say that? With governments and powerful figures paying millions for the service? Process our troublemakers and launder their ideas for us."

"Then there is Emmy Winchurch," she said. "Not quite sure how she fits in, I must say."

"Maybe the wealthy get their kids mentally 'improved and modified'. Just like intelligence enhancements before important exams," he claimed.

"Don't forget that you were a patient yourself," Pixie added.

"There's one fact I don't need to be reminded of," he commented. "Most of all I rely on you. Effectively I turned up as a complete stranger."

"We still don't know exactly how you lost your memory," Pixie said.

"There are moments when I slip back into unconsciousness," he admitted.

"You must come back around. We can't lose you."

A frightened look broke her cool masque, like the first crack in a mirror, a sudden fissure in an ancient glass.

"I suffer blackouts," he confirmed. "Apart from changes in light and temperature, it's hard to calculate how long. I still feel the effects of whatever they did to me. But what should we do from here?" he agonised.

"I can return to the hospital. There's evidence about the detention of prisoners by individuals and companies. I have to return to make my own record," Pixie argued. "What's preventing me from reporting to the authorities?"

"You'd take a giant risk by doing that," Clive told her.

Pixie tried to look as if she was not putting her life in danger, simply by agreeing to meet him.

"It's more dangerous than arguing that I'm a good guy. Sep can take that, because he thinks you're a deluded lover. He's got a thing about you. He dreams about turning Emmy into somebody like you. I've heard some of those messages he used to leave for you. But he'll have to drop the paternal smile if you get some hard evidence," Clive warned.

"Don't imagine that I'm going to leave you alone in this," Pixie assured him.

She darted him an anxious gaze of expectation, as if there was an emotional point to settle.

This connected irresistibly to Pitt's feelings. In that moment he moved closer and kissed her. They remained in this embrace for a long time.

37

Clive felt all the guilt of a married man, since his wife had not divorced him. Noreen probably didn't know about his present movements or whereabouts. On the other hand she hadn't fully informed him; so he had no information about what she may be doing over there. His ex-wife had absconded to Seattle on a safer bet, taking their son with her. No doubt she was settling into the new house, enjoying the new lifestyle, establishing the new business over there. Why hadn't she been in contact at all? Or had he missed her communications, due to his erratic movements? After all he only had second-hand explanations of her actions and motivations.

Yet, for all his conflicted thoughts, he felt a powerful attraction to Pixie. Their mutual attraction was intensified by the danger he faced, *they* faced. Their passion was inflamed by an existential sense of only having each other; of only being able to depend on each other.

This isolation induced vertigo and dread in Clive. He was in an impossibly fragile place in his life, which no man could envy. The sensation contrasted with the excitement of holding Pixie in his arms, absorbing her passionate kisses, of feeling her smooth cheeks against his face, of breathing her exquisite feminine scents. There was a dizzying unreality to this combination.

"Are you coming back to the hotel with me?" Clive wondered.

"That wouldn't be a clever move," she demurred.

"Yes, but I thought you'd feel safer... if we stayed together," Pitt insisted.

"It's true that we only have each other," she concurred.

"I definitely want to make love to you," Clive said.

"When we feel more relaxed," she told him.

"That's when I can repair my thoughts," he told her. "When I can bring back vital evidence of the deal, with your support."

"But I don't know where you put your memory either. I'm literally as lost as you," she reminded him.

"Fair enough, but if I could get a clue about my strategy at the time," he said, squeezing his mind again.

"Sadly you didn't include me on that, Clive."

There was a hint of fear and panic etched into her refined features. Superficially at least the scene was normal; they didn't stand out. The Square was punctuated with such lovers, from home and abroad, on holiday or after work; as varied and cosmopolitan as the patients at the ZNT hospital, having their minds and ideas set.

"We may be safer if we separate," Pixie replied.

"How can we possibly separate? I want to stick with you now!"

"We are being watched again," she told him.

"Are you serious? How can they find us here?" he lamented.

"They've literally caught up with us again...unless we are unlucky to attract the attention of those creepy guys over there. Do you see?"

"Where are they?" Pitt said. He attempted to look back over his shoulder, without making the fact too obvious.

"Enjoying a beer outside that bar, under a striped canopy in the plaza....do you see? Do you recognise them?"

"Where do you mean? Are you sure they are suspicious?"

"Unless we are interesting to a group of voyeurs," she remarked.

"You get all types here. You picked a right place to meet, didn't you?"

"They seem very concentrated on us. Although at this moment they have no idea we are watching them back," she added.

"Now I see them," he told her. "What a bunch of charmers. An unmistakable combination of designer labels and obsessive gym work. Maybe we've already met, but after a while they all look the same," Clive remarked.

He observed them, as secretly as possible; took in their burning goggle eyed looks, and discomforted shuffling between strained conversations, attempting to seem casual over inflated tourist beers. In truth nobody gave even this group of heavies a second look. Leicester Square is a marginal space, where people could operate freely.

"They are watching us," he noted.

"I told you."

"What concerns me is that they've seen you, with me. It's the first time they have linked us, since my return. These things get around you know." Nerves made him joke at this stage. He was secretly devastated that she was identified and involved.

"They already think that we are lovers. Now they have literally seen us kiss and hug. Hopefully they imagine I am a silly girl... that I don't understand anything. Anyway I know about personal danger. When I was a schoolgirl in Geneva my boyfriend was on the run from national service. He faced prison and disgrace in his own country. I felt an intense risk every time we met in public... we usually met under the bridge in the old town," she recalled.

"Try to land softly at the bottom of Sep's heart. Don't let him realise that you're even more rebellious than his daughter," he urged her.

"Sep has no idea that I looked through hospital databases."

"Then don't ruin his illusions, Pix," he told her. "Let him be fond and foolish."

"Do you have any other ideas Clive?" she replied. "We must literally separate now. We should dash into the crowds in opposite directions. We'll be hidden immediately if we do that. I'll get towards Shaftsbury Avenue and you can go into Piccadilly Circus. Just get on the tube as normal, do you understand?"

"They must have found where I'm staying now... the hotel. I'm not going back to that place...together or alone," he argued.

"You see I had a clever idea in meeting in Leicester Square, because there are always crowds. It will be difficult for them to isolate us."

"I'm not exactly in a hurry to separate from you," Clive said. "You'll need a bit of protection at this point. We should try to get out of the country together. I'm serious. That isn't a guarantee of safety. But it will confuse them and give us more time."

"If you gave up fighting the deal," she said. "If you were able to forget..."

"You should know the chances of that," he replied. Warily, cautiously, he kept an eye on that bunch of guys, who were eyeing him back, nervously across the square.

"Why don't you borrow another phone and call me up? When you feel there's a proper moment?" Pixie suggested.

"What happens if they ask you about our date?" he replied tensely.

"There's no more information to report back," she insisted.

Pitt was sceptical of her chances, but he kept his fears to himself. "All right Pixie, I agree that I'm going to call you later... at the first opportunity."

"Then kiss me again Clive and say good night."

He carried out this instruction and then, without hesitation, they dashed into opposite directions. Immediately Pitt felt himself surrounded by other bodies, trying to squeeze through packed spaces; trying to get between those hordes of visitors, making their ways in multiple directions, towards the numerous attractions of the capital city.

She was gone, like a bottle top in a rip tide; even while he retained impressions of her touches and kisses. He was pressing towards the even more intense crush of Piccadilly Circus, as she had suggested.

38

Pitt slogged out the West End pavements, negotiating an aggressive rush of traffic. He threaded and squeezed through a good-time crush, constantly looking back over his shoulder, along every shadowy side street. He slipped up a garbage strewn alley into Chinatown; half hidden among lantern lit restaurants and shops, but didn't feel like a free man. He wouldn't go back to that hotel room to soak in the bath like a rubber duck.

Get out of the country, assume a different identity, he told himself; lead a different existence; become anonymous. He could pull off his own vanishing act and reappear when he chose - if at all. Except that he didn't have the resources to achieve that, or an exchangeable identity. He didn't want to continue as a criminal since, it had already been established, and there was not a single warrant or police officer out against him.

Most basically he didn't possess a passport. Forgeries were easily obtainable from a Nigerian contact in New Cross, but there wasn't time to make such a transaction. For his enemies passports were as obtainable as fishing licences. These people didn't respect national borders except, with passion, their own. They usually had violent nationalism as a personality trait. Rather he didn't have his own valid passport at hand. Probably it was with his wife in the US, reviled or mourned over in a forgotten box.

He could head for Victoria coach station or the rail station, sleep rough overnight and purchase a ticket in the morning. Except these days that route was not an escape, because Europe was like the Isle of Wight. If he flew to the continent then he could get the boat from Cadiz to Casablanca, smuggle himself into North Africa - people smuggling in the opposite direction was unproblematic.

But even in those places he would struggle to survive, to get basic shelter and food. The resident populations of those countries had a few troubles of their own, the 'Arab Spring' notwithstanding, as night follows day. His only chance to escape was through his associate, his friend, Doug Breadham. The guy was a financial lawyer and had useful contacts, not only with banks and corporations; he had freedom to manoeuvre and no doubt resources. Clive would restrain himself from trying to communicate to Pixie, to avoid making the link for them. She was already linked, it was far too late, but why dispel their doubts?

Clive retraced his steps to confound his enemies. He went back to the recognisable environment of his old home. They would never expect him to do that. He had the profound sense of being like a ghost, as his intimate memories and regrets returned. He was disturbed by a weightless feeling of being unconnected, just as he was unable to access any communication or information.

There was only a blanket of stars and a freezing temperature over his back. His fingertips were frozen and a chill spread up his arms. Then Pitt trudged on to the next village, like some folk myth to frighten the impecunious, on the road to Doug's estate. Obviously there was nothing for Clive at his original home. It was also an empty shell, he judged. There were just the haunting sounds of owls from a nearby barn and the alarming screams of foxes, scurrying at the edges of fields and hedges, denied a meal or a mate.

On calling at Gatemead however, Reg explained that Breadham was staying over in London; at his apartment in Chelsea. Fortunately Reg wanted to make amends for his past rudeness and obstruction. He gave the Chelsea address and useful directions, which Pitt took gratefully - thanking him profusely - before turning back up the long gravelled drive towards the lawyer's leonine gates. It was a given that the contemporary world couldn't be approached on foot. At least Reg the man-servant had tagged his employer and wasn't such a bad guy.

But returning to London, he had problems finding Doug's apartment by the naked eye and unassisted mind. The narrowly serpentine highway of the King's Road was choked with traffic, as he set off from the Royal Court theatre. Customers were milling about the theatre, as well as restaurants, bars and clubs of the borough. In former days, before Pitt's troubles began, he enjoyed socialising after hours at his favourite bars in Shoreditch. That was in another life it seemed. The idea of enjoying himself now felt completely unlikely. Indeed such behaviour was eccentric, even sinister. What was it like to relax with your friends and colleagues? Such normal scenes of people having fun in public, now struck him as other worldly, as for a battle weary soldier.

Pitt felt as if he could measure his own reduction by these activities. There were reasons to be watchful, but the situation was affecting his personality; it was changing his neural responses. Only Pixie provided a thread to normal existence, by a single touch or a single word. The pair of them were cuffed together as if by invisible links.

But was it ethical to make her play this game of double jeopardy?

After some fun and games Clive located Doug's address. The apartment was within a complex of redeveloped and renovated buildings around Chelsea harbour. There was an intercom and security camera system. After stubbing his thumb on the button he listened to static noise for a while - as if the lawyer was lost in deep space - until a tinny voice emerged in response.

"Yes?"

"Hi."

"Who is it?"

"Clive."

"Clive?"

"That's right, mate."

"What are you doing here?"

"I've come to see you."

"Whatever for?"

"I need advice."

"Advice? Private?"

"Yes, I'd appreciate that, mate."

"Now?"

"There's no other time."

"You alone?"

"Yes."

"Is this important?"

"What do you think?"

"You're still in a mess?"

"Up to my nose."

"It's kind of awkward Clive, at the moment, to be honest."

"Why awkward?"

"I'm not alone."

"Sorry, mate."

"Can't leave you I suppose."

"Thanks."

"Come on up."

There was a sustained buzzing, signalling for him to push and to enter. Clive took the hint and was presented with a narrow walkway, a row of wooden post-boxes, and then a winding stairway, comprised of stone steps worn-down at the centre, as if by giant feet. Time had this heavy tread, aided by stevedores and commodity brokers. As Pitt ascended he seemed to be imitating these, with his heavy weary tread.

He climbed three levels, turning into a claustrophobic passage. This was barely wide enough to admit his bulk; poorly lit by electric nautical lamps, which only revealed oppressively rough stone walls. He had the feeling of wandering the corridors of a Victorian jail, dark and cold, like Newgate. He had to peer and grope to find the correct apartment number (wondering who would seriously choose to dwell here).

Pitt thumped the door and waited, trying for composure and to disregard humming nerve ends. He had the constant sensation of a tremble through his body, like electricity or radiation. Was this just stress, or had he been poisoned at some stage? Feeling as if he couldn't inhale properly, to get enough oxygen into his body, and on the edge of consciousness. Pitt waited for his friend to answer.

Pitt endured an unnerving delay, as when voicing his doubts face to face to a ZNT executive team. They expected him to be professionally useful and positive throughout their discussions; not to be critical or obstructive. They couldn't handle that. Eventually Doug seemed to locate his front door: there was the shifting of bolts and locks, before the lawyer revealed himself, smiling in a chummily forced way.

At such an hour Breadham could only manage to smile for girls. Nocturnal hours formed a private transaction. He conducted an active on-line sex life, hooking up with pretty young women in search of a sugar daddy. Breadham used his address for such liaisons, as it was a safe distance away from his office. He only went into the country at weekends or Bank Holidays, where he was happy to slip into the quiet role of an eligible bachelor. This allowed him to recharge his batteries before another hectic week, when he would again swap his cocktail glass for a cocktail dress.

The lawyer was attired for bed. "Thought you'd lost your way," Doug declared - as if he hoped this would be the case. "Take your shoes off, will you." It was hard to keep cool, even for a polished City lawyer.

"No problem, mate," Clive replied, sheepish. "I appreciate this. Some place you have here," Clive said, scanning.

"Thank you, Clive. Glad you like it."

Pitt entered a room which felt immense in comparison to the passageways. He began to relax into the warm comfort of the space. Long and high-ceilinged, with a wide window at the end, there was a view to the canal, where small boats were moored along romantically lit jetties.

"What happened to your new set of clothes? You know, that I purchased for you?" he observed.

"I went through them," Clive informed him.

"Oh? Really? I think I may have kept the receipts... if you wish to -"

"I wouldn't be bothered with that," Pitt said, laughing painfully.

"Did someone buy you some more new clothes?"

"Another anonymous benefactor," Clive returned.

He considered the point, before moving on. "Been to this apartment before?" Breadham wondered.

"Very impressive," Pitt agreed, swivelling his eyes again. "But, no."

"Are you sure?"

"Not really."

"Have you been out somewhere?" Doug asked. Was he sarcastic? He was surprised by Pitt's comparative neatness. This was a few degrees short of the horror show he'd been expecting.

"You're with someone?" Clive recalled.

"Mm, yes. I asked her to get her things together. She's on her way out."

"She can stay, if you would like her to."

"But she's made her mind up."

"At this hour?" Pitt wondered. "You think that I have something to hide?"

"There's a cab coming. Who can read a woman's mind?" Doug replied. "Best to let her shoot off, if that's what she wants." He exercised his facial muscles under strain, even while keeping an amiable gleam.

"Well if this girl's determined to leave, I'm not going to stop her."

"That's the attitude," Doug said.

Pitt strolled across the room, to gaze through the window to outside; to enjoy a glimpse of freedom.

The people sitting outside the pub were on a different planet. He expected to rely on Doug's pragmatic approach. They had probably been friends for a long time, although their first meeting had been a professional matter; as far as he recalled. They dealt in the same circles because Doug worked with prestige clients, including banks and hedge funds, and even took on occasional spats between foreign oligarchs. This must have been where they first met and became friendly.

Clive's attention was caught by movement in one of the adjoining rooms. He turned about to see a tall red-headed girl, striding across the rug in his direction. As expected she was an ultra-beautiful, glamorous young woman; she was a fragmented chip from an exotic mineral. London had a virtual army of these beautiful girls; a veritable Warsaw Pact of glamour. These were lovely girls of great promise who found that travel itself didn't always add up to happiness. Even if the grass was greener on this side of Europe it hid some peculiar creatures. Even if the advertisements claimed otherwise, beauty could not be traded so easily for wealth. Sometimes you were cheated out of your goods.

It was hard to read this girl's emotions. She was trained to hide her feelings. This was an essential shield. Emotion might short-circuit to suffering and to poverty. She showed a blank mask and swished her long hair as she swivelled over the lawyer's Afghan carpet.

Doug spoke to the girl in a commiserating tone. Then he put a hand on her long narrow waist and guided her toward the exit. Clive observed his friend's authentic silk Chinese robe (probably a gift), cinched around pampered flesh, in an extravagance of red dragons on green. Pitt repressed a feeling of antipathy towards the man. The girl was wearing a red twin-set that must have come from Liberty's or Harrods. On principle she only went for expensive brands. But she finally slipped outside, without a word or an expression.

Tomorrow was another shopping day.

"Someone special?" Clive asked.

"What can I do for you?" Breadham stated. He was not best pleased.

"I need your help, mate," Clive admitted. His posture slumped to bridge a gap.

"How precisely?"

"There's really no escape for me. Other than to...to get out of the country," Clive answered, in a tone of bleak certainty.

"Where have you been, since we last spoke?"

"All over," Clive said.

"Have you given up?" Breadham asked, stood astride in his silk gown.

"There's a range of dangerous people toying with me. I don't think I can keep away from them much longer. I don't believe my innocence is their real concern."

"You understand their concerns?"

"They aren't looking out for me," Clive said.

"Then why don't you speak to the authorities?" Doug said.

"Not unless I get my evidence against them," he stressed.

"Any chance of recovering it?"

"I still don't remember."

"You can trust me with that information," Doug said.

"I put the dossier somewhere."

"Isn't there a copy?" Doug wondered.

"It was even more dangerous to keep a copy," Clive reminded him.

"Didn't you tell somebody else, as a safeguard?" Breadham insisted.

"They don't know either," Pitt replied caustically.

"You have to remember."

"What were you doing on this same evening, last year?" Clive asked.

"Last year?"

"Do you know?" Pitt challenged, wild eyed.

Doug reached into his mind and his brow creased. "Of course I don't remember. Who would?"

"You don't remember for the life of you!"

"I'm glad you have a party trick. But your memory has become other people's business," the lawyer argued.

"So I gather. But all the data is lost. Either though I put the information in a box, or stashed it away in hyper-space," he considered. "They smashed my mind while trying to get the truth out of me. Without that the police aren't going to believe me. The financial authorities will have nothing to go on. Are they going to listen to me, against the word of Sir Septimus Winchurch? To contradict the arguments of prestigious clients? Some of whom oil our political system?"

"That's quite a serious allegation. Agreed you are in a tight spot," Doug agreed. "Even if your views are rather cynical."

"I can only leave the UK, assuming these guys are a step behind."

"Money's no problem, if that's what you need," Doug said, dismissively.

"I assume that all my accounts are frozen," Clive admitted.

Every feature of this conversation between them was awkward.

"As much as you need, but..." Breadham floundered. He began to wander abstractedly about the room, butterfly silk flowing behind. "Does this imply an assumption of guilt?"

"Certainly not, mate." Clive studied his movements with curiosity. "I'm caught up in a tangle of circumstances."

"Are you really in such desperate straits?"

"Yes, and I'm dragging other people behind me...such as Pixie Wright."

"Her again? Does she know much?" Doug returned. "Or is she helping you?"

"There, I've dragged her back into this," Pitt objected - feeling the slip like a missed kerb. "I've trusted you with a lot, Doug. Maybe I can trust you with this. I left her a few hours ago. She was running back into Shaftsbury Avenue with a couple of ZNT assassins following. Maybe she should have come with me," Clive considered.

"So you split up? Where do you plan to flee?"

"North Africa is at the top of my list right now. I can disappear there."

"Good luck," Breadham replied.

"But I don't have my passport on me... as you might expect."

"What's a passport? Are you sure you have clearance at the border?"

"Let's try, shall we?"

"Give me a couple of days." Doug halted across the room, as if considering all his woes, with his shimmering back turned.

"Reserve a seat for me, will you? I don't like to put you out... but there's nowhere else to turn."

"Don't you sense they will find you? Wherever you go?"

"I can try to clear my name," Clive essayed.

"You need at least one night's rest to recover your bearings," Doug argued. He set off on his travels around the apartment again. Thought and movement went together as any lawyer can testify.

"You're inviting me to stay?"

"For a single night. Until we figure your plans. As you are in a tight corner. You don't want to draw attention to yourself."

Clive had to reluctantly agree. "If I can leave the UK early tomorrow. Can you make some arrangements? Is that too tight?"

"Let's see what I can do, shall we?" Breadham replied.

"I want to put as much distance between myself and these guys as possible," Clive explained. "Until these gaps in my memory are restored."

"Meanwhile I can find you a safe place in Budapest. Just let me talk to my contacts in Hungary and they may be able to hide you."

He was as good as his word. He switched on his gadget and, judging by the movements of his fingers, had a number of conversations. Eventually he put the gadget aside, looking tense and twitchy.

"Listen carefully, because I have your itinerary."

39

Pitt accepted a meal and a glass of wine. He related his latest adventures, starting from when Doug had dropped him back at the station.

Doug listened with a drink in hand. As a lawyer he knew how to pace. He had many expressive styles of covering a floor. Pitt could gauge the lawyer's attitude and mood from these melodramatic movements.

"What do you have to say then?" Clive asked. "What's your opinion?"

"You want a summing up?" Breadham retorted. "Why do you think that I can help you? I can offer advice, but I can't be your brain."

Pitt was taken aback. "You're sitting on the fence, mate? Let me help you down. ZNT are taking people from their own countries and putting them into this old hospital... these victims are dissidents of various types. Here they are being treated, or rather chemically modified, *and experimented* on... so they no longer pose a risk to their native regimes. Pixie believes they are probably entering the country with regular visas, maybe described as embassy staff. So what's your reaction to that?"

"Your mind is under severe stress," Breadham deduced.

"At least I am capable of interpreting events."

"Should I remind you that I'm not a human rights lawyer? You require a different counsel."

"That's marvellous, so you don't want to help?" Clive assumed.

"A conspiracy theory is the best you can do?"

"At this stage paranoia is rational."

"Is that the case, Pitt? So who is the mastermind of this arrangement?"

Breadham had come around the living room; he stopped in front of Clive, looking quite angry, as if dicing with a contrarian judge.

"I can't be completely sure," Clive admitted. "There's this bloke, who heads up the Swiss fund... Viktor, isn't it."

"Viktor di Visu?" Doug returned.

"That's the bloke," Clive agreed. "Viktor's shy of the limelight. Despite heading up ZNT he would not talk to my team or to me directly."

"Did you require him to lead negotiations?" Breadham remarked.

Pitt considered his yet shadowy recollections. "No... no, but it would have been unusual. But I knew Viktor's role. I had some questions about him. Viktor's not the only offender perhaps, when you look at the companies now listing... but I raised issues about his governance. Viktor doesn't understand the principle of transparency or probity."

"Not only is Mr di Visu a brilliant designer," Douglas argued, "but he is proprietor of a business empire, including a merged folio of leading luxury brands. Don't you expect him to be busy? Are you so easily offended?"

"Then you are already familiar with him," Pitt deduced. "So how did that come about?"

"Everybody who operates in the City has heard of Viktor di Visu."

"Oh? Maybe I recognised one of his signature perfumes," Pitt said, "earlier this evening? When that girl walked past me? What do you think?"

"You still have your sense of smell," Breadham replied.

"Viktor has a sensitive side, doesn't he... with all his frocks and perfumes," Clive remarked.

"Do you have anything against it?" replied Breadham.

"As a side-line he's the major shareholder in Imperial British Pharmaceuticals. That's the business I was bothered about," he said. "The profits from pharmaceuticals must help finance his other hobbies. I would guess he's able to launder money

294

through his more legitimate activity. He's able to do favours for unsavoury regimes and be rewarded for that too, I'd guess. What d'you think?"

"His father was one of the richest men within the CIS region," Breadham argued. "So why would he require extra capital for those purposes?"

"Who invested in his sexy frocks? Who bankrolled his studies in the first place?" Pitt speculated.

Doug stared directly - just a flicker of irritation about his pupils.

"Viktor is amusing himself. Not only is he king of the catwalk, he's now on the cutting edge of drugs and medical research. He's also exploiting those resources, for political reasons."

"You have a lot of new theories. Can you substantiate these allegations?"

"Pixie says that they are working on brain function. At these facilities their research is about the mind. In the name of science, just like the old days. They will do this by finding new drugs and treatment."

"Can we set aside your conspiracy theory?" Doug complained. The lawyer stood in a challenging pose, akimbo, waving around a heavy bottomed whiskey glass.

"They seek to destroy their critics, both at home and abroad."

"You are definitely living in a fantasy land."

"You really think so, mate? Just consider what's been going on here in London over recent years," Pitt objected. "Don't you think that these fantasies originate with them? Rather than with us stiffs... we handmaidens of the banking world?"

"There's only so much they can achieve. In the City or in the UK, that is."

"Winchurch needed kickbacks from ZNT to survive. He took big hits during the last financial crisis. He stared into the face of bankruptcy. The hedge fund - no doubt in the shape of Viktor - offered Sep free money, non-dilutive capital, in return for fixing the price for BIP. Sep's firm undervalued the share price and pushed forward the sale. And there are places for fund managers on the Winchurch's board now. So I understand," Clive said.

"Perhaps, who knows? You don't have any proof to hand?" Breadham suggested, offering the faintest satirical smirk.

"I have encountered Viktor a few times lately," Pitt replied.

"You have? Are you sure?" Doug said. He began to pace out a new pattern over the floor - an innovation. "Why would he wish to see you? If he didn't want to meet with you before?"

"Well, he's a kind of a devil. Or that's how he casts himself. He's trying to manage this unpredictable situation... to use me against my former boss and company. Sep is too furious about the attack on his daughter, to understand such machinations. How can he take me seriously? Viktor wishes to destroy us all, with me as the instrument. This can be achieved after he has neutralised my case. He's indescribable, but not a figment of my imagination," Pitt insisted.

"Well, I'm prepared to help you leave the UK, aren't I? I'm even offering you a bed for the night? Doesn't that put me at risk too?" Breadham declared.

The barrister's circles had degenerated into staggers, as he'd taken several refills.

"Well, I can appreciate that, mate."

That crowd outside the pub could watch Doug tottering about behind glass. Breadham gave the impression of being pressed against something dangerous and repellent. Budapest was arguably a good distance for both of them; though he doubted if any place offered suitable cover and protection.

An alternative plan was for Pixie to retrieve evidence. She had been able to hack into the ZNT hospital files, to bypass security and to decipher encrypted information. But even if she could achieve such a feat, Clive was reluctant to allow her, as she would leave traces. The ZNT recruited brilliant young technicians, often directly from the courtroom; offering these 'hackers' irresistible packages; so able to beat competition from state security organisations; as well as phishing around the computers of agitators and activists.

He wanted to shield Pixie. Hopefully Winchurch retained a soft spot for her, to keep her away from Di Visu.

"I believe it's time for some shut eye," Breadham argued.

"There are these nasty clowns on my heels. I don't want them to get the same holiday plans," Clive remarked. "I don't want to put you into danger either."

"Where would you go at this hour? In this town?"

"I will go back on the street, if you're worried."

"No, I made a promise. I'm not going back on my word. I never go back on my word," Doug insisted.

"If you regard me as some kind of unhinged maniac, then I would prefer to leave," Clive stated.

"There's no need for this. I shall prepare a guest room."

The palms of his hands fell on Clive's chest. He felt himself in the position of a half-cut tart desperate for a trick. He noticed a quiver of distaste momentarily distort Pitt's face. He removed his hands in alarm and pulled away.

"I couldn't abandon you at this stage. Let me fix you a drink. Something hot and harmless I mean. Before I show you into your bedroom." Fortunately he was one of those people for whom drink didn't slur the speech. But inwardly he'd lost his professional cool hours before.

"That's generous of you, mate," Clive said, distrustfully. He was dog tired and grateful for a bed in any circumstances.

"I trust that you don't suffer from claustrophobia," Doug said.

"What do you mean exactly?" Clive asked.

"It's a small room. That's what I mean. A former store room," he explained.

"Oh, right then. I just want a night's sleep, not to buy the place."

"Point accepted," Doug replied, leading the way through, in his colourfully streaming garment. "The bed is wonderfully comfortable. Three pillows?"

"I shan't feel them tonight?" Clive predicted. He set off in pursuit.

"I'll show you the way then. No time for breakfast I suspect."

The room was as very cosy, as advertised. Also it was completely windowless. After a rudimentary introduction to the facilities, Doug withdrew. Pitt didn't feel so confident about his 'friend' anymore; he was relieved to see him go. It was scary, as he thought about it, that he couldn't recall his true friends, other than Pixie Wright.

A heavy door was secured against him. He felt locked up, yet the door was not locked when he checked. He was at liberty to move about the apartment, to the bathroom and so on, as he pleased. This was reassuring. The nature of the building could not be changed. Until morning he would have to endure confinement. Then he would acquire wings, to fly off to another land, where he would be safe from vindictive clutches.

40

Nevertheless, once he'd switched off the light, settled under the covers, the sides of the airless chamber began to oppress. Sleep was as elusive as a taste of sweetness in salt water. Yet if he wished to sleep, he had never expected to succeed; only to gain respite until dawn; just waiting for the sun to clamber back over the skyline of London and to sink its claws back into his pulpy mind.

He couldn't sleep but he suffered waking nightmares. All of the events and experiences of the past replayed in his mind; while he stared into the darkness of that space. Again he staggered down the lumpy furrows of Close Copse, a devilish guy squeezing his arm and forcing him along. Worst of all he returned to the column of light that revealed Emma's terrified eyes. He was tearing at her clothes and her screams tore at his ears. He was betraying the excitement and trust of a passionate young woman. Clive felt that he would never be able to escape these terrible images. He realised that he'd been right at the centre of such cynical brutality.

Pitt lost physical feeling and his body became light to the point of incorporeality. It was like staying at the ZNT Hospital in a quiet room amidst the English countryside. He felt locked into his own head; entirely composed of mental images. Instead of getting some rest he progressed through interminable patterns of chaos.

The nightmare continued: He tumbled again out of the City sky; even reliving the obscure events of another lost year. This time he was entirely in the dark and alone, understanding every moment, yet detached, as if sitting in a theatre or cinema - an old London fleapit of the mind - to watch those terrible events played out.

Everything ran through his mind's eye, across a mental screen. Rather than being the participant or victim he was just a spectator; he was telling his own story. But where exactly was he situated? Clive began to doubt that he was simply beginning to drift into sleep, however uncomfortably. He had the sense of being very distant, more deeply unconscious, even hallucinating or in a coma. Was he delusional as a consequence of trauma?

At some point he heard men shouting, pushing him around, shaking his shoulders and screaming into his face; although he couldn't recognise them. He was unable to distinguish or identity any of the participants. After a while there was a ringing in his head, tuning in and out, splitting him in two.

Clive was desperate to wake, to find out who was around, and what exactly was happening. As if stranded at the bottom of a deep pool of heavy unconsciousness, held under a dead salty sea - making out vague shapes, voices and actions - he couldn't return to the surface: He could see glimmers of light and movement, on a surface many fathoms above him, which aroused a flicker of interest.

But he was unable to free himself from that stagnant tank. He couldn't shake himself, in fact could barely move a limb in the struggle. His body and will were weaker than his opponents.

This felt close to drowning. He felt as if all the blood was gushing towards his head - he could feel unbearable pressure, behind his eyes and around the skull - as if he was turned upside down. He felt as if somebody was striking his face, slapping him about, even pulling his hair. Then the empty pool was suddenly filled with water, running water, heavy and strong, so that it was choking him. It was then a struggle to breathe: the blood was heavy, like a fist into the brain, while the water - distantly icy - was gushing over his face, like a sheet of rippled ice over his vision, through his mouth and nose, partly into his lungs. He was convulsed with choking, as if some heavy guy was sitting on his chest, so he couldn't breathe any more. Somehow the icy water was transformed into searing fire in his chest and lungs. His heart burst like a paper bag filled with hot blood.

The guy was shouting at him: "Where is your dossier Pitt?! Where is your dossier?!" Clive had the strange perspective of seeing an upside down face; the world was upside down again.

There it was; the large round face of Viktor Di Visu, like a cynical infant. As described, Viktor resembled the devil with a point of beard at the very end of his chin. He wore a neat pony-tail at the back, a blood-diamond stud in one ear, above a lovely black cashmere rolled-neck sweater, which clung to every ripple of designer muscle. The sleeves were pushed elegantly a few centimetres up firm forearms, as if he was doing something interesting but slightly messy. A waft of exquisite Di Visu's new *Blades pour Homme* fragrance almost masked the hot fetid air within Doug's boxed, windowless spare room, which was filling up with fear and stress like a slave ship in a storm. Pitt noted Viktor's presence and was aware of his background presence, waiting and scowling, orchestrating.

"Give us the information," echoed a heavy voice. "Give us the information you son of a bitch!"

"He can't speak. You dumb fuck. Don't you see? Allow the bastard time to speak!"

"Give back the information that does not belong to you. Where have you stored that? Do you hear us, where are you storing our data, Mr Pitt?"

"We are going to kill you now, Pitt, if you do not speak."

He felt the world swivel, as blood and water surged with gravity. His vision was obscured as sopping hair streaked over his eyes. His bursting lungs apparently gasped and spluttered water as he lurched for oxygen. Then he felt himself dropped onto the stone floor, crushing the side of his head; except he was not horizontal, he realised, he'd been heaved up against the wall, so that his ribs were cracking.

"He doesn't understand you, fuckers. Can't you see what's happening?" Vi Visu challenged.

"Where is it Pitt? Do you want more of this? Then you tell us immediately!"

"There's no point to this. He isn't going to say anything."

"We'll come back again tomorrow. Give us another day, Viktor."

"Get out of here all of you. Leave us alone. We must eliminate him now. Don't you see that you are ruining his looks?" came the voice of Di Visu. "I'm tired of these ugly scenes. Don't you realise I am creative? Artists don't like such ugliness. This is disgusting for me to even look at. This is a beautiful guy. Give this bitch something to loosen up his arse," Di Visu said. "Then go away, will you? Let me get something pleasurable out of this!"

There was a clearing of the space. Then Clive felt himself being hoisted under the arms, pulled back across the room by his hair. He was not sensible enough to feel the full pain such an action should have provoked. Somebody had their hand in his mouth after that, forcing his jaws apart, before he was thrown down to the ground again. There was something inside his mouth that he was forced to swallow, as this was the only method to get rid.

Di Visu was stood biting at the back of his neck, focused as intently as a mating dog. Clive had the sensation of elegant yet forceful hands painfully in the small of his back. He was too physically weak and disorientated to resist. After which he felt himself dropping back down, descending into the dark, until he was no longer conscious, far away from any point of light. For hours and hours he was content to fall into a state of unconsciousness, this dreamless sleep.

41

Then a point came back, like a needle entering a cave. He was able to focus on a feature of the room; to become aware of his physical situation; the twitching of a hand, a building pain in his knee. He had a distant awareness of movement in the area around; an exchange of fuzzy voices. Clive edged agonisingly back, forcing himself to concentrate. This pinprick kept him company like a cigarette on an endless and freezing night.

Coarse, thick features clarified in front of him: a face peering at him from a high, stiff shirt collar. There was a jagged scar on the guy's wide chin, slick with sweat and hair. Over this gent's shoulder was another thick-neck, set off by an identical bowler hat. There was a blinding flash, like a primitive camera flash, that fully Illuminated Breadham's claustrophobic guest room, filling it with smoke and sulphur. Clive clung precariously to the sharp sides of his consciousness. He hoped that this purgatory suspension, much worse than hell, would draw to an end. Maybe the whole ordeal would finish there, he wondered, and he could face eternal damnation or salvation with a degree of relief.

However the revelatory light turned out to be issuing from a standard bulb (albeit diffused through a frilly pink shade). Pitt began to understand that detectives were standing around the bed - he was in the bed - when his vision cleared as if by a miracle cure.

"What's the time?" he enquired.

"It's the afternoon, sleepy head."

"Sorry to disturb your dreams. Did you have a bad night?" remarked the other.

Clive recognised the guy who'd received an unconventional blow from a croquet mallet. The other bowler hatted figure stepped forward in support, looking down with a vengeful grin and grimace.

"What's been going on?" Pitt declared.

"Mr Breadham kindly put you up."

"Oh, right, he put me up all right. But where are the other people? Like Viktor?"

"You took full advantage of the bathroom facilities," someone jested.

Pitt was in a vulnerable position, his head splitting, stretched over a bed in his underpants. He was walled into this suffocating enclosure.

A sequence of events, spending the night at Doug's apartment, filtered back into his thoughts. So had he been in this space all the while? Perhaps - yet his head was killing him, his jaw ached, and every part of his body seemed to hurt; to the roots of his hair. Had he fully awoken?

He couldn't help a certain curiosity about these men, the detectives; what did they precisely want? Clive was trying to articulate these questions when another figure showed: a small guy, nimble on his feet despite relative age, wearing a well-cut black linen suit, throwing into relief a kinky quiff of silver hair. This was Sir Septimus Winchurch on night duty; if it was still night-time.

"Don't move a muscle Pitt," the financier warned.

Although not physically imposing, even regarded from the horizontal, the eminent banker had presence.

"Where is your master?" Pitt returned.

"Viktor Di Visu? Your interview is over, I understand. It doesn't matter because I am taking control of the situation. He's passed you on," Sep said.

"Are you back in touch with Viktor?" Pitt returned.

"You're in talkative mood again? Viktor informed me of your lethal reticence. I understand you have been entertaining lately," he chuckled darkly. "Isn't that your social philosophy? Been to any good parties lately?"

"Very funny, you little swindler, but you're a poor judge of character," Clive replied. "You have a dangerous choice in friends."

"Oh, very sorry to disturb your toilette Pitt," Sep told him, rattling the bedstead in annoyance. "But who are you to lecture me on friendship?"

"Where's Doug meanwhile? Has he betrayed me?" Clive wanted to know.

"Do you claim not to remember him? Douglas Breadham has an excellent legal brain, as you may recall. He underwrote our agreement with Mr Di Visu and the ZNT consortium. Surely that didn't escape your grasp? Didn't you ask him any questions? Surely you knew he's one of the best financial lawyers in London. Didn't you understand that?"

"Doug Breadham is a good friend of mine."

Despite himself, the financier laughed.

"He covered himself very well," Clive remarked.

"How well do you think you know Douglas?" the financier asked.

"For some time ," Pitt considered, vaguely.

"Who and where are your true friends? Don't you find it strange that you have not called on them, or even recalled them?" Sep told him gleefully.

"I was quite popular," Clive volunteered. But he couldn't quickly produce any names or faces.

"It's always a pleasure to work with young Douglas and his team at *Beds Whetter Breadham & Gross*. Of course we have spent a lot of time discussing your personality flaws, when you first went off the rails."

"Wait until I get my hands on him. After I have finished with you and these two circus freaks," Clive snarled.

The pair shifted from foot to food unhappily.

"Defiant to the last. But you are already a name from the past Pitt. You're a talking corpse, really. Can't you at least change your tune? Where is your expectant audience these days? Everybody has forgotten you, including a toothless FCA."

"Then why come and keep me company?" Pitt wanted to know.

"You're my responsibility. You used to work for me, didn't you? Before you were deleted. We all agree. You don't know your own mind. You've lost your thread. I'm glad to have this opportunity to... to tie up loose ends. It's been a long time I must say," he chuckled.

"What's happened to me? It's like someone's been running me under their boat," Clive said, coughing. "I feel just terrible!"

"Yes, it must have been torture, Pitt. But what does it feel like now? That you too are practically naked, defenceless and under threat? You should have stuck around my hospital to ask my daughter," Winchurch said, losing the smile. "Did her screams put you off? Is that why you took to your heels?"

The banker leant forward indignantly over Pitt; although he was dwarfed between the shoulders of those meaty investigators. His claret red animosity contrasted with the detectives' professional detachment.

"Insult me," Clive said. "Pour scorn as you wish." He clutched his knees and drew up the eiderdown. "If you were honest you wouldn't be in this situation. You refuse to recognise peril with an offshore account."

"Huh, when it comes to the City, young man, you are stupidly naïve. Why, I hesitate to call you a banker any more. Didn't you decide to opt out? Join another profession? You are half my age, yet you are stuck in the past, aren't you. You long for the age of pinstripes, bowler hats, rolled umbrella at the ready and... and a copy of the FT tucked under the arm," Sep scorned. "What do you think City finance involves, eh?"

"Oh yes finance has adapted, just as the climate is changing," Clive observed. "Just look at the kind of guys you've been mixing with."

"What about them?" Sep wanted to know. "I know how to play them... but you ran back into the pavilion, didn't you? Too many hard balls around your head."

"Even worse your associates in Europe, linked to organised crime, offered kick-backs. Are you calling that a game of bloody cricket," he declared.

"What persuaded you to transform yourself, Pitt, from a trusted employee, a brilliant banker, in to some ninny? As an insider you don't start acting like an outsider. Why not volunteer in a charity shop, if you feel that strongly? You knew this was a rough game, when you signed up. The financial markets never smelt sweetly," Sep argued.

"We claim to be a vital and legitimate business," Clive objected.

"What do you know, you innocent mill boy? During the Napoleonic wars my ancestors were raising finance... to pay for Wellington's armies. That's right, we go that far back. During the Peninsular war. Did you hear of that?" he challenged. His large face had flared and he was on the ends of his pointy shoes.

"Was there anything crooked about that? I wonder."

"It isn't our role to find moral questions. I'm not here to complain about other people's imperialism, after we lost our empire. Wealth changes but money remains the same," Winchurch argued. "Even these individuals that you term 'crooks' spend their money to the population's benefit," Sep argued.

"So these crooks can do their Christmas shop down the King's Road," Pitt replied.

"What a provincial little Englander you are, Pitt. I should have known. My father didn't squander his investment. He knew what he was paying for. What did yours get? All we offer these high worth customers is wise investments... regardless of origin, or social or political backgrounds. It's all as sound as Adam Smith would advocate."

"You apply the same principles to Mr Di Visu, do you?" Clive challenged.

"We don't have anything against Mr Di Visu. Viktor is fundamental to ZNT. He also runs an extremely successful fashion house. He's moved this firm into the new global situation. His ZNT colleagues have become admirable members of my board. You couldn't wish for more charming fellows. They aim to diversify and to purchase a larger basket of luxury brands.

This company is ready to help them; according to our historic ethos. I recognise good business and will always back a winner."

"This guy lured me to ruin my life, as well as to harm your daughter. As part of the ZNT group he exploits a UK research hospital to render prisoners from abroad...political dissidents and opponents. He doesn't merely launder currency but human souls. Are you aware of these practices?" Pitt declared. He tried to struggle up into a more forceful posture.

"That's your insane interpretation!" Sep declared.

"You even hope to modify your daughter's personality. That's right, Sep, to stop her being an embarrassment to you. Yes, you might succeed in getting me out of the way, but Di Visu and ZNT are making themselves at home. Viktor and his cronies have occupied the economic driving seat. Crime and corruption are undermining business. Don't even mention governments and the law!"

"A shame you've lost your mind Pitt," he commented.

"You wouldn't be treating me this way, if you thought so."

The financier stared deeply, with apprehension, into Clive's eyes; eyes that were red and narrow with trouble. "What is this? Paranoia? Conspiracy theories? Miss Wright made hints about you... while I was driving her to the hospital. She suggested that you were not in control of yourself. You lost your memory - couldn't recall what happened during the past year. Well I can tell you, I don't go for that escape clause," he argued.

"I was kidnapped, drugged, brain washed," Clive argued.

Winchurch's acid expression proved he was not won over.

"During that period terrible events took place. I spent time in that hospital of yours, this psychiatric prison...undergoing some form of treatment, as it were."

"You managed to escape from this psychiatric prison, didn't you?"

"Viktor must have arranged for me to get out. You believe that he saved your bacon. You shouldn't make any more mistakes like that, as he was the guy that arranged the attack on your daughter."

Sep's facial muscles flickered. "You are the man who is responsible for the rape of my daughter, nobody else."

"You wish to trade your own daughter, for the survival of your precious family firm?" Clive demanded.

"You're nothing better than a contemptible scoundrel," Sep barked.

"Did you suspect that I was capable? You got some warning sign? Then how did I get away from the scene? Didn't you suspect there must have been others?"

"There were witnesses. You went into the woods with her," Sep insisted.

"Did you forget how your daughter followed me? Don't you think the events are strange? Wasn't she behaving in an unusual way, for all her nightclub antics?" Clive argued.

"You knew exactly what you were doing. You executed your plan with cold calculation. Miss Wright may have been gullible about you. She was a great disappointment to me as well. I had my doubts about her, but I hoped for the best. I sometimes question my judgement in regard to Pixie. Do you really expect me to believe your paranoid excuses? That you are prepared to follow someone's instructions? Drugged? Brain washed?" Sep scoffed.

"De Visu wanted to criminalise me to neutralise my case. He gambled that you would never go to the police. That you would be determined to avoid scandal in the media."

"That was quite a risky gamble for Viktor, wasn't it? Maybe as a father I would be determined to have the police involved."

"Viktor is nothing but a gambler. He's dancing between life and death, like the red and the black. How did his family enrich themselves to begin with? The City resembles a Sunday picnic to that guy. Then why didn't you get the police involved? Your girl was attacked and you didn't even want to tell the authorities? Ask yourself why these events took place during the previous year. I don't have any recollection of that period. I might just have been a different guy."

"That's mad. You knew what you were doing," Sep insisted.

"Why allow Viktor's thugs to smash me about?" Clive wanted to know. "Was that going to clear my head?"

"What evil genius persuaded you to ruin your career?" he asked. "Didn't you know that I would shoot you down? Striking your pose as the whistle-blower?"

"You were involved from the beginning. You understood what the ZNT flotation involved. What did my career mean to you?"

"Why are you being so bloody stubborn? Viktor doesn't know, nobody knows!" Septimus declared, giving a nimble, indignant jump.

"You knew well that the ZNT deal was a bombshell. You'd turn into a black legend in the financial world. You'd be dodging camera crews outside the high court. As a preamble to years in a cell...even tighter than this one," Pitt said.

"You were motivated out of envy and revenge," Winchurch insisted.

"We don't think alike, you can be sure about that," Clive said.

"Your marriage was on the rocks. Didn't she leave you and go off to America? I agree, you had information that didn't make me look good," Sep admitted. "But how did you respond to pressure? You began to crack up, that's what you did. You lost professional judgement. You went to pieces. You had your eyes on Pixie from the day she walked into the office. Oh yes, Pitt. Your hands, as ever, were not far away from your thoughts. Did you imagine she'd help you forget your problems?"

"Pixie helped me to untangle that business," Clive insisted.

"I don't want to speak ill of her now, the poor creature. Only you forgot to think about the consequences of your behaviour. That's entirely typical in my experience. I wouldn't dare to insult animals by making a comparison," Winchurch said, ignoring the laughter of his lackeys. "There's no harm in a healthy sexual appetite, but I wouldn't describe yours as being healthy."

"You've been through a lot as Emmy's father," Clive agreed. "But how can it help to send suggestive messages to a female employee? You know who I'm referring to, Sir Septimus. I've listened to a few of Pixie's recorded messages," he confirmed.

"A few kind words in her voice mail?"

"Scented endearments that you sprinkled after yourself," Clive said.

42

Pitt continued under the spotlight of that narrow cavern. His former boss had caught him in an eternal moment.

"I'm beginning to think," Sep commented, "that you are some type of comedian."

"Oh yes, I want to join in. Just lying here in bed having the time of my life," Clive said.

"You're the butt of this joke. That treacherous, cunning grammar school boy...that grubby boy from one of those dark Yorkshire towns, who should have been selling pet insurance for a living... but was given an opportunity in the City... and suddenly had the world at his feet. Who did you have to thank for that? How did you repay that risky judgement, Pitt?"

The financier paced around that little iron caged bed. He had a broad chest, yet his structure was dwarfish; a pointed-toe gait on thin bowed legs, emphasised by drain-pipe Armani's. He peeled away to lean into a shadowy corner, glowering for a few moments, observing like a circus trainer with a mangy lion; before skipping back into the spotlight to menace his helpless charge.

"You are not even ashamed of yourself," Sep argued. "What a self-deceiving piece of valley trash you are, Pitt."

"How can I be ashamed of what I don't know? The extreme nature of those events proves that," Clive argued.

"Is that really the case? Does a man with memory-loss pack his suitcase one bright morning? Can he decide to run away to his mistress? Then does he pack his suitcase on another bright morning - after falling out with this fancy woman - and go and move in with another woman instead? Is that the behaviour of a confused and disorientated individual?"

"Why not?" Pitt retorted, rucking up the bedclothes underneath.

The two bowler hatted investigators shuffled in confusion. They turned to Sep for help who, for all his diminutive stature, was a superpower.

"Let me explain your private life, Pitt," Winchurch offered, lowering his resonant voice to a whisper, and putting an ironic forefinger to his temple. "Let's go back and have a look through your diary, shall we?"

"Why are you obsessed with my personal life? How does that relate to the ethics of that deal? It's nothing but a smoke screen for their actions. The main issue is the behaviour of the fund and of Di Visu... as well as your conduct in a potential scandal," he added. "Face the facts, Sep. I loved my wife and I still do, if you must know. What further proof do you require?"

"*You* are the scandal," Septimus declared. "We all know what happened after the attack on Emmy. You went back alone to Pixie's place... her flat above a shop in Hampstead. After that you signed the register at a small hotel near to Hyde Park. Next morning you made an early start and ordered a full English breakfast, room service."

"Come on, Sep, how is all this relevant to my work?" Pitt insisted.

"It highlights your character ... and typical condition of mind," Septimus argued. There was a waspish quality to his gestures. It seemed as if he wished to strangle Pitt and restrained himself. "You went into a bank and drew out most of the money in a current account. It takes time to close an account altogether, as you obviously realise. I assume you learnt that much on your father's knee. Obviously these are the desperate actions of a dazed amnesiac."

"Draw your own conclusions," Clive said. "I really don't remember."

"Is that the fact? Not a single detail? It's simple to lose trace of one's past experiences. After all, where are all of our memories stored? The mind is a curious agent. That's what the doctors tell me, you know. How complete and accurate is anyone's memory of a year passed?" Sep remarked. For a moment his face fell into a disconsolate mask of bafflement.

"Then how exactly does this incriminate me?" Pitt retorted.

The financier's mask changed back to rage and his nose came within an inch of the disgraced young banker's. "Don't imagine that I could ever forgive you, Pitt."

"I'm not looking for forgiveness," Clive said.

Septimus disentangled himself. He cut a pattern of strides like a guardsman in a sentry box. "What charity did you offer my family? Having drawn out the money - much of which belonged to your wife - you rented a small basement flat off Ladbroke Grove. After wrecking people's lives you decided to live quietly," Sep recalled. "In fact technically you continue to rent that room, as you paid the lady in advance. My investigative team discovered this bolt hole."

The team in question swapped satisfied grimaces and leers.

"For me it was a matter of survival... I needed a base," he considered.

"There was a suit in the wardrobe... just back from a dry clean and press. You were not depriving yourself of creature comforts. There was a bottle of claret on the table... a supply of upmarket television dinners. You were keeping up your reading... in economics and the City. Newly published books, making negative arguments about us," Winchurch hissed.

"There were some leaks about the deal? Was I the source?" Clive asked.

"You went to read articles in current journals at the British Library," Sep added, raising his voice. "You were conducting a research project, or rather a campaign. Quite the student."

"We always believed in self-improvement," Clive replied.

"*The lad did good!*" Sep exclaimed hoarsely - he found a temporary hitch within his vocal folds - his stare glittery and watery. "Not only this, but you went out to look for another job. What's more you soon found one... a consultancy at a rival corporation... after lying about previous employment. I couldn't keep tabs on all your connections in the City."

"You can't expect me to sit about at home, can you, twiddling my bloody thumbs," Pitt argued.

"The rest of the time you were plotting from Clerkenwell. At least until you left the gas on," Sep said, alluding the ransacking of Pitt's office. "You'd take your lunch at the Working Men's Chop House. Do your thinking time in the pews of St James church. A position in the City, in a company of rising stock, just three streets away from us, with a desk of your own."

"Sounds reasonable," Pitt observed. But he hadn't seen this coming.

"It's utterly scandalous, that's what it is. We're not going to stand for it any longer," he hissed.

Clive was amazed. Yet the details accorded well with what he might have done. He'd been continuing his investigations into the deal.

"The bizarre point is that I lost track of everything."

"Your plea is not acceptable," Sir Septimus replied. "You are a traitor."

"I'm not joking. I must have even left my jacket behind. My possessions are stored somewhere. Those would include my briefcase... all my devices. Most importantly there is the evidence. I was thinking about where the heck I might have put those memory files."

"You chanced across poor Pixie in the street," Sep insisted. "You couldn't resist her and this drew you back to the firm, didn't it?"

"That's complete rubbish. Why would I do that?" he spluttered.

"From that moment we were able to track you."

"Are you telling me Pixie informed on me?"

"Certainly she didn't expect to see you... outside our building," the financier explained.

"Then she betrayed me, even if she didn't intend to," Pitt concluded.

"Scum like you cannot be betrayed," Sep rebuked. He took a grip on the bedstead with his oversize hands and gave it an alarming shake. "But for the record... not to say anything unkind about the girl... she didn't betray you. We really shouldn't say anything unkind about Pixie now. Later she was willing to defend you. She was ready to repeat all your excuses. She claimed that you were the victim of a plot, orchestrated by Viktor."

"Then you think she's a liar too," Clive insisted.

"You'd won her over. Soon after that you were back together. The girl betrayed herself, as soon as she opened her mouth. Why should she want to sell me junk like you?" he snarled.

"I just hope she's all right," Clive considered.

"A charming, well brought up girl like her... connected to a Norwegian shipping magnate...a girl who was skiing down Swiss mountains in her romper suit... mixed up with a plebby northern climber like you... the narrow minded son of an out-at-the-elbow building society manager, invited down to London and selected by this firm, offered a generous position, constantly with his foot in his mouth. *Of course you manipulated her*," Septimus argued.

"You were jealous, you little crook. You're still jealous. Let me tell you, she called the shots in our relationship. It's no business of yours if she chose to go out with me," Clive told him.

Sep's eyes rounded in righteous indignation. Such was his loathing of Clive it was almost a pleasure to talk to him.

"Let's go along with this, shall we? Maybe I was feeling let down by her. She never told me her new address. How did you win back her confidence? You even took her in twice. I couldn't understand that."

"Is she all right?" Clive asked, worried. "You haven't killed her, have you?"

"It was a blow to understand she was helping you... feeding you information. She hacked into our hospital records. She browsed encrypted files of patients..."

"She knows how to switch it on, you know," Pitt said.

"Many of them important patients... from clients abroad. Indeed she does. Paying a lot of money for treatment. Such a breach of trust and security. She was prepared to do this. When I had such a high opinion about her!"

"What's happened to her?"

Sadness clouded Sep's eyes for a moment. "Unfortunately, if you didn't know, Pixie has met with a most unfortunate accident."

"What are you talking about? What sort of accident?" Clive persisted.

"That's right, in an accident. A most dreadful incident. Terrible. She stepped out into the path of a van. She didn't look both ways, no... she didn't look where she was going," Sep explained, "and she went into the path of a transit van... a support workers' van. The chap wasn't speeding, so far as I gather...but he must have been going at a... He had no chance to stop, any more than Pixie could avoid being hit."

"When did this happen?" Clive pressed. He struggled to find his voice again.

"Does the timing matter to you now?" Winchurch asked.

"So you're telling me Pixie's dead? Is that it? She's been killed? Another terrible coincidence?" Clive accused.

"Pixie wasn't killed. Do you think I was a witness? No, she was critically injured, but the ambulance came and took her to hospital immediately. She was badly injured, yes, rather shaken, but she's making a recovery."

"How exactly is she hurt?" Pitt asked.

"She was extremely lucky. Not to have been killed, I mean. However she will never be the same girl again... she suffered head injuries. The collision has rather changed her personality. You'd be forgiven for thinking that Pixie is quite another girl," he mused. "She is so quiet, so restrained, compared to how she used to be. We might say that this awful accident has altered her character."

"I can't bear to listen to this," Clive said. "Is she conscious? Does she know the people around her?"

"How could she ever forget you?" Sep remarked. "Just don't expect her to collaborate in your fantasies any more...or to add to your conspiracy theories. I expect that her hobbies will be much gentler. Of course she'd be difficult to replace on that desk...but she wouldn't be able to concentrate or reason properly. Sadly I couldn't trust her judgement or her speed of reaction."

"You arranged this, or you were involved... as with the entire affair."

"This was just an accident Pitt. An awful, heart breaking accident," he said, in a gravid aside. "Some brain damage, a change of personality, was part of the injuries she suffered. I'm sorry that this occurred. In some ways she's an even nicer girl than before. At least she keeps her looks," he added.

"I will have to speak to her. Visit her in the hospital. How can I?" Clive agonised - he was thinking out loud.

"There's no way you're going to visit her," Winchurch retorted.

"Doesn't she have a right to meet with me?"

"Shouldn't you take some responsibility? This wouldn't have happened without you. Or do you seriously think she was in love with you? Don't you feel any remorse, Pitt, after all the feelings you have offended? Not to mention the lives you have destroyed?"

"I have never hurt Pixie in my life," he replied.

"For a self-confessed amnesiac, you speak with amazing conviction!"

"Viktor pushed me into those actions."

"You admit that you raped my daughter," Sep challenged.

"What do you really know about me?"

"Enough. More than you do, apparently."

"I was hard-working, dedicated, conscientious...wasn't I? Look at my P&A year in year out."

"You cling to a high opinion of yourself, don't you. You can't admit to any gaps of self-knowledge. Why are you sure about your own character? My investigators found some interesting downloads at your flat in Ladbroke Grove. Hard core pornography I believe is the popular description. At my company that means instant dismissal."

"You think a bit of naked flesh condemns my character?" Clive replied. "Try again."

"I wouldn't touch you with the jaws of a sand dredger," Winchurch argued.

The detectives' loose grins broke out into chuckles.

"For years our minds were your fortune," Clive argued.

"Oh, yes, really? That's how you saw your situation?" Winchurch found a pair of soft leather gloves in his jacket pocket and peeled them back over his chubby fingers. "They also found an intriguing collection of exotic sexual instruments there in your seedy bedsit... not merely a filthy contaminated hard drive."

"That's impossible," Pitt rejoined. "I deny all knowledge of these objects, which were obviously planted."

"Clearly you don't recognise the inside of your own mind," Sep remarked.

"I admit to looking at pornography... from time to time. I admit that's a bit embarrassing. But this stuff about fetishist objects is nonsense. It would be just as revealing to break into your interior mental world, Winchurch. That's without any reference to your gangster-ism in the City."

"What a lurid imagination you have, Pitt. Mr Muldrow and Mr Oblomov here made enquiries on a wider scale. They investigated a series of attacks on women in the west London area. Yes, I have my facts straight. They didn't only make a record of your curious metal and rubber collection. They read through police files and went to the borough library to read back editions of local newspapers."

The two slogs grinned at each other from either side of the bed.

"You claim there was a connection to me, do you?" Clive replied.

"True, these were not rapes. Victims were able to describe your physique and appearance... more damningly these women described objects of a type that my detectives found in your bedsit."

"That's impossible. This is fabricated evidence," Clive retorted.

"You can't deny responsibility for these crimes," Sep argued. "They'll lock you up for years. The felons will beat you senseless!"

"Somebody already stuck the boot into me," Clive said.

"There was some rough justice there! No more than you deserved."

"Don't ask me how it was brought off. Certainly I went through some process of mind bending or washing. Anyway, some form of influence to control my thoughts and movements."

"I fear you've lost your marbles," Sep told him.

"You put me into a psychiatric ward...along with dissident intellectuals. What did they put me through?" Clive bemoaned.

"You talk about your sufferings. Of your life in ruins," Sep retorted brokenly. "But what about the effect on my daughter? On her mother and family? And even on your former colleagues?" he barked.

"That was a strike ball for ZNT," Clive countered.

"Stuff and nonsense was it."

"Who gave you this raging thirst for revenge?" Clive argued.

"You really think Viktor has arranged this?" the financier considered.

"The very man," Clive told him. "I'm his inside trade."

"Viktor seems more interested in couture...in acquiring his prestige labels."

"That's all a fig leaf, I can tell you."

"Perfumery and frocks?" Sep replied. "What can possibly be sinister about dear Viktor? You are merely envious of his drive and ambition, his genius."

"You fixed a flotation of BIP for the fund. You set up a surprisingly low share offer. The firm was skimming off commission from fraudulent profits. You believe they saved your company, but the company's in their pocket. ZNT are the fund and your firm is merely part of the hedge! They can destroy the firm at any time, or simply call it ZNT or even *Di Visu* for fun. Why not? What's to stop them?"

"What a ridiculous allegation! No, you were master of yourself, Pitt," Sep argued. "Now get your clothes back on. Face the consequences."

"You have no authority. I demand to speak to the City of London police. They can put me in touch with the Serious Fraud Squad."

"They wouldn't give you the time of day," the financier insisted.

The detectives pounced on him and there was a struggle. Gripping Pitt's arms, they dragged him off the rickety bed, which clattered on its side. They managed to drag him over the floor, banging his spine, until pushing him up against a wall. As Muldrow or Oblomov put a huge mitt around his windpipe, the other one forcefully clothed him. It was like having a pair of brutal male nannies; as if Pitt could only recruit a dresser from Brixton prison.

Meanwhile Winchurch observed proceedings, until he revealed a neat little silver pistol, female in its concision. But he managed to squeeze a finger on the trigger, and he began to wave the gun about self-consciously. Toting small arms was different to handling a shotgun on a grouse shoot. He perspired, flourishing it around, like an incompetent music conductor during a difficult passage, hoping everybody would catch up with his gestures.

"How could you allow them to hurt Pixie?" Clive remonstrated. "Are you so spineless? You're complicit. You'll be held responsible."

"You can say goodbye to Pixie Wright. You'll never hear her voice again or look into her eyes... nor fall into her soft embrace. From now on you'll be enjoying the careful attentions of my detectives. You'll be looking into their eyes instead... feeling the caress of *their* hands on your body," Sep remarked. "You'll never experience her love again."

Clive felt cramps and pains where Di Visu's thugs had already worked him over. There was a burning effect in his throat and lungs, from the water.

Sir Septimus cast a satirical eye over him, before signalling for the prisoner to be dragged away.

It was a relief to escape the terrible nightmares of the past night, or week or month - whatever period of time had elapsed. He was glad to leave that 'spare bedroom', even under threat, slick with water and sweat. He exited with a gruesome henchman on either side; not to mention the narrow aperture of an elegant pistol at the base of his skull. Like God's forefinger touching Adam.

Douglas Breadham was nowhere to be seen - maybe he'd left for work - as Pitt was hauled like a dead dog across the financial lawyer's luxurious living room.

43

Outside in the street - regardless of some passers-by - Clive was bundled into the back seat of a company BMW. This vehicle was used for ferrying visitors to and from the airport and between meetings. He was squeezed between that pair of lumpy and malodorous detectives, with Sep back in the driver's seat, perched on his tartan cushion. All he saw of Winchurch was a patch of wavy silver hair that poked under a head rest.

The automobile's cream upholstery was gentle on bruises, and created an insulated atmosphere, although the compartment was even more claustrophobic.

Sep roared out of the cobbled lane, heading back towards town. Apparently it was very early in the morning, as the sky was pitch black. The passing streets were practically deserted. Only buses and a scattering of other traffic circulated. Clive hadn't often travelled through these London streets at such an early hour: only during the intense period of the BIP flotation; when he would be coming and going from the office virtually around the clock. They rode the markets night and day, as if they span against the globe, or someone had designed a programme to banish nature.

Pitt's incredulity had increased - disbelief turning to anger - as he had scrutinised the ZNT proposals in detail, examined all proposals for the takeover, with Sep's notes and endorsements added, so that his initial enthusiasm completely guttered. After that every trip to the office had involved a violent inner conflict. He had turned his attention to the frauds, numerous massive illegalities, with a feeling of outrage, which could be blamed on his father's infuriating small-town integrity.

"Where are we headed?" Clive asked. "Planning on dumping me somewhere?" He'd endured a lengthy silence, with London's grand architectural parade gliding past on both sides.

"Glad you are still curious about your fate. Thought you were nodding off back there," Winchurch replied. "Must have been exhausting for you."

"What's next?" Clive persisted.

"I'm the kind of chap who likes to get things done. You know that. Sometimes rules are there to be ignored. It's like having a moral accountant. Creative justice, of the mind, so to speak. I'm a City man to the bone and I enjoy paying people back in kind. There's still something of the old gent' in me, Pitt. Yet while we may be involved with numerous charities, many worthy causes, we are certainly not one. Don't you think that shows generosity of spirit?"

Pitt made a lunge at his former employer. Finding his hands free he thrust them around the headrest. His fingers sank into bristly skin and rough sinew.

Yet despite squeezing as forcefully as possible (until the veins and bones of his own neck bulged) no noise issued from the front, where his old boss was presumably being strangled. The car over-revved a touch, but didn't even lurch or change direction; just cruised in the same line. Such was the determination, the self-control and resilience of the financier. After all, his direct ancestor had bargained loans and bonds with Lord Liverpool (not known for his compassionate heart) and with many of the crowned heads of Europe.

Soon the crude detectives, in a state of alarm and panic, struggled to unlock Clive's grasp. They made expert thrusts to the vulnerable areas of his anatomy. Within seconds Clive was safely back within their grasp, squashed back into the seat, like a schoolboy who had tried to flee on a museum trip.

Finally choking noises gathered at the front. Despite his toughness Winchurch was not immune to physical pain and damage. Although remaining calm and in control he'd been half throttled by his errant employee.

"Was that a desperate attempt..?" Sep enquired hoarsely. Then there was the explosion of a cough. "Is that your final word?" The broken pieces of his voice box began to reassemble. "Any more excuses?" The timbre of his voice had been damaged.

"You're going to bump *me* off, aren't you!"

"Don't go jumping to obvious conclusions," Sep retorted.

"What else can you do?"

"I could decide to retain you. Who can tell my plans?"

"You're having a laugh, aren't you? How can you keep me on, after all this?"

There was no immediate response. They listened to the restful ticking of the indicator as Winchurch turned his BMW into the Strand.

Sep tuned into a financial news programme on the radio. Not that he was paying much attention to the analysis - the volume was soft - but he required reassuring habit. Between revenge and anger there was a jangling of nerves; silent perhaps but felt as violently in his limbs as feedback guitar.

Those grand buildings continued to slip sombrely around them. Traffic increased as morning drew on. The city shook off its relative slumber as the conventional working day commenced. Opposing red and white car lights gathered at junctions, like clogging spores: before they were released to circulate, as if dislodged by a gust. Pitt wished he was back as an independent agent, walking over those pavements that unravelled beyond the car's windows. There was a young tramp going through spilling rubbish bins he noticed. Even social isolation was better than being trapped in this company.

"What a vicious and ungrateful chap you have been," Sep remarked.

"As you like," Pitt retorted.

"I'm making you a new job offer. Are you turning me down?"

Clive made a contemptuous noise.

"Admittedly it isn't as attractive as your previous job," Sep confirmed.

"Stop piking me."

"I'm deadly serious about this, Pitt. We'll offer you a contract."

"I joined the firm ten years ago, it has to be now," Pitt recalled. "Full of hope and expectation...yes, and ambition too... youthful energy...maybe a bit of greed, who can deny it? Starting off in a great career at Winchurch Brothers...the pride and fear of my family. And how did you reward me in the end?"

"You didn't keep your bond of trust," tolled his employer's voice.

"Do you think that was easy for me? To consider turning whistle-blower?"

"You're going to stick with us through thick and thin. How do you think it was for us? It'll be just like the good old days of tight regulation. When we could play by gentlemen's rules," he said teasingly.

"Now we're the servants of criminals," Clive said.

Sep jeered. "You're still satisfied with your performance? Even as head of that team, you were never indispensable. But you can redeem yourself. Even after being dismissed you can find a new place... there's unfinished business."

"You can say that again, mate," Clive replied, shuffling his bones.

"Quite correct, so let's concentrate on terms and conditions. You made a dossier about the BIP deal, about ZNT...even my involvement."

"Do you think that gave me any pleasure?" Clive replied.

"Fair enough... you don't know where your memory files may be stored right now." Septimus concentrated on a turning. He emitted a groan as he relaxed into the next street. "You don't have any clue what you did with them...even encouraged by Viktor's staff...to bring them back. Viktor tried every technique available to him. Were you going to inform the police, or were you plotting to blackmail me?"

"The plan was to hand everything over to the authorities," Clive insisted.

"So you're not a blackmailer?" Winchurch considered.

"Did you think I could be?"

"I have a duty of care towards Winchurch Brothers. The way I structure this company, steer through the present climate... to secure our future financial health... my management style is designed to benefit everybody... as well as the board and shareholders. Everything I do is for this company and for my family," Sep insisted warmly.

"Even when you're ignoring the law," Pitt argued, stubbornly.

Sep continued to navigate the streets smoothly and to keep his eyes on the road.

"Do you think that I approve of everything our clients do? Of all the individuals we deal with here, in all their colourful variety?" the financier challenged. "Didn't you learn to hold your nose, Pitt, from time to time...for the good of the company? Even for the good of UK plc.?"

"You put me into a terrible position, by asking me to break the law," Clive objected. "Then to cover everything up. Or to pretend not to notice."

"You're not remiss to say that ZNT practices were not legal... or transparent. Viktor has his own management style... with an international, if nationalist outlook. Exposure would have ruined my reputation, harmed us on the markets. I might have been forced to resign."

"For a time the company had tanked. You faced bankruptcy," Clive insisted.

"Did you really think you could disgrace me? Bring down such an influential figure? No, this was a little indiscretion among powerful friends. No, I had the Chancellor's ear...*GQ*'s young politician of the year no less. It is you who is the diseased cell, Pitt, which has to be eradicated."

"This new job definitely sounds less attractive," Pitt remarked.

"Ah, you need to read the small print."

"You would have faced a fraud squad investigation, a parliamentary committee, a public enquiry. Not to mention those reporters and photographers waiting for you outside the Old Bailey."

"The establishment of this country doesn't want to upset us. Not even after we overreached ourselves last time. They don't know how to put the international house in order. You can see that Pitt, the world economy needs to breathe, but it has to be strangled too. They're too afraid we'll unplug our algorithms and relocate to a small duchy... sacking our UK labour force, stop paying any UK taxes and dividends - such as they are - as a consequence," Winchurch mocked.

"We're supposed to serve the nation...raise finance to boost business expansion...to help produce a successful economy. Aren't we?"

The financier guffawed. "Is that what your old Dad used to tell you, Pitt? When he was listening to some Halifax social worker, deciding whether to offer him a loan for a new patio... or not?"

"They'll put us bankers in our place one day," Pitt vowed.

"Not very likely, as we always had these politicians by the short and curlies. What's a small City player like you going to do, anyway? You tried to take us on. Did you get to the top of your profession? Our transactions bankroll the public sector... the entire UK welfare state, actually. We deliver twelve billion in tax, in return for a light touch. We're the electricity for Frankenstein. The British government knows that. We are the chaps keeping our ignorant thugs off the street... bankrolling single mothers' clubs, leisure centres...and drug addict drop-in centres."

"We've been an extra tax on the economy," Pitt argued. "We're basically skimming off the profits to...to do what? Hand out bonuses to ourselves, inflate our salaries, and to enrich a select group of robber barons!"

"Nonsense, Pitt, they know who's buttering their bread... keeping their society from breaking down altogether...these socialist or social liberal types. Do they want complete honesty and transparency? Or do they want a percentage?"

"Are you serious, Winchurch? Half of the business is about avoiding taxes," Clive said.

"If only you had the same dedication to your job... your former job. You could have continued to live the life, couldn't you? ...to enjoy spending it all," Winchurch argued. "Didn't you enjoy putting on the style? You could have stayed inside the bubble, rather than trying to pop it... hiding out in Clerkenwell... conducting your investigations into my affairs...running your little office there... like some kind of financial Mickey Spillane. But where is your damning evidence now, Pitt? Where did all your work get you, exactly?" he taunted.

"The location of my evidence...remains obscure," Clive admitted.

"You're absent minded, aren't you? Now you've lost your records. In fact you've lost everything, haven't you, Pitt," he laughed. "While you were labouring to destroy me, to blow apart the deal, you actually ruined your own career."

"But I don't regret it. I know that this report existed...I note your determination to retrieve the evidence contained," Clive noted.

"Do you, actually?"

"That would totally vindicate my accusations, you tricky little fraudster!"

"I will not tolerate you prying into private and company affairs. You broke the trust and loyalty we placed in you. You betrayed us. Ruining our reputation! Not only is it dishonest and disgraceful, it is loathsome."

"Whatever you say," Pitt told him.

"Luckily we caught you red handed. There was also an attempted break-in at Viktor Di Visu's house near Regent's Park."

"Are you saying I tried to break into his place?"

"Do you remember his marvellous house? A burglary narrowly foiled by his returning early from the Lord Mayor's banquet last year... incidentally."

"What a relief for the nation," Clive remarked.

"I would have sacked you years ago," Winchurch declared. The temper rose in his voice, although he kept control. "At least I don't have to throw myself at the arcane mercies of that haunted house," he remarked. He was referring to the Old Bailey, the law courts, which they had then driven past.

"You could have distanced yourself from ZNT," Clive suggested.

"Allowed myself to be screwed, do you mean?"

"We could have recommended a rejection. On the basis of the company being undervalued, of improper governance ... we might have stopped the fraud and pitched for another buyer."

"No Pitt, you reached your limits, you lost your nerve. You fell back on your bloody-minded provincial ethics. You developed a vendetta against the company. Against me. You even transformed yourself into an Occupy style campaigner, didn't you? Nothing would get done here, with ninnies like you."

"You can't see how Viktor has played this?" Clive commented.

"You would like to have a gram of the talent he has."

"He's a destroyer of the world," Clive replied.

"Bullshit, Pitt. You're paranoid...envious. He's a highly creative young man, who conducts himself in a modest and democratic style," Winchurch claimed. "Despite his enormous resources and his untold influence."

"This guy tortured me to get information. He has no more respect for democracy or human rights, than he does for the rule of law!"

"Many of these tactics can remain within the law," Sir Septimus claimed.

"Do we depend so heavily on these guys? Or are we just afraid of them?" Pitt asked.

"Our brokerage may not interest the authorities at all. A big fund like ZNT has to play the game. Welcome to the real financial world, Pitt. You didn't join your building society after all, did you... as I keep reminding you," Sep argued.

"There's nothing enlightened about your self-interest," Clive said.

"What a tragedy that your attitude didn't extend to my daughter. You didn't treat my girl with so much respect. You didn't show any moral squeamishness about her, did you, Pitt?" he scoffed.

"This reflects the true respect they have for you, Sep. You said that Viktor has to play his game, but he's aiming to take us all out. Like a bunch of awkward minor officials in his own country. He turned you speechless and knocked you out."

"Revenge came in the form of my daughter. You humiliated me. But you should know that you can't break my balls so easily. We've been a part of the establishment for centuries. Some callow grammar school kid ... surely you can do the maths there!"

"Now you offer me another job? Can you be as cynical as all that?"

"Are you going to tweet about this?" Winchurch observed. "I do understand that my proposal is strange. This isn't the normal interview and selection process. Talking of your former position, it is out of the window. I did consider throwing you out of a window, by the way. That would have been a medieval form of justice, would it not?"

"Why don't you get to the point?" Pitt suggested. This prompted further digs into his ribs from the offended detectives.

"Let me run this idea by you, Pitt. I want to lock you down in the basement, for the rest of your working life... so you can toil for me undisturbed, around the clock."

"What sort of job do you call that?" Clive snorted.

"Exactly. It's going to be horrible for you."

"You can't be serious," Clive objected.

"Our business is very abstract, when you analyse it. Wouldn't you agree with me there? Millions of people around the globe survive on less than a dollar a day...while we print billions of dollars out of thin air...or whichever currency it may be...just to add fiscal stimulus. The Americans have done it, we have done it."

"Are we heading towards the office now? Are we meeting someone? Di Visu maybe?" Clive said anxiously.

"You're pulling my leg now, aren't you? Viktor doesn't want to speak to you again. He's sick of the sight of you. You proved a very incommunicative friend. Some help you were to him. You wouldn't help him with your memory. He can only assume it's lost altogether. Now you're lost too."

Clive noticed that they were back in the square mile, apparently on course for Winchurch Brothers building, as if it was business as usual.

But, as it transpired, further changes were afoot.

44

Sir Septimus chose to remain silent as he accelerated along Queen's Street. Traffic was sporadic, consisting of speeding postal vans - perhaps one of these had struck Pixie - and early buses, ferrying auxiliary staff.

This was the subterranean life of the City that Pitt rarely observed, and which he was too busy to comprehend even now. The thought of Pixie's accident continued to trouble him. He thought of her with sadness and loss, as he recalled her way of talking, how her smile tightened the skin around her eyes, her rapid panther way of walking; lost.

"If you're curious," Sep remarked, "I thought I'd take you over docklands way. I'd be interested in your reaction. We're moving HQ out there, you see. A plot became available. Viktor is prepared to sink in extra capital. The ZNT people want something to rival the Arabs over at the Shard. It's a matter of personal and national pride to Viktor, you see, to erect a 'scraper here in London. It's an upheaval for our staff, admittedly, but we have to move with the times."

"Very interesting, Sep," Clive agreed. "Then are you implying that I will have a desk in the new building?" Pitt speculated.

"There will be changes with this new board," Sep agreed. "This has been a turbulent year for the company... back from the brink of bankruptcy after two hundred years in business... working with new clients... adapting to new market conditions. But after the BIP flotation and our partnership with ZNT, we are healthy again," Sep claimed.

"Thanks for sharing the news with me," Clive told him.

"I'm confident that you'll adapt to your new role. My employees' troubles are my troubles," Winchurch argued.

The financier peered back between seats, grinning and more generously disposed.

Meanwhile he pressed silkily through the crisp morning air. A route was negotiated between those monstrous iced cakes of the City. Although it was near dark outside, with only a sparkle from Jupiter, artificial lights pierced from interiors.

Overseas labour was busy cleaning. Security staff crossed the trading floors in ritual dawn blessings. Eventually Winchurch's car sped into the eastern boroughs, as far as Limehouse, and turned on to the East India Dock Road.

Pitt was not familiar with surroundings this far east. Like anyone taken to an unfamiliar terrain he experienced a mix of fear and vague elation, not knowing which was most appropriate. Was this to be a short journey?

"Not far now," chipped Winchurch.

"I'm not interested," Clive said.

"Don't get shirty with us now," replied his boss.

"In working for you, I mean."

Silence was enforced until the ride was over. The BMW came to a halt with a gentle post-coital deflation. The smooth efficiency and calm power of this car was meant to casually intimidate, as well as to shield. This was impressive technology designed to carry either saints or tyrants - no questions asked. All they had to do was to hand over sufficient cash; this was a universal principle. If we are travelling to environmental collapse then we may as well go in style.

"All right everybody. You can all get out now," Sep ordered, genially.

Pitt was grappled by the investigators, who made sure not to let him free for an instant. They shook him out, more or less, with his feet and legs dragging, cutting grooves through dried mud and sand. From there they all four traversed a parking area, in the direction of a wire-link perimeter fence.

There was the usual material and machinery of a large scale building project; now in the final stages. The breeze was fresh and immediate, at this hour, with a tang in the air, suggesting the proximity of the Thames. Their probable destination loomed in front - a spanking new building, reaching up thousands of feet, designed in a post-modern style - or styles. Not far west the Shard rose into the high clouds, as Clive gazed upwards. The new Winchurch Building, as it had become, strained every architectural sinew to beat the record height for a 'scraper in London.

"This must be setting Viktor back a few notes?" Clive said, awed.

"Don't worry Pitt, you're not paying," Winchurch replied.

"Only a few tax pounds, any roads," Clive suggested.

"God knows you young rascals must owe me a few millions," he protested jokily. "Throwing good money after bad. Gambling away my family inheritance."

"Who was running the show anyway?" Pitt objected.

"Tony didn't want us to kill his golden goose, did he? Then there was poor old Gordon, tampering with the pension funds."

"Not if they wanted to avoid becoming a banana republic," Pitt countered.

"Stuff and nonsense Pitt. If it hadn't been for oil and finance, cheap labour and deregulation, this country would have been third class decades ago."

Winchurch unlocked padlocks, releasing heavy gates. He began to grow animated and bounced ahead. They had to crane their necks to get a view of the building's magnitude. Winchurch's undersized buoyancy was annoying to Pitt, as was that beam of self-satisfaction and the pride of ownership; even if he was really no more than a rent paying tenant.

"What a magnificent edifice!" Sep called back. His voice was thin in the air. "This is to be our new headquarters."

"Thanks to the ZNT bankroll," Pitt remarked.

Sep assumed the vanguard, paying no heed when he nearly tripped, hampered by his higher than normal heels. "Look at the architecture here - magnificent! The twenty first century personified."

"Hubris and squandering of resources," Clive said.

"You stick in the mud, stubborn Yorkshireman. You can't recognise ambition, the drive for something impressive and better than ever before!"

Finally Sep waited for the other three to catch up; Clive pinned between those two beefy detectives. The latter pair tended to gape in the direction of the new 'ZNT Winchurch Tower', but with a detached uncomprehending expression, as if the first stone hadn't yet been laid.

"This is a complete folly, mate! Do you think this can save you, once the details emerge?" Clive remonstrated.

Sir Septimus laughed dismissively. "What do you know of the subject?"

The diminutive financier stood arms akimbo, waved silver hair flying loose. He checked back on their progress, while tossing up his glance, with a slight groan of discomfort, to the very pinnacle of the new skyscraper.

"Don't tell me. Viktor Di Visu helped towards the design," Clive guessed.

"You're a cynic if you are nothing, Pitt," he said.

"Now you're going to make people work here? Did you even manage to half fill all this extra office space?"

"I'd advise you to get a feel for the place. In a few years every square metre will be occupied...as has been proved before. The basement is reserved for you," Sep added, with a leer.

"I should tell you this is a classic second-hand hit. You want to cover for him? Do the dirty work? A man of your standing? Don't you feel any shame about that?" he complained.

Septimus snickered darkly. "This is a pleasure for me. This is justice for my little girl. What does a monster like you understand? Don't worry about that. Your memory, along with our history, completely erased. You are obsolete. You don't pose any risk," Sep growled.

"These goons are only protecting Viktor. Life is cheap for those ZNT guys...they snub out their enemies over coffee break... but Viktor still needs to protect himself in regard to the deal. So they have to involve you too. Are you proud of your consultancy? You feel like doing time for those guys? While Viktor designs his frocks and tests his chichi perfume?" Clive said.

"You're a paranoid chap," Sep said. "You fully deserve this extra bonus. I want you to take a symbolic role."

The rays of an aggressive sun, emerging from the water, spilt around his restless silhouette.

The breeze ruffled Clive's fringe, which was stuck together with blood and sweat in parts. He could barely stand on his own feet. "How symbolic?" he wondered.

"Honorary, if you prefer. I have to consider everybody's feelings. Including Esmeralda's. Although I agree she presently has no role, until she graduates with a first class business degree, when she agrees to enrol. Her doctors are fully confident about her full recovery. I'm sure she can turn the corner."

"You still hope she's going to be your ideal candidate? Will she meet the same fate as Pixie, if she fails to impress?" Pitt scorned.

"We spent a lot of money on our Emmy. She is undoubtedly a clever and pretty girl. Who needs an eldest son in this day and age? What kind of father would allow her to go astray? What a future we can promise her these days. Now you can play your small part too, Pitt."

"Let's get this over with," Clive suggested. "Do Viktor's cheap hit."

"Don't give up. You sound resigned. That's what I told my bright young quants straight out of university...when they were losing me millions every hour, a few years ago. Never lose hope, raise the stakes, when your next hunch could be your winning bet!"

"I was never a loser in this firm," Clive reminded him. "You made me a key holder...you promoted me."

"I trusted you, sonny boy," Winchurch agreed. "I put my balls on the block."

"You involved me with the BIP sale...you appointed me head of the team."

"Bring him up gentlemen!" Sep urged, with a raised note.

Clive resisted again but the detectives were able to comply.

"What marvellous entrance steps," Sep observed, jogging up. "Senatorial in grandeur."

"I demand to be taken to Bishopsgate police station," Clive said.

"Do you really? You want to talk to the filth?" Sep satirised. "Anyway they're not interested in your case. How coherent is it likely to be?"

"You don't know that," Pitt insisted.

"Try to retain your dignity."

Clive was drowning in cold sweat, given an icy surface by the waterside. Usually, before the oven heat of another late summer day, this breeze would have refreshed. This morning, he considered, it felt more like a frosty breath prefiguring eternal flames.

Clive was dragged to the top of three flights of marble steps. At the summit the diminutive, black-clad figure of Winchurch awaited. The financier was rummaging in his pockets for something; then he brought out a key. He soon managed with the chunky contractor's lock and gestured for them all enter the building's lobby.

As the group moved into the dusk of a cavernous lobby, the hefty investigators shoved Clive ahead. The place was empty except for bare carpentry and other finishing materials. Shafts of sunlight punctured surrounding dirty glass. The vast internal atmosphere glittered with a nebula of concrete dust.

"Witness my success...while confronting your own failure," Sep suggested.

His voice, usually baritone in his beer barrel chest, echoed flatly.

"That's where your promises lead," Clive commented.

"You see where your arrogance got you?" Sir Septimus invited.

"That's fine coming from you, isn't it?"

"If only you knew where your quibbles would lead."

"I should have wised up," Clive replied.

"But you can still play your part in our triumph... even if your memory has to perish with you."

"It has to be somewhere. Aren't you afraid it will turn up?" Clive said.

"In the event of your death, do you mean?" Sep glinted, with a curl of his top lip.

"I begin to see what you have in mind," Clive stated.

"What took you so long to figure that out... a chap with such a head for figures?"

"What brilliant cover for Viktor," Clive said. "Gets you to behave like a cheap gangster. How does it feel?"

"Feels wonderful, if you're interested," Sep retorted. "Adjust yourself to your unpaid situation. Consider this a personal compliment. Not every social deviant deserves such an end. What a way to enjoy the new office. What an honour to have you," Winchurch declared. "Better than a plaque at the entrance, wouldn't you say?"

The henchmen took Clive further inside, as their boss dashed ahead. There were lofty half completed vaults above their heads. The men stopped before a huge hole in the ground, ready for a central supporting column.

"Take a look down, Pitt. There's your new desk," Septimus told him. "Can you see?"

"What are you talking about?" Pitt replied, suddenly vertiginous.

"Not such a high climber now. But at least it's a start... with every chance of promotion," he joked. "Throw him down gentlemen. Time is money, Pitt."

"Get your mitts off me, you apes!"

"No, I'm not going to shoot Pitt, as suggested. Viktor told me to shoot you in the back of the head, you see. That isn't my way, you know. Viktor should understand... I'm not an assassin. I'm not some SS henchman, you know. Let Pitt feel every bump as he tumbles. Let him suffer as much as possible. Remember what happened to my daughter."

"You really intend to throw me down there?" Clive shouted.

"This is the end of the line for you, Pitt."

"You're a complete monster."

"That's quite something coming from you," Sep said. His hilarity ricocheted.

Pitt's terrified outrage rang around the cavern. Yet the detectives got the better of Clive. They dangled him out over an abyss.

Their boss observed satisfied, with arms crossed, steeled against the noise, beaming with malevolent satisfaction.

Sep then reached forward with his petite weapon. He placed the chilly nozzle of the pistol into the nap of Clive's neck. But this was merely symbolic and his finger was off the trigger. Clive should fall down and sense his bones breaking as he bounced around the vault.

"Are you having fun, Pitt? You want to take the long view? Well, I think this is the time to sell, sell, sell."

"You're doing their dirty laundry, yet again," Clive said; finding calm as he contemplated destiny.

"Please mind the gap, will you?" Sep replied. There was a mad gleam in those hard crinkled eyes.

The detectives dangled Clive, giving him a perfect view. Without any more to do, they let him go.

Clive fell and fell and fell.

Until his mind span out of consciousness and succumbed to oblivion.

45

There came an inner voice, or voices, urging him to return to the surface; to drag himself out of this cavern of night: "Clive, are you there? Do you recognise me? Will you open your eyes now?"

Clive wasn't strong enough to clamber back to the surface. As yet he wasn't able to recognise or to decipher these messages; nor to locate the direction or source. It was impossible to rouse his volition. He'd lost any proportion of time again.

A painful humming sensation developed in his hearing. He felt that he was asleep, perhaps trying to rouse himself; having great difficulty doing that; with a point of consciousness far away. His mind fixed on the prick of light, like a trapped potholer. In a sense he was like that lost explorer, trapped under a mountain, tons of granite and other materials above his head. Or it was a type of 'buried alive' nightmare.

These voices made spikes into his mind, from time to time; talking encouragingly, asking him to rouse himself and to seek an escape. Was he able to discover the identity of these speakers and to respond?

Rather than to reconstruct the trauma, when those flunkies had tossed him into the foundation, he tried to enjoy a sensation of calm. He became convinced that he must be dozing under shady trees in his favourite square. He wondered if the whole ordeal had been a just a bad dream, playing out his worst fears to a fantastic level. He might wake soon and return to solid reality; he craved this from the depth of his consciousness; the entire drama played out within the dark watery globe of his own head.

He would be able to open his eyes soon, to return to the City; and to the usual scenes of London's working life. After that he'd check off his watch and get back to the office, careful not to be late after a rare lunch out. He had the sensation that it was Friday, the end of the week, he thought with relief. This evening he would get home promptly, so that he could arrange for a babysitter, when the wife and he went to the rugby club bar; before setting off to a restaurant and a club.

But then what about Pixie Wright? Was he intending to discount her as well?

When he did come around, as he sensed, he found himself setting in a narrow seat next to a small round window. It was too dark to see anything through this porthole. He understood that it must be an aeroplane; he was aboard a flight!

The huge engines whined through the air and turbulence shook the whole craft. He gazed about the cabin in astonishment, trying to acclimatise. It was the feeling of life returning to normal that had been the illusion. But had he managed to cheat death, or murder, and to escape from Septimus?

His last memory was of being thrown into the void of Winchurch Brothers' Tower. Yet his memory was proven to be unreliable.

He couldn't explain what he was doing aboard an aircraft. Was he on that early morning fight to Budapest after all?

Maybe Douglas hadn't betrayed him. The lawyer had friends in that country; or contacts from land and property deals. If so Doug had been playing a clever double bluff with Septimus. In mysterious circumstances Breadham had smuggled Clive to Heathrow or to the City airport and out of England. How was this bizarre rescue possible? There was no recollection of going through airport procedures.

Pitt didn't understand why his memory should be erased again.

"Clive, are you listening? Do you hear me? Will you try to follow?" persisted the voice.

But he tried to relax in the airline seat; to understand the new situation. He was the only passenger in the row of seats. But he saw that there were other passengers, occupying seats in other rows. Nobody was taking any special interest in him; this was a normal in-flight atmosphere. There was a hum of companionable conversation that put him at ease. He was approach by a young woman. She was an air steward.

"You can unfasten your seat belt now, sir," she advised.

"Oh, right. I didn't realise I was wearing one, to be honest. Do you mind me asking...where are we flying?"

"Can I fix you something to drink, Mr Pitt?"

"You know, what's our destination?" he remarked.

"How about a whiskey, sir? It's excellent whiskey?"

"No. Do you have a pint of bitter? Then make it a Gin and tonic. Why are you referring to me by name? What happened to cheap flights? Did we just leave London?" he enquired. He was gabbling with curiosity.

"Yes sir, from London."

"Heathrow?"

She shrugged. Then she went off to mix his drink with a deeply sexy sashay and reassuring coping-with-everything smile.

Clive pushed back into the seat, exhaled deeply: "Whatever you do, keep calm, keep calm."

Engine noise reintroduced into his senses, putting those inner voices to the back of his thoughts. For a while he followed the gestures of a couple conversing in an adjacent row. The girl resembled Pixie and the guy was like Cohen from the office, he thought; although he could only see the back of their heads.

There was comfortable chatter within the cabin. This helped to block out the other voices that called him; with the persistency of his Mum telling him to stop playing and come back indoors. Shouldn't he check to see if that was Pixie, no matter how coincidental it was? Anyway what was she doing with Cohen and other guys from the office? Hadn't she been in a terrible accident that had altered her personality?

"Don't be afraid, Clive. You are safe now. Do you hear me? You are safe now. Just say something to me, will you?"

Clive searched for an in-flight magazine without success. There was a sick-bag and, amazingly, a copy of the Winchurch Brothers Company Report for the previous year. On the front of this publication was an image of Sep and Viktor, stood on the marble steps before the new tower, locked in a firm and friendly handshake.

The air hostess returned. She pressed a G&T into his hand, without taking any more questions. In the meantime he sipped the drink, which tasted intensely fantastic. He could taste again. Indeed he could live again.

On second thoughts the girl was very much like Pixie. Wasn't that her after all? He would have to go and see. But his decisive action was stalled by a new voice; an announcement:

"Good evening ladies and gentlemen. This is your captain speaking."

Clive accepted the competent tones of a trusted professional. "I foresee a calm flight. There may be some turbulence later. For those of you interested we are now flying at sixty six thousand feet below."

"*Below*?" Pitt mouthed.

"The conditions are as expected at our destination. About three million degrees centigrade. Cloudy with light showers. The morning's fire storms have passed over. Once we arrive at the terminal you may experience delays. This is due to your souls departing from your body. We request patience until our staff can dispose of your mortal bodies. Thanks for choosing to fly with us today, and taking out your life membership. Refreshments are now being served. Our President looks forward to seeing you. In the mean time I wish you a pleasant flight."

The airhostess returned with a fixed smile. Except this time she was accompanied by two burly stewards, two heavily muscled men in the same branded red and black uniform. To his astonishment and protest, these guys reached over and lifted him from his seat. What was going on here? His tumbler bounced to the ground and G&T spread over the narrow carpet like transparent blood.

Pitt was being whisked down the aisle like some miscreant who'd been caught smoking in the toilet. Yet his offence was more serious apparently, because they pulled him towards the cockpit, along the blue lighted and carpeted aisle.

"Get your paws off, you meat heads," Clive urged.

The hostess continued to smile - as if to reassure the other passengers - yet the shit-house bullies were squeezing the juice out of his muscles, so that he couldn't coordinate himself.

Was the idea to disgrace him in front of the pilot? Maybe he was effectively being arrested. To be handed over on landing to the Hungarian authorities.

But that wasn't the scenario. Instead he was taken to the front entry and exit door. They faced him up to the porthole with arms twisted up behind his back. Clive was forced to stare through the Perspex window, towards the darkness shown outside. He heard the rush and suck of freezing air outside.

A still smiling hostess unlocked this barrier; she had to use her whole strength. Clive didn't think this was possible to achieve. Was she trying to kill them all? Yet she cracked open the air-locked capsule. She exposed a torrential darkness outside. It was a terrifying sensation. Like the sight and sound of all hell breaking loose. The male stewards took him to the edge, shook him in reprimand, and then, as he felt their fingers in his back, shoved him out of the aircraft.

46

Pitt lost the sense of security that came from being in the aircraft; far behind. He fell and fell and fell, snapping in and out of consciousness.

He had the sensation of flying above the square mile, peering down at the towers below, at the Gherkin, the Shard on the south bank, the shapes misty and abstract.

It was definitely one of those "my life is flashing before my eyes" moments. There was a feeling of elation, euphoria even, as if he was only dreaming about flying, as many people did. But this was not a dream, because he could feel the air, powerful currents, and saw all objects on the ground. This experience was too real, too superbly scary, suspended there in the gaping space, with only a super jumbo above his shoulder. Perhaps this was the very plane he'd been ejected from, on his way to sanctuary. Only idiots are not afraid at all. Guys without a frontal lobe, or a damaged frontal lobe: which he confidently didn't suffer from.

There was not time to look along the Thames to fully enjoy the view. He felt himself swooping, gliding and swinging downwards, drifting and circling. Soft and beautiful, as he shut out noises and smells; the clamour and frenzy of the City. He didn't sense speed or weight until he touched the ground again.

"Clive you have to come back around now. Can you hear me, sweetie? Can you pick up my voice, darling?"

"Yes, I hear your voice," Pitt responded. Finally he had to reply to those voices, as they were insistent, yet sympathetic and encouraging.

There was a group around him, a circle of people; various anxious faces. They leant forward over him, as he seemed to be horizontal. Following his reply they gave a collective gasp of surprise and relief. Why should they be amazed at the sound of his voice? There was a type of commotion around him - a stirring of the atmosphere and a change in mood - a sense of tears and laughter.

"Can you open your eyes for me, Clive? You do hear me, don't you? Are you coming back to me now?"

"I don't know," Clive replied. "I hear your voice. Whoever you are... Who are you?" But there was a circle of bright lights above his head, like undercarriage lights from a space ship.

"You've been through a terrible trauma, darling."

"I'd reckon so," he agreed.

"He's definitely coming back around now," remarked a male voice.

"Try to open your eyes and look at me."

"Where am I? I feel bloody terrible!" Pitt complained. "Who put my head in a vise?"

"Don't worry Clive. Keep talking. This is your wife."

"Pixie? Didn't I just see you on the flight? With Cohen?"

"This is your wife. It's Noreen here with you!"

"Have patience with your husband."

"How is that possible? Noreen? What type of hoax are you carrying out?"

"There are no tricks now. What don't you try to see now?"

"He's opening his eyes."

"I thought you were in Seattle. What are you doing here?"

There were bright lights, strobes. Yet he painfully opened his eyes and adjusted to intense spots. Sure enough he began to distinguish elegant dark features, his wife's face, the tender Semitic eyes, a long thin nose, the grey flecked hair and cutely pointed chin - the familiar features of a woman he'd loved and married.

"It's true. I went to Seattle with him. I felt that was the right thing to do. But how do you feel, Clive? Try to keep your eyes open. Don't close your eyes again. Speak to me darling. Speak and clarify your thoughts."

She was gripping his hand and wiping his forehead.

"Why don't you explain? You took Josh with you States side?"

"He's coming around nicely now." It was an authoritative remark.

There was a bunch of nurses in peculiar uniforms and more white coats.

"Yes, that was true, Clive. Don't you remember anything at all? We made a plan together. I would go with my friend to the States, to Seattle, Washington State. We hoaxed a separation between us, you know, after you were in dispute with your boss. They were trying to bring you down, actually, over the deal. The idea was that we would pretend that our marriage was in trouble. There would be a period of separation leading to divorce. Wilson agreed to pose as my boyfriend. He already had a business over there. Wilson is our true friend, Clive."

"Definitely a cunning plan," Pitt said.

Other faces around his wife were clarifying. Somehow the figures were connected and uniform, like heads from a single body.

"We made a copy of your dossier. I took the secret over with me to Seattle," she explained. "Remember, my sister already lives over there. I had somewhere to go. We knew you were in danger. We knew that your company wanted to destroy the evidence. Thank God we managed to reach you now, Wilson and me."

"You really have my dossier on the ZNT deal?"

"Yes, I know where your memory files are located. I have access ... all that you need. For a whole year I have posed as a new emigrant to the USA and as the future spouse of Wilson."

"Exactly where am I?" Clive wondered. He was on his back blinking at those blinding lights.

"You're in Westminster Hospital. You nearly died Clive. We nearly lost you."

"Tell me that this hasn't all been a dream?"

"You've had a near death experience, sweetie."

"Really? Then what's true?"

"They tried to kill you, actually. They threw you into the foundations of their new building."

"That actually happened?" Clive replied.

"But they failed," Noreen explained. "They also failed to locate me in Seattle this year. I was under a different identity. Wilson has contacts with the CIA." The large dark eyes were dense with feeling. "When I was informed about your 'accident' we came rushing back to London. Your colleague Pixie Wright was in contact with me. She decided to look me up. I caught the earliest flight. I've been at your bedside these last few weeks... hoping that you would survive...that you'd come out of this terrible deep sleep."

"Now I'm in the clear? I'm vindicated?" He lifted his head, although the rest of his body was inert.

"Your dossier was delivered to the City police on my return."

"When was this?" he wondered. He tried to scramble up on his elbows.

"About three weeks ago, twenty days ago...The FCA has been studying the details, actually... and they are preparing a prosecution against Septimus. He will also be charged with attempted murder. The Criminal Prosecution Service is processing the case. The Serious Fraud Squad is involved of course, in examining the documents around the deal, that you stored."

"Why can't I move my legs? Am I paralysed or something?"

"No Clive, nothing like that. But you broke some bones and fractured others. It's going to take a lot of time, darling. Let the doctors resolve those physical problems. You suffered an awful assault."

"By Viktor Di Visu," he assumed.

"That's proven Clive. This chap and some of his friends attacked you in that lawyer's apartment. They raped you and beat you to an inch of your life."

"Oh no, God help us. I've had a few inches now in my life," Clive said.

"Exactly so, my darling."

"You know everything about this, Noreen?" he wondered.

"About the rape and beatings? He downloaded a film on to the internet. Yes, the idiot put this on a porn site, for other maniacs to enjoy. Why did he do this? Good question Clive, because it was really stupid. Yet I suppose it is stupid to rape someone in the first place, so no less stupid to share the same scene with other maniacs."

"That's incredible. What sort of character is this?"

"He is a brute, needless to say."

"For how much longer?" Clive remarked.

"Well, I'm afraid that Viktor Di Visu took off in his private jet. He escaped from the City of London airport... on the way to a friendlier nation."

"We can't get him!"

"Unfortunately British law doesn't stretch there... nor international law, actually... and a government plea for extradition has been turned down."

"Laughed out of court?"

"That's right, Clive, sweetie. How is your head now? Does it ache badly?"

"The FCA and police are unable to obtain Di Visu."

"They are unable to retract the ZNT agreement."

"We can't run history backwards," Clive agreed.

"That will take a ruling," she replied. "But I think they'll get there in the end."

"They can't stop Viktor, at this time, any more than the nuclear bomb can be un-dropped," he agonised.

"They just have the auspices to charge Septimus. Meanwhile Viktor has moved out of his London home. He's gone back home. ZNT HQ is listed in Geneva. But they have various international locations..."

"What else?" Clive pressed.

"That hospital in Buckinghamshire is under investigation. There will be a public enquiry," Noreen explained, brushing his face again.

"How about Pixie Wright?" he said.

"She is not too bad, Clive. After the accident she is rather... slow in her thoughts. But she survived, didn't she. She appears to be content, actually… living with her grandmother in Sussex now."

"Then it's true."

"I'm afraid so, darling." There wasn't much feeling in the hand she was holding, as if it belonged to another man.

"Oh my God, what did I do to her?"

"They will be closing that hospital. They will no doubt be liquidating Winchurch Brothers."

"Not the end of Viktor and his operations. He'll still be running his fashion empire; cruising the world in his yacht, bankrolled by the carbon industry."

"For the time being, unless we can make international law stretch. Everybody is trying to curtail him," she insisted.

"Then how about me?" Clive asked. "Where am I now? Where do I stand?"

"I understand there's an accusation again you."

"Yes, love, I know what you're referring to," he admitted.

"Septimus didn't bring a charge against you, did he, before. With these other, very serious charges against him… he is prepared to bring that prosecution. He wouldn't allow that to drop. You shouldn't worry about all that now. You have to get better. I can't believe that you've come back to me!" she declared.

"There's no mistake?" he replied.

"You should explain yourself… at the first opportunity."

"Do they know my actions were manipulated?"

"They already ran some tests on you, actually," Noreen explained. She took him in excitedly; her large brown eyes shining.

"Yeah, Pixie took some blood samples from me. A friend of hers…a nurse. We suspected that I had been slipped something."

"You think they drugged you?"

"There was some chemical… hormonal or steroid influence. Pixie took that sample to an independent clinic. They tested for various chemicals. Which may have been injected into me, during that hospital stay…"

"You mustn't allow him to go back to sleep," announced the doctor. "We mustn't allow him to slip back. He may not return to us."

"The suspicion is that my levels of testosterone and adrenaline were much higher than normal," Clive explained.

"They definitely tested this sample," Noreen confirmed.

"Of course in my job, my old job, in the City, we thrived on high levels of testosterone. Adrenaline, natural steroids... the stress levels were amazing"

"I know, darling."

"But we thrived on that. We loved the pressure. It was bloody in tooth and claw. The excitement. The aggression of the office. Sometimes. The incredible rush was normal. It was necessary for survival. It was a fuelled environment. But this was way above all that. I was pumped up when I attacked Emmy."

"The sample came back slightly above normal, that's true. But apparently your levels were within the normal range," Noreen told him.

"Then it's clear," he muttered. "Isn't it?"

"Don't let him drift back Mrs Pitt. Keep him conscious. He must remain conscious."

"You got a last message from Pixie. It was received on the morning before her accident. It was confused, in the way it was expressed. But, basically, she reminded you that Emmy was blindfolded. Her eyes were covered as she was attacked. She couldn't possibly have seen the face of the guy who raped her. Do you understand the implication?"

THE END